DEAD MAN'S REACH

DEAD MAN'S REACH

D. B. Jackson

A Tom Doherty Associates Book

NEW YORK

DEAD MAN'S REACH

Copyright © 2015 by D. B. Jackson

Map reproduction courtesy of the Norman B. Leventhal
Map Center at the Boston Public Library

A Tor Book
Published by Tom Doherty Associates, LLC
175 Fifth Avenue
New York, NY 10010

www.tor-forge.com

Tor® is a registered trademark of Tom Doherty Associates, LLC.

The Library of Congress Cataloging-in-Publication Data is available upon request.

ISBN 978-0-7653-7114-0 (hardcover)
ISBN 978-1-4668-3819-2 (e-book)

Tor books may be purchased for educational, business, or promotional use.
For information on bulk purchases, please contact the Macmillan Corporate
and Premium Sales Department at 1-800-221-7945, extension 5442,
or write to specialmarkets@macmillan.com.

First Edition: July 2015

Printed in the United States of America

0 9 8 7 6 5 4 3 2 1

For Alex and Erin,
words cannot begin to express my love

A PLAN of
THE TOWN of BOSTON

CHARLESTOWN

HARBOUR

MILL POND

Hudson's Point

Barton's Point

North Battery

North Boat Water Mill
E. to N. Mill Dam

Valley Acre

THE

South Battery

Rowe's Wharf
Hubbart's Wharf
Wheelwright's Wharf
Whitehorn's Wharf
Griffin's Wharf

Battery March
Kings Road

Sea Street
Cow Lane

Ship Yard
Gardner's Wharf

Belle Wharf

Windmill Point & Battery

Hill Wharf & Stillhouse

Mr. Austin's Pasture

Summer Street

Rowe's Field

Golden Field

Henchay's Wharf & Stillhouse
Arbuthnot
Walters Wharf & Stillhouse

Cow Lane
Pond Street
Short Street
Orange Street

Burying Ground

THE MARSH

The Island

all this Part is dry at Low Water

Dry at Low water except in the Mill Channel

Wind Mill Point

Sea Mill

The Neck Road

References to the Town.

A Christ Church
B Old North Meeting
C Anabaptists Meeting
D Faneuil Hall
E Town Hall
F Old Meeting
G Prison & Court House
H Kings Chapel
I Work House
K Granary Public
L Province House (General hope)
M Old South Meeting (the Riding House)
N Trinity Church
O New South Meeting
P Hollis's Meeting
Q West Meeting

Scale of Yards.

0   60   120   180   240

180 or Half a Mile.

DEAD MAN'S REACH

Chapter
ONE

Boston, Province of Massachusetts Bay,
February 21, 1770

*E*than Kaille slipped through shadows, stepping from one snow-crusted cobble to the next with the care of a thief. He held a knife in one hand, his fingers numb with cold. The other hand he trailed along the side of a brick building, steadying himself as a precaution against the uncertain footing.

Dim pools of light spilled onto the street from candlelit windows. Flakes of snow dusted his coat and hat, and melted as they brushed against his face. Every breath produced a billow of vapor, rendering his concealment spell all but useless.

The air was still—a small mercy on a night as cold as this one— and a deep silence had settled over Boston, like a thick woolen blanket. Even the harbor, her waters frozen near to shore and placid where they remained open, offered not a sound. In the hush that enveloped the city, Ethan's steps seemed as loud as musket fire.

Will Pryor, who had stolen several gemmed necklaces and brace-lets from the home of a merchant in the North End, lived here on Lindal's Lane, in a room above a farrier's shop. Ethan had followed the man for two days, and though he'd not yet seen the jewels in Pryor's hands, he had little doubt but that the pup still possessed them, and was merely biding his time until he could sell them without drawing undue attention to himself. Ethan was determined to keep him from finding a buyer. He feared, though, that the uneven sound of his footsteps would be enough to wake Pryor from a sound slumber, much less alert the thief to his approach.

Ethan reached the worn wooden stairway leading up to Pryor's room and began to climb, wincing at every creak, eyeing the window, which glowed faintly. It wasn't until he heard the murmur of voices, however, that he thought to examine the steps with more care. Leaning forward, squinting in the murky light, he felt his stomach clench.

Footprints in the snow. Several pairs.

Seconds later, an all-too-familiar voice called out, "Come and join us, Ethan. We've been waiting for you."

"Damn it!" he muttered, teeth clenched.

He kept still, snow settling on his shoulders, and he pondered his options. Realizing that he had none, he pushed up his sleeve, cut his arm, and whispered an incantation to remove his concealment spell.

A glowing figure appeared beside him, russet like a newly risen moon, with eyes as bright as flames. He was the ghost of an ancient warrior, tall, lean, dour, and dressed in chain mail and a tabard bearing the leopards of England's Plantagenet kings. He was also Ethan's spectral guide, the wraith of an ancient ancestor who allowed Ethan access to the power that dwelt at the boundary between the living world and the realm of the dead. For years, Ethan had called the ghost Uncle Reg after Reginald Jerill, his mother's waspish brother, of whom the ghost reminded him.

Reg regarded Ethan with an expression that bespoke both amusement and disapproval.

"I didn't know she was here," Ethan said.

Reg scowled, as if to say, *No, but you should have.*

Ethan could hardly argue. For years, Sephira Pryce, the so-called Empress of the South End, Boston's most infamous and successful thief-taker, had been interfering with his inquiries, swooping in at the last moment to take for herself items he had been hired to recover, stealing his clients and with them the finder's fees they paid. She reveled in tormenting him, although most times she seemed content to taunt and ridicule. On occasion, she set her toughs on him, allowing them to beat Ethan to a bloody mess. And every now and then, she threatened to let them kill him, and dump his body in the leas of Boston's Common.

That she and her men had reached Pryor first should have come as no surprise at all.

"Don't stand out there pouting, Ethan. It's only a few pounds. Mister Wells should never have gone to you in the first place. A man of means, of culture. He should have been mine."

Ethan glanced at Reg. "I'd gladly pay a few pounds if it meant a moment's peace and an end to her mocking."

Reg grinned and faded from view. Ethan cut his arm again before climbing to the top of the stairway and pushing open Pryor's door.

Three of Sephira's men stood before him, blocking his way. One of them, a brute named Afton, was as large as a British frigate and almost as welcoming. He had dark, stringy hair and a broad, homely face. Next to him, smaller, also dark-haired, stood Nap, a flintlock pistol in his hand, full-cocked and aimed at Ethan's heart.

The third man held a blade instead of a pistol. He had pushed up the sleeve on his left arm; a trickle of blood ran from a cut on his fore-arm, twin to the gash Ethan had carved into his own skin. Gaspar Mariz was a conjurer like Ethan, and though in private conversations he had declared himself Ethan's friend, he still answered to Sephira. Ethan had no doubt that if she ordered him to kill Ethan with a spell, he would attempt it. He stared at Ethan, his expression grim, the lenses of his spectacles catching the light of a candle so that they appeared opaque.

Behind these three were three others. Will Pryor, lanky, youthful, with yellow hair and dark eyes, sat in a chair, blood seeping from his nose and split lip, as well as from a raw wound on his temple. He watched Ethan, clearly uncertain as to whether his arrival presaged an escape from his predicament or a worsening of it. Another brute loomed over him: Gordon, as big and as ugly as Afton. And beside these two, a look of smug satisfaction on her lovely face, stood Sephira.

There could be no denying that she was beautiful; even Ethan, who had as much cause to hate the woman as anyone in Boston, had to admit as much. Ringlets of shining black hair fell over her shoulders. Her eyes, bright blue and dancing with mischief, shone in the candle-light. A black cloak that he assumed must be hers—it was far too fine to be Pryor's—lay on the thief's bed. She wore her usual street garb:

black breeches, a white silk shirt opened at the neck, and a black waist-coat that hugged her curves with the ardor of a lover.

But though she was exquisite and alluring, her beauty put him in mind of a cut diamond. She was hard, remote, cold, and sharp enough to draw blood. He had never met anyone more ruthless or better suited to a life of thuggery and deception. She could be cruel as well as charming; he had known her to be shrewdly calculating one minute and utterly capricious the next. There was no predicting what she might do under any given circumstance, which was one reason why she could be so confounding as a rival.

Another reason: she—or at least men in her employ—bore responsibility for a good number of the thefts she investigated. She stole from the wealthy and then took their money as reward for returning their property, all the while basking in their praise. "She can solve any crime," they said, their praise as fatuous as it was fulsome. "No thief in Boston can elude the Empress." Those like Ethan, who encountered her in the streets, knew her for what she was: a brigand, bonny and winsome, but villainous. To the rest of the city, however, including its wealthiest and most powerful citizens, she was a heroine.

And tonight she had bested Ethan yet again; she would claim as her own the three pounds Mr. Wells had promised him. Ethan felt reasonably sure that this would be the extent of his loss for the evening. But he couldn't be entirely confident that the night wouldn't end in his death. Such were the risks of any encounter with Sephira Pryce.

She smiled at him as she would at an old friend, but then her gaze fell to the cut on his arm, and her mien turned icy.

"You shouldn't have done that."

"And you shouldn't be surprised that I did. You're going to have Nap take my knife. All your men are armed. Did you expect me to walk in here without any means of protecting myself?"

Sephira stared daggers at him, but then nodded once to Nap, seeming to concede the point.

Nap stepped forward and took the blade from Ethan's hand, all the while keeping his pistol trained on Ethan's heart.

"Will, how are you bearing up?" Ethan asked.

The thief swallowed. He cast a wide-eyed, fearful look Ethan's way, but a second later his gaze was drawn back to Nap's pistol. At last he gave a tentative shrug. "I don't know."

"He's quite the intellect," Sephira said, regarding Will with unconcealed scorn. "I find it hard to believe he eluded you for as long as he did."

"Aye, well thieves are easier to find when you have another thief-taker doing all the difficult work for you. Why are you here, Sephira? Have times grown so difficult that the Empress of the South End must abandon the warmth and comfort of her home for a mere three pounds?"

She tipped her head to the side, a coy grin on her lips. "I never see you anymore," she said, purring the words. "I've missed you."

Ethan offered no response.

Sephira began to pace the room. As she strolled past Will, she traced a finger lightly down the bridge of his nose. The pup looked to be on the verge of wetting himself.

"Wells is one of those clients I'm not sure you ought to be working for," she said at last. "You've seen his estate, you know the sort of men who live on his street." She halted, her eyes finding Ethan's. "I thought I had made myself clear on this point."

"You have," Ethan said, his tone light.

Arguing the point would have been useless. Sephira had told Ethan more times than he cared to remember that she expected him to limit his thieftaking to a clientele of her choosing. He could work for families of limited means, while leaving the wealthier clients for her. And he could work for those who came to him explicitly because they believed their property to have been spirited away by someone with access to the same conjuring powers that he possessed. This was her notion of an equitable arrangement. She appeared not to care in the least that he had never agreed to her terms, despite her threats of beatings at the hands of her men should he violate their "agreement."

"Yet, you took on the inquiry anyway," she continued, "without regard for my wishes. Will here is no conjurer, so I know that you didn't take the job because witchery was involved. Therefore, I can only assume that you deliberately ignored my previous warnings."

"That's right."

"And still you ask why I'm here."

It was his turn to concede the point. He did so with a shrug. "So have I earned another beating?" he asked. "Or do you plan to do worse this time?"

"Neither, actually. I'll take the gems, which Will was clever enough to hide on top of that table there. And I'll claim your fee from Mister Wells. I'll do the same with your next job, and the one after that. Perhaps, with time, you'll decide that working without being paid makes little sense, you'll concede that I've beaten you in this, as in everything else, and you'll start taking on the sort of clients I've been telling you to work for all along."

Ethan watched her, waiting for more: for the threats, for an order to Nap and his companions to bludgeon him a bit. But she said nothing else. She merely stared back at him.

"What?" she asked in unfeigned innocence—odd in and of itself coming from Sephira.

"That's surprisingly . . . restrained of you."

"I can have them beat you, if you'd prefer," she said, sounding bored.

"No. Thank you, though." He tipped his head toward Will, who was listening to all they said and looking more anxious with every word. "What about him?"

"You know what Mister Wells would say."

"I do," Ethan said.

Wells, like others who had hired him to retrieve stolen items, would want to see the pup punished as severely as the law allowed. Indeed, if he was as vengeful as some for whom Ethan had worked, he wouldn't care about the limits of the law, and would want Will killed for his transgression.

"What?" Will asked, his gaze darting from one of them to the other. "What would he say?"

Before either of them could answer, several things happened at once. A pulse of conjuring power hummed in the floor; Ethan couldn't say with any surety whence it had come. He thought he saw a flash of light as well, but he had no opportunity to see what it was, or to ask Mariz if he had felt the spell.

Because at that moment, Gordon, without uttering a word, or giving any indication of what might have provoked him, stepped directly in front of Will, and began to beat the pup with his cobble-like fists. A blow to the side of the head nearly knocked the lad from his chair. A second broke his nose, so that blood gushed over Will's mouth and chin. One more, and the pup fell over, his chair toppling with him.

But Gordon wasn't through. He aimed a vicious kick at Will's side—Ethan heard ribs break.

At first, it seemed all of them were too shocked by the sudden assault to do more than gape. For seconds that might as well have been hours, none of them moved to intervene.

Sephira was the first to act.

"Gordon!" she shouted, the name echoing in the small room.

No response. The brute kicked Will a second time, then wrapped one fist in the pup's bloodstained collar and hoisted him to his feet, his other fist drawn back to strike again.

By this time, though, Afton, Nap, and Ethan had emerged from their stupor and were converging on the man. Afton grabbed Gordon's arm. Nap and Ethan wrested Will from the tough's grasp and set him back in his chair, which Sephira had set upright. The pup's head lolled to the side. He was unconscious; Ethan feared he might be dead.

Gordon struggled to free himself from Afton, the room quaking as the two behemoths wrestled each other.

Sephira planted herself in front of them. "Gordon, stop it!"

But still he fought, as if in a blind rage.

Another conjuring thrummed, this one coming from within the room. Gordon staggered, slumped in Afton's arms. Afton eased him to the floor, where he lay still, his chest rising and falling gently.

"Is he alive?" Sephira asked, turning back to Will.

Nap knelt beside the pup and put a hand to Will's neck, feeling for a pulse. "Barely," he said after a few seconds.

"What did you do?"

They all turned to Mariz, who alone among them had not moved, though the blood had vanished from his arm, expended in the sleep spell that subdued Gordon.

He glared at Ethan, his knife poised over his arm, ready to cut himself and conjure again.

"I don't know what you mean," Ethan said, knowing that he sounded slow-witted.

"What did you do to him?" Mariz repeated, his accent thickening as his anger flared.

Sephira snapped her fingers. Immediately, Nap stood once more and raised his pistol.

"You're saying that Kaille used his witchery on Gordon? That's why—?"

"I did not!"

"I sensed a conjuring, Kaille," Mariz said. "And for just an instant I thought I saw your spectral guide appear."

Ethan shook his head, even as he considered the magick he had sensed and the flash of light he thought he saw before Gordon struck his first blow at Will. He pointed to his forearm, which was still red with blood. "Look," he said, holding it out for Mariz and Sephira to see. "The blood's still there. Had I conjured, it wouldn't be."

Mariz blinked once, his brow creasing.

"Mariz?" Sephira said. Ethan sensed that she was seconds away from ordering Nap to pull the trigger.

"There are other ways for him to conjure. But the blood on his arm would have been easiest."

Sephira appeared unconvinced. "Unless he wanted to hide what he was doing, isn't that right?"

Mariz shook his head. "Even then I would see his guide, and feel his spell."

"But you say that you did—you saw the ghost and felt a conjuring. That's what you said."

"I thought his guide had appeared. It was there, and then it was gone. I might have imagined it."

Sephira frowned. Since the previous summer, when Ethan and Mariz had worked together to defeat a conjurer named Nate Ramsey, she had been distrustful of their friendship. Mariz's uncertainty was only making matters worse.

"Why would I make Gordon beat the lad?" Ethan asked her. "I'm the sentimental one, remember? That's what you always say. I was prepared to plead for Will's life. It's you who usually argues on behalf of vengeance for the client."

She didn't answer, but instead turned to Mariz once more. "How long will he sleep?" she asked, dipping her chin toward Gordon.

"Not long. But if we wake him, I can offer no assurance that he will not resume his attack."

"I want him to tell us what happened."

"He can," Ethan said. "And we don't have to wake him." He and Mariz shared a look. "A *revela potestatem* spell would show the color of the conjuring that hit him."

"It will show my sleep spell," Mariz said.

"Aye, but if you word it correctly it will also show the previous conjuring."

"What are you two talking about?" Sephira asked, the words clipped.

"You've seen the spell before; more than once. We can use a conjuring to show what spells have been used against him. You'll see that I had nothing to do with what happened."

She made a sharp, impatient gesture that might or might not have been meant to indicate her acquiescence. Ethan didn't ask her to clarify.

"*Omnias magias,*" he said to Mariz. "All magicks. That's the wording."

"Yes, I know it," Mariz said, and cut his arm. Blood welled; he put some on his fingertip and dabbed it across Gordon's forehead and down the bridge of his nose to the base of his neck. When he had finished doing this, he spoke the incantation. "*Revela omnias magias ex cruore evocatas.*" Reveal all magicks, conjured from blood.

The spell rumbled in the walls and floor. Mariz's spectral guide, a young man in Renaissance clothing who resembled the conjurer and glowed with a warm beige hue, appeared beside him. The radiance of a conjuring appeared on Gordon's body, but in only one color: Mariz's beige.

"What did that mean?" Sephira asked, sounding cross. Ethan knew that she neither understood nor trusted spells and spellmaking. And she hated being at a disadvantage when Ethan was anywhere near her.

"There was nothing," Mariz said. "No color at all aside from mine. Nothing from Kaille, nothing from another conjurer." He looked up at Ethan, the lenses of his spectacles flashing again. "Perhaps there was no spell after all."

Sephira's scowl had grown more severe. "So, now you're not even sure that a spell was cast."

"I felt something," Ethan told her. He turned back to Mariz. "We both did. And both of us thought we saw something, as well—a light of some sort. It could have been the spectral guide of some other conjurer."

"Or it could have been nothing," Mariz said. "Lightning from outside, or the gleam of some distant conjuring."

"Maybe. Has Gordon ever done anything like that before?" Ethan asked Sephira. "Has he ever taken it upon himself to beat someone without a word from you? For that matter, have you ever known him to ignore a direct order, as he did when you told him to stop?"

"No," she said, and while she had sounded unsure of herself when speaking of spells, there was no hesitation in this response. "He may not be the smartest of my men, but he does as he's told."

"I thought as much." Ethan looked down at Gordon, and then at Will, who had yet to regain consciousness. There had been something odd and deeply chilling about Gordon's behavior. His attack on the pup had been savage, and yet devoid of provocation. And without any evidence to indicate that a spell had been cast, it was hard to imagine what could have caused him to lose control so suddenly.

"Perhaps Pryor said something we did not hear," Mariz said, echoing Ethan's thoughts. "Or maybe he made some rude gesture toward the *senhora* that we did not see. Gordon is very protective of her."

Ethan frowned. "Yes, maybe," he said, unable to keep a note of doubt from his voice.

Sephira said nothing, but she regarded Ethan, Mariz, and Gordon in turn, seeming in that moment to trust none of them.

Chapter TWO

Like Mariz, Ethan also feared that if they woke Gordon in the presence of Will Pryor, the brute might attempt to renew his assault. And though the room belonged to Will, it seemed easiest to move him rather than risk stirring Gordon. Not to mention the fact that with the possible exception of Afton, there was no one there who could lift Sephira's man.

Ethan and Mariz draped the lad's arms around their shoulders and bore him down the stairway to the icy street. There they both cast healing spells to repair some of the damage Gordon had done in his unexplained rage. Ethan mended Will's broken ribs, while Mariz tended to the pup's jaw and nose, both of which were also broken.

"How confident were you that you caught sight of my spectral guide?" Ethan asked as they conjured.

Mariz glanced his way. "I cannot say. When I saw it, I was quite certain. But in . . . What is your word? In retrospect, I am less sure. It lasted not even a second—the blink of an eye. Nothing more. I am sorry. I should not have accused you."

Ethan shook his head. "That's not why I was asking. As I said, I spotted something, too, and I'm not at all convinced that it came from the window."

"Did you see a figure? A color?"

"No. I saw a flicker of light. That's all."

"Do you still believe it was a spell that made Gordon do this?"

Ethan didn't know how to answer. Sephira's man had behaved as would one under the influence of a control spell. But control spells were among the most powerful of conjurings, and Ethan couldn't imagine how a conjurer might conceal one from an *omnias magias* spell.

The door to Will's room opened and closed, and boots scraped on the landing outside the room and then on the snow-dusted stairway. Seconds later, Sephira joined them on the street, her black cloak draped over her shoulders.

"He's awake," she said.

What little light reached that corner of the street came from Will's window, above and behind Sephira. It made a halo of her shining curls and left her face in shadow.

"And?" Ethan asked.

She shrugged. "And he seems perfectly normal, or at least as normal as Gordon gets. He remembers pummeling the noddy, but he can't recall what set him off, nor can he explain why he wouldn't stop. He keeps apologizing to me for ignoring my order to stop, but when I ask him why he did it, he merely shakes his head and tells me again that he's sorry."

Ethan wasn't sure what to make of this, and to make matters worse, he wasn't entirely certain whether he could trust what she told him. She had no reason to lie about the episode, but his mistrust of her ran deep, and old habits were not so easily broken.

"Do you think that if he saw Will, he would try again to attack him?"

"I don't know," Sephira said. "I don't think we should take that chance."

Mariz looked up. "I agree."

"How is he?" Sephira asked.

"Another blow or two and I expect he would have died," Ethan said. "As it is, he won't be doing much thieving for a while."

"Then, I suppose some good came of this."

He couldn't tell if she was joking.

"If you'll take Gordon back to your home, Mariz and I will return Will to his bed."

"Yes, all right." She started to turn away, but stopped herself. "I believe you and I have more to discuss."

"No, we don't, Sephira. You'll be watching me, I know. And you'll be displeased if I take on other wealthy clients. I've heard it before."

"Very well, Ethan. But one day, after you've once again ignored my warnings, you'll find that my patience has run out. When that happens, you'll have no one to blame but yourself." She looked at Mariz. "When you're done here, return to the house. I have more questions for you."

"Of course, *Senhora*."

She climbed the stairs to Will's room and called to Nap and Afton from the doorway. Ethan and Mariz moved Pryor a short distance down the lane, so that Gordon wouldn't see the lad as he left. Once Sephira and the others were gone, they carried Will back up to his room.

"You did not answer my question before," Mariz said, as they settled the pup on his bed. "Do you still believe Gordon acted under the influence of a conjuring?"

"I don't know. It was all rather strange, and everything happened quickly. If only one of us had felt a conjuring and seen that light, I'd be willing to dismiss it as coincidence, or something imagined. But both of us . . ." He draped a blanket over Will and straightened. "Sephira is going to ask you the same question. What will you tell her?"

"That I am unsure of what I saw and what I sensed. That my spell indicated no conjuring had been used against Gordon. And that I am convinced you had nothing to do with whatever happened to him."

"You've told me in the past that our friendship has made Sephira and her other men less trusting of you. Is that still so?"

"It is," Mariz said. "She does not like you, Kaille. And yet she speaks of you with more respect than you might think. I believe if she had her way, you would be working for her, not I. Yours is an odd relationship."

"Aye. That much I know." He proffered a hand, which Mariz gripped. "Thank you."

"For what?"

Ethan gestured toward Will. "For helping me heal him. And for telling Sephira that I wasn't responsible for the spell."

"I believe I suggested first that you were."

"Aye, that you did. But I probably would have done the same."

They let themselves out of the room and closed the door behind them.

At the bottom of the stairway, they parted ways. Ethan intended to go to the Dowsing Rod, the tavern on Sudbury Street where he spent much of his time. First, however, he walked through Cornhill to Marlborough Street and turned southward. At the corner of Winter Street, he turned up a small walkway and followed it to the door of a modest house with a gabled roof. Candles shone in the windows, and pale gray smoke rose from the chimney. Ethan rapped on the door with the simple brass knocker.

The man who opened the door was tall, though his shoulders were stooped. He had deep-set eyes, a prominent nose, and long, powdered hair that he wore in a plait.

"Yes? What can I do for you?"

"Forgive me for disturbing you so late in the evening, Doctor Church. My name is Ethan Kaille—"

"Ah, yes! The thieftaker who doesn't wish to be associated with Samuel Adams or the Sons of Liberty."

Ethan offered a wan smile. "I'm surprised that you remember, sir. It's been some time."

Several months before, as Ethan tried to rid Boston of Nate Ramsey and his army of wraiths, he was summoned to the Green Dragon tavern by Samuel Adams. There he met with Adams, Benjamin Church, James Otis, Joseph Warren, and Paul Revere, who thanked Ethan for conjuring attacks on warehouses belonging to merchants who had not honored the nonimportation agreements. These agreements, which were intended to halt the sale in Boston of British goods, were the work of Adams and his allies, who believed that Ethan had thrown in with their cause at long last. But Ethan had nothing to do with the attacks; it turned out they were Ramsey's doing. And at that meeting, as on previous occasions, Ethan refused to join with Adams and his allies in their struggle against the Crown.

"Yes, well," Church said. "It's not every day that one meets a man with the gumption to say no to Samuel." He stood to the side and waved Ethan into the house.

Ethan removed his hat and entered. It was blessedly warm within; a hearty blaze burned in the hearth.

"If I remember," the doctor went on, "that was not our first meeting. Trevor Pell brought you to me some years ago. You had been beaten and shot, but most of your wounds had already been healed with what some might call witchcraft."

Ethan recalled that evening vividly as well. Sephira and a large retinue of her toughs had taken Ethan out to the Common, fully intent on killing him. Only the timely intervention of Reverend Pell, with the unwitting cooperation of Sheriff Stephen Greenleaf, had saved Ethan's life. He had healed the worst of his wounds with spells, and while Dr. Church had been surprised by this, his response had been notably measured. This was why Ethan had come to the doctor tonight.

He took a breath and faced the doctor. "Aye, sir. That's my memory as well. Again, I'm flattered that you have such clear recollections of our encounters."

"Can I offer you some wine or something to eat?"

"No, thank you."

Church looked Ethan up and down. "You appear to be in a far better state this evening than you were that night. Is this a social visit then?"

"No, sir. There's a lad who lives above a farrier's shop on Lindal's Lane. His name is Will Pryor. He's taken a terrible beating, and while I've done what I can to heal the worst of his wounds, I was hoping you might go to him in the morning and make certain that he's on the mend. I would pay you, of course."

"I see," Church said, his voice hardening. "And were you responsible for the beating?"

"No, I wasn't."

"Then why would you pay me?"

"Because I wasn't able to prevent the assault, and because my ability to care for the lad is limited."

The doctor considered him. "Very well, Mister Kaille. I'll go to him first thing tomorrow."

"I'd be most grateful, sir. How much shall I pay you?"

"One and ten should be enough."

Ethan narrowed his eyes. "One shilling, ten pence. That's all?"

Church lifted his shoulders, a small grin tugging at his lips. "It sounds as though you've already done most of my work for me."

"But surely—"

"It's all right, Mister Kaille." He gestured in a manner that encompassed the whole of the sitting room. It was comfortably furnished, its appointments tasteful if not lavish. A pair of upholstered chairs stood near the hearth, and a sofa sat along the far wall, before a low oaken table. "As you see, I'm not about to go hungry."

"Thank you, sir." Ethan pulled out his worn leather purse, removed the coins, and handed them to the doctor. "There you are."

Church pocketed the money without bothering to count it.

Ethan started back toward the door. "I'll leave you to enjoy your evening."

"Pryor, you said?" the doctor asked, following him.

"Aye. Will Pryor. On Lindal's Lane."

"Above the farrier's shop."

"Just so. Again, my thanks."

After the doctor saw him out, Ethan turned once more onto Marlborough Street and followed it toward the Dowser, satisfied that he had done what he could for Will.

As had been his habit since the beginning of the British occupation of Boston in the fall of 1768, Ethan followed a somewhat roundabout route to the Dowser so that he would not pass too close to the intersection of Brattle Street and Hillier's Lane, where the regulars of the Twenty-ninth Regiment were billeted.

Still, Ethan could not avoid entirely the British military presence in the city. Regulars patrolled the streets night and day, and with tensions rising, everywhere they went they encountered the taunts of young men inflamed by drink or simply the folly of youth.

Walking on Treamount Street, he could hear cries of "Damn the king and his men!" and "You have no business here, you bloody bastards!" aimed at the soldiers stationed a block away near the Town House. He heard as well the usual insults: "red herring," "lobsters," "thieving dogs," "bloody-backed scoundrels." Each time he was abroad in the streets, he expected these jeers to be met with the report of a musket, but miraculously—so far—the city had been spared that sort of tragedy. He didn't approve of the occupation, and he had long since stopped referring to himself as a loyalist, or a Tory, as men of such thinking were called. But there could be no denying that thus far the soldiers had demonstrated remarkable forbearance.

Treamount met Sudbury Street a bit north of where the soldiers were based, and from there it was but a short walk to the Dowsing Rod.

Upon entering the tavern, Ethan was greeted by the usual savory aromas. Kannice Lester, the tavern's proprietor, and Ethan's lover for nearly seven years, made the finest stews and chowders in all of Boston. Tonight, she was serving the fish chowder; Ethan could smell the cod, as well as the bay and thyme Kannice used in her recipe. The aroma of the chowder was overlaid with the scents of fresh-baked bread and roasting chestnuts.

The air within the tavern's great room was warm and welcoming. A thin haze of pale pipe smoke hung over the tables and chairs, and the incomprehensible din of laughter and dozens of conversations brought a smile to Ethan's lips. He rented a room above Henry Dall's cooperage on Cooper's Alley in the South End, but for years now, this tavern had been as much a home as he'd ever known.

He crossed to the bar, squeezing past the wharfmen and shipwrights who sipped ales while trading stories and jests, and caught the eye of Kelf Fingarin, Kannice's mountain of a barman.

"Good evenin', Ethan," Kelf said, as always running his words together in a rapid jumble.

"Well met, Kelf. I'll have the Kent pale, and a bowl of the chowder."

"Ale'll be right up. Chowder should be out in a few minutes."

Ethan dropped a half shilling into the man's massive hand.

Kelf nodded toward the back of the great room as he filled Ethan's tankard with the Kentish pale ale Ethan preferred. "Diver's in his usual spot, with Deborah. I'll bring the chowder to you."

"All right. Where's Kannice?"

Kelf reddened to the tips of his ears. "She's in back cookin'." Abruptly the barman wouldn't look Ethan in the eye.

"I take it she's still angry."

"I mind my own bus'ness, Ethan. You know that about me." Kelf placed the tankard in front of him.

Ethan grinned, though it took some effort. "That would be a yes, then."

"Not for nothin', but I happen to think she's right about this."

"I never said she wasn't. All I said was, a cove's got to work, and times being as they are I can't be turning down any jobs. You understand that, don't you?"

Kelf's crooked grin conveyed more than a bit of sympathy. "Aye. But she can be hard sometimes. You know that as well as anyone."

"Aye." Ethan took his ale. "My thanks, Kelf." He pushed away from the bar and waded through the throng toward the back wall of the tavern, where his friend Diver—Devren Jervis—usually sat.

As he wound past tables of workers and artisans drinking flips or Madeira wine, and eating oysters and chowder, he saw many faces he recognized. Kannice's fine cooking had earned her a loyal clientele. But though most of these men had seen Ethan here day after day, few of them offered anything by way of greeting; most refused to make eye contact.

For as much as they cared for Kannice, they thought the worst of Ethan. He supposed they had cause.

As a young man, about the age of Will Pryor, he had put out to sea as second mate aboard the *Ruby Blade*, a privateering vessel. The initial legs of the ship's voyage went poorly, and before long the first mate, a silver-tongued ruffian named Allen Foster, had talked much of the crew, including Ethan, into mutinying. Somehow Foster had learned that Ethan was a speller, and he convinced him to use his conjuring abilities on their behalf. Only after the captain and his supporters had been subdued did Ethan come to realize that Foster was cruel and arbitrary, a worse commander by far than the captain had been. Ethan freed the captain and helped him retake the ship.

That act of repentance saved Ethan from the hanging he probably deserved. It could not keep him out of prison. He served for close to fourteen years as a laborer on a sugar plantation in Barbados. There, in a hell of backbreaking toil, disease, unbearable heat, and brutality at the hands of the plantation's overseers, he lost part of his foot to a stray blow from a cane knife. He lost as well his first love, Marielle Taylor. She broke off their betrothal upon hearing of his involvement in the mutiny, but she was even more appalled to learn that he was a conjurer, something he had concealed from her during their courtship. Hardest of all, Ethan lost the bright future he and Elli had planned together, as well as any chance of realizing his ambitions of becoming a successful merchant captain.

He had done all right for himself in the years since his release from servitude, and among those who knew him solely as a thieftaker, he had a reputation for honesty and competence, not to mention the notoriety that came with pitting himself against Sephira Pryce.

But to many who spent their evenings in the Dowsing Rod, he was little more than an ex-convict, an unrepentant mutineer, and a man dogged by rumors of witchery. He understood why Kannice's patrons shunned him and whispered that she was too good for him. Half the time he agreed with them.

The one person who welcomed him back to Boston after his release, in 1760, was Diver. Ethan would never have remembered him—Diver had been but a boy working the wharves when Ethan sailed from Boston aboard the *Blade*—but Diver remembered Ethan, and didn't seem to mind at all that he was a convict and a reputed witch. In those early days after Ethan's return from the Caribbean, Diver was the only friend he had.

The intervening years had been kind to his friend. Aside from a few strands of silver hair amid his dark curls, Diver had conceded nothing to age. He still had a youthful face, a lean build, and a smile that could have won the heart of the queen consort. On this night, he sat near the back wall of the tavern with Deborah Crane, a red-haired beauty Diver had been courting for more than a year. He held her hand in his, their heads close together as they spoke.

Ethan cleared his throat as he approached their table. The two young lovers looked up.

"Am I intruding?"

"Not at all, Mister Kaille," Deborah said, favoring him with a smile.

Diver nodded to Ethan, but there was something stiff in his manner. Ethan took the chair opposite his and sipped his ale.

"Something on your mind, Diver?"

Deborah glanced between them, appearing uneasy.

"Nothing that you haven't already heard from Kannice. If she can't convince you, what hope have I got?"

Ethan took a breath, his eyes fixed on his ale. "She told you?"

"She asked me to speak with you. But to be honest, I'm so furious that I don't know what to say."

Ethan had expected as much. He wanted to be angry—who was Diver to tell him which clients he could work for and which he couldn't? He had no more right than did Sephira. But he couldn't bring himself to look the younger man in the eye.

In the past, Ethan had taken on but one client at any given moment, but these were lean times, and even wealthy men like Josiah Wells weren't paying as much to thieftakers as they had in past years. Ethan had little choice but to work for whomever would hire him.

In recent months, as dissatisfaction with the occupation and British policies deepened, the nonimportation movement in the city had grown stronger. Agreements to eschew all imports from Britain had been circulated among Boston's merchants, and those who refused to sign the agreements faced increasing pressure from the Sons of Liberty and their allies. Many had been harassed in the streets. The shops of noncompliant merchants had been vandalized, and mobs threatened worse.

Ethan had been approached by several noncomplying merchants who wanted protection, and, needing the work, he had agreed to help one of them. Kannice, who had long been sympathetic to those who resisted the Crown's attempts to impose ever-greater fees on the colonies, made it clear to Ethan that she disapproved. Now it seemed she had enlisted Diver in her cause.

"I'm not helping anyone violate the agreements," Ethan said, his voice low. "I'm merely trying to keep shops from being burned to the ground. Is that so bad?"

"Some of them deserve to be burned out," Diver said with quiet intensity.

"You don't mean that," Ethan said. "Violence is—"

"Violence is all we've got. If these merchants break the agreements, then the movement fails and we're stuck with the Revenue Acts and all that comes with them. Is that what you want?"

Deborah had been good for Diver. In their time together he had matured, and had managed to find steady employment as a clerk in a shop near where she lived. But, like Kannice, she was a supporter of Samuel Adams and his friends, and at her urging Diver had joined the Sons of Liberty. Ethan enjoyed the company of the new, mature Diver; he was less sure about this political Diver who was so fervent in support of a movement he had all but ignored until a few months before.

"I'll tell you what I don't want," Ethan said. "I don't want any part of 'liberty' if it means that those who don't agree with you and your friends can have their businesses destroyed, while those who do the deed go unpunished. And I think if you were to consider it even briefly, you'd agree with me."

Diver glowered at him, but said nothing.

"I believe, Mister Kaille," Deborah said after a brief silence, "that Derrey fears for you."

"Why is that?"

She hesitated, seeming to search for the right words. "People see you with these men, and they assume that you're in agreement with them, that you think they're right to defy the agreements."

"And then they see me with you," Ethan said to Diver, his choler rising in turn. "And they think the worst of you, as well. Is that it?"

"People know where I stand," Diver said. "Deborah's right: I'm worried about you."

"So am I."

Ethan swiveled in his chair. Kannice stood behind him, a towel draped over her shoulder, loose strands of auburn hair falling over her brow. There was a fine sheen of sweat on her face, and her cheeks were flushed. She looked lovely, as always.

He could smell the lavender in her hair, and the faint scent of Irish whiskey on her breath. It was a combination he had come to know and love in their years together. He hoped that she would stoop and brush his lips with hers, as she usually did when she greeted him. But she merely gazed back at him, a pained expression in her periwinkle blue eyes.

It had been over four weeks since last Ethan stayed the night with her. In all their years together, this was the longest they had gone without making love, and Ethan had little hope that she would invite him back into her bed any time soon. Unless he gave up working for the noncomplying merchants.

"Do you think it's right," Ethan asked, looking from Kannice to Diver, "that mobs cover the windows and doors of these men's shops with dirt and shit? Do you think it's right that the merchants should be so afraid for the safety of their wives and children that they can no longer live in their own homes, but instead must hide in the houses of the few friends they have left?"

"I can't say if it's right or not," Diver said. "But I do know that they brought this on themselves."

"Is that what you think as well?" Ethan asked Kannice. "If Tories did those things to the Dowser and justified their actions by saying that you brought it on yourself when you cast your lot with Samuel Adams and his fellow radicals, would you agree?"

She opened her mouth, closed it again, the look in her eyes hardening. After a moment, she turned on her heel and stalked back to the bar.

Ethan could do little more than stare after her.

"You don't want people thinking you're one of them," Diver said. "And I can tell you that people are already talking."

Ethan continued to watch Kannice, though she steadfastly refused to look his way. "Of course they are. That's what people around here do best."

"Ethan—"

"And what are they saying?" He faced Diver once more. "Are they calling me an ex-convict? A mutineer? A witch?"

"They're calling you a traitor."

"Odd, isn't it, that I can be a traitor and a loyalist at the same time? Except that I'm neither. You and I both know that."

"You make it hard for people to believe."

Ethan took a long drink of ale before setting down his tankard smartly. "They'll believe what they want to, regardless of what I do."

"What if they come by your place, and do to Henry's cooperage what they've been doing to the shops?"

"How are they going to find me, Diver? Are you going to tell them where I live?"

"That's not fair, Mister Kaille!" Deborah said, her cheeks reddening, her eyes shining with candlelight. "Derrey defends you at every opportunity. I've heard him."

Before Ethan could answer, Kelf arrived at their table with Ethan's chowder and a small round of bread.

"There ya go," the barkeep said, placing the bowl and bread in front of him. "Anything else, Ethan?"

Ethan shook his head. The barkeep looked at each of them in turn before starting back toward the kitchen, a frown on his broad face. Long after Kelf left them, Ethan continued to regard his ale.

"I'm sorry, Diver," he said at last. "I shouldn't have said that." The younger man didn't answer. Ethan looked up. Diver was staring down at his tankard, much as he had been.

"I need the money," Ethan said. "Surely you can understand that. In my line of work, I don't always get to choose my clients. They choose me, and if they're offering coin, I can hardly refuse."

"You could refuse this," Diver said, sounding more sad than angry.

Ethan knew there was no point in continuing their argument. He had said his piece, as had Diver. He picked up his spoon and began to eat, though his appetite had long since left him. He scanned the tavern for Kannice and spotted her near the bar. She was chatting amiably with a man he didn't recognize, a man younger and taller and better-looking than he was. At one point she laughed at something he said, and laid a hand lightly on his arm. Ethan looked away, fighting a powerful surge of jealousy.

She could do better than him. Ethan had known that for some time. She was smart and strong and beautiful and as kind as anyone he had ever known. He knew that any man in his right mind would want her. This might finally have occurred to her, as well.

"Maybe you could work for Adams and the rest," Diver said, after several minutes.

Ethan glanced up at him, not bothering to mask his skepticism.

"I'm serious. Maybe they have jobs that you could do, and then you wouldn't—"

Deborah laid a hand on his arm. "Have done, Derrey," she said softly. "It's enough."

He pressed his lips thin and sat back in his chair. "Anyway," he said after a brief pause. "It's getting late. We should probably go."

It couldn't have been much past eight in the evening, which had never been late for Diver before. But Ethan didn't try to stop them.

Diver stood, and Deborah did as well, her brow creased with concern.

"Good night, Ethan."

"Diver."

Ethan's friend began to wend his way to the door. Deborah lingered at the table.

"He really is frightened for you. You're like an older brother to him."

"I know."

"Mister Kaille—" She broke off, appearing to think better of whatever she had meant to say. "Good night."

"Good night, Deborah."

She offered a sad smile and hurried after Diver.

Ethan watched them go before turning his attention back to his food. He ate a bit of his chowder and a few bites of bread. He chewed slowly, making himself eat, oblivious of taste. He couldn't even bring himself to finish his ale.

Kannice still stood near the bar. The man with whom she had been speaking was nowhere to be seen, but she continued to avoid Ethan's gaze. Once he had given Diver and Deborah time enough to put good distance between themselves and the tavern, he stood and left as well. He was sure that Kannice saw him leave; he felt her watching him as he crossed to the door. But she made no effort to stop him, and Ethan gave her no indication that he wished to stay.

THREE

than slept poorly. His room was cold, and he spent much of the night bundled in his blankets, hovering at the edge of sleep and drifting in and out of dreams in which he argued once more with Diver and Kannice. He awoke tired and hungry and chilled to his very core.

He dressed with haste, donning his heaviest woolen stockings and shirt, a waistcoat and coat, and pulling on an old woolen greatcoat over all of that. He would be hard-pressed to push up his sleeve for blood should he need to conjure, but he had not yet had to rely on spells for this job, and he didn't expect that he would today, either. Still, before leaving his room, he slipped into his pocket a full pouch of mullein, a powerful conjuring herb, and he strapped on his blade. Last, he set his tricorn hat on his head and slipped his hands into fingerless woolen gloves.

He had thought his room cold, but when he stepped outside onto the wooden stairway that led from his room down to the street, he shuddered. The sky had clouded over as he slept, leaving it as white as the snowy rooftops. The air remained bitterly cold, and even the gentle breeze blowing off the harbor was enough to make Ethan's cheeks ache and his eyes tear.

A large gray and white dog waited for him at the bottom of the stairs, seemingly unaffected by winter's grip on the city. She wagged her tail as Ethan approached, her tongue lolling. Henry Dall, the cooper, had adopted Shelly years before, along with her mate, Pitch, a beautiful black dog with long, silken fur. Pitch had died several years ago. More accurately, Ethan had killed him, using the poor dog for what conjurers called a killing spell, a casting that drew upon the life of another for its power. The conjuring saved Ethan's life and that of a boy, the son of Elli, his former betrothed. But to this day, he wasn't sure that these ends excused what he had done. Of all the dark deeds Ethan had committed in his life, including those that led to his imprisonment, casting that spell was the one he regretted most. It had been nigh on five years, but still, upon seeing Shelly, Ethan had to resist the urge to apologize to her for taking her companion.

"Well met, Shelly," Ethan said, squatting down to scratch her head. She licked his hands.

"I've no food for you," he said. "Nor for me, for that matter. My apologies."

He straightened and started toward the North End. Shelly trotted alongside him, perhaps hoping that he would buy them both a bit of breakfast if she stayed with him long enough. As he neared the Town Dock, she seemed to decide that Ethan would be providing no meals; she turned and started back toward the cooperage.

The closer Ethan drew to the North End, the heavier his steps grew. The truth was, in all his years as a thieftaker, he had never harbored greater misgivings about taking on a job. His words to Kannice and Diver notwithstanding, he wasn't entirely convinced that the merchants who violated the nonimportation agreements deserved protection. Those who argued that the Townshend Duties helped to pay for the ongoing occupation of Boston by British soldiers, an occupation of which Ethan disapproved, made a compelling case. But Ethan did need the money, and jobs were as hard to come by now as he could remember.

Making matters worse, Theophilus Lillie, the merchant who had hired him, was among the most outspoken of the importers, and, as a result, one of the most despised men in all of Boston. He owned a dry goods shop on Middle Street, a short distance north of Mill Creek, where the North End began. In person, he was quiet, polite, and unassuming. But on those occasions when he chose to write in defense of his stand against the nonimportation agreements, as he had most recently the month before in the Boston *News-Letter*, he could be every bit as acerbic as the most talented Whig writers. To Ethan's mind, much of the abuse directed at his shop was well deserved. Of course, he kept this opinion to himself.

When Ethan reached Middle Street, he found Lillie outside in the lane, surveying the latest indignities heaped upon his establishment. The windows of the shop had been smeared with tar and feathers, and a large wooden sign in the shape of a hand had been attached to one of the iron posts in front of the building. The sign, which appeared to be pointing toward Lillie's door, read, "A very inoffensive man, except in the offense of importation."

A second sign, this one bearing effigies of four noncomplying merchants, including Lillie, had been erected nearby.

The signboards were annoyances; the tar on the windows could be removed eventually, although probably not until the air turned warmer.

Ethan was far more alarmed by the presence in the street of several dozen young men. They stood together a short distance from the shop, their hands in their pockets, their shoulders hunched against the cold. A few of them glanced toward the shop and Lillie, but mostly they talked among themselves, punctuating their conversations with occasional bursts of laughter. Ethan feared, however, that they would not be content for long to mind their own affairs.

Ethan halted a few feet from the merchant, his eyes on the mob.

"I suppose I should be flattered that they think me otherwise inoffensive," Lillie said, frowning at the damage done to his windows. He leaned in closer, peering at the besmeared glass over the rims of his spectacles. "That tar won't come off easily."

"No, sir, at least not today with it being so cold. For now, I think you should go back inside."

Lillie glanced at Ethan and then toward the crowd of young men. "Yes, you're probably right." He heaved a breath. "Could you have prevented this?" he asked.

"I don't know."

"I hired you to protect my shop, my family, and me. And yet, they managed to do this despite the money I'm paying you."

"If you remember, you hired me to watch your shop by day. I told you what it would cost to hire me at night; you balked at the amount."

"You were asking for a lot of money," Lillie said, facing him.

"Be that as it may."

Lillie scowled and surveyed the windows once more. "It might well have been worth the expense."

Ethan held his tongue, hoping the merchant wouldn't change his mind and ask him to work past sundown. As bad as it was working for Lillie at all, it would be worse by far spending his evenings here instead of at the Dowsing Rod.

Boys and young men continued to stream from all directions onto Middle Street. Watching them greet one another, it occurred to Ethan that this was no chance gathering. The same rabble who in recent weeks had tried to intimidate other importers with loud demonstrations, acts of mischief like the dirtying of Lillie's windows, and even wanton destruction of property, had chosen on this day to direct their ire at Mr. Lillie.

"Sir, I do think we need to get you inside."

The merchant eyed the mob once more. "Yes, very well."

He stepped into the shop, and Ethan followed close behind, shutting the door and securing the lock.

Lillie turned at the sound of the bolt. "I'm open for business, Mister Kaille. My purpose in hiring you was to remain open despite these threats."

"I understand, sir. And as soon as a customer approaches, I'll unlock the door. I'll even hold it open. But until then, I intend to keep it locked."

Lillie didn't look pleased, but neither did he argue the point further. He removed his cloak, revealing a deep green coat and matching breeches and waistcoat—a ditto suit, as such sets were called. He wore as well a powdered wig that made him look a good deal older than his years; Ethan guessed that Lillie was actually a few years younger than he. He had a round, pleasant face, dark eyes, and a weak chin. He didn't look to Ethan like a man who could so inflame the passions of the mob that lingered out in the street.

The young clerk who worked in the shop knelt before a shallow hearth and stirred the fire burning there. It was still chilly within but it wasn't nearly as cold as it had been outside.

Ethan removed his greatcoat, and, with his back turned to the merchant, pulled a few leaves of mullein from the pouch hidden in his pocket.

He had planned to cast a warding spell on the shop door, but now, holding the leaves in the curl of his fingers, he reconsidered. Lillie had gone behind the counter and was readying the shop for a day's business. Ethan wasn't sure a warding that allowed patrons to come and go as they pleased would have any effect on those with darker intentions.

Staring out through the filthy windows, he could see that the crowd continued to grow. More, many of the young toughs had positioned themselves closer to the shop and in the middle of the street.

"Sir, you might consider closing for the day."

Lillie turned. "What? I'll do no such thing! As I've said, you are here—"

"I'm here to protect you and your shop. I believe you would be safer at your home, and I believe that if you were to close, only for today, that mob would count it a victory and would be satisfied. As long as you remain and try to keep your doors open, they'll stay out there and will do everything in their power to keep customers from your door."

"I'm not interested in giving them a victory, Mister Kaille. I'm interested in running this establishment as I see fit, without interference from these so-called champions of liberty. Where is my liberty to do as I please with my shop?"

"I understand all that, sir," Ethan said, trying to keep his tone level. He almost told the merchant that he even agreed with him, but he couldn't bring himself to speak the words. He was no longer certain of his own mind; as much as he argued with Kannice and Diver, he couldn't bring himself to take Lillie's side, even in a conversation his friends could not hear. "I'm trying to keep you from coming to harm. That is my greatest concern."

"Then I would suggest that you get out there and see what you can do about clearing the street and allowing me to earn a bit of coin."

Ethan saw no point in this, although he did see great risk to himself.

But Lillie had hired him, and was watching him now, an expectant look on his face.

He left his greatcoat where it was, willing in that moment to trade warmth for greater agility. And as he walked out the door and pulled it closed behind him, he muttered under his breath in Latin, "*Tegimen ex verbasco evocatum.*" Warding, conjured from mullein.

Uncle Reg appeared beside him, pale to the point of translucence in the bright glare of the snow and clouds.

"Stay with me," Ethan said in the same low voice. He started toward the nearest cluster of toughs, Reg matching him step for step.

"Are there any conjurers among them?"

The ghost shook his head.

That was a small grace.

"Good day," Ethan called, raising a hand in greeting as he approached them.

The toughs stared back at him, stony-faced.

"You work for him?" one of the pups asked, nodding toward Lillie's shop.

"He's hired me, yes. It's my job to see to it that his shop is not vandalized and his person not abused."

The pup grinned. "Looks like you didn' do too good protectin' his shop. I don' suppose you'll do much better guardin' 'his person.'"

The other toughs laughed.

Ethan glanced around. Others were listening to their conversation, eyeing him with manifest hostility. He didn't wish to trade threats with the lad, but he felt compelled to make some attempt to do as the merchant had asked. "I should tell you that if you molest Mister Lillie's customers or do anything to keep them from his door, he'll have no choice but to summon Sheriff Greenleaf."

"Oh, not the sheriff!" the pup said, feigning terror, and drawing more chuckles from his companions. He sobered. "The sheriff has about as much chance of clearin' us from the street as you do."

"The sheriff may bring soldiers."

The lad smiled again though there was not a hint of mirth in his pale eyes. "Let him."

Before Ethan could say more, the lad turned away from him. "Are we afraid of the lobsterbacks?" he cried.

The mob replied with a deafening "No!"

He faced Ethan again. "Go back an' tell your importer friend that he's free to summon the sheriff, or the gov'nor, or Gen'ral Gage. Hell, he can summon the goddamned king for all we care."

The other toughs had sidled closer, and they cheered the lad. Ethan knew that if he didn't retreat now, he might not have another opportunity.

Tipping his hat to them, he said, "Very well. Good day, gentlemen." He turned and started back to the shop.

"You hear that?" the lad said, laughing once more. "Gentlemen he calls us. Good'ay to you, too, gov'nor!"

They continued to laugh at him, but they let him go, which Ethan counted a small victory.

No sooner had he reentered the shop than the mob began to converge on Lillie's establishment.

"What did you say to them?" the merchant asked, sounding angry and frightened. He had come out from behind the counter and now stood at the window, marking their approach, his cheeks wan.

"I told them that I was here to keep your shop from harm, and I suggested that they refrain from molesting your customers lest you call the sheriff to disperse them."

"Apparently you weren't very convincing."

Ethan laughed. "Did you truly believe I would be?"

Lillie shot him a filthy look.

The young men were shouting, although aside from hearing "importer," and "traitor," and a few other imprecations, Ethan could make out little of what they said. Some of them were also pelting Lillie's door and window with snowballs and pieces of ice. Fearing that the glass might shatter under the onslaught, Ethan thought about casting another spell. But before he could retrieve more mullein from the pocket of his greatcoat, Lillie said, "What in the Lord's name is he doing?"

"Who?" Ethan asked, stepping closer to the window.

Lillie pointed.

Gazing in the direction the merchant indicated, Ethan spotted an older man scrutinizing the wooden hand and effigies with a critical eye. He wore a tricorn hat and a bright red cloak much like Lillie's. He had a kerchief wrapped around his neck and the lower part of his face to protect him from the cold, but still Ethan thought he recognized the man as Ebenezer Richardson, Lillie's neighbor.

As much as Lillie had made himself an object of scorn among Boston's Whigs, his unpopularity was nothing compared to that of Richardson. Several years before, Richardson had been exposed as an informer for the Customs Board. He had alerted officials of the Crown to the smuggling of goods, including French wine, by merchants acting in defiance of Parliament. When these merchants, most of whom were Whig sympathizers, attempted to shame Richardson publicly, he was unapologetic. In the years since, he had been employed by the Customs Board in a more formal capacity, which did nothing to improve his reputation. Nor did his habit of referring to himself as "a magistrate" and ordering people about without any real authority to do so.

"He's going to get himself killed," Ethan said. Most of the lads had yet to take notice of the man, but when they did he would be in peril.

"Go help him, Kaille," Lillie said.

"That's not my job. I have no desire to risk my neck for Ebenezer Richardson."

"You said it yourself: They'll kill him."

Ethan glanced at Uncle Reg, who still stood beside him, his russet glow more pronounced inside the shop. Of course Lillie, who was no conjurer, could not see him. The specter gave a halfhearted shrug.

"Very well," Ethan said. "I'll use the rear entrance."

"Aye. That's a fine idea."

Ethan exited the shop through the door in back and returned to Middle Street by way of a narrow alley. By the time he reached the front of the shop, however, Richardson was no longer standing in front of the signs. Scanning the mob, Ethan spotted the man talking to the driver of a horse and cart, and gesturing back at the effigies. Ethan hurried toward them.

". . . Run them down!" Richardson was saying.

"No, sir," the cart driver replied. "Even if I were inclined to, it might hurt my horse or my cart."

"It will do neither." When the driver said nothing more, Richardson dismissed him with a wave of his hand. "Fool!"

"Mister Richardson," Ethan said, "you need to get off the street."

Richardson rounded on him. "And who are you to tell me what I ought to be doing?"

"My name is Ethan Kaille, and I'm—"

"You're that thieftaker who Theophilus hired."

"Yes, sir. Mister Lillie is concerned for—"

"You're not doing much to earn your wage, are you Kaille? These signs and such are a disgrace. They need to be torn down."

"I'm less concerned with the signs than I am with keeping Mister Lillie safe. And he's concerned about you, sir. This mob is getting more agitated by the moment, and you're not exactly their favorite person."

Richardson dismissed this remark much as he had the cart driver. "I don't give a damn about that. Let 'em come on me. I've got my guns loaded." He turned a quick circle. "Ah! You there!" He bustled off toward a charcoal carter who was making his way through the throng.

Ethan didn't bother to follow, but he watched as the customs man, his gesticulations growing ever more animated, tried to convince the charcoal man to knock down the signs with his cart. Once again, however, Richardson was rebuffed.

By this time, more people in the crowd had noticed him. Some were pointing; others shouted his name.

Richardson paid them no heed. He was as a man possessed. Unable to find a cart driver to knock over the offending signs, he strode to a small chaise that sat near another shop. Its driver had stepped away to speak to a few of the street toughs, and before this man could stop him, Richardson climbed in and grabbed the reins, shouted at the horse, and steered the chaise toward the effigies.

Aware now of what the customs man was up to, the mob blocked his way and tried to pull him from the carriage.

Fearing for Richardson's life, Ethan clambered toward him, pushing his way through the sea of men and boys. He knew though that he wouldn't reach Richardson in time.

But to his surprise, Richardson escaped the chaise on his own and beat a hasty path toward his home. Several men accosted him, and the boys shouted "Informer!" again and again.

Richardson answered the taunts of several of the men with cries of "Perjury! Perjury!" And when at last he reached his door, he turned, and said to those baiting him, "By the eternal God, I'll make it too hot for you before night!"

With that, he shut the door in the men's faces.

Relieved that Richardson had reached the safety of his house without injury, Ethan turned, intending to make his way back to Lillie's shop.

"Come out, you damn son of a bitch!" one man shouted at Richardson's door. "I'll have your heart out! Your liver out!"

To Ethan's amazement and consternation, Richardson opened his door once more, and jumped out into the street, his fists raised.

"C'mon, you bloody bastards! I'll fight all of you. I'll make it hot for every one of you!"

The mob of men and boys that had gathered around Lillie's door swept toward Richardson's house as if compelled by a tide, calling him an informer and shouting other insults.

"Go off!" Richardson warned, his voice carrying along the street. His wife joined him in front of the house, and shouted most unladylike epithets at her husband's enemies.

The mob laughed at them both.

"We've as much right as you t' this street, informer!" one young man called.

His companions cheered.

Snowballs, chunks of ice, and pieces of refuse rained down on the Richardsons, forcing them to retreat once more into the house. Ethan hoped that this time the customs man would have the good sense to remain inside. He should have known better.

The door opened again, and Ethan drew breath to shout a warning. Richardson held in his hands what Ethan took at first for a longrifle, though as Richardson shook it at the mob and traded more insults with them, he realized it was nothing more threatening than a stick. Again the customs man ducked back through his door, but this time instead of closing it, he threw a brickbat out at the mob. It didn't hit anyone, but it further enraged his harassers. A man grabbed the brick and threw it through one of Richardson's first-floor windows.

A roar went up from the mob. They pressed forward, pelting the home with sticks, rocks, eggs and pieces of fruit from nearby shops, and anything else they could lay their hands on. More windows shattered. A woman cried out from the upper floor. A man Ethan didn't know leapt up onto the doorstep and, after speaking briefly with Richardson, was ushered into the house.

The door was barred, even as more projectiles flew at the windows and door. In short order, most of the glass on the front of the house had been broken. One man called for Richardson to be dragged from his home and hanged. Several other men—older than most of those in the mob—tried to dissuade the toughs from doing more damage, but the crowd seemed to be beyond reason. There were as many young boys as there were men. A number of them were laughing, seeming to think it all a great game. The scene reminded Ethan of the Pope's Day riots that used to pit North End gangs against ruffians from the South End.

Ethan watched the house, thinking—hoping—that at last Richardson had tired of the confrontation. Perhaps if the customs man kept out of sight for a time, the crowd would disperse, or at least turn their attention back to their less combative demonstrations in front of Lillie's shop.

But even as he formed this thought, he felt a low thrum of power in the icy street. A spell? Reg, still beside him, though ethereal in the daylight, cast a sharp look Ethan's way.

"That was a conjuring, wasn't it?" Ethan asked the ghost, whispering the words.

Reg nodded, his eyebrows bunched.

"Do you know where it came from?"

A shake of the ghostly head. *No.*

He had other questions for the specter, and he sensed that there was more Reg wished to communicate to him. But he had no opportunity to ask. Richardson appeared at a downstairs window, and this time there could be no mistaking the musket he held in his hands.

He knelt and rested the barrel on the windowsill, seeming to take careful aim. But though it seemed to Ethan that he pulled the trigger, nothing happened. With a crash, the mob broke through Richardson's door. Those closest to the house appeared to be taken aback at what they had done; no one entered. But volleys of rocks and ice still flew at the structure. Richardson stepped away from the window, though only briefly. Seconds later he was back, kneeling again.

The second man stood behind Richardson, also holding a musket, but it was Richardson who aimed at the crowd once more.

And this time when he pulled the trigger, the weapon fired with a report that reverberated through the lanes.

For the span of a heartbeat, all was still save for the receding echo of that gunshot. Then the stunned silence gave way to shouts of outrage and screams of panic. More stones hit off the façade of the house and flew through the unglazed windows. Someone cried, "He's shot the boy!"

Richardson yelled back at the mob, aiming his musket again. The second man moved to the window and aimed his weapon toward the open doorway. Some who had advanced on the entrance retreated again. Several ran around toward the back of the house, no doubt hoping to gain entry that way.

Ethan spotted a young man being led away from the Richardson home toward another house. There was blood on his hand and on both of his thighs, but that appeared to be the extent of his wounds. He had been fortunate; all of them had. It seemed Richardson—the idiot—had fired pellets into the crowd, endangering dozens.

And in that moment, Ethan caught sight of the second lad.

He was slight, with wheaten hair, and he couldn't have been more than twelve years old. His coat had been peeled away to reveal the front of his shirt, which had several holes in it and was soaked with blood.

Two men carried the boy, their faces pale, though not so much as the child's. His face was white as the snow, and contorted in a rictus of pain. They took him to one of the other houses and shut the door on the mob. A few seconds later two men rushed inside this same structure; Ethan hoped they were physicians.

He felt sick to his stomach. The battle for Richardson's house went on; he could hear men battering the rear, but he hadn't the heart to watch more. He walked back toward Lillie's shop.

Before he was halfway there, he turned and made his way to the house into which they had taken the boy. He couldn't try to save the boy without revealing to everyone there that he was a conjurer. But he wouldn't forgive himself if he didn't make the attempt. Reaching the house, he rapped hard on the door.

Almost immediately it swung open. The man who blocked Ethan's way into the house had blood on his coat and breeches.

"Are you a surgeon?" he asked.

Ethan hesitated for no more than an instant. "I have experience healing wounds of this sort."

The man seemed unsure, but he stepped aside. Ethan rushed past him into what appeared to be the dining room. The boy lay on the table in the center of the chamber. His shirt had been removed; his chest and abdomen were a bloody mess. A man stood beside the table, his hands crimson, shocking. Ethan assumed he was a physician.

"Who are you?" the man asked.

"My name is Ethan Kaille, Doctor."

"Your name is not familiar to me. Are you a surgeon?"

Ethan stepped closer to him. He was aware of Reg hovering at his shoulder, eyeing the boy. "I have the ability to heal," he said, keeping his voice low and holding the man's gaze. "Do you understand what I'm saying?"

The doctor's eyes widened. "I believe I do," he whispered.

"I can close the wounds, stop the bleeding."

"The bleeding is only half the problem," the doctor said. "The boy was struck with swan shot. At least one of the pellets seems to have lodged in a lung. There may be others in his heart or his stomach. Unless we can extract them, he's going to die."

Ethan sagged and stared down at the boy.

"Can you get them out?" the doctor asked. "Is that within your . . . your talents?"

"No," Ethan said, his voice thick.

The doctor grimaced.

Ethan thought he still might be able to help the lad, but before he could say as much to the doctor, a second gentleman hurried into the room, halted at the sight of Ethan, and scrutinized him with a critical eye.

"Who is this?"

"My name—"

"Are you a physician?"

"No, sir."

"Then off with you. The boy needs care, not more trouble with rabble and ruffians."

The doctor appeared ready to tell the man that Ethan was a speller, but Ethan stopped him with a shake of his head. The boy needed a surgeon; he needed more than the crude healing Ethan could offer.

"I'll be going," he said to the doctor. "I'm sorry I couldn't do more."

"We've called for other surgeons," the man said. "I'm sure they'll come; one of them might be able to save him."

Ethan paused, although he didn't look back. "I hope so."

"Pray for the boy."

I believe in neither prayer nor God, Ethan wanted to say. But he kept this to himself and left the house.

Chapter
FOUR

Ethan stepped back onto Middle Street. A church bell had begun to peal nearby and more men had surrounded Richardson's house. He could hear raised voices from within the residence, and he assumed that some of the mob had managed to get inside. He wondered if they would kill the customs man or merely turn him over to the sheriff. He couldn't say that he cared much one way or another.

Reg was still with him, watching Ethan as he walked. Ethan didn't know what the spirit expected of him, and he was too angry and too disturbed to treat with him just then.

"*Dimitto te,*" Ethan whispered. I release you.

Closer to Lillie's shop, a few men lingered near the sign and effigies that Richardson had tried to remove, but they barely took notice of Ethan. They were watching the mob and seemed to have all but forgotten the importer Lillie.

Ethan knocked on the door. The merchant unlocked it, waved him inside, and shut it again, taking care to secure the lock once more.

"What happened?" Lillie asked. "Where have you been? I thought I heard a gunshot before, but I can barely see through that window, and I didn't dare venture outside. Is Ebenezer all right?"

"Ebenezer?" Ethan repeated, picking up his greatcoat. "You're worried about Richardson?"

"Of course. He and I have been friends for years. And if you remember, it was your concern for him that drove you out into the street in the first place."

Ethan could hardly blame Lillie for being concerned for his friend. The merchant hadn't seen the shooting; he didn't know what Richardson had done. But at that moment Ethan was too enraged and grief-stricken to care.

"You all but ordered me into the street," he said.

"And did you help him? Is he all right?"

"I haven't the faintest idea." He shrugged on his coat and headed toward the door. "To be honest, I hope they kill him."

"What? How dare you say such a thing!"

Ethan whirled, leveling a finger at Lillie with such passion that the merchant fell back several paces. "He fired into the crowd, without a thought for who he might hit!" He pointed in the general direction of the house in which the boy lay dying. "There's a boy—I doubt he's seen his thirteenth birthday! And he's dying, murdered by your friend!"

Lillie paled, but raised his chin. "If he was in that mob, with the rest of the rabble, he probably deserved it. Ebenezer wouldn't shoot a child without cause."

"Aye, he would. I've just seen it."

Ethan pulled the door open.

"Where are you going now?"

"I'm done here for today. I'm going to the Dowsing Rod for an ale."

"I hired you! You leave when I tell you to!"

"No, sir. I leave when I'm good and ready. You pay me by the day. You can have this morning for free. The afternoon is mine."

"But that mob—"

Ethan wanted to put as much distance between himself and this shop as he could. But he read genuine fear in Lillie's round face and so paused on the threshold.

"They no longer care where your goods come from. Not today they don't. I don't know what they'll do to Mister Richardson; I meant what I said before: I don't care a whit about him. But I believe that you and your shop are safe, at least until tomorrow. Go home, Mister Lillie."

Ethan swept out of the shop and pulled the door closed with a bang, intending to make his way back to Sudbury Street and Kannice's tavern. But the mob had worked itself into a frenzy once more, and Ethan could guess why. He squeezed through the throng until he had a clear view of the Richardson house.

The customs man, and the other gentleman who had entered the house and brandished a musket alongside him, stood together near the doorway. Young toughs gripped their arms so that they couldn't escape. Another man held the muskets, and yet another held a cutlass; Ethan didn't know where he had gotten it. Richardson and his companion had been beaten. Their faces bore cuts and bruises, and their clothing was torn and bloodstained. The mob shouted obscenities at them. One man held aloft a rope that had been tied into a noose. Seeing this, the crowd cheered. Richardson and his friend were borne down to the street none too gently and dragged toward a post, which the fellow with the rope was already turning into a makeshift gallows.

Without giving much thought to what he was saying, Ethan had told Lillie that he hoped Richardson would be killed. Now, with that outcome seeming likely, he had second thoughts. Hanging the villain in the street would only confirm for Lillie and other Tories that the crowd was made up of ruffians and bloodthirsty miscreants.

Apparently, he was not the only person on Middle Street thinking this way. Another man stepped forward from the crowd and approached the would-be hangman. He was tall, broad-shouldered. Ethan recognized him as one of the leaders of the mob, and thought he might have seen him on other occasions when men took to the streets to make their case against the importers.

This gentleman and the hangman conversed for several moments; their exchange appeared, at least from a distance, to be most congenial. At last the hangman pulled down his rope and shook hands with the tall man. Many in the crowd jeered.

Soon enough, however, the mob found another means to make sport with Richardson and his friend. They bound the two men's hands and then began to drag them through the lane, while men and boys in the throng kicked and beat the prisoners and pelted them with stones and refuse.

Ethan wondered if the two would have been better off with ropes around their necks. Rather than remain there and watch, he walked southward along Middle Street, away from the revelers and back over Mill Creek. By the time he reached the Dowsing Rod, he could no longer hear the crowd, though the church bell still pealed in the distance.

When Ethan entered the Dowser, Kannice and Kelf were at the bar, she polishing the wood, he drying tankards. A few British soldiers sat at tables, drinking ales and eating oysters, but otherwise the tavern was empty.

Kannice smiled at the sight of him. "You're here early."

A couple of the soldiers swiveled in their chairs to see who had come, but after regarding Ethan for a few seconds, they went back to their meals.

"Aye," Ethan said, crossing to the bar. "My work's done for today."

She frowned. "Done? I don't understand."

"I left. I had no interest in collecting this day's wage."

Her frown deepened.

"I thought you'd be pleased," Ethan said, his voice falsely bright. "We haven't passed a day together in weeks."

She knew him too well.

"I don't like the sound of this. What's happened, Ethan?"

He glanced at Kelf, who filled a tankard and placed it in front of him. "My thanks, Kelf." He took a long pull, draining most of the cup's contents.

"Ethan?"

"There was a mob there today. I think they planned to make an example of Lillie, as they have some of the other importers in recent days. But then Ebenezer Richardson showed up. He tried to bring down some signs they'd put up, and before long the mob turned their ire on him. One thing led to another and . . . and he fired a musket into the crowd."

"May the Lord have mercy," Kannice whispered.

Ethan shook his head. "If only. He shot a boy. I doubt the lad will last the night."

"And Richardson?" Kelf asked.

"He's being dragged through the streets as we speak. I'm not sure he'll see the morrow either."

Kannice canted her head to the side, her brow furrowed as she searched his eyes. "And Lillie sent you away?"

"No. As I said, I left. He was more worried about Richardson than the lad; he said the boy probably deserved what he got. I should have quit on the spot, told him I wouldn't be coming back." He looked away. "Some would say I should have done that some time ago. But all I did was leave. I suppose I'll be going back in the morning. I'm not sure what that makes me."

"What will you tell him when you go back?" Kannice asked.

Ethan sighed. "I don't know." He couldn't bring himself to look at her. "I know what you'd like me to do."

"You have to decide what you want, Ethan. You need the money; I understand that."

"Aye, but now there are other considerations."

Lillie had been paying him fifteen shillings a day, which, while not a fortune, was more than enough to keep him fed and housed. As much as he wanted to end their arrangement, he wasn't sure that he could afford to take so drastic a step. Besides, in all his years as a thieftaker, he had never abandoned an inquiry or stopped working for a client before his job was done. He was known to be reliable as well as honest and competent. He didn't wish to mar this well-earned reputation.

But could he bring himself to work for the man after all that had passed this morning?

"No one would blame you if you quit," Kannice said, reading the doubt on his face.

"Lillie would. And so would his friends."

"You don't have to work for them. There are other jobs. Even if you give up this one, you won't be idle for long." A smile crossed her lips. "And while you're looking for a new employer, you and I could make up for lost time."

"I'll be in the back," Kelf said, stomping into the kitchen, his ears bright red.

"So you'd be willing to take me back if I stopped working for Lillie?"

Kannice's expression turned serious. "I've been ready to take you back all along, Ethan. You're the one who wouldn't stay."

"I was waiting for an invitation."

"And I was waiting for some indication that you wanted one."

He gave a small, mirthless laugh. Kannice took his hand, and laced her fingers through his.

"Let me get you some bread and chowder. I'd wager every coin in my till that you haven't eaten a bite today."

"You'd win that wager." He fished in his pocket for a half shilling.

"Ethan, don't."

"I'm not so desperate that I can't pay for my supper. Not yet at least."

She glared at him, trying with only some success to look stern. At length she relented and held out her hand. "Very well."

He gave her the coin and she started back into the kitchen to get his meal. But then she halted and faced him once more.

"Do you know the boy's name?" she asked.

"No. But I have a feeling we all will before long."

Christopher Seider.

He was the son of a German laborer. And he was eleven years old.

The other young man who had been shot was Samuel Gore, the son of a captain in the colonial militia.

Word of the shootings spread through the city like smoke from a fire, until by nightfall no one was speaking of anything else. Gore was expected to recover, although Dr. Joseph Warren, who had treated the young man, said that he might never regain the full use of his hand.

Seider's condition was far more grave. He was alive still, though only barely. Several doctors, including Warren, had tried to remove the shot from his lung, but none had succeeded. Most said it was merely a matter of time before the lad died.

Kannice's tavern filled up as it always did, but on this night her patrons were unusually subdued. They ate and they drank, but conversations were spoken in hushed voices. Ethan heard not a thread of laughter.

Diver and Deborah came in and walked to a table a good distance from Ethan's. Diver wouldn't even look at him. Ethan considered joining them and telling Diver that he had decided he would no longer work for Lillie. But he was still wavering on what he should do come the morning, and he wasn't convinced that Diver would care even if he did choose to terminate his arrangement with the merchant. He had been working for Lillie this morning, when Christopher Seider was shot. Nothing else mattered.

Instead, Ethan sat alone, sipping an ale. Like every person in the Dowser, he awaited news of the boy's condition, looking toward the door each time it opened. But again and again he was disappointed.

As he sat, he turned over the morning's events in his mind, sifting through his memory of what had been said and done. And so it was that at last he recalled something that should have been foremost in his mind.

"*Veni ad me*," he whispered. Come to me.

Uncle Reg winked into view in the chair across the table from him, his eyes burning as bright as brands. He had balled one of his glowing hands into a tight fist; with the other hand he gestured wildly. Ethan had no idea what he was trying to convey, but he didn't think he had ever seen the ghost more angry.

Calm down. Ethan said this in his mind. No one who wasn't a conjurer could see Reg, and Ethan didn't wish to draw the attention of every person in the Dowser by appearing to speak to himself. *You're angry with me. Because you didn't want me to dismiss you earlier today?*

Reg threw his arms wide. Ethan knew that if he were capable of speech, he would have berated him.

I'm sorry. I was thinking about the boy and nothing else.

The specter's expression softened. He offered a curt nod, and then opened his hands: a questioning gesture.

There's been no word yet, but I fear the worst. You wished to tell me something?

Another nod.

You felt a conjuring a short while before Richardson fired into the crowd. I did*, too. At the time, you couldn't say where it came from. Do you know now?*

Reg shook his head.

Do you know what kind of spell it was?

No.

So then it's possible that the conjuring had nothing do with what happened on Middle Street.

Reg did not respond at first. After a few seconds he gave a slow shake of his head. He tapped his chest with his fingers and then made a sweeping motion with his hand.

You believe the spell was related to the shooting of the Seider boy. I understand that much. But the rest . . . Ethan shrugged. *I'm sorry. Sometimes I really wish you could speak.*

The ghost nodded at that.

Were there other conjurers there today? Did you sense that anyone was casting spells on the street?

No.

Is there a conjuring I can try that would—

Reg held up a hand, forestalling Ethan's question. He tapped his chest again.

"You," Ethan whispered.

Reg nodded. He made that same sweeping gesture again.

Ethan shook his head. "I don't—"

The ghost frowned and rubbed a hand over his face. After considering the matter, he placed an open hand to his brow and swiveled his head, as if he were searching for something.

You were looking around. On Middle Street?

A nod. He pointed to his chest again, then to his eyes, and once more to his chest.

I don't— A chill passed through Ethan, making him shudder. "My God," he said under his breath. *You were looking around, and you saw a ghost, a spectral guide, a being like you.*

Reg nodded with great enthusiasm.

A ghost, Ethan said within his mind, wanting to be clear on exactly what Reg was telling him. *Not an illusion spell.*

Reg tapped his chest again, more emphatically this time. A ghost.

Ethan's heart had started to labor. "Was it one you had seen before?"

A man seated at an adjacent table glanced Ethan's way, his expression a blend of dismay and alarm. At that moment, Ethan didn't care who heard his question or what they thought of him speaking to himself.

"Was it Nate Ramsey's guide?"

Nate Ramsey was the merchant captain and conjurer who, during the previous summer, had nearly managed to kill Ethan, as well as Mariz and Ethan's friend Tarijanna Windcatcher. He did kill Gavin Black, another friend and an accomplished conjurer in his own right. The captain had raised an army of shades by desecrating graves throughout the city, and had come within a hairsbreadth of rendering powerless every conjurer in Boston except himself.

During their final confrontation on Drake's Wharf, Ramsey set a warehouse ablaze and appeared to perish in the conflagration. But though Sheriff Greenleaf had men of the watch search through the rubble, no one ever found the captain's body. To this day, the possible implication of that fruitless search haunted Ethan's dreams, and lurked in the back of his mind during his waking hours.

To Ethan's profound relief, Reg shook his head. *No.* It wasn't Ramsey's ghost.

You're certain?

Yes.

Could it have been one of the ghosts Ramsey controlled last summer? Is he trying to deny us access to our spellmaking power again?

Reg shook his head yet again.

Ethan didn't realize until he exhaled that he had been holding his breath. *You didn't recognize this specter?*

No. He tapped a finger to the side of his head, beside his eye, and then raised his hand to his brow again, as if searching.

But you think it was watching, or rather, that the conjurer was watching through the ghost. You think he cast the spell when he did for a reason.

Reg sat back in his chair and nodded, a look of relief on his lined face.

I see. Thank you.

The door to the tavern opened, and a man stepped inside. Every person in the Dowser turned to look at him.

"Richardson and Wilmot have been before Justices Ruddock, Pemberton, Dana, and Quincy," the man said, his voice carrying through the great room. "They've been sent to the gaol and will be tried before the superior court on the thirteenth of March."

"We don' need the court!" someone shouted back. "We all seen what they done. They should be hanged, and good riddance to them!"

Others cheered this.

The man at the door shrugged. "That's not for me to say. I'm only tellin' you what's happened."

"What about the lad?" another voice called.

"I've no word on him. I'm sorry."

He tipped his hat to Kannice, and left the tavern.

Ethan turned back to Reg. *Is there anything else you wanted me to know?* Reg shook his head.

Very well. Thank you. I'll be more attentive next time and I'll try not to send you away before you've had your say.

A rare smile curved the ghost's lips.

Dimitto te. I release you.

Reg faded from view, leaving Ethan to ponder the implications of what his spectral guide had seen. The pulse of a random spell could be dismissed as mere coincidence, even if it did come only moments before Richardson fired his musket. But if there had been a specter there, watching all that happened, waiting for the precise instant when a spell might do the most harm . . . that was a different matter.

He recalled Gordon's sudden attack on Will Pryor the previous night, and the spell he and Mariz thought had preceded the assault. Were the two incidents related? Ethan didn't see how they could be— one mattered only to himself and to Sephira Pryce. The other had implications for all of Boston. Once more he wondered if he and Mariz had imagined that pulse of power the night before.

On that thought, something else occurred to him. It seemed like folly, but before this night was through he might have no choice but to test his theory.

He had few ideas of how he might proceed, none of them very good. But he couldn't sit there doing nothing. Making up his mind, he drained his tankard, stood, and walked to the table Diver shared with Deborah.

"May I join you?"

Diver looked up at him, but said nothing.

Deborah eyed her beau before indicating the chair between them. "Of course you may, Mister Kaille. Please, sit."

Still Ethan waited, watching his friend. At last Diver offered a slight shrug, which Ethan took as an invitation.

He sat and, holding up his tankard, caught Kelf's eye. "Can I buy you one?" he asked Diver.

"No, thank you."

If Ethan needed further proof of the depth of Diver's anger, here it was: He couldn't remember the younger man ever refusing a free ale.

"I was there today," he said. "I saw Christopher Seider get shot."

"I thought you might have." Diver didn't face him, but at least he replied. "I knew that they were going to be at Lillie's shop, and I know that you're working for him."

Ethan's anger flared. Diver had known that there would be a mob on Middle Street, and he had given him no warning. He held his tongue, knowing that no good would come of another confrontation. But something in his chest tightened. Once he had been Diver's closest friend; now, apparently, Diver felt greater loyalty to the Sons of Liberty than to him.

"I have been working for him. I don't know if I can anymore."

At these words, Diver met his gaze.

"Truly?"

"He made excuses for Richardson; he said the boy deserved what he got." Ethan cringed. "How can I take his money after that?"

Diver leaned forward. "You can't," he said. "He doesn't deserve to have you working for him, Ethan." It was the nicest thing Diver had said to him in months.

Kelf arrived with Ethan's ale and glanced first at Diver and then at Ethan. "It's nice to see the two of you chattin' so amiably," he said, the words a great jumble.

A smile crossed Diver's face, though it vanished as quickly as it had come. Once Kelf was gone he said, "I owe you an apology, Ethan. With all the fool things I've done over the years, and all the times I've made trouble for you—and you've always stuck by me. I shouldn't have said all those things to you last night."

"It's all right," Ethan said, waving away the apology. "I have to ask you, though—" He dropped his voice. "Do the Sons of Liberty ever use conjurers to help them with all they do?"

Diver fairly beamed. "You're ready to join the cause?"

Ethan was too pleased by the civil turn their conversation had taken to disabuse Diver of the notion. Also, he didn't think Diver would take well to being told that Ebenezer Richardson might have been the victim of a spell, and was not the villain so many thought him to be. "For now I'm asking out of nothing more than curiosity," he said, hoping that he sounded coy rather than evasive. "Do they have access to spells?"

"Well, not that I know of, but I'm still new to the Sons. I've been to only a few meetings."

"Of course."

"But if you want me to ask—"

"No, that's not necessary."

"Right," Diver said, grinning. He cast a look at Deborah. "Our friend here has had dealings with Samuel Adams himself. You don't need my help talking to them, do you, Ethan?"

"At some point I might, and I'll be sure to let you know when that time comes." He sipped his ale.

Diver did the same, clearly pleased.

An instant later, though, the Dowser's door opened again and a different man stepped inside.

"He's dead," this man said, his voice forlorn. "Chris Seider's dead."

Ethan placed his tankard on the table and closed his eyes, a dull pain in his heart.

"God grant him rest," came a voice from near the bar.

"To Chris Seider," another man said. "May he rest in peace."

"Chris Seider," the other patrons answered, the lad's name resonating like a spell through the tavern.

Ethan opened his eyes again. Deborah was crying. Diver had walked around the table to where she sat and put his arm around her shoulders. Ethan searched the tavern and soon spotted Kannice near the bar; she was already looking his way. Her cheeks were dry, but he could see grief in her lovely eyes.

He stood with a scrape of his chair legs on the tavern's wooden floor, and picked up his hat off the table.

"Where are you going?" Diver asked.

"There's something I need to look into. I told you, I was on the street today when Richardson shot him, and while I was there . . . well, it's hard to explain."

Diver's face fell. "You're not going to try to prove that he didn't do it, are you? I know that you protect people when they're innocent and all, but this—"

"He did it, Diver. I saw him pull the trigger. I could no more prove Ebenezer Richardson innocent than I could teach him how to fly."

"Good," Diver said. "I want to see him swing for this."

Chapter
FIVE

Kannice was not happy to see him leaving, but he assured her that he would be back before long, and that he would try to explain where he had gone and why.

Leaving the warmth of the tavern, he found the icy street hushed save for the tolling of several church bells around the city—no doubt a tribute to the fallen lad. He had feared that a new mob might take to the lanes upon hearing the news of Christopher Seider's death, but for now at least, all remained quiet. A pall had fallen over Boston.

He headed south on Sudbury to Queen Street, which he followed toward the city gaol. On most occasions he took pains to keep his distance from Brattle Street and Murray's Barracks, but on this night there could be no avoiding the soldiers occupying the city. Indeed, Ethan was headed to the very seat of the Crown's military presence in Massachusetts.

As he came within sight of the gaol, however, he saw a large crowd gathered in the street outside the austere building. Here, at last, was the gathering he had thought to find in the lanes. Many carried torches, and though from this distance he could not make out what the throng was shouting, he could imagine easily enough. He retreated a short distance and found a lonely byway in which he could remove his greatcoat, cut his forearm, and whisper, *"Velamentum ex cruore evocatum."* Concealment, conjured from blood.

His conjuring hummed in the street, and Reg appeared before him, vivid against the whites and grays of the city in winter. At the same time, the spell settled over Ethan, like a fine cool mist.

"This might be incredibly stupid of me," he said.

The ghost grinned and vanished.

Once more, Ethan headed toward the gaol, placing his feet with care so as to make as little noise as possible on the lane. Even so, his shoes crunched the ice and snow. Fortunately, by the time he was near enough to other people to be heard, the clamor from the mob was enough to overwhelm the sound of his footsteps.

He slipped through the crowd, avoiding any contact when he could, and when he couldn't, making it seem that some other person was responsible for the gentle jostle or shove.

"Give 'em to us and we'll be on our way!" one man called to the young regulars guarding the prison door. Several men laughed.

Cries from others gathered there were less humorous.

"They're murderers, and should be dealt with as such!"

"Damn lobsters! Protectin' child killers!"

"Richardson and Wilmot deserve what's comin' to them! And so do them what keeps 'em safe!"

With each new imprecation, the mob grew increasingly agitated, until Ethan wondered if he would be able to extricate himself before the gathering became a riot. He could find no path of escape; the throng had closed in on all sides. He could do nothing but continue forward, pushing his way closer and closer to the front of the crowd and the façade of the city gaol.

When at last he slipped free of the mob, with a final shove that left a tall young man glancing about in confusion, Ethan found himself even closer to the gaol's ancient oaken door than he had expected. From so near, the four regulars posted in front of the gaol appeared younger and more frightened than they had from the rear of the crowd.

He saw no way past the men, nor could he think of any means by which he might enter the gaol through the door without drawing notice.

With slow, deliberate steps, he circled around the building and made his way back to where he knew the prison cells were located. There were several small windows along the wall—each looking in on a cell. But they were too high for Ethan to reach, and even if he could have climbed the brick walls, he couldn't accomplish much from outside.

Reluctantly, he concluded that he had but one choice. Leaving the prison, he cut across a snowy lea, strode past the church grounds of King's Chapel, and turned onto Marlborough Street. From there, he continued south to West Street, where lived Sheriff Stephen Greenleaf.

Greenleaf's spacious stone mansion stood a short distance from the edge of the Common. It was a stately home with extensive gardens that were, during the warmer months, among the most admired in all of Boston. It was, Ethan had decided long ago, a finer home than the good sheriff deserved.

Greenleaf might well have had the most difficult job in the entire Province of Massachusetts Bay. As sheriff of Suffolk County, he was responsible for keeping the peace in Boston. Any and all crimes committed within the city and its environs fell under his jurisdiction. But other than the men of the night watch, most of whom were either incompetent or dishonorable, or both, the sheriff had no men under his command. He was expected to see to the safety of Boston's citizens, and their personal property, almost entirely on his own. It was no wonder Ethan and Sephira had worked for so many clients over the years.

The near-impossible duties with which the sheriff was tasked should have made Greenleaf a sympathetic figure. As it happened, though, the sheriff's abrasive manner prevented that. He and Ethan had been at odds practically from the day they met. The sheriff had long been determined to see Ethan hanged as a witch; only Ethan's discretion, and a few strokes of uncommon good fortune, had kept Greenleaf from following through on his frequent threats. Moreover, when the sheriff wasn't trying to prove that Ethan consorted with the devil, he was often working with Sephira Pryce to hinder one of Ethan's inquiries.

Still, on those rare occasions when the sheriff required Ethan's aid—more often than not to investigate crimes that involved conjurings—he did not hesitate to press Ethan into service. And every now and then,

Ethan had no choice but to turn to the sheriff for help, as he did this night.

He walked up the path to the sheriff's front door and rapped twice with the brass knocker.

Only then did he remember that he was still under a concealment spell. Sparing not a moment, Ethan yanked off his greatcoat, slashed his arm, and whispered in Latin, *"Fini velamentum ex cruore evocatum."* End concealment, conjured from blood.

The spell pulsed in the ground and Reg issued forth once more. But concealment spells did not take effect or wear off instantly, and when the door opened, revealing the formidable figure of Stephen Greenleaf, Ethan knew that he was only partially visible. The sheriff wore his usual garb—a coat, waistcoat, and breeches—and he bore a candle, which threw his face, with its hook nose and steep forehead, into sharp relief.

He raised the candle higher and peered into the night through narrowed eyes.

"Who's there?" he said, the words coming out as a low, menacing growl.

"Sheriff Greenleaf, it's Ethan Kaille."

"Kaille?" the sheriff said, leaning forward. He had spotted Ethan, but still he squinted. "Is that really you?"

Ethan took a step toward him. "Aye. I'm sorry to disturb you at this hour."

Greenleaf held his candle still higher. "I couldn't see. It's like your witchery hovers over you, blending you with the night."

"I require your aid," Ethan said.

"My aid? Why should I give my aid to you?"

"I can't offer you any compelling reason why you should. Helping me will bring you no tangible benefit. But I'm hoping you'll listen to my request anyway."

"So you want a favor from me, and while you, no doubt, will profit nicely from whatever it is I'm supposed to do, you offer nothing in return."

"Actually," Ethan said, "there's no profit in this for me, either."

That, of all things, seemed to give the sheriff pause. "What is this about?" he asked.

"Ebenezer Richardson."

Greenleaf straightened and lowered the hand holding his candle. "What about him?"

Ethan hesitated, searching for some way to tell the sheriff what he wanted without as much as admitting that he was a conjurer. "I can't tell you everything—"

"Witchery," the sheriff said, spitting the word.

"Conjuring."

"Call it what you will, Kaille. It's still—" The sheriff stopped, his mouth hanging open. "You admit it?"

"I admit nothing about myself. But yes, I do believe that a conjuring may have played some role in the events that unfolded on Middle Street."

"What kind of conjuring? Done by whom?"

"I don't know yet. That's why I require your help."

"Ebenezer Richardson—"

"Is guilty of murder. There's no question of that. I was there today. I saw what happened."

"You were there, eh? Then isn't it likely that any . . . conjuring used against Richardson came from you?"

"It wasn't me," Ethan said.

"Then how can you be sure that anything unnatural happened?"

Ethan winced inwardly. It was not a question he could answer without incriminating himself. "I thought I might have felt something: a spell."

"You *thought* you felt something?" Greenleaf's grin was cold and smug. "Aye, I'll wager you did. That's practically an admission, Kaille. I might even be able to convince a magistrate to let me put a noose around your neck."

"Only if you manage to find a noose that can hold me."

The sheriff's smile slipped.

"You and I both know all too well what harm a rogue conjurer can unleash in this city. If there's even a chance that some dark spell played a part in today's tragedy, don't we owe it to the people of Boston to investigate?"

"You're the only rogue conjurer I know. Well, you and that crazy old witch who lives on the Neck. Windcatcher, isn't it?"

"It wasn't Janna, and it wasn't me."

"So you say."

Ethan gritted his teeth. "I don't have time for this. *We* don't. This is no trifle I'm speaking of. The entire city may be in danger. I sensed something similar last night. So it's happened twice in two days."

"And before that?"

"Nothing. Last night was the first time."

Greenleaf seemed to weigh this, his gaze fixed on the frozen water-front. "All right, assuming for a moment that I believe you, what is it you require of me?"

"I need to see Richardson. Alone."

"You don't ask for much, do you?" the sheriff said, scowling.

"I may be able to determine if something was done to him."

"Why do you have to see him alone?"

"Witchery can be dangerous, Sheriff. I wouldn't want anything to happen to you."

Greenleaf raised his chin. "I don't believe you. You've said similar things to me in the past; I think you wish to frighten me, to keep me away while you use your devilry to cause all manner of mischief."

"Sheriff—"

"I know you're a witch, Kaille! Why do you deny it?"

"Why do you let me live?"

Greenleaf blinked.

"If you're so convinced that I'm a witch, and that my being a witch makes me an instrument of Satan, you should put a bullet through my head, here and now."

The sheriff stared back at him, saying nothing, and looking un-characteristically diffident.

"You may not like me, but you need me, much as Sephira does."

"Miss Pryce?" Greenleaf appeared to grow more confused with each word Ethan said.

Ethan shook his head. "It's not important. The point is, we can help each other. You know we can—you've come to me in the past when you've needed help with . . . inquiries of a particular kind. You can call it witchery if you like; the point is, in the hands of the wrong person, it can do tremendous evil. You and I have seen as much, be it with Nate Ramsey or the Sisters Osborne. I can't say for certain that a conjurer had a hand in Christopher Seider's murder. But neither can I rule it out until I've seen Richardson."

"You still haven't told me why you wish to see him, or what you plan to do once you're there in his cell."

"And I still have no intention of telling you."

"How do I know you won't try to kill him? There are plenty in the city who would like nothing better than to see the man put to death. An eye for an eye, and all that."

"I suppose you'll have to take my word," Ethan said. When the sheriff's expression didn't change, he added, "I'm not going to kill him. I hope he swings for what he did. Even before the conjuring, he was threatening the mob, making an ass of himself. The man's an idiot. But tonight I have other matters on my mind. You have my word that no harm will come to him, at least not by my hand."

Greenleaf still glared at him; Ethan stared back, refusing to be cowed. At last the sheriff gave a shake of his head.

"I must be mad. Wait here, Kaille."

He went back inside the house and closed the door, only to emerge again moments later, a heavy cloak draped over his shoulders and a flintlock pistol in his hand.

"You should know that there's a mob gathered at the gaol," Ethan said, as they walked out to West Street and started toward the city's prison.

"Aye, I expected as much."

They walked in silence for some time, vapor from their breath rising into the night sky.

"What would a conjurer have to gain by making Richardson shoot the lad?" Greenleaf asked.

It was a fine question, one that Ethan hadn't considered.

"Conjurers have their political leanings," he said, "just like the rest of us. Is it so hard to believe that there are some who wish to foment violence in the city?"

The sheriff glanced his way. "The Sons of Liberty, perhaps."

Ethan shrugged, then nodded, conceding the point. "Perhaps."

They covered the remaining distance without saying more. Seeing the mob outside the gaol, Greenleaf faltered in midstride, but only for in instant.

"Stay close," he said, his voice low.

As they neared the outer edge of the crowd, Greenleaf halted.

"You won't be seeing Ebenezer Richardson tonight," he said, his words echoing in the lane. "Go home."

The men turned as one.

Someone called out, "He deserves to hang!"

"And he might before this is over. But that's not going to happen tonight." His smile appeared genuine. "You lot know me. When there's a hanging, I don't make a secret of it. If Richardson swings, you'll all have a fine view."

A few people laughed.

"This has been a hard day, and a sad one. Go home, or better yet, go to a tavern and raise an ale to the memory of Chris Seider. But get the hell away from my gaol."

Ethan expected the men to refuse, to respond in anger to the sheriff's words. These men knew the sheriff to be, at least on most occasions, a servant of the Crown and its representatives here in Boston. Back in the fall of 1768, as the occupation of Boston began and General Gage and his staff attempted to billet a thousand uniformed regulars, the sheriff had been at the fore of efforts to evict Elisha Brown and his companions from the Manufactory so that it might be used as a barracks. The sheriff was unpopular among those who had gathered outside the gaol, as well as those who had been on Middle Street earlier in the day, harassing importers and trading insults with Ebenezer Richardson.

But while these men might not have liked Greenleaf, they did harbor some respect for him, or at least a modicum of fear. Ethan noticed that the sheriff still held his pistol loosely in his right hand, its barrel glinting dully with torchlight. He had no doubt that many in the throng had seen it as well. If the mob turned on them, the sheriff would have time to fire off only a shot or two before they were overwhelmed. But Ethan doubted that any of the men wished to be the unfortunate soul whom Greenleaf managed to shoot.

Slowly, with obvious reluctance, the men started to disperse. A few shouted threats at Richardson, no doubt hoping that the customs man could hear them in his cell. Others glared at Greenleaf, though the sheriff didn't appear to notice. But within a few minutes, the street had cleared.

"That was well done," Ethan said.

Greenleaf rounded on him, a fearsome look in his eyes, as if he were searching for some sign that Ethan was mocking him. Seeing none, his expression eased. "Thank you." He indicated the gaol with an open hand. "After you."

Ethan walked to the door, eyeing the soldiers as he approached.

"Good evening, Sheriff," one of the men said. He studied Ethan, a faint sneer on his angular face. "This another prisoner?"

"Sadly, no," the sheriff said. "We need to see Richardson."

The man produced a key, unlocked the prison door, and pulled it open with a creak of the great iron hinges.

Greenleaf surveyed the street. A few stragglers still lingered near the corner of Treamount and Queen Streets. "Lock the door again once we're inside. Don't open it for anyone but me. Do you understand?"

"Aye, sir."

Greenleaf waved Ethan inside. As soon as Ethan crossed the threshold, the stink hit him, calling up unwelcome memories.

Not so long ago, again around the time of the occupation, Greenleaf had led Ethan into the gaol as his prisoner, and had left him there, chained to a wall in a fetid cell.

It seemed the sheriff was thinking of this as well. "Have you missed the place?" he asked, watching Ethan.

"Hardly."

But by now his recollections had carried him past his brief incarceration in this gaol, to darker memories of his imprisonment after the *Ruby Blade* mutiny: rancid food, the vermin-infested pile of straw on which he slept, backbreaking labor beneath a scorching tropical sun, and overseers who reveled in abusing and beating Ethan and his fellow prisoners. Even now, years removed from that living hell, Ethan couldn't think of these things without breaking out in a cold sweat. He had come to the gaol voluntarily—he had all but begged the sheriff to bring him here. And still his legs trembled so violently that he could barely stand.

"Are you all right?" Greenleaf asked, sounding more impatient than concerned.

Ethan nodded, swallowed the bile rising in his throat.

"You're sweating."

"You may recall that I have . . . an aversion to prisons."

The sheriff scowled his disapproval. "This way," he said, stepping past Ethan. He led him down a narrow corridor and halted before the third cell on the left.

Ethan joined him and peered into the cell through a small barred window in the door. Richardson sat on the stone floor, his back against the rough wall. His face was a mess: bruised, swollen, caked with dried blood. His clothes were filthy, torn almost to rags, and stained with blood as well. And still Ethan knew that he had been fortunate to survive this day.

"Who the hell are you?" The words sounded thick, muddled; his lips were split and it appeared that he had lost at least one tooth in the melee.

"I was on Middle Street today," Ethan said. "I'd like a word."

"What is this, Sheriff? Are you going to let him finish me off?"

"If I wanted to let someone finish you, I could make a fair bit of coin," Greenleaf said. "They'd line up all the way from Queen Street to Long Wharf and back again, and they'd pay me well to have five minutes alone with you." He grinned. "You're a bit short on admirers these days, Richardson."

The customs man looked away.

"No, Kaille isn't here to kill you. He wishes only . . ." The sheriff glanced at Ethan. "He came to talk."

"Kaille," Richardson repeated, eyeing Ethan again. "Lillie's man?"

Ethan bristled at the description. "Aye. Mister Lillie hired me. You and I spoke this morning, when you were trying to tear down the signs outside his shop."

"I remember now. If you had done your job, those signs never would have been there, and none of this would have happened."

"I seem to recall warning you to get off the street."

The man turned from him once more. "Go away, Kaille."

Greenleaf unlocked the door and motioned for Ethan to enter. Ethan stepped into the cell, expecting that the sheriff would close the door behind him. Instead, Greenleaf followed him inside.

"I told you that I need to see him alone," Ethan said.

"I know what you told me, but I never agreed to all of it." He leaned closer to Ethan, and said in a whisper, "We're going to settle this once and for all, Kaille. I know what you are, and tonight, at last, I'll have my proof."

"I don't want either of you in here!" Richardson said, glaring up at them. "Can't you leave me in peace?"

The sheriff scowled. "Shut your mouth, Richardson!" He faced Ethan again, and flashed a smiled. "Go on then, Kaille. I promise you won't swing tonight, or even tomorrow. It could be years before I decide to rid this city of you, but that will be my choice to make."

Richardson regarded them both, obviously perplexed by what the sheriff had said. For his part, Ethan was damned if he was going to allow Greenleaf to watch him conjure. Fortunately, as on several occasions in the past, he was helped by the sheriff's ignorance of spellmaking.

He had been planning to put Richardson to sleep with a conjuring before attempting any other magick. Directing the spell at two men was really no more difficult than directing it at one.

He didn't move, and he kept his gaze locked on that of the sheriff. But drawing upon the mullein he still carried in his coat pocket, he recited the incantation to himself. *Dormite ambo ex verbasco evocatum.* Slumber, both of them, conjured from mullein.

The conjuring sang like a harp string, vibrating in the stone walls, floor, and ceiling of the cell. Reg appeared, bright as a newly risen moon in the dim, inconstant light of the torches, but Ethan watched the sheriff. Before long, the man staggered, his eyelids drooping.

"Wha—?"

As he started to fall, Ethan caught him and eased him down to the floor, propping his back against the nearest wall.

"I believe you've been working too hard, Sheriff," he muttered.

Greenleaf snored softly.

Richardson had toppled onto his side. Ethan righted him and leaned him against a wall as well. He drew his blade and cut his arm. As blood welled from the wound, he traced a line of it across Richardson's forehead, down the bridge of his nose, and over his chin.

"Revela omnias magias ex cruore evocatas," he whispered. Reveal all magicks, conjured from blood.

This spell rumbled in the stone as well, and Ethan saw his own russet power flicker across Richardson's body: the residue of the sleep spell he had cast. But his conjuring revealed no other evidence of spells. None.

"The conjuring revealed my sleep spell," Ethan said to Reg. "So I know it worked."

Reg frowned and nodded.

Ethan cut himself again and rubbed blood on the man in the same pattern. *"Revela originem magiae ex cruore evocatam."* Reveal source of magic, conjured from blood.

This conjuring yielded much the same result, showing evidence of Ethan's spell, but no others.

"Is it possible that the spell we felt on Middle Street wasn't directed at Richardson?" Ethan asked.

Reg shrugged.

Ethan considered once more the tragic sequence of events from the morning. The hum of that distant spell had preceded by mere seconds the appearance of Richardson with his musket. He didn't fire at first, though he aimed the weapon at the mob. Seconds later, he aimed again and pulled the trigger. As Ethan thought about this, he realized that he had seen Richardson pull the trigger twice. It wasn't that he didn't try to shoot the first time he took aim; rather, it seemed that the musket misfired.

Of course it was possible that Richardson had every intention of firing his weapon, and that whatever spell was cast had nothing at all to do with Christopher Seider's death. Ethan knew enough of the customs man to think the worst of him. But the coincidence was too striking to ignore, particularly in the wake of Gordon's attack on Will Pryor.

"I don't understand any of this," he said to the ghost.

Reg glowered down at Richardson, his jaw set.

"I know. I don't like him either. But if a spell made him fire, I want to know it." A thought came to him. "George Wilmot," he whispered, "the other man being held here. Is he a conjurer?"

Reg shook his head.

"Right, because that would have been too simple."

He didn't think that he could do much more here, which left him with one final task. It promised to be unpleasant.

Ethan gave Richardson a hard shake, and said, "Wake up."

Then he crossed to Greenleaf and squatted down before him. "Sheriff," he said, shaking him as well, though more gently. "Sheriff, are you all right?"

Richardson stirred, as did the sheriff.

Ethan took hold of Greenleaf's arm and helped him up. The sheriff swayed, and Ethan tightened his hold on the man.

"Have a care. We wouldn't want you to fall again."

"What happened to me?" the sheriff asked, his voice weak. "What am I——?" He glanced around, taking in the cell, the torches. At last his gaze came to rest on Ethan, the look in his pale eyes hardening.

"What did you do to me, Kaille?"

"What did *I* do to you?" Ethan repeated, opening his eyes wide in feigned innocence. "What do you remember?"

"I——You were standing there, just as you are now, watching me. We were . . . we had been arguing. You wanted me to leave, but I wouldn't. And then . . ."

"And then what?"

Greenleaf jerked his arm out of Ethan's grasp. "You know damn well what! You used your damned witchery against me!"

"Did you see me do anything?" Ethan asked. "Did I speak, or wave my hands about?"

The sheriff looked like he had sucked on a lemon. "No."

Richardson let out a low groan.

The sheriff looked past Ethan to the customs man. "What happened to him?" he asked, an accusation in the words. He stepped around Ethan and planted himself directly in front of Richardson. "What is it Richardson?"

"I . . . I don't know. I feel odd."

"Did you fall into a swoon as well?" Greenleaf glared at Ethan.

"I think so."

"And I take it you had nothing to do with that, either, did you Kaille?"

Ethan didn't flinch from the sheriff's glare. "Richardson took quite a beating today," he said, his tone mild. "He's lucky to be alive. Have you had a surgeon in to look at him?"

Greenleaf shook a thick finger in Ethan's face. "I should chain you up right now. That cell back there has held you before; it can again."

"Aye, it has. But you may wish to wait until we're certain that . . . that 'witchery' isn't behind all of this. You wouldn't want to face a villainous conjurer on your own."

Greenleaf lowered his hand, though he continued to eye Ethan with unconcealed distrust. After some time, he glanced at Richardson again and then asked Ethan, "Are we finished here?"

"Aye."

The sheriff turned on his heel and stomped out of the cell; Ethan had little choice but to leave as well. Greenleaf locked the cell door once more and led Ethan out of the gaol. Even after they were outside in the cold, blessedly fresh air, he said not a word. He mumbled a curt "Good night" to the soldiers and started up Queen Street in the direction of his home. Ethan sensed that Greenleaf expected him to follow, and so he did.

Once they were beyond the hearing of the regulars, the sheriff said, "I want to know what you did to me in there."

Ethan angled away from the man toward the Dowser. "Good night, Sheriff."

"Damn you, Kaille!"

"I'll make some inquiries," Ethan called to him. "If there is a new conjurer in the city, one who intends to use his powers to sow such

mischief, I'll find him. And I'll bring him to you. In the meantime—"
He stopped himself, unwilling to give voice to the thought that flashed
through his mind. "In the meantime," he said instead, "I won't trouble
you again."

"What did you learn from Richardson?"

"Nothing," he said. "Nothing at all. And that bothers me."

Chapter SIX

Almost as soon as he entered the Dowser, Kannice came out from behind the bar to greet him.

"Where were you?" she asked.

Ethan scanned the tavern, his tricorn hat in his hands. Diver still sat near the back with Deborah. When he saw Ethan gazing his way, he lowered his eyes.

"I think you know already," Ethan said.

Kannice took his hand. "Don't be angry with Derrey. I made him tell me."

Ethan gaped at her. "Am I imagining things, or did Kannice Lester, proprietor of the Dowsing Rod, come to the defense of Devren Jervis?"

A grudging grin crept across her features. "It's not likely to happen again." She tried to look stern. "Don't tell him."

"Your secret is safe with me. For the moment."

"You went to see Richardson?"

Ethan looked around, to make sure that they weren't overheard. "Aye. I needed to know if he acted today under the influence of a conjuring."

Her brow furrowed. "And did he?"

"Not that I could tell, no."

Kannice took a long breath. "Well, I'm glad. I prefer to think that he's cruel and heartless. If he had been . . . controlled in some way, if there was a conjurer out there making him do something that terrible, I'd be truly frightened."

"As would I," Ethan said. He didn't tell her that he *was* frightened; that while he had found nothing, he was convinced this was because the conjurer had hidden his spells too well. Again, though, he should have known that he couldn't dissemble with her, not about this. Not about anything, really. It was one of the reasons he loved her.

"What is it you're not telling me?"

He glanced back at Diver again, then scanned the somber faces in the tavern—anything to avoid looking her in the eye.

"Ethan?"

"Today, before Richardson fired at Chris Seider and young Gore, I felt . . . something."

Her eyes widened. "And by something you mean . . . ?"

"Aye, a spell. I felt one as well last night, just before one of Sephira's men attacked a lad who had done nothing to provoke him."

Kannice brushed a strand of hair from her brow. "And Sephira's other man—the one who conjures—he had nothing to do with this?"

"No. He sensed it as well, and at first, all but accused me of bewitching his friend."

"Could it be a coincidence?"

"I suppose," Ethan said.

She smiled, though the crease in her forehead remained. "You're humoring me."

"I'm not. I'm casting about for answers. If anything, what I've seen and learned thus far points to all of this being coincidence, as you say."

"But?"

He shrugged. "But I don't believe it is. Probably I'm imagining things."

She ran a hand down his cheek. "I've not known you to imagine things of this sort before. Why would you begin now?"

"I don't know. My spells are telling me one thing: that no one used a conjuring to make Richardson fire into that mob. But my heart and my head, not to mention Uncle Reg, are telling me something else."

Kannice's cheeks went white. "Uncle . . . You mean your . . . your ghost?"

"Aye. He tells me that there was another shade like him there today, watching all that happened. He's as sure as I that someone cast a spell."

"And you trust him."

Ethan could only nod. He did trust Reg, in all things. But he couldn't help wondering if the old ghost was wrong about the specter he saw on Middle Street. It wasn't that Ethan doubted the figure had been there. Rather, he wondered if Reg had been too quick to conclude that it wasn't a shade he had seen before.

Moments earlier, in Richardson's gaol cell, Ethan had been so sure that his *revela* conjurings would show a residue of Nate Ramsey's power—a brilliant aqua hue that to this day still haunted Ethan's nightmares—that he had flinched as he cast the spells. During that one horror-filled week in July of the previous year, Ramsey had both tormented and tortured him; the captain had come very near to killing him. Ethan didn't know if Ramsey was alive or dead; he had no reason to believe that the man had played any part in the events of the past day. But Ethan's fear of him ran every bit as deep as his fear of prisons—he had never thought that he could possibly be so frightened of one man. Then again, Ramsey was no ordinary man. He was a conjurer of exceptional ability. He was also vengeful, vicious, cruel, as unpredictable as the New England weather, and utterly mad. Knowing that he might one day return, and anticipating that day with dread, Ethan had spent the past several months learning new conjurings and honing his spellmaking as he had not since he was a boy, new to his power. And even so, he knew that he remained utterly unprepared for a new confrontation with the man.

"There's still more to this than you're saying," Kannice said. "I can tell when you're keeping things from me."

He shook his head. "It's nothing. I—This has been a long, difficult day." He could tell from the way she regarded him that his denials hadn't convinced her. "When I know more, I'll tell you more. Right now I'm certain of nothing."

"I understand. I'm sorry, I don't mean to pry . . ."

Ethan toyed with the brim of his hat. He was keeping secrets and she was apologizing to him. Worse, they were speaking to each other as if strangers. "You're not prying. I . . . I've missed you."

She met his gaze. "I know. I've missed you. Stay with me tonight. Please."

He took her hand. "I'd like that." He raised her hand to his lips and kissed it.

"I have work to do. Go sit with Derrey." She stepped closer, raised herself onto her tiptoes, and kissed him on the lips. "And don't you dare leave again," she whispered.

"Yes, ma'am."

He released her hand and walked back to where Diver and Deborah were seated.

"It's nice to see you and Kannice getting on again, Ethan," Diver said, sounding a bit too enthusiastic.

"Don't worry, Diver. I'm not angry with you."

Diver exhaled, and smiled with relief. "Well, good. She made me tell her where you'd gone. I swear it. I don't know how you keep a secret from that woman."

"Oh, it wasn't that bad," Deborah said, a reproach in the words. "Honestly, Derrey, you didn't put up much of a fight."

Diver's cheeks reddened. "What did you find out, anyway?"

"Very little. But I did get to put Sheriff Greenleaf to sleep with a spell, so the evening wasn't a total loss."

"Now that's a story I'd enjoy hearing," Diver said.

Deborah reached across the table and patted his hand. "Another time, perhaps. It's getting late, and you've work first thing."

Ethan's friend looked as put out as a boy denied a sweet. "Aye, that I do."

Diver and Deborah stood. As Diver stepped past Ethan's chair, he laid a hand on Ethan's shoulder. "It is good to see you two together again," he said, his voice low this time. "I meant that."

"I know you did. And the fact is, I don't like to keep secrets from her, and I wouldn't have it any other way."

Diver bade him good night and followed Deborah out of the tavern.

Not long after they left, Kelf brought Ethan an ale. Ethan sipped it, his back to the wall, as the tavern crowd slowly thinned. He couldn't take his eyes off Kannice as she wiped the bar clean and bid good night to her patrons. She was willowy, yet strong, stubborn, yet quick to smile.

He had never known another woman like her, and perhaps their time apart had the unintended benefit of reminding him that this was so.

Before long, only she, Kelf, and Ethan remained. She and the barman made short work of the night's last chores and then she let Kelf out, and locked the door.

She crossed the great room to where Ethan still sat, blowing out candles along the way. He reached for his empty tankard, but she said, "Leave it."

She held out a hand to him. He grasped it, stood, gathered her in his arms, and kissed her deeply.

Wordlessly, she led him up the stairs and through the narrow corridors to her bedchamber. There they lit a single candle and kissed again. Ethan began to unlace her bodice; she unbuttoned his waistcoat and then his shirt. The chamber was cold, but neither of them cared. Kannice laid him down on the blankets and straddled him, her hair like spun gold in the candlelight, her skin soft and smooth and cool. It occurred to Ethan that he had forgotten just how lovely she was. After that he lost track of time, and later, of thought itself.

They made love with a fierce tenderness that was as urgent and intense as the nights Ethan recalled from the first months of their love affair. Fueled by grief and passion and hunger too long denied, they came together again and again, until at last, sated and exhausted, they fell into a deep slumber.

Ethan woke early, as the first silvery light of the morn seeped into Kannice's room around the shutters on her window. Usually she rose before he, but she still lay beside him, her breathing deep and steady, her body warming his.

Though reluctant to leave for any reason, much less an appointment with Theophilus Lillie, Ethan swung himself out of bed, making every attempt to move silently. But as he dressed hurriedly, shivering in the cold, he heard Kannice stir.

"Where are you going?" she asked, sounding sleepy.

"Mister Lillie is expecting me."

She watched him, her brow furrowing once more, as it seemed to so often these days when they spoke of his work. There had been a time, only a few months before, when she had tried to convince Ethan to give up thieftaking and join her in running the Dowsing Rod. He had done little to encourage her hope in this regard, and it had been some time since last she even mentioned the possibility. But occasionally he caught her looking at him in a way that told him she still wished he would consider a change in profession. She regarded him in that manner now.

But all she said was "Be careful. It could be dangerous there today."

"Aye, I will." He finished dressing, and bent to kiss her.

"Are you sure you can't stay a while longer?"

"I'm sure that if I stay for a minute it will turn into an hour, and if I stay for an hour, I'll lose the entire day."

She kissed him again. "You would consider such a day a loss?"

"Not at all. But I think that I had best leave now, while I still can."

"But you'll be back tonight?" she asked. Her smile lingered, but he could tell that she had asked the question in earnest.

"I promise that I will."

"Good. Then go on."

He left her, took a bit of bread and butter from the kitchen and left tuppence in the till, and let himself out of the tavern. Gray clouds still covered the sky, but the air had grown warmer. Ethan thought he could smell a storm riding the wind.

His hands buried in his pockets, he followed his usual circuitous route past Murray's Barracks and into the North End. He found Middle Street largely deserted. Richardson's house appeared to have been abandoned; Ethan saw no sign that Richardson's wife and daughters remained within. The door had been propped up against the house, but the entryway was not secured. The broken windows had not been boarded. The façade of the structure bore stains from the eggs and pieces of rotten food thrown at it by the mob the day before.

Closer to Lillie's dry goods shop, the wooden effigies and the hand-shaped sign lay in the street, broken and trampled. The structure itself, though, was unmarred, save for the tar and feathers that still covered the windows.

Ethan did not see Lillie moving about within, and when he knocked no one answered. He stood by the door, bouncing on the balls of his feet to stay warm, and waited for the merchant.

He didn't have to wait long.

A few minutes later, Lillie turned onto Middle Street from Cross Street to the north. He halted upon spotting Ethan, and even took a step back; Ethan thought he might flee. But recognition flashed in his eyes and he came forward, glancing about as he did.

"I didn't expect to see you here, Mister Kaille," he said.

"We have an arrangement, sir. I feel that I owe you the courtesy of an explanation before I terminate it."

The words crossed Ethan's lips before he gave much thought to their meaning. But as soon as he heard himself speak them, he knew that this was why he had come.

Lillie scowled. "What makes you think that I have any interest in hearing your explanation?"

Ethan grinned, feeling better than he had in days. "Frankly, sir, I couldn't care less whether or not you wish to hear what I have to say. You will hear it. And then I'll be on my way."

Lillie dismissed him with a wave of his hand and turned his back, fumbling with the keys to his shop. Ethan strode forward, grabbed the man by the shoulder, and spun him around so that they were face-to-face. The merchant shrank away, cowering like a cur expecting a beating.

"I just want to be left alone," he said, his voice quavering.

"And so you shall be. But understand, you will listen to me first."

"Why should I? To hear more insults? More threats? You're all the same, you riffraff. I am a simple merchant, trying to make an honest wage. I've done nothing wrong, and yet I'm bullied and beaten. My wares are stolen, destroyed." He slapped his leg, the sound echoing across the empty street. "I have done nothing wrong!"

Ethan laughed, which only seemed to infuriate the man more. "You count me with those who were in the street yesterday? You're a bigger fool than I thought. They hate me because I've been working for you. What's more, I've refused to ally myself with the Sons of Liberty because I believe their tactics to be . . . irresponsible. They have too little respect for the sanctity of a man's property and too much confidence in their own righteousness. But you . . ." Ethan shook his head.

"Men like you and Ebenezer Richardson are worse by far than even the greatest fools in that rabble gathered here yesterday. Because you would dismiss their calls for liberty without a thought. Of course they're naïve. Of course they're blinded by their ardor for the 'great cause.' I would even grant that many of them have been driven, at least initially, by parsimony, by their desire to avoid another tax. But they are, in the end, fighting for something other than the weight of their own purses."

"You think me greedy?" Lillie asked, clearly outraged.

"I think you selfish and small."

"You do me an injustice, sir!"

"If he was in that mob, with the rest of the rabble, he probably deserved it."

Lillie paled at the repetition of his own words. His gaze, so angry a moment before, slid away. "I didn't mean that," he said, his voice low. "Ebenezer is an idiot. He should never have fired into that mob. I didn't know at the time that the boy was so grievously wounded."

"I told you he was."

Lillie nodded. "You did. But I didn't believe you. I thought you were exaggerating, that your passions were inflamed by all that you had seen."

"They were," Ethan said. "They still are."

Lillie looked him in the eye, though this simple act seemed to take a great effort. "So, you no longer wish to work for me?"

"No, sir. I don't."

"I can make matters difficult for you, you know. I may be hated by the rab—" He licked his lips. "By those who support Samuel Adams and his kind. But I'm still an influential man. There are families who, at a word from me, would never deign to hire you."

"Aye, I'm sure there are. Fortunately, crime cares not at all whether a man is Whig or Tory. There are plenty who will hire me. There are some who will be more inclined to do so if they hear you speak ill of me."

Lillie didn't argue. He stared at Richardson's house, taking in the damage. "They're threatening us all, you know. I stayed last night at the home of a friend. My wife and children are there now. To be honest, I expected to find my shop in ruin this morning. I expect that one of these morns I will."

"Yes, sir."

"I'm considering leaving Boston. My wife believes we would be safer in the country, and I'm inclined to agree with her."

"She may well be right, sir."

Lillie's expression soured. "Very well, Mister Kaille. I suppose matters are settled between us. You worked for the wages you received, and I owe you nothing more."

"That's my reckoning as well."

"Fine. Off with you then."

Without another word, Lillie turned back to his door, his keys jangling once more. This time Ethan left him, relieved to be done working for the man, and, he had to admit to himself, embarrassed by his own outburst. Lillie had spoken true: He hadn't done anything wrong, at least not in a legal sense. He bore no responsibility for Richardson's crime. But change was coming to Boston, to all the colonies. Legalities were fast being overtaken by politics, and Lillie was on the wrong side of the looming conflict. Of that much, he was certain.

Ethan intended to make his way back to Cooper's Alley, where he rented a room above the cooperage of Henry Dall. But his thoughts still churned with memories of the previous day, and with fears born of the previous summer. He walked northward from Middle Street, crossing through the heart of the North End, skirted the base of Copp's Hill, and soon reached the waterfront near Drake's Wharf, where he, Janna Windcatcher, and Mariz had their final confrontation with Nate Ramsey. He could almost smell the smoke from the blaze Ramsey started that summer day in his attempt to escape.

He scanned the wharves arrayed before him, looking for the *Muirenn*, Ramsey's pink. The night before he had almost suggested to Greenleaf that he do the same, but Ethan trusted no one with this task but himself. If Ramsey's ship was hidden with a conjuring, the sheriff would walk right past it. Ethan wanted to believe that he would sense the conjuring, or would recognize signs of a concealment spell that others might miss.

Or maybe he was misleading himself. The truth was, as soon as it occurred to him that Ramsey might be alive and back in Boston, he had known that he himself would have to search the waterfront. Because even if the entire British army were to take on this task, and even if the king's soldiers could sense the lightest touch of a spell, Ethan would want to look anyway. He feared the captain too much to place trust in anyone else's assurances.

Most of the harbor was frozen. Few ships could have docked in the past week or two. But still Ethan resolved to search for the captain's ship. He followed Lynn Street from Ruck's Wharf to Thornton's Shipyard. At North Battery, the street name changed. It did so again at Hancock's Wharf, and at Lee's Shipyard. But Ethan maintained a slow, steady gait, ignoring the cold and the freshening wind, and the pain radiating up his bad leg into his groin. He stared hard at every moored vessel, his eyes watering in the frigid air, tears running down his cheeks and into the raised collar of his greatcoat, where they formed a rimed edge that rubbed against his chin. His fingers grew numb with the cold, and his cheeks, nose, and ears ached.

After crossing the creek back into Cornhill, Ethan turned onto Merchant's Row so that he could scan the wharves of the South End. He turned at Long Wharf, and walked the length of the dock into the very teeth of that wind. At the wharf's end, he turned back and then followed the lanes past the point where he usually would have turned to go to Cooper's Alley and past Fort Hill, so that he could view the wharves along Belcher's Lane and Auchmutty Street, which jutted out into the water like spines on a sea urchin. He continued onto Orange Street, so that he could see the piers located along Boston's Neck, and didn't conclude his search until he had walked all the way to Gibbon's Shipyard near the town gate. He had never known Ramsey to moor his ship at any of these wharves, but he refused to take anything for granted.

He had seen a few ships that resembled in superficial ways the *Muirenn*—all were pinks of a size similar to that of Ramsey's ship. But Ethan made a point of examining the escutcheon on each vessel, and he also looked closely at the crewmen. Ramsey had inherited the ship from his father, whom he revered; he took pride in being the second Nate Ramsey to captain the *Muirenn*. And he had gathered a crew whom he could trust to fight on his behalf, and who accepted that he was a conjurer. Unless Ramsey had replaced most of his men and re-christened the vessel—and Ethan did not believe that he would do either—none of these pinks were his.

Staring back over icy waters, he railed at himself. First Reg had assured him that the shade he saw was unfamiliar to him, and now Ethan had wasted half a day in pursuit of a vessel that wasn't here, that might never return. Perhaps he had allowed his imagination and his fears of Ramsey to get the better of him.

As it happened, the Fat Spider, Tarijanna Windcatcher's tavern, stood but a short distance from Gibbon's Shipyard. Drawn by the promise of a warm hearth and a bowl of one of Janna's savory, spiced stews, Ethan hurried on to the publick house.

The Spider had changed little in the span of Ethan's friendship with Janna. It was small for a tavern. Its wood had been worn to a pale shade of gray by the summer sun and winter snows and more storms in spring and fall than Ethan cared to count. The roof sagged alarmingly and the walls stood crookedly, astagger under the building's weight. The very first time Ethan saw the tavern he thought it one strong gust of wind away from collapse. In the years since, gales had come and gone, but still the Spider endured. Ethan had come to wonder if Janna used conjurings to reinforce the structure, but he had never asked, fearing that she might take offense.

He entered the tavern, and without even pausing for his eyes to adjust to the dim light, walked to the bright fire burning along the far wall of Janna's great room.

"Is that you, Kaille?"

"Aye, it's me." Belatedly, Ethan removed his hat.

Janna came out from behind her bar and joined him near the fire. The Spider was crowded with people and thick with the aromas of stew and fresh bread, of clove and cinnamon, and, overlaying it all, the acrid smells of woodsmoke and spermaceti candles.

"You look half froze to death. Where have you been?"

"All over the city."

Janna shook her head, wearing her familiar scowl. She was diminutive; she looked almost frail, wearing a simple linen dress and a woolen shawl wrapped tightly around her bony shoulders. As if being a self-proclaimed marriage smith didn't make her enough of a curiosity, Janna was also one of the few free Africans living in Boston. Her skin was the color of dark rum and her hair, as white as snow, was shorn so short that Ethan could see her scalp through the tight curls.

She rarely talked about how she had managed to remain free, but over the years, Ethan had pieced together a story that made a certain amount of sense. Born in the Caribbean, she was orphaned at sea as a young girl and rescued by a ship out of Newport. She might have been taken in by a family, or she might have been passed from household to household; either way, she was never sold into slavery. Eventually, she met a wealthy shipbuilder who fell in love with her. Because of her race, they could not marry, but the man provided for her, and, when he died, left her with enough money to buy the Spider and to secure her freedom for the rest of her life.

Janna claimed to have no memory of her family name. Sometime between her rescue at sea and her arrival in Boston, she took the name Windcatcher, because she liked the way it sounded.

Ethan would have walked through fire for her, and he was convinced that she would do the same for him. But with Janna, it wasn't always easy to tell. To say that she could be difficult was to understate the case, like saying that the kings of England and France didn't always see eye-to-eye. She was as prickly as anyone Ethan knew. She was also as smart, as strong, and, when he had need, as reliable a friend. Her knowledge of conjuring dwarfed his own, and she didn't care who knew that she could cast spells. A placard on her door read "T. Windcatcher, Marriage Smith. Love is Magick." She made no secret of the fact that she sold herbs, oils, talismans, and other items intended to enhance conjurings. Ethan sometimes wondered if she wasn't daring all of Boston to hang her as a witch. Thinking about it though, he realized that before last summer's battle with Nate Ramsey he had rarely seen her conjure, and never when there were people about who weren't also spellers. Perhaps she was more careful than he credited.

She eyed him now as if he were mad. "What are you doin' wanderin' around the city in this kind of cold? Are you tryin' to catch your death?"

Ethan shivered, though the fire was already warming him. "Something like that," he said, his voice low. He reached into his pocket and pulled out a half shilling. "Can I have some stew and an ale?"

She took the coin. "Course you can." She pointed toward an empty table. "Sit yourself down there and I'll be right out."

He remained by the fire for a few moments more before taking a seat at the table. His fingers had started to tingle as they warmed, but the skin on his face still felt tight. He kept his greatcoat on, at least for the time being.

Janna brought him his stew and a small round of bread. "I'll get you your ale," she said, after placing the food in front of him.

"Wait, Janna."

"I can't talk right now," she said over her shoulder. "You see how busy this place is."

"I was searching the wharves," he called to her.

She halted, turned.

"That's what had me out in the streets."

Janna had stilled, like a cat stalking a sparrow. Her gaze darted around the tavern. At last she walked back to Ethan's table. "You were lookin' for Ramsey's ship?" she asked, her voice low.

"Aye." He faltered, feeling like a fool. But he couldn't keep himself from asking the question that burned in his chest. "Do you know if he's back, Janna?"

"If he was back, and I knew it, I would've told you first thing."

Some of Ethan's apprehension sluiced away. "I know. But you have a tavern to run." He smiled. "And I know you don't venture outside when it's this cold."

"You don' understand, Kaille. If he was back, and I knew it, I would tell you, even if it meant I had to close this place down, and walk through hip-deep snow." She crossed her arms over her chest. "Why were you lookin' for him?"

Ethan indicated with an open hand the chair beside his. Annoyance flickered in Janna's dark eyes, but she sat.

Speaking in a low voice and offering only those details that he deemed essential, he told her about Gordon's beating of Will Pryor, and recounted all that he had seen and felt on Middle Street the day before.

When he finished, Janna gave a small shake of her head. "That all doesn't sound like Ramsey to me. When he comes back, he's gonna come back hard, and he's gonna come straight at you."

"You may be right."

"I ain't sayin' that this is nothin'. Some conjurer is messin' with things better left alone. But I don' think it's Ramsey."

"I hope you're right. My thanks, Janna."

She stood. "I have more stew on the fire. When you're ready for another helpin' you let me know."

"I will."

She left him, returning a few seconds later with his ale.

Ethan ate slowly, savoring the warmth of the meal and the rich spices Janna used in her cooking. Kannice's chowders were the best Ethan had found in all of Boston, but he was well-nigh as fond of Janna's island stews. They were made with fowl and white beans, and flavored with nutmeg, pepper, and a blend of other spices he couldn't name. No other publick house in Boston served anything like them. The ale she sold, on the other hand, was weak and barely worth drinking, unlike the Kent pale that he enjoyed at the Dowser.

As he sopped up the last of his stew with his bread, Ethan tried to take comfort in Janna's certainty that Ramsey was not responsible for the conjurings he had been feeling. He had doubted Reg, and even what he had seen—or not seen—with his own eyes. But surely he could trust Janna, who had taught him so much over the years. And yet his doubts remained. His fears of the captain had begun to consume him, as they had in the first weeks after the fire at Drake's Wharf.

When Ethan had finished eating and could stomach no more of the ale, he stood and crossed to the bar. Janna was wiping the wood and watching a pair of men sitting near the back of the tavern.

"Those two have been there for most of the day, and they've barely bought a thing," she said, her gaze hawklike. "I think they're only in here to keep warm."

"Maybe you should chase them out."

"I might." She looked at him. "So you searched all mornin' for Ramsey's ship, and you didn't find it."

"No, I didn't. Nor did I see or feel anything to make me believe that his ship is moored but concealed by a spell. On the other hand, he could be on the harbor or the Charles, or any of the other surrounding waters."

"You can make yourself insane thinkin' that way. If Ramsey is here, and he's determined that you ain't gonna find him, there's nothin' you can do."

She was right.

"Good day, Janna. Again, my thanks."

He started for the door, but stopped when Janna called his name. Turning, he saw that she had come out from behind the bar.

"You said there was a ghost there yesterday, when that boy got shot."

"Aye," he said.

"You know Samuel Adams, don't you? That's somethin' you might want to talk to him about."

The same thought had crossed Ethan's mind. "I will."

He walked to the door, pausing to button his coat before stepping outside into the cold. The wind was blowing even harder now, and though the air was warmer still, it was cold enough to scythe through his clothes and sting his face. He held his hat in place with one hand, shoved the other hand into his pocket, and strode toward Cooper's Alley, leaning into the strengthening gale.

Ethan had hoped that once he was off the Neck, with its open leas, the houses and shops of the South End would offer some relief from the elements. They didn't. Wind blasted through the narrow streets and alleyways, keening like a wild beast.

He walked as swiftly as he could, eager to reach his room, though he knew that it would offer scant relief from the cold. As he neared Dall's cooperage, however, he saw that several soldiers, resplendent in red and white, had gathered outside Henry's establishment. And standing with them, of course, was none other than Sheriff Greenleaf.

"There he is," the sheriff said upon spotting Ethan.

Ethan slowed, then stopped, wondering what he had done now to draw the sheriff's attention. Perhaps he had been foolish to conjure the man to sleep the previous night.

"You're to come with me, Kaille," Greenleaf said, leading the soldiers in Ethan's direction, his expression grim.

"Am I under arrest?"

"Should you be? Is there something you care to confess?"

Ethan shook his head. "What is it you want, Sheriff?"

"I want nothing to do with you. But someone else wants a word."

"Who?" Ethan asked, but already he knew. Few men had the authority to send the sheriff on such an errand.

"The lieutenant governor," Greenleaf said. "Thomas Hutchinson."

Chapter

SEVEN

hough still lieutenant governor in title, Hutchinson had been acting governor of the Province of Massachusetts Bay since the previous summer, when Francis Bernard left the city for England. Bernard had been vilified by Boston's citizenry, many of whom considered him the man most responsible for the continuing occupation. But Hutchinson enjoyed little more goodwill than did his predecessor, and the Crown's unwillingness to make his appointment as governor official had done nothing to enhance his standing.

Ethan had met Hutchinson on several occasions, each time under difficult circumstances. Back in 1765, after mobs protesting Parliament's new Stamp Tax ransacked Hutchinson's home, the lieutenant governor summoned Ethan to his chambers in the Town House. At the time, Ethan had been hired by Abner Berson, one of Boston's wealthiest merchants, to investigate the murder of his elder daughter. Hutchinson sought to convince Ethan that the same rabble who destroyed his home were responsible for the murder, and he hoped that blame for both crimes would fall on Samuel Adams and his associates. Ethan's inquiry led to a different conclusion: The riot and murder were the work of a conjurer acting on behalf of some in England intent on weakening the very agitators whom Hutchinson wished to blame.

Three years later, as the occupation began, Ethan was hired by agents of the Customs Board to find the conjurer responsible for the murders of nearly one hundred men aboard HMS *Graystone*, a ship in the occupying fleet. On this occasion, with the beginning of the occupation going poorly, Hutchinson gave Ethan a mere five days to find those responsible. If Ethan failed, the lieutenant governor warned, he would put to death every conjurer in the city. Ethan found the killers with barely any time to spare, but still Hutchinson spoke of purging Boston of all who dabbled in magick. Nearly eighty years after so-called witches were executed in nearby Salem, Massachusetts, Ethan believed Hutchinson remained willing to repeat that barbarity.

"Be careful how you use that witchery of yours," the lieutenant governor had said at the end of their last conversation. "I'll go to my grave believing that it's an abomination, and I know that I am not alone in my belief."

Ethan thought back on that exchange as the sheriff and soldiers led him through the icy streets to the Town House. He wondered if he would have been better off refusing the summons, although he couldn't imagine that Greenleaf would have any compunction about dragging him to Hutchinson's chambers against his will. It seemed that in this case he had no good choices.

Ethan and Greenleaf walked together behind the regulars; for now at least, the sheriff was not treating him as a prisoner. Still, some stopped to stare at Ethan and his escort as they progressed through the city; most ignored them, however. Uniformed soldiers were, by this time, an all-too-familiar sight in Boston.

They soon reached the Town House, an impressive red-brick building, famous for its graceful steeple, gabled façade, and ornate clock. While the soldiers waited outside, Greenleaf led Ethan into the building and up to the second floor. There he rapped once on the door to Hutchinson's chambers, and, at a summons from within, opened the door and waved Ethan inside.

Hutchinson stood at a large desk, poring over a sheaf of parchment. He half turned at the sound of their entrance and removed a pair of spectacles from the bridge of his nose. "Ah, Sheriff Greenleaf, Mister Kaille. Thank you for coming so quickly."

"Of course, Your Honor," Greenleaf said.

"Sheriff, please leave us for a time."

Greenleaf's face fell. He cast a dark look Ethan's way, but then let himself out of the chamber.

Ethan and the lieutenant governor eyed each other in silence for a few seconds, like men preparing to duel. Hutchinson was tall with large eyes, a high forehead, and a long, aristocratic nose. He had narrow shoulders that he held thrust back, as if constantly standing at attention, so that he appeared barrel-chested. His hair was gray, and in the year and a half since their last encounter the lines in his face had deepened considerably. The occupation of the city had not been kind to him.

"You have some idea of why I've summoned you?" the lieutenant governor asked.

"Is it to accuse me of causing Christopher Seider's murder? Or perhaps to tell me that all of Boston's witches are responsible and will be put to death at the morrow's dawn?"

Hutchinson's cheeks turned pink, but he did not rail at Ethan for his effrontery, as Ethan expected. Instead, he looked away, the corners of his mouth quirking. "I suppose I deserve that." He placed his spectacles on his desk. "Would you believe that I have come to regret the way I treated you during the *Graystone* affair?"

It was one thing to confront the lieutenant governor with his own words and actions. It was quite another to call him a liar.

"Aye, sir. I believe it."

Hutchinson nodded, still not looking Ethan in the eye. "I asked the sheriff to bring you here after he described for me your visit to the gaol last night."

Ethan said nothing. Did he refer to Ethan's eagerness to see Richardson, or the fact that he used a conjuring to put Greenleaf to sleep?

At last Hutchinson lifted his gaze. "You suspect that . . . that an act of magick caused Ebenezer Richardson to fire at that mob."

"I believe it's possible, yes."

"I've had my own dealings with mobs, as you may recall. And I understand the impulse to draw a weapon in one's own defense. But firing blindly as he did . . ." He shook his head. "Richardson is an idiot."

"Yes, sir, he is."

A faint smile touched Hutchinson's lips. "At least we can agree on that."

Ethan grinned as well. "At least."

"The sheriff mentioned no names, save yours of course. I would like to know if you have in mind a certain—what is it you call yourselves?—a certain conjurer?"

Even Hutchinson, who knew so little about conjuring, would have heard Ramsey's name mentioned the previous summer. He was not about to give the lieutenant governor cause for panic in the absence of any evidence. "No, sir, I don't. Not yet at least."

"Are there people of your kind living in Boston who might be capable of doing something as dark as this?"

"None of whom I'm aware, Your Honor. I suspect that if a conjurer is responsible, it is someone from outside of the city. A recent arrival perhaps. But really all of this is conjecture. Right now, I'm afraid I know very little."

"Yes, the sheriff indicated as much. He seems to believe that you might be responsible."

"Imagine my surprise."

Hutchinson said nothing, but continued to watch him.

"If this were my doing," Ethan said, "why would I bring it to the sheriff's attention in the first place? I would simply cast my spells and let them work their mischief. Seeking him out as I did would make no sense at all."

"No, I don't suppose it would, though I do not pretend to understand the workings of a witch—of a conjurer's mind." Hutchinson began to pace the chamber. "Tell me, Mister Kaille: Have you discussed this matter with Samuel Adams or his fellow radicals?"

"No, sir, I haven't. And if I may, whatever you might think of Adams and his allies, I do not believe that they would sacrifice the life of a child for their cause."

Hutchinson halted. "Is that right?" he asked, his tone sharpening. "Perhaps if you knew them as I do, you would place less faith in their scruples." He resumed his pacing, his thick eyebrows bunched. "Oh, they wouldn't be so crass as to have the lad killed, but I've no doubt that they will seek to turn this tragedy to their advantage in whatever way they can. Already, I have received word that they intend to organize some sort of public display a few days hence."

"What sort of display?"

The lieutenant gave an impatient shake of his head. "I've no idea. It doesn't matter; whatever they do will only make matters worse and lead us inexorably toward the next crisis."

He stopped again and faced Ethan. "I know that you have had dealings with Adams and the rest. I asked you about them before not because I seek to blame them—though I refuse to believe that they are blameless—but rather to ask that you prevail upon them to put an end to these unlawful and perilous assemblies."

"Sir—"

"Clearly Adams didn't pull the trigger. Not even I believe the man or his colleagues capable of such barbarity. But don't you see? He didn't have to. He ordered those scoundrels onto Middle Street to make an example of Theophilus Lillie—a man you were paid to protect, if I understand correctly."

Ethan didn't deny it.

"Adams and his kind organize these mobs with the express intent of fomenting unrest. Surely you understand that." The lieutenant governor was growing more animated by the moment, his face reddening, spittle flying from his mouth. "They incite the rabble to a frenzy and set them loose upon the city, knowing that all manner of violence and mayhem will follow. Adams might have been comfortably ensconced in his tavern over on Union Street, but he bears responsibility for the Seider boy's death. He may as well have loaded Richardson's musket and thrust it into his hands."

Ethan stared down at his tricorn, which he held before him, and he kept silent.

"You disagree," Hutchinson said with a hint of asperity.

"Whether or not I agree is unimportant. You want me to convince Samuel Adams to go against his very nature. There isn't a man in Boston who could do that. I'm sure I can't. Adams and I are acquaintances and nothing more. To be honest, we don't particularly like each other. You may find this hard to credit, but he thinks me too much a Tory to be trusted. And I—" Ethan stopped himself. "Well, let's say simply that I don't always agree with his tactics."

"Apparently we agree on that as well," Hutchinson muttered.

"As I've already told you," Ethan said, "I don't believe that Adams would sacrifice a child's life for his cause."

Hutchinson's laugh was bitter. "Where do you think all of this leads, Mister Kaille? Are you truly so naïve? Adams and the others want separation from England. Do you believe the Crown will simply allow the colonies to leave the British Empire?"

"No, I don't suppose—"

"Of course not. So then it's war we're talking about, isn't it? Before this is over, how many lads do you think will die for Adams's cause? A thousand? Ten thousand? More?"

"That's not the same, sir, and you know it. If you're right, the king will send lads to fight here. Do you impute similar motives to His Majesty?" Hutchinson did not deign to answer and Ethan thinned a smile. "I thought not. As for Adams, I have no influence with the man. If you want someone to speak with him, I would suggest you seek out one of those whom he keeps in his confidence."

"Who? Otis? Warren? Revere? They won't treat with me. They are as besotted with the notion of 'liberty' as Adams."

"Be that as it may."

The lieutenant governor shook his head, his frustration manifest in his expression. "So you refuse to help me."

"I don't believe I can help you."

"I can pay you. Or rather, the Province of Massachusetts Bay can pay you."

"Pay me to do what?"

"To . . . to find the witch—the conjurer—who cast that spell you felt on Middle Street."

"If you would care to engage my services as a thieftaker I would consider it an honor to work on behalf of the province."

"Five pounds?"

Ethan nodded. "Done."

"And Adams?"

"For that you'll need to find another man."

Hutchinson's mien soured once more. "Yes, very well. Good day, Mister Kaille."

"Good day, sir."

Ethan turned and walked to the door. Before he could pull it open, however, the lieutenant governor said, "Hold, Mister Kaille."

Ethan faced him.

"I have a proposition for you. You doubt that Adams would use the death of the Seider boy to advance his political aims. I know that you're wrong. I will accept that you don't wish to speak with him on my behalf. But I would ask this: If in the next several days you perceive that I am right and you are wrong about the man's scruples, you will go to him, as I've asked."

Ethan weighed the proposal. "And if it turns out that I'm right?"

"In that case, our original arrangement stands, with this one amendment: If you find the conjurer, I will pay you from my own purse another three pounds above the five I've already promised you."

"All right," Ethan said, grinning.

"You find this amusing?" Hutchinson asked.

"Not the circumstances, no. But I will admit that I never imagined when Sheriff Greenleaf was bringing me here that our congress would end with a wager."

"We're living in interesting times."

"Aye, sir. That we are."

"We have an agreement, then?"

"We do, sir."

He left the lieutenant governor's chambers and found the sheriff waiting for him in the corridor.

"Well?" Greenleaf asked.

"I have a job," Ethan said, donning his hat and stepping past the sheriff. "And a wager."

When Ethan reached Dall's cooperage, the sky was already starting to darken. He could hear Henry hammering away within, and Shelly sat in front of the door, her tail thumping on the cobblestones as she marked Ethan's approach.

The cooperage had been built by Henry's grandfather some sixty years before and, though weathered and worn, it remained a sturdy building. A sign over the oaken door read "Dall's Barrels and Crates," and a second on the door itself read "Open Entr." Ethan pushed the door open, removed his hat, and slipped inside.

It was quite warm within the cooperage, and it smelled of smoke, freshly cut wood, and sweat. A fire burned brightly in the hearth along the back wall. Henry stood at his workbench, hammering the last stays in place on a barrel. He waved at Ethan but continued to pound away at the stays, until at last he tossed the hammer onto the barrel and dropped himself onto his bench, wiping sweat from his brow.

"All right, Henry?"

The cooper shrugged. "I gueth," he said, with his usual lisp, a product of the large gap where his front top teeth used to be. "Working too hard. You?"

"About the same."

"I saw that the sheriff was here for you, with a few lobsterbacks. What'd they want?"

"They took me to see Thomas Hutchinson."

Henry looked impressed. "You in trouble?"

"Aren't I always."

The cooper cackled at that, but soon sobered. "This is no time to get in trouble with them soldiers, Ethan. Not after yesterday."

"I know," Ethan said. He paused, then, "I was there when Christopher Seider was shot."

"You were in that mob?" Henry asked, sounding surprised.

"Not exactly. I was working . . ." He didn't finish the thought. He couldn't bring himself to admit to the cooper that he had been working for one of the nonimportation violators.

"It's a bad business," Henry said with a slow shake of his head. "And it's going to get worse before it gets better."

"Where do you stand on all of this, Henry?"

The cooper regarded him solemnly. Ethan and Henry had never

before discussed politics, and Ethan feared that he had given offense by asking.

But eventually Henry shrugged again. "I guess I think that if Samuel Adams believes we should have more liberty, I believe it, too."

"You like Adams."

"I liked his father. He stood up for what he thought was right, and he wasn't afraid of anyone, not even the people with money who came to hate him. I respected that. I think the son has a bit of his father in him." He picked up a metal cup that had been beside him on the bench and sipped what Ethan assumed was water, all the while eyeing Ethan over the rim of the cup. Placing it back on the bench, he said, "I've always figured you for a Tory. Am I wrong?"

"You wouldn't have been a few years ago," Ethan said. He gazed at the fire. "The occupation has changed my views."

"It's changed a lot of people's views."

"Aye, that it has."

They sat in silence for a minute or two. The wind rattled Henry's door.

"I think more snow's coming," Henry said. "It been pretty cold up in your room?"

"Aye. I'll probably be at the Dowsing Rod tonight." Ethan stood. "It's good to see you, Henry."

The cooper gave a gap-toothed grin. "And you, Ethan. Maybe now that you're not a Tory, I'll see more of you."

"What do you mean?"

Henry sat a little straighter. "I've been going to some of the assemblies," he said, pride in his voice. "It's mostly young fellas, but they made room for me. And there's bound to be more now, after what's happened. Word is Adams already has plans for something big."

Ethan thought of his conversation with Hutchinson, a tight feeling in his gut. "Do you know what it is?"

"No. But I'll be there. You can count on that."

"Well, be careful, Henry."

"Oh, I will. Good evening, Ethan."

Ethan forced a smile and let himself out of the cooperage. He paused by the door to scratch Shelly's ears before climbing the stairway to his small, cold room. Enough daylight still seeped in through his window to let him see without lighting a candle. He considered using a spell to light a fire in his hearth, but he didn't plan to stay long, and he had only a small supply of firewood remaining. He merely sat on his bed, his elbows resting on his knees.

He was working for the Crown. He hadn't given much thought to what this meant when he agreed to Hutchinson's proposal, but now he regretted their arrangement. What would Kannice think? And Diver?

True, he had only been hired to find the conjurer responsible for whatever spell was used against Richardson—if such a spell had even been cast. But still, it felt like a betrayal. What was more, Henry believed—as Hutchinson did—that Samuel Adams had it in mind to use the death of Christopher Seider as justification for further agitation against the Crown. Which meant that Ethan would have to speak with Adams on the lieutenant governor's behalf. Neither Kannice nor Diver would be happy about that.

But what was he supposed to do? He had stopped working for Lillie, for his own sake as well as for them, at significant cost to himself. Two nights before, he had lost yet another payment to Sephira. He needed to eat and to pay Henry for his room. Perhaps the Empress of the South End could afford to refuse those jobs she found distasteful or beneath her station, but Ethan couldn't.

"I'm a thieftaker," he murmured in the gathering gloom. "This is what I do."

Surely Kannice would understand. And still he sat, not yet ready to face her, unsure of when he would be. Ultimately, it was the wind and the cold, and the growling of his stomach, that forced him to his feet and out into the night.

Once outside, he beat a hasty trail to the Dowser, ignoring the pain in his leg, and shivering with every new gust of that cutting wind. As he crossed the city, a few flakes of snow fell, whipped along by the gale. Ethan remembered winds of this sort from his days as a sailor; usually they augured great and terrible storms.

When he reached the Dowser he found it far less crowded than usual. The great room smelled heavily of smoke, and Kelf knelt by the hearth, working a bellows, his face pink and his eyes watering.

Ethan joined him there. "Can I help?"

Kelf shook his head. "I don't think there's anything to be done. It's burnin' well enough, but every time the wind blows the smoke comes back down."

"Where is everyone?"

Kelf dropped the bellows and stood with some effort. "At their homes, most likely. Word is, this is going to be a big one."

Ethan gave him a sharp look. "Do you have that from Adams?"

"Adams?" Kelf repeated, eyeing Ethan as he would a madman. "You mean Samuel Adams? What in God's name would he know about it?"

"What are you talking about, Kelf?"

"The storm that's comin', of course. Word is it's a big one. What were *you* talkin' about?"

"The next . . ." He shook his head. "It doesn't matter. My mind's on other things."

Kelf regarded him with a deepening frown. He gestured for Ethan to follow and lumbered back to the bar.

"There's chowder," the barman said over his shoulder. "Do you want some?"

"Please. And an ale."

As they reached the bar, Kannice emerged from the kitchen carrying a stack of bowls. Seeing Ethan, she smiled and leaned across the counter to kiss him. "I was afraid you wouldn't get back tonight; it's blowing something fierce out there."

"Aye. Snow's starting to fall."

Her expression grew more guarded. "How was it with Lillie today?"

"I only stayed long enough to tell him that I wouldn't be working for him any longer."

She beamed. "Really?"

"Aye. There's blood on his money. I don't want it."

"You did the right—"

He held up a hand, stopping her. "Before you say more, you should hear the rest."

Her smile faded. She nodded for him to go on.

"The sheriff paid me a visit earlier today. Thomas Hutchinson wished to speak with me. It seems Greenleaf related to him what I thought I felt before Chris Seider was shot. Hutchinson wants me to find whoever was responsible."

"So, you're working for Hutchinson?"

"I'm working for the Province of Massachusetts Bay."

"But only to find . . ." She glanced around and leaned closer to him. "Only to find the conjurer, right?"

"Aye, to find the conjurer." Perhaps he should have mentioned as well that he would need to speak with Samuel Adams, but he couldn't bring himself to tell her just then.

"Well," she said, "if there's someone using spells to hurt children that way, he should be dealt with. And who better than you to find him?"

"So you're not angry with me?"

Kannice shrugged. "How much is Hutchinson—or rather the province—paying you?"

"Five pounds, if I succeed."

"And how much of that will you be spending on me?"

Ethan laughed. "A good deal it would seem."

"Then no, I'm not angry." She grew serious once more. "You need to earn a living, Ethan. I understand that."

He cupped a hand around her cheek. "Thank you." They kissed again. "Will you be closing early tonight, Missus Lester? On account of the weather, I mean."

Candlelight danced in her blue eyes. "That's my plan. On account of the weather."

It was another late evening.

Throughout the night, the storm raged outside the Dowser, rattling the shutters on Kannice's bedroom window and filling the chamber with billows of smoke from the blaze in her hearth. Falling snow scratched at the shutters and every new gust of wind seemed to suck from the room what little warmth came from the low-burning fire.

Ethan woke often throughout the night, and knew that Kannice did, too. He knew as well, though, that in a storm such as this, there would be few people abroad in the streets. He had nowhere to be, and Kannice had no reason to open the tavern. Shortly after dawn, he fell into a deep sleep, only to be awakened again sometime later by a deep rumble of thunder.

"Did you hear that?" he whispered, wondering if perhaps it had been a pulse of magic.

"Aye," Kannice whispered. "I can't remember the last time we had thunder during a winter storm."

He let out a breath, relieved that she had heard it, too. Thunder growled again, closer this time. From the frenzied scrabbling at the shutters, it seemed that the snow was falling harder than ever.

Kannice moved closer to him, her skin warm against his. "I think we're stuck here for the day."

He ran his fingers through her hair and down over her back. "Now that," he said, "is a shame."

Hunger drove them from her bed some time later. They dressed and went downstairs to the kitchen, where Ethan, savoring a rare morning of leisure, cooked them a grand breakfast of pancake, bacon, and eggs. Thunder continued to shake the tavern, and lightning flickered around the edges of the window shutters.

While they were eating, and sipping English tea that Kannice swore she had purchased months before the nonimportation agreements took effect, there came a pounding at the tavern door.

"Could that be Kelf?" Ethan asked.

Kannice stared at the door, a frown on her face. "I suppose. But he and I agreed last night that if the storm was as bad as some said it would be, he wouldn't come to the bar until late in the day, if at all."

Ethan stood, drew his knife, and pushed up his sleeve. They approached the door together. Kannice drew the lock key from within her bodice.

Whoever had come hammered at the door a second time.

"Who's there?" Kannice called.

"Kannice?" came the reply. "Ethan? It's me, Diver. Derrey."

Kannice looked back at Ethan and rolled her eyes. She unlocked the door and pulled it open.

Diver stood before them, his coat, scarf, and Monmouth cap caked with snow. Beyond him Ethan could see that the entire city was blanketed in white. There must have been at least a foot of snow in the street, and it was still falling so hard that he could barely see the shops on the far side of Sudbury Street.

Diver made to enter the tavern, but Kannice planted herself directly in front of him.

"Don't you dare!"

"But, I'm cold!"

"And you can get warm as soon as you take off those boots," she said, gesturing at his feet, which were completely covered in snow. "But you will not track all that snow into my tavern."

Diver looked at Ethan, a plea in his dark eyes.

Ethan held up his hands. "I can't help you, Diver."

"Well, at least give me a shoulder to hold on to."

Ethan moved to the threshold, putting himself as close to Diver as he could without stepping into the snow himself. Diver gripped his shoulder with one hand and wrestled off his boots with the other.

"All right?" he asked Kannice when he was done.

She regarded him with a critical eye, then pulled off his hat and shook the snow off it. Still holding it, she brushed snow off his coat.

"Very well," she said at last, stepping aside.

Diver hurried past them both to the hearth. Kannice and Ethan shared a smile. Kannice closed the door and Ethan joined his friend before the fire.

"What possible reason could you have for being out in such a storm?" he asked.

"You *haven't* heard then. I told Deborah that you wouldn't know."

Ethan's pulse quickened.

"Know what?" Kannice asked.

"Samuel Adams is arranging a funeral for Chris Seider. It's to take place the day after tomorrow. He expects it will draw a crowd the like of which the lobsters have never seen."

Chapter
EIGHT

Ethan's conversation with Henry had prepared him for this, but still he didn't want to believe what Diver was telling them.

"He's going to use the boy's funeral to gather another mob?"

"No!" Diver said. "It's not like that. Not really."

"Tell me how it's different."

Diver opened his mouth, closed it again. "Well, what do you expect, Ethan? Richardson shot the lad while trying to defend Theophilus Lillie and the other importers, didn't he?"

Ethan shook his head. That wasn't precisely what had happened. But thinking about it he knew that for Adams's purposes it was close enough. "Go on."

"So, it's like people are saying. Chris Seider died for the cause of liberty. He's the first, but probably not the last. And he deserves a hero's funeral."

Kannice had joined them by the hearth. She slipped her hand into Ethan's. "You say this will be in two days?"

"That's right. Monday. We're to gather at the Liberty Tree."

Ethan shuddered. The Liberty Tree had long been a symbol of Adams's cause, beginning back in 1765, when effigies of Andrew Oliver and other Crown officials were hung from its branches. But the tree was also significant for Ethan. That same summer, he was chained to its trunk and tortured by the conjurer who killed Jennifer Berson. He managed to win his freedom and kill his captor, although, ironically, only after Adams shot the man.

He gave Kannice's hand a quick squeeze and then released it. "I have to go," he said.

She rounded on him. "Go? Go where?"

"I have to speak with Adams."

"Why?" she asked, narrowing her eyes. "Does this have anything to do with your new employer?"

She was as clever as anyone he knew.

"Aye, it does."

"Who are you working for now?" Diver asked, looking from one of them to the other.

Ethan caught Kannice's eye and gave a small shake of his head.

"Ethan?"

"It doesn't matter, Diver. But I have to go."

Kannice didn't look at all happy, but she said, "Come back when you're done."

"I will."

He retrieved his greatcoat from her bedroom, pulled on his scarf and gloves, and put on his hat.

"You didn't finish your breakfast," Kannice said, as he came back down to the great room.

"Give it to him," he said, waving a hand at Diver.

He stepped to the door, but halted and faced his friend again. "Is Adams at his home or at the Green Dragon?"

"I'm not sure," Diver said. "The Dragon, I think."

"My thanks."

Ethan pulled the door open and squinted against the glare of the snow. The air was thick with flakes, and the wind still blew, though not as fiercely as it had. Thunder rumbled in the distance. Ethan struck out southward on Sudbury.

The distance between the Dowser and the Green Dragon was not great. But the streets were choked with snow, which made for slow going. With every step, Ethan sank knee-deep, until his legs and feet were wet, heavy, and cold. Snow flew into his eyes and gathered on his shoulders and back. His bad leg ached, and though his face and hands were freezing, by the time he reached the Dragon, he was sweating within his greatcoat.

The tavern was housed in the basement of a plain, two-story brick building that was owned by the Freemasons. A cast-iron dragon sat perched over the entryway, its wings raised, tongues of sculpted flame issuing from its open mouth. Ethan paused in the doorway to shake the snow off of his hat and coat before descending a dim stairway to the tavern.

The storm might have kept much of Boston's citizenry at home on this day, but the Green Dragon overflowed with people, their voices raised in a din of conversations. A few drank ales or ate from plates of oysters. Most however, appeared to be there to talk and plan. Ethan threaded his way through the patrons, searching for Adams and moving in the general direction of a small room at the back of the tavern where he last had encountered the man.

Reaching the door, he knocked once.

Immediately the door opened, revealing a chamber as crowded as the great room, its air hazed with pipe smoke.

Ethan didn't recognize the young gentleman who blocked his way.

"Who are you?" the man asked, sounding more harried than threatening.

"Ethan Kaille. I'm looking for Samuel Adams."

"You and half of Boston. He's busy right now."

The man started to close the door. Ethan put out a hand to stop him.

"Now see here—"

"Mister Adams and I have had dealings before. And today I bear a message from Thomas Hutchinson."

The man's expression turned cold. "And why should any of us care what he has to say?"

"Because like him or not, he is the acting governor."

"Aye. Fine. Give me your message. I'll see that it reaches Samuel."

Ethan shook his head. "No. I'm to give it to him personally."

"I don't think so."

A second man, one Ethan recognized, appeared at the shoulder of the first. He was young as well, tall, with expressive dark eyes.

"What is this, John?" Joseph Warren asked.

He glanced at Ethan, looked a second time. Recognition flashed in his dark eyes, though his expression was no more welcoming than that of the first man.

"Mister Kaille, isn't it?"

"Aye, Doctor Warren. It's a pleasure to see you again, sir."

"He wishes to see Samuel," John said. "He claims to bear a message from Hutchinson himself."

"Is that so?"

"Aye," Ethan said. "I know that Mister Adams has more important things to do than treat with me. But I need a moment of his time."

Warren looked over his shoulder at the throng, leading Ethan to believe that Adams stood at the center of it. He faced Ethan again, and Ethan was certain that the doctor would send him away. But he said, "Yes, very well. Wait here, Mister Kaille." He patted the other man on the shoulder. "It's all right, John. Thank you."

Warren wandered back into the crowded room, leaving John to guard the door. He made no effort to shut it in Ethan's face, but he did seem determined that Ethan would not, under any circumstances, enter the chamber.

After several minutes, Ethan saw Warren detach himself from the cluster of men in the room. He was followed by a shorter figure wearing red breeches and a matching waistcoat. This man had gray, plaited hair and penetrating dark blue eyes.

Samuel Adams was but a few years older than Ethan, but, as with Hutchinson, the occupation of the city had taken its toll on him. His face, while still pleasant and open, appeared somewhat sallow. The palsy that had afflicted him all his life was more pronounced than Ethan remembered; his head and hands shook noticeably. Nevertheless, he smiled as he proffered a hand.

Ethan grasped it. Adams still possessed a firm grip.

"Mister Kaille," he said, speaking softly and yet managing to make himself heard over the voices of the men around them. "It's good to see you again."

"And you, Mister Adams. Thank you for agreeing to speak with me. I know how busy you are right now."

"More than at any point in our struggle. But perhaps that is why you're here." He turned to Warren. "Joseph, Mister Kaille and I require a few moments alone. I believe we'll find a bit of privacy upstairs. In the meanwhile, you should continue with the arrangements."

"Of course."

"With all the snow that has fallen today, it will be more difficult than usual to communicate our intentions to those most likely to attend the funeral. We'll need to use the *Gazette* and other sympathetic papers. Have James and Paul work on an announcement."

"Very well." Warren's gaze flicked toward Ethan. "Don't keep him long," he said.

Before Ethan could answer, Adams chuckled and said, "He'll keep me no longer than I wish to be kept, and no shorter either." He gestured toward the great room. "This way, Mister Kaille. To the stairway."

Ethan and Adams began to wend their way through the packed room, but progress came slowly. At last, Adams stepped past Ethan and said in a ringing voice, "Please make way, gentlemen."

He might as well have been Moses with his great staff. The crowd parted as by divine intervention, allowing Adams to lead Ethan to the stairs.

By the time they reached the top of the stairway, Adams was breathing hard and his face was flushed.

"Do you need to rest, sir?" Ethan asked, masking his alarm.

Adams waved off the question with obvious impatience, and led Ethan down a corridor to what appeared to be a small office.

"This belongs to the junior warden of the Freemasons," Adams told Ethan over his shoulder. "Usually I wouldn't presume, but he won't be coming today, and I doubt he'll mind."

He shut the door behind them and went to the glazed window that looked out onto the building's grounds. The snow was piled so high on the outer sill that the bottom half of the window was obscured.

"It's still falling," Adams said. "Perhaps God doesn't wish for us to go ahead with our plans." He turned to look at Ethan. "I know the lieutenant governor does not. Is that not why you've come? To tell me that Hutchinson requests our forbearance?"

"I've come for a number of reasons, sir."

"Including that one. I'm disappointed in you, Mister Kaille. There was a time when I thought you might join our cause, when I saw in you a man who would come to embrace the notion of liberty. And now here you stand: a messenger for the greatest enemy of liberty in all of Boston. How did this happen?"

Ethan bristled. "You mistake me for a servant of the Crown, sir. I am not. I remain, as I have always been, a subject of the British Empire. Beyond that, as you well know, I'm a thieftaker and a conjurer, and it is in those capacities that I stand before you."

A small smile played at the corners of Adams's mouth. "You have some fire in you, Mister Kaille. One need only stir the coals a bit to see it."

Ethan tried to maintain a hard glare, but before long he had to look away. He allowed himself a small breathless laugh. "Since the day we met, you've reveled in provoking me. Why is that?"

"It is, as I've said, because of the potential I see within you. I still hope that someday you'll join the patriot cause."

"You and everyone else," Ethan muttered.

Adams quirked an eyebrow. Ethan wished he had kept that thought to himself.

"In recent months, a friend has joined your cause. And there is . . . someone else as well who would like to see me a . . . a patriot, as you put it."

"A woman."

Ethan laughed again, openly this time. "Is it so obvious?"

"Always," Adams said.

"In truth, sir, I can imagine a day, not long from now, when I'll be willing to join you and the Sons of Liberty. But this is not that day. We have other matters to discuss."

"Very well, Mister Kaille. Proceed."

"First, you should know that I was on Middle Street two days ago when Christopher Seider was shot. I had been working for Theophilus Lillie."

Adams's expression clouded. "Had been working?"

"Aye. After Richardson shot the boy, I told Lillie that I would no longer take his money."

"I suppose that's admirable, though I believe you should have scrupled to take his coin when first he offered it."

Ethan swallowed the first retort that came to mind. "Times have been hard," he said instead. "I make no apologies for trying to earn a living."

Adams appeared to think better of a reply of his own. "So you were there when it happened."

"That's right. And before Richardson fired, I felt a conjuring."

"A conjuring." Adams said, his eyes widening. "Magick, you mean? Do you think that's why he did it? Are you saying that some form of witchery forced him to kill the lad?"

"I believe it's possible. Beyond that, I can say nothing with any confidence. But I have to ask you—"

"No! I know full well what you wish to ask, Mister Kaille, and the answer is no! Think what you will of me, but I am no murderer, nor would I ever countenance an act of such savagery!"

"Then allow me to offer my most sincere apologies for even suggesting as much."

"Is this what Hutchinson sent you to do? Does he believe that we are responsible?"

"No, sir. Never in my conversation with him did he suggest that you or anyone else in the Sons of Liberty wished to see Christopher Seider killed. And please let me be clear. I don't believe that you would ever sanction the murder of anyone, much less a child. In fact, I defended you to the lieutenant governor—that, as much as anything, is why I'm here. But I need to know if, to your knowledge, there are conjurers among the men downstairs."

Adams did not appear mollified, but after considering the matter he shook his head. "Not to my knowledge. But really, Mister Kaille, how would I know such I thing? I know that you're a conjurer because you tell me so, and because once, some years ago, I saw things that to this day I don't fully comprehend."

"I understand, sir. In that case, with your permission, when we're done here, I'll accompany you downstairs so that I might determine for myself if there are conjurers among your brethren."

"Yes, all right." Adams rubbed a palsied hand across his brow. "If this . . . this conjuring that you felt is what made Richardson fire into the crowd—"

"I don't know that for certain."

"But if it did, then he would not be guilty of murder, would he?"

"He pulled the trigger. Hundreds saw him do it. He will be charged with murder, and though I'm no attorney, I find it impossible to imagine that he won't be found guilty."

"That's not really what I asked," Adams said, a haunted look in his eyes. "In the eyes of the law, he may be guilty, but you're suggesting that he may not have acted of his own volition."

"Aye."

"In all of our dealings—yours and mine—I have tried to accept that your ability to conjure does not make you a devil in the eyes of God. But it seems to me that whenever we speak, it is to discuss some new atrocity committed with these same powers that you possess. Forgive me for saying so, but I fear your witchery."

"Many feel as you do, sir. I can only respond by telling you that I've done great good with my spells. I've healed wounds, saved lives, and discovered the perpetrators of crimes who might otherwise have gone unpunished."

Adams nodded, but said nothing.

After a brief, uncomfortable silence, Ethan said, "I should allow you to return to your friends downstairs."

"Not so fast, Mister Kaille. There is still the matter of Hutchinson to discuss. You've indicated that he doesn't think me a murderer, at least not yet, for which I am grateful. But you also said that you defended me in his presence, which is why you're here. I would like you to explain that."

Ethan's cheeks burned. He fixed his eyes on the floor in front of him. "The lieutenant governor suggested that while you might not kill a child, you would not be above using the lad's death to your advantage and that of your cause. I disagreed, and told him that you would never make use of tragedy in that way. Mister Hutchinson is paying me, in his capacity as leader of the province, to find the conjurer who cast this spell, assuming that the spell was directed at Richardson. And we agreed to a bit of a wager. If I was right about you, and you made no effort to turn Christopher Seider's murder to your purposes, he would pay me extra. And if I learned that he was right, I was to come to you on his behalf and try to convince you not to organize yet another assembly."

Adams said nothing at first, but turned and walked back to the snow-covered window.

"And here I've been speaking of being disappointed in you."

"Mister Hutchinson fears that another gathering like the one on Middle Street will lead to more bloodshed." Ethan paused. "Truthfully, sir, I fear that as well."

Adams turned. "So do I. So does every man downstairs. But what are we to do? Even if Hutchinson's expressions of concern are sincere, his solution, essentially, is for those of us who agitate in defense of liberty to surrender. The lieutenant governor stands on the side of angels and exhorts us simply to give up. And if we refuse, then we are cold-blooded and self-seeking. I'm sorry, Mister Kaille. We must carry on with our plans."

"As I told him you would."

"Do you think so ill of me?" Adams asked through a brittle smile.

"I don't think ill of you, sir. I know that the cause of liberty is the foundation of your life's work. And I know as well that Hutchinson's request was as much a political calculation as it was an attempt to prevent further violence."

Adams grinned. "Indeed. Are you sure you won't join us, Mister Kaille? We could use a man who thinks so clearly."

"Thank you, sir, but no. I will be there on Monday, however, at whatever sort of assembly you have in mind. I wish I could have saved the boy's life, but I was as powerless against his wounds as the surgeons who treated him. I want to pay my respects to the lad."

"Very well," Adams said in a solemn voice. "Shall we return to the Dragon? I have a good deal of work to do."

"Yes, sir."

They left the warden's office and descended the stairs once more. Before they reached the tavern's great room, Ethan whispered in Latin, *"Veni ad me."*

Uncle Reg appeared beside him, gleaming like the moon in the dim light.

"Did you say something, Mister Kaille?" Adams asked.

"No, sir."

Reg watched him as they emerged from the stairway, an avid look in his bright eyes.

I need to know if there are any conjurers here, Ethan told him silently. *And if there are, I don't want them to know that I'm aware of their powers. Can you search the tavern without allowing yourself to be seen, even by those who can cast spells?*

Reg nodded and vanished, though not before grinning like a thief in a rich man's home. Ethan assumed that the ghost followed as Adams led him to the small room at the back of the tavern.

Because Ethan was accompanied by Adams, no one tried to keep him from entering. John, the man who first greeted him at the door, eyed him with obvious mistrust, as did James Otis, whom Ethan had met on several occasions.

Ethan lingered in the room for a few minutes, which he hoped would be enough time for Reg to conduct his search. Then he approached Adams and bid the man farewell.

"Have you found . . . anyone?" Adams asked in a whisper.

"Not yet, sir. Perhaps in the great room."

"Very well, Mister Kaille. We will meet again soon."

They shook hands and Ethan left the small room for the main part of the tavern. He stood beside the door for some time, scanning the great room for any sign of Reg. Before long, he saw the image of the ghost flare beside the bar for no more than the blink of an eye.

Ethan pushed through the crowd to the bar. Reg appeared again beside a small man who stood drinking an ale, speaking to no one.

This one? Ethan asked.

Reg nodded.

Anyone else?

No.

Can you tell how powerful he is?

Reg shook his head again.

Before Ethan could ask the ghost anything more, the man let out a gasp. He had spotted Reg—as the lone conjurer in the tavern other than Ethan, he was the only person who could see the shade.

"He's with me," Ethan said.

The man turned with such haste that he slopped ale onto the bar and down the front of his own waistcoat.

"Who are you?"

"Ethan Kaille." He held out a hand, which the man gripped with some reluctance.

"Are . . . are you with the Sons of Liberty?"

"No. I'm a thieftaker. I'm wondering if you would be so kind as to summon your spectral guide. Just for a moment."

"Why should I?"

"As a courtesy to me."

"What? I have no—"

Ethan silenced him with a raised finger. "As I said, I'm a thieftaker. I'm conducting an inquiry and would like very much to see your ghost. If you refuse, I'll have little choice but to assume you do so out of fear that your role in the crime will be discovered."

"This is outrageous! What crime?"

Ethan shook his head. To Reg he said, "He leaves us no choice. I'm sure the sheriff will be eager to speak with him."

"Now, wait a second. There's no need to involve the sheriff."

"I quite agree," Ethan said. "Your ghost?"

The man placed his tankard on the bar and whispered, "*Veni ad me.*"

A glowing figure appeared beside him: a woman dressed in finery, who glowed with a pale orange hue. She was rather homely, with curled hair and a haughty expression. She regarded Reg with unconcealed hostility.

"Is this the ghost you saw two days ago?" Ethan asked his own spectral guide.

No.

"Does the color of his power look familiar?"

No.

Ethan wasn't sure whether to be relieved or disappointed.

"Are you satisfied?" the man asked, sounding self-righteous and angry. Ethan could hardly blame him.

"I am. Please accept my apologies, sir, and my thanks for your co-operation."

"I'm not much inclined to accept either."

Ethan donned his hat. "No, I don't imagine." He started toward the stairway. "Good day, sir."

"I want to know what crime you thought I had committed."

Ethan halted, turned. "I beg your pardon."

"The crime for which you were ready to blame me. I should like to know what it was. I believe you owe me that small courtesy."

"I don't believe I owe you anything, sir."

"You were lying. There was no crime."

The man spoke bravely, but when Ethan took a step back in his direction, he quailed.

"What is your name?" Ethan asked.

"Why should I tell you that?"

"Small courtesies."

His eyebrows bunched in a way that told Ethan he didn't appreciate having his words thrown back at him. But he said, "Jonathan Grant."

"I wasn't lying, Mister Grant. And you might consider that accusing a stranger of such a thing, when you don't know how powerful a conjurer he is, might not be so wise. The crime in question is not one others know about, but it was committed on Middle Street, two days ago."

Ethan walked away again.

"Two days—Hold on there."

He didn't stop, and was halfway up the stairs when he heard Grant behind him.

"Please wait."

Once more Ethan halted. He looked down at the man.

"Two days ago?" Grant said. "On Middle Street?"

"Aye."

"You were there, and you felt a conjuring."

"That's right."

"Damn," Grant whispered.

"I probably shouldn't have told you that," Ethan said, walking back down to where Grant stood. "But you were right: I did owe you as

much after threatening you. Please, breathe not a word of this to anyone else."

"Could it have been Richardson who cast?"

Ethan shook his head. "I don't believe so."

"What sort of spell was it?"

"I don't know that, either. Mister Grant, I would prefer—"

"Fear not, Mister Kaille," Grant said in a weak voice. "Whom would
I tell? No one here knows that I'm a conjurer, and as a clerk working
for the Customs Board, few at my place of business know that I spend
my free hours in the Green Dragon."

Ethan grinned. "A clerk with the Customs Board? I believe, sir, that
I misjudged you. You might be the bravest man in the tavern."

"Hardly."

"Since you work with the Customs boys, I would imagine that you
know my brother-in-law, Geoffrey Brower."

The smile Grant pasted on his face didn't fool Ethan at all. "Of
course. He's a fine man."

"You're kind to say so. I think he's an ass." Ethan proffered a hand,
which Grant gripped. "Your secrets are safe with me, Mister Grant."

"And yours with me, Mister Kaille."

Ethan tipped his hat to the man, and left the Dragon.

The snow had not abated at all; it might well have been falling
harder than before. Ethan's walk back to the Dowser proved nearly as
difficult as the walk to Union Street had been. He could see the furrow
in the snow where he had walked, but already it was covered with new
snowfall. It would be days before the city's streets were clear. If the air
remained this cold, or grew more so once the storm blew through, it
might take a week or more.

Adams could plan day and night, but with this much snow on the
ground, Ethan did not expect that his funeral for Christopher Seider
would amount to much.

Chapter
NINE

he storm ended that night, leaving more than two feet of snow on Boston's streets and rooftops. As Ethan expected—his years at sea had taught him to read the sky and the wind—after the storm passed, the air turned frigid once more, even as the clouds cleared away, leaving a sky bright with stars.

Kannice did not open the Dowser at all that day, and Kelf never made it to the tavern. Ethan and Kannice enjoyed a rare evening alone. They ate a modest meal before retreating to the warmth of her bedroom.

Lying with her, listening to the crackle of the fire burning in the hearth, Ethan realized that he could hear no other sounds. Outside, the streets were empty, the air had gone still, and the snowfall had ended. He had never known Boston to be so utterly silent. It was both eerie and wondrous.

At one point, he and Kannice opened the shutters on her bedroom window and peered out into the night, staring in awe at the blanketed city, which appeared to glow with starlight. Then they closed the shutters once more and burrowed under the blankets to escape the cold.

On Sunday morning, the streets of the city came to life again, not with commerce and carriages, but with families wading through the snow to church, and then, once the day's sermons were over, with children lured out into the snow by the promise of sledding and snowball fights. From within the tavern, Ethan could also hear the muffled scrape of metal shovels on snow-covered cobblestone.

Kelf reached the tavern at about midday, his breeches caked with snow and his face ruddy. Not long after, Diver arrived, his coat and hair damp. He grinned sheepishly at Ethan.

"Got into a bit of combat with the lads on Treamount," he said, crossing the great room to stand before the hearth. "They threw snowballs at me, I threw one back, and before I knew it, we were in a pitched battle. There were at least six of them, but I gave as good as I got."

Ethan sipped a toddy. "I'm sure."

Even Kannice seemed amused.

"Where's Deborah?" Ethan asked.

"She's back in her room. I only came out because I had matters to see to on Union Street."

Ethan straightened in his chair. "The Sons?"

Diver glanced at Kannice, perhaps fearful of her response. On most nights, she did not allow in her tavern discussions of politics—or anything else that might lead to a row. But she ignored Diver's remark, even though Ethan was sure she had heard him.

"Aye," Diver said, facing Ethan again. "They want each of us to bring as many people as possible. Adams is hoping for a huge crowd."

"He's still planning to do this tomorrow?"

"Of course. Why shouldn't he be?"

"Have you looked at the streets, Diver? He'll be fortunate to get a dozen people there."

Diver grinned. "I think you're wrong. It's going to be the biggest assembly this city has seen in many years. But if you'd care to place a small wager on the matter, I'd be more than happy to lighten your purse by a pound or two."

"I don't think so," Ethan said.

"A half sovereign?"

"An ale," Ethan said. "Kannice's Kent pale. I don't want you buying me some swill from another tavern."

Diver's smile broadened. "Done."

Ethan spent the rest of that day and much of Monday at the Dowser. Kannice took advantage of the lack of customers to straighten up her kitchen and bar, something she had wanted to do for months. Ethan helped Kelf lift, carry, and clean as she directed, enjoying the work far more than he would have guessed. He was glad to labor and sweat without giving a thought to spells and shadowy conjurers, to Sephira and her toughs, and to the possible whereabouts of Nate Ramsey. He felt no conjurings, and even started to question whether he had been too quick to assume that the spells he had noticed in recent days were responsible for Gordon's attack on Will Pryor and Richardson's shooting of Chris Seider.

Late on Monday afternoon, Ethan, Kelf, and Kannice set out from the Dowsing Rod for the Liberty Tree. Some effort had been made to clear the streets of snow, and many merchants and craftsmen had shoveled paths to the doors of their shops. Still, Ethan found it hard to believe that more than a handful of people would come to the Seider funeral.

He and the others hadn't been abroad in the city for long before he realized how wrong he had been.

Though the streets remained covered with a thick layer of snow that made them only barely passable, Ethan soon found himself in a broad stream of men, women, and children filing through the lanes toward Boston's Neck. The farther he, Kannice, and Kelf walked from the Dowser, the more people he saw. They came from the North End and Cornhill, the waterfront and the South End, all converging on Marlborough Street. There, they continued in silence, with grim purpose, bathed in the golden light of late afternoon. By the time they reached the corner of Orange Street and Essex, where stood the famed Liberty Tree, they numbered at least a thousand.

A large sign had been erected near the tree. On it were several biblical quotations that someone—Adams perhaps—had deemed appropriate for the occasion.

"Though Hand join in Hand, the Wicked shall not pass unpunish'd," read one.

And another said, "Thou shalt take no satisfaction for the life of a MURDERER—he shall surely be put to death."

As it turned out, the men and women who had walked with Ethan, Kannice, and Kelf to the Liberty Tree represented but a fraction of those who had come to honor Christopher Seider. A far greater number of people awaited them along Orange Street south of the tree. Adams and his allies had already begun to arrange the procession that would march through the city streets. Hundreds of schoolboys had been lined up in twin columns, their cheeks red with the cold. Behind them, flanked by six more boys—pallbearers, it seemed—lay on the snow a small, wooden coffin with Latin inscriptions painted in silver lettering along its sides and at its head. A cluster of perhaps three dozen men, women, and children stood next in line. Many of them wept openly, and when Ethan walked past, he heard snatches of conversation in German. He gathered that these were Seider's parents, relatives, and friends.

Behind these unfortunate souls, the rest of the mourners, already numbering in the hundreds, had taken their places. Ethan thought that with all those he had seen on his way to the Liberty Tree, the number of marchers would exceed two thousand.

In the distance, at the very rear of the procession, more than two dozen carriages and chaises waited for the parade to begin, their horses snorting clouds of vapor in the twilight air.

As Ethan, Kannice, and Kelf made their way toward the back of the procession, they passed one luminary after another. Joseph Warren and James Otis had joined the throng, as had Paul Revere and Benjamin Church, Benjamin Edes and John Hancock. Samuel Adams walked the length of the column, calling encouragement and instructions to those he passed, while his cousin, the lawyer John Adams, stood with a woman Ethan assumed was his wife, appearing somewhat awed by what Samuel had wrought.

Near the back of the line, they found Diver and Deborah, who greeted them with solemn expressions and made room for them. If Diver took any satisfaction in being right about the size of the assembly, he gave no indication of it. He shook Ethan's hand and Kelf's, gave Kannice a quick kiss on the cheek, and then stood facing forward, his chin raised, his hands clasped in front of him.

Ethan continued to look around, amazed at what he was witnessing. It was a sight as humbling as it was spectacular. Adams had outdone himself. Ethan could only imagine what Thomas Hutchinson would think of this display. No doubt he would think it a spectacle and nothing more, a cynical attempt to turn tragedy to political gain. Ethan had resolved to be here because of what he had seen four days before on Middle Street, but he had expected that he would feel much the same. As the procession began, however, as he strained to see those six boys lift Christopher Seider's coffin onto their shoulders and plod through the snow, he understood how wrong he had been about this as well.

It took some time before Ethan and the rest of those near the back of the column could begin walking. Even as he started to tread through the snowy lane, he guessed that by the time the carriages rolled forward, the first of the lads leading the parade would be near the center of Cornhill.

Kannice walked beside him, tears coursing down her cheeks, no doubt as moved as he by the city's outpouring of grief and resolve. He took her hand.

Still more people had gathered along the side of the street to watch the procession as it followed Orange, Newbury, Marlborough, and Cornhill Streets up to the Town House. It then snaked through the North and South Ends before turning back toward the Neck, and the burying ground where Christopher Seider's body was to be interred. As the sky darkened and night fell, those lining the lanes handed torches to the marchers so that the procession became a river of light flowing through the city.

But as the coffin passed once more within sight of Murray's Barracks, where so many British soldiers were billeted, Ethan felt a conjuring pulse in the street. He halted, forcing his friends to do the same. The men walking behind stumbled into them.

"What is it?" Kannice asked.

Ethan opened his mouth to answer, but then shut it again, his heart hammering in his chest. He hadn't noticed at first because several of the people around him carried torches. But Uncle Reg had appeared by his side, and was eyeing him, his eyes as brilliant as the brightest flames.

"I didn't summon you," Ethan whispered. "Why are you here?"

Before Reg could offer any sort of answer, Ethan heard shouts from up ahead.

"What are the lobsters doing now?" one of the men behind him said.

Diver looked back. "Let's go find out."

Several of the men started forward, Diver among them.

Ethan made to follow, but Kannice still held his hand.

"Ethan—"

"I need to go with them," he said.

Kelf still stood on Kannice's other side, although he was watching Diver and the others, and appeared to be on the verge of following. "Kelf, can you get Kannice back to the Dowser?"

"What? Well, I suppose, but Ethan—"

"Please," Ethan said.

"I don't understand what's happening," Kannice said, staring after the men who had gone forward.

"I don't either. But I don't think it's safe in the street right now. I think you should go back."

"But the funeral."

He stepped closer to her, and whispered, "I've just felt another conjuring, and my ghost is here; I don't know why. Please do as I ask, Kannice."

"I'll not be scared off the streets by whoever's doing this," she said, keeping her voice low despite the fierce expression on her face.

"You're right. You shouldn't have to be. And you know I'd never let anything happen to you. But in protecting you from a spell, I might let others come to harm. Neither of us wants that. Please," he said again.

She hesitated, doubt creeping into her eyes. At last she nodded. "Yes, all right."

"Maybe you should take her back, Ethan. Diver and them others might need help, and I think we both know who would be more valuable in a fight."

At another time, Ethan might have found this amusing. Kelf was as large as a Dutch merchant ship and as strong as any man he knew. But he had no idea that Ethan could conjure.

"I'm hoping to prevent a fight," Ethan said, "not tip the balance of one."

The barman glanced once more in the direction of the raised voices. Ethan wanted to scream at him to make up his mind, but he kept silent, and at length Kelf said, "Aye, all right. I'll take her. You watch yourself, though."

"I will. Thank you, Kelf."

With one last quick look at Kannice, and what he hoped was a reassuring smile, Ethan started after Diver. All of those mourning Christopher Seider had done at last what shovels had failed to do: much of the snow was packed down, making the lanes passable.

Diver and his companions had a head start, and Ethan's leg slowed him. By the time he reached the commotion, it was already threatening to turn into yet another tragedy. A group of perhaps a dozen British soldiers stood in the street, their uniforms bearing evidence of a pelting of snowballs; two of them had lost their hats, which lay in the snow at their feet. All of them held their muskets at waist level, their bayonets gleaming with the inconstant light of dozens of torches.

At least fifty mourners, most of them young men and boys, were shouting taunts at them, calling them "lobsters" and "bloody-backed scoundrels."

"What are you goin' to do, ya thievin' dogs?" one man shouted. "Shoot all of us like you did Chris Seider?"

More snowballs flew at the men.

"Murder'rs!" a boy called out.

"Murderers!" came the reply. It didn't take long for the epithet to became a chant. "Murderers! Murderers! Murderers!"

The soldiers, none of whom was much older than those harassing them, looked frightened, and who could blame them? They might have been armed, but they were facing a mob that outnumbered them, and at any moment they could find themselves surrounded by literally hundreds more.

To their credit, Diver and the men who had walked forward with him had not joined the fools who were shouting insults and throwing snowballs. But neither had they attempted to make the pups break off their attack.

"Diver!" Ethan called. "Help me stop this."

Without waiting for his friend to answer, Ethan stepped between the young men and the soldiers, his back to the uniformed regulars.

"Stop this now!" he shouted at the mourners. "We're here to honor Chris Seider! Not to cause another tragedy!"

"Maybe we want to pay 'em back for what they done to Chris!"

Ethan shook his head. "These soldiers had nothing to do with that! It was Richardson, and he's in the gaol."

"He's right!"

Ethan glanced to his left. Diver had joined him in the street, as had another of the men who had been in the procession with them. It was this third man who had spoken.

Several of the pups held snowballs in their hands and were staring past Ethan and Diver at the soldiers.

"We don't want anyone else getting shot," the other man said. "Be smart lads."

One of the men tossed his snowball aside and regarded Ethan and his companions with disgust. The others did the same.

"Lobster lovers," one of them said. But already they were turning away.

Ethan turned to Diver and the other man, intending to thank them for their help. He opened his mouth to speak the words, but then faltered at the touch of another spell thrumming in the street. Reg's gaze snapped to Ethan's face. Before Ethan could ask the ghost what had happened, one of the soldiers rushed them, his bayonet leveled at Diver's gut.

Ethan didn't have time to strip off his greatcoat and cut his arm, nor did he wish to make a conjuring spectacle of himself in front of so many. Instead, he bit down hard on the inside of his cheek and tasted blood.

"*Pugnus ex cruore evocatus,*" he whispered. Fist, conjured from blood.

The advancing soldier staggered, as if punched in the jaw. But then he righted himself and closed on Diver.

Ethan bit himself again and repeated the spell, aiming this blow at the man's midsection.

The soldier doubled over, retched. A second later, though, he straightened.

Ethan bit down on his cheek a third time—he was going to curse these spells later—and whispered, *"Dormite ex cruore evocatum."* Slumber, conjured from blood.

It was a more dangerous spell to use, simply because its effects were more obvious to those around him. But short of lighting the soldier on fire, Ethan didn't think that anything else would stop the man. The regular staggered again; he halted and swayed. At last he collapsed in a red heap on the snow.

"Did you see that?" one of the lads called. "He was gonna kill that cove there. He was gonna to stick him like a pig."

He and his comrades stalked back toward the soldiers.

"Diver," Ethan said, his voice low. "Say something. Tell them to yield."

"Why should I?" Diver said, rounding on him. "The lad's right! He was coming right at me with his bayonet ready. I don't know what happened, but he might have killed me."

"I stopped him," Ethan whispered. "And it was another spell that set him on you. Now tell them to leave it be."

"What do you mean?" Diver asked, his voice too loud for Ethan's taste. "You stopped—" His eyes widened. "Oh," he said, breathless, whispering at last. "And someone else . . . someone made him do that?"

"That's right."

"It's all right, lads," Diver called to the young men, raising his hands to placate them.

"He's asleep!" the third man said, bending over the soldier. He looked up, clearly amazed. "The bloody fool fell asleep!"

"You see that?" Diver said. "He must have been drinking. No harm done."

"He wasn't drunk!" said one of the soldiers, as if enraged at the mere suggestion.

Ethan glared at him. "You'd rather they thought he was sober and willing to kill a man? Don't be an idiot. Take your friend, and go, before someone gets hurt."

The regular eyed the mob of young men, who appeared to be spoiling for a fight once more. Perhaps taking Ethan's words to heart, he gave a quick nod and signaled to one of his fellow soldiers. They hurried forward, lifted the sleeping regular, and bore him away, his arms draped around their shoulders.

The lads whistled and shouted more insults at them, but they didn't pursue the soldiers, apparently preferring to declare victory in the face of the regulars' retreat.

"That may have been the oddest thing I've ever seen," said the man with Diver. "He . . . he fell into a slumber, without any warning."

"Aye," Ethan said, his gaze flicking in Diver's direction. "It was quite odd. My thanks to you, sir, for standing with me."

The man shrugged. "It was like you said. We're here for Chris. There was no sense in getting someone else shot." He patted Diver's shoulder and started away after the rest of the mourners, who were now far ahead of them. "I'll see you around, Diver."

"Good night, Peter."

Ethan and Diver watched the man go. The lads had moved on as well, leaving them alone in the snowy street.

"What was that about, Ethan? Why would someone cast a spell to make a soldier attack me?"

"I don't know. If it makes you feel any better, I'm not convinced that any of it was directed at you specifically. That regular could as easily have gone for your friend."

"I don't take much comfort in that."

Ethan shook his head. "To be honest, neither do I."

"The day Chris was shot, you tried to tell me . . . You said that you felt something on Middle Street. Was it the same as this?"

"I don't know—"

"But you suspect."

Ethan hesitated before saying, "Aye. I wish it had occurred to me at the time to put Richardson to sleep. I could saved the boy's life. But I didn't know what would happen."

"Of course you didn't. Thank you for saving me tonight."

"If I'd been thinking, I wouldn't have. I'm afraid I owe you an ale."

Diver grinned. "That's right. I'd forgotten."

"I'm heading to the Dowser. Care to collect your winnings now?"

"I can't," his friend said, sobering. "I have to find Deborah. She'll be wondering where I've gone."

"Of course. Good night, Diver. My thanks for your help with those pups."

"Good night, Ethan."

Diver headed back toward the Liberty Tree, which was near the spot where the Seider boy was to be buried. Ethan continued along Cornhill Street past Dock Square up to Hanover Street, which he followed to Sudbury, where stood the Dowsing Rod. It wasn't the most direct route, but on this night especially he wished to avoid any more encounters with soldiers and so went out of his way to avoid Murray's Barracks.

Uncle Reg still walked beside him, and as Ethan neared the tavern he slowed. He needed to have this conversation while alone save for the ghost.

"What did you feel?" he asked, halting to face the specter. "There was a spell, isn't that right?"

Reg held up two fingers.

"Aye, two spells. Were both of them directed at the soldier?"

Reg didn't seem to know how to answer that. He offered a tentative nod, but Ethan had the distinct impression that he had asked the wrong question.

He regretted not having the opportunity to use a revealing spell on the soldier, though he assumed that like the spells cast on Gordon and Richardson, it would have shown little.

"Was this the same sort of spell you felt the day the boy was killed?"

Reg responded the alacrity this time. *Yes.*

"And was the other ghost there again? The one you saw that day?"

Again the ghost nodded, though with less certainty.

"You believe so, but you're not sure."

Yes.

"Were their other conjurers in the procession, aside from me?"

Reg shook his head.

Ethan frowned. He had expected a different answer. "Not even Jonathan Grant, the man we met in the Green Dragon?"

No.

Of course. The man was a clerk for the Customs Board. It was one thing to go to the Dragon, where he could be confident that only fellow patriots would see him. But to march in the funeral procession, on display for the entire city, could well have cost Grant his job.

It occurred to Ethan to ask another question of his spectral guide, but at the thought of it, his pulse quickened, and his thoughts returned once more to the night Gordon attacked Will Pryor.

"I didn't summon you tonight," Ethan said. "I didn't have to. Why is that?"

Reg stared back at him; it seemed that his eyes blazed brighter than usual.

"The spells you felt tonight—where did they come from?"

Reg lifted his hand and pointed at Ethan.

Chapter TEN

*E*than had known that the ghost would tell him this, and yet he didn't understand how it was possible.

"I didn't conjure," he said. "You know that I didn't."

Reg nodded. But once more he pointed at Ethan, his glowing finger gleaming like a polished blade.

"I didn't cut myself, or draw blood in any way. I didn't—"

He broke off and fumbled in the pocket of his greatcoat for the pouch of mullein. Pulling it open he saw that it was still as full as it had been.

"It's all there." He held it open for Reg to see, though the ghost showed little interest in looking. "So if I drew no blood, and used none of the herb, how could the spell have come from me?" He began to pace; he could feel Reg's gleaming eyes following him. "An illusion spell wouldn't have been powerful enough to make a soldier behave that way. Never mind that I didn't utter a single word in Latin." He stopped and stared at the ghost. "What you're telling me isn't possible. How could I cast such a spell without meaning to, without being aware of doing it?"

Reg shook his head, but then pointed at him again.

"Yes, I understand! I cast the spell. I'm asking you how that can be."

Reg opened his hands, a rare look of sympathy on his ancient features.

"Did both spells come from me? The first that precipitated the conflict, and the second that made the soldier attack Diver?"

The ghost nodded.

"It has to be Nate Ramsey. Who else could cast in this way?"

Reg offered no response.

"Do you sense him? Is he in Boston again, or perhaps out on the harbor, beyond the ice?"

The ghost shrugged and shook his head.

"Search for him, please. I walked the length of the waterfront three days ago, before the snowfall. I can do it again, but I don't think I'm going to find him that way. I need your help."

Reg grinned and saluted.

"Thank you."

The ghost faded from view, leaving Ethan in darkness on the street outside the Dowser. Stars shone overhead and the barest sliver of a moon hung low in the western sky beyond the dark mass of Beacon Hill. He had no proof that Ramsey had returned, no reason even to suspect that the captain was back save the unexplained conjurings that had done such grave harm in recent days. And yet Ethan felt as though an unseen blade were pressed against his throat.

He tried the tavern door. Finding it locked, he knocked once. Heavy footsteps approached the door.

"Who's there?" Kelf said, growling the words.

In spite of all that had happened this night, Ethan smiled in the darkness. As reluctant as the barman might have been to leave the funeral, he would have battled the entire French army to keep Kannice safe.

"It's Ethan, Kelf."

The lock clicked and Kelf pulled the door open. He held a cleaver in his free hand.

"Took you long enough," the barman said.

"Have you been worried about me?"

Kelf glowered. "Joke all you like, but she *was* worried. And I'm the one who has to put up with it."

Ethan schooled his features. "I apologize. I'm not going anywhere else tonight, so if you want to be on your way, she'll be fine."

The barman waved him into the tavern and shut the door. "What happened, anyway?" he asked.

"Yes," Kannice said, emerging from the kitchen. "I want to hear this as well."

"There's not a lot to tell, actually," Ethan said, keeping his gaze on Kelf. "A few young pups thought they'd insult some soldiers and throw a snowball or two. It could have been worse, but they tired of their sport before too long, and the king's men kept their heads."

Kelf gave a shake of his head. "Them lobsters shouldn't be here at all. The sooner they leave, the sooner we can get back to livin' our lives."

Would that it were so easy, Ethan thought. To Kelf he said, "I'd wager that every person who was in that procession tonight feels as you do, myself included."

"Aye, but no one asks us, do they?"

Ethan grinned. "No, they don't."

Kelf turned to Kannice. "All right then; I'll be on my way."

"Thank you, Kelf," she said.

The barman nodded to her and to Ethan and let himself out of the tavern. Once he was gone, Kannice stepped out from behind the bar, drew her own key from her bodice, and locked the door. Then she put her arms around Ethan's neck and kissed him.

"Now," she said, "I want to know what really happened."

"As do I."

Her brow creased.

"I felt a spell, and Uncle Reg appeared. And as soon as those things happened some lads started a confrontation with a group of soldiers. I did my best to keep them from hurting one another, and thought I'd succeeded. But then a second spell pulsed in the street, and one of the regulars charged at Diver, his bayonet fixed. I had to cast three spells to stop him."

"Is Diver—?"

"He's fine. But the soldier would have killed him; I'm sure of it."

"And you have no idea where those other spells came from?"

"None."

"What about your ghost? Can't you ask him?"

Ethan forced a smile, knowing that it couldn't mask his fear. "That's the strangest part of it all. He swears that the spells came from me."

Kannice took a step back. "I don't like the sound of that at all. You didn't cast them, did you?"

"Of course not. Some other conjurer has found a way to use my power for his or her own spells, to conjure through me, as it were."

"Is that something you can do?"

"I didn't even know it was possible until now." He frowned and rubbed a hand over his face. "The odd thing is, these spells don't appear to leave any residue. Usually when a conjurer casts, there remains a hint of his or her power that another speller can reveal with a particular kind of conjuring. But that doesn't happen with these spells. There appears to be no residue at all, neither mine nor anyone else's. I'd almost feel better if there was; that at least would make some sense. It would mean whoever is casting wants others to believe I'm responsible for the violence these spells are unleashing. But to leave nothing . . ." He shook his head.

"Who do you think is doing this?"

Ethan's gaze slid away from hers toward the hearth. "I don't know."

"Ethan."

"I don't know, Kannice. I'm . . . I don't know."

"But you suspect, don't you? I know you do. You believe it's Ramsey."

He chanced a look at her. Despite the dim light in the great room, he could see that her cheeks had gone pale.

"Aye," he said in a whisper. "I can't think of another conjurer who possesses both the skill and the ill nature to do something this . . . evil. But I don't even know if he's alive."

"Of course you do."

He dipped his chin, closing his eyes. "I've assumed all along that he survived the fire at Drake's Wharf, and that he would return eventually. I had hoped it wouldn't be so soon."

Kannice put her arms around him again, and he pulled her close.

"He nearly killed you last time," she murmured, "and now he has more cause than ever to hate you."

There was little Ethan could say; she was right on both points.

"What will you do?" she asked, looking up into his eyes.

"I'll find him, I'll learn what he wants this time, and if I have to, I'll kill him."

She took a deep breath and rested her head against his chest.

"First, though, I need to speak with Mariz, and perhaps I should see Janna again as well. It may be that they know more about this type of conjuring than I do."

"Well, you're not going out again tonight, so take off that coat and come upstairs with me."

He was in no mood to argue. "Yes, ma'am."

⁘

Dreams of Nate Ramsey and their previous encounters haunted Ethan's sleep and woke him for good early in the morning. He slipped out of bed, dressed without waking Kannice, and descended the stairs to the tavern. Once more, he took some bread from the kitchen and left a few coins in the bar till. He stirred the coals in the hearth of the great room, and put two more logs on the gleaming embers. Soon he had a fine blaze burning. He settled into a chair by the fire and chewed his bread.

When he had finished, he pulled his knife from the sheath on his belt, pushed up his sleeve, and cut his forearm. *"Locus magi ex cruore evocatus."* Location of conjurer, conjured from blood.

The spell rumbled in the floor and walls of the tavern, and his conjuring spread through the city, like ripples in a pond.

"Good morning," Ethan said to Reg, who had winked into view near the fire.

Reg stood straight-backed, his head cocked to the side, as if he were waiting to see what the spell revealed.

"Did you find Ramsey?" Ethan asked.

The ghost shook his head. Despite his disappointment, Ethan was hardly surprised. Ramsey would never make things so easy for him.

For the same reason, he didn't expect his simple finding spell to work on the captain, but he still held out hope that some other conjurer was responsible for the spells he had felt. His finding spell revealed a conjurer in the North End; he assumed it was Grant. He also sensed two more a good distance to the south: most likely Mariz and Janna. And there seemed to be one more conjurer in the center of Boston, not far from the Dowser; he wasn't sure who this might be. But he found no conjurers near the waterfront or on the harbor. He would need to find this fourth conjurer, though he thought it unlikely that Ramsey, if he were alive, would venture so far into the city.

Reg watched him, avid, eyes glowing.

"Perhaps it's not Captain Ramsey after all," Ethan said to the ghost. "We might have to do some hunting later today."

The ghost grinned, then faded from view. Ethan stood and pulled on his greatcoat. As he did, he heard Kannice stirring upstairs.

"Ethan?" she called down to him.

"I'm still here. But I was about to leave."

She descended the stairs, wearing a robe, her hair still disheveled. "Where are you going?"

"Sephira Pryce's estate."

"Are you serious?"

"I told you I wished to speak with Mariz. That's where I'll find him."

"Haven't you told me that she doesn't approve of your friendship with Mariz?"

He made no effort to conceal his amusement. "Aye."

She arched an eyebrow. "There are times when it seems that you go out of your way to antagonize her."

"Well, a man needs a hobby."

"I'm serious, Ethan. She's no more fond of you than you are of her, and she has never been shy about threatening your life or ordering her brutes to beat you bloody."

"She hates Nate Ramsey more than she hates me. When I tell her that he may be back, she'll be willing to let me speak with her pet conjurer. And I've just sensed another conjurer here in the city. She might want to know about that as well."

Kannice narrowed her eyes. "Do you think she's beautiful?"

"I don't think it," he said, without pausing to ponder his words. "I know it."

She pressed her lips thin. "That was not the response I was looking for."

Ethan walked to where she stood and took her hands in his. "Am I to understand that you're jealous of Sephira Pryce?"

Kannice's gaze dropped. "Well, you could have been a bit less ada- mant about how lovely she is."

"You're right. I don't know what I was thinking. She's a hag, toad- like in appearance. I've seen sows that were more attractive."

She laughed.

"Would you have believed me if I'd said that?"

"Probably not, but it would have been nice to hear."

He lifted her chin with a finger, making her look him in the eye, and he kissed her softly on the lips. "First of all, Sephira Pryce, while beautiful, is the cruelest, most wicked, least trustworthy, most self- affected person I have ever met. And second, her beauty, while un- deniable, is nothing next to yours."

Kannice smiled. "Now that was much better. You should have started with that."

"All right. Ask me again."

She laughed once more. "That's not—"

"Ask me again."

She rolled her eyes. "Do you think Sephira Pryce is beautiful?"

"Sephira Pryce," he said, scratching his chin. "I'm not sure I know who that is. Oh, of course. You're referring to that mean old sow who lives on Summer Street. I suppose she might be attractive to some— mostly the blind and the infirm."

"Leave," Kannice said, a thread of laughter lingering in her voice. She pushed him toward the door.

"But I haven't gotten to the part where she's not as lovely as you."

"I don't care. Go away."

"I'll be back later."

"I'll have moved to Newport."

It was his turn to laugh. She followed him to the door so that she could unbolt the lock. He stepped out into the bright daylight, but then turned back to her. "Lock the door."

"Kelf will be here soon."

"And when he arrives you can unlock it."

"My lock is not going to stop Nate Ramsey."

She was right, of course, though he didn't care to be reminded of this.

"Humor me," he said.

There was a note of indulgence in her voice as she said, "All right."

He struck out southward along Sudbury Street, which soon became Treamount. The lanes were more crowded this day, and the snow had been trampled down further, making walking far easier than it had been even the night before. Carriages and chaises steered past him, the hoofbeats of their horses muffled, the turning of their wheels on the packed snow as quiet as the gliding of sleigh runners.

The sky was a deep azure and cloudless. An eagle circled on splayed wings high overhead, white and chestnut against the blue. Lower, gulls soared in great flocks, their cries sounding thin and mournful.

It was a sparkling morn, brighter than any Boston had seen in recent weeks. Yet those Ethan encountered in the streets seemed uncommonly solemn. Ethan wondered how long it would be before the pall from yesterday's funeral lifted.

As Ethan walked along the edge of the Common, he considered what he might say to Sephira. Notwithstanding what he had told Kannice, he wasn't yet ready to share with the Empress of the South End his fear that Ramsey had returned. He knew nothing for certain; he was not entirely convinced that his suspicions were based on anything more than his lingering dread of another confrontation with the captain. There was another conjurer in the city; he knew that now. Though he could not yet shake the conviction that Ramsey was responsible for all that had happened in the past several days, the evidence he had gathered thus far—his own fruitless search of the waterfront, Uncle Reg's assurances, the fact that he had yet to see Ramsey's aqua power on any of the men affected by the spells—pointed him in a different direction.

More to the point, Sephira hated Ramsey with a passion that surpassed Ethan's own, and with good reason. The previous summer, during a pitched battle between Ramsey's crew and her toughs, Ramsey killed Nigel Billings, the yellow-haired giant of a man who had been Sephira's most trusted lieutenant. If Ethan so much as suggested that Ramsey might be back, she would tear the city apart searching for him, with potentially tragic results for herself, her men, and any innocents who chanced to get in her way.

But without mentioning Ramsey, Ethan didn't know how he might convince Sephira to allow Mariz to help him. She did not approve of their friendship, and she would be reluctant to do anything that might deepen it. Though he racked his brain, trying to come up with ideas, he still had not thought of anything by the time he reached her home.

Sephira's mansion stood at the south end of Summer Street, near the Old South Meeting House and across the lane from d'Acosta's Pasture, an expanse of grazing land that was usually filled with lowing cows and flocks of crows.

The cobblestone path leading from the street to Sephira's house had been cleared, but otherwise the snow blanketing her yard remained pristine, making her impressive white marble home appear even more stately than usual. Ethan approached the front door. Most days Sephira had at least one of her toughs posted outside on the portico, but not this morning. He rapped once with the brass lion's-head knocker.

A moment later the door swung open, revealing Gordon, who looked as huge and ugly as usual. The brute frowned at the sight of Ethan, his ears turning red.

"What do you want?"

Ethan considered a gibe—something about the nap Gordon had taken that night in Will Pryor's room, and how Sephira might have been working him too hard. But he had come to ask a boon of the Empress of the South End. Angering one of her men would not help his cause.

"I need to speak with Sephira," he said. "And with Mariz as well. Please."

Apparently, Gordon had expected mockery; Ethan's courtesy deepened his frown.

"Wait here."

He shut the door before Ethan could say more. Ethan stepped off the portico back into the sunshine of the path. He stamped his feet to get the snow off his boots and breeches.

The door opened again and Gordon waved him inside.

Ethan entered the house, and waited while Gordon closed the door again.

"Your knife," the tough said, holding out a meaty hand. "And those plants you like to carry around."

Ethan smirked. "Do you mean the mullein?"

"Sure, whatever you call it."

He pulled the blade from the sheath on his belt, flipped it over, and handed it to Gordon hilt-first. Then he dug in his coat pocket for the pouch of mullein and gave that to the man, too.

"That all of it?" Gordon asked. At Ethan's nod, he said, "In that case, she's in the dinin' room."

"My thanks."

He had been Sephira's guest enough times to know his way around the ground floor of the mansion. He walked through the grand common room, to the dining room. Sephira sat at the end of a long table of dark polished wood. She looked as lovely as always, in a black waistcoat and white silk shirt. Her hair was down, and a large purple gem shone at her throat.

Nap, dark and lean, and Mariz, a blade already in hand and his sleeves pushed up, both stood by the entrance to the chamber. Afton stood behind Sephira, his massive arms folded over his chest.

"How nice to see you, Ethan," Sephira said, hardly sparing him a glance as she perused a newspaper: the *Boston Evening-Post*, the city's most prominent Tory publication.

"Good day, Sephira."

"To what do we owe this pleasure?"

Having failed to come up with any viable falsehoods, Ethan opted for a version of the truth.

"I've come seeking your help. And more to the point, help from Mariz."

The conjurer frowned, his spectacles catching the light from the nearest of the glazed windows.

Sephira looked up from her paper, her expression no warmer than the air outside. "Help with what?" she demanded, biting off each word.

"In the past several days, I've sensed spells that I can't explain, and for which I can find no residue of power, nothing at all that would let me determine who cast them. I don't believe that Mariz is responsible for these spells, but I do think that he can help me find the person who is."

Sephira turned her attention back to the newspaper. "Why should I care that another witch is troubling you. It sounds as though I should offer this person a job, or at least a reward."

"I can understand why you feel that way. But these spells could affect you as well. In fact, one of them already has."

She put the down paper once more. "What are you talking about?"

"Five nights ago, when Gordon here nearly killed Will Pryor."

Gordon twisted his mouth to the side like a little boy accused of stealing.

"It's happened again?" Sephira asked.

"Aye. Not exactly the same thing, of course; the circumstances have been different. But several times over the past few days I've felt these conjurings, and each one of them has led directly to violence."

"And what exactly do you believe Mariz can do?"

"To be perfectly honest, I don't know. I need to speak with another conjurer, someone who understands spellmaking. This is a puzzle, Sephira, the like of which I've rarely encountered. I need help figuring it out."

"Why must it be Mariz? Why not go to that mad old woman who lives on the Neck? Windcatcher. Why not ask her?"

"I intend to," Ethan said. "But surely you can see the value in speaking to more than one person."

"All right, ask him what you will." Her smile was as thin as smoke.

"I'd prefer to speak of this in private."

"I don't care what you'd prefer," Sephira said, firing the words back at him.

"I came here as a courtesy to you, Sephira. I knew that you wouldn't be pleased by my request, but I thought it proper that I ask rather than seek out Mariz's advice without your knowledge. I can just as easily leave now, and approach him another time. Would you prefer that?"

If Sephira could conjure, she would have turned him into a human torch. She glanced at Mariz before turning her glare back to Ethan. "Five minutes," she said, her voice so low that at first Ethan wasn't sure he had heard. "You can speak outside on the portico."

"Thank you, Sephira."

Ethan left them there, knowing that Mariz would follow eventually, but that Sephira would wish to speak with him first.

He let himself out of the house, and stepped to the edge of the portico to stare out across the snowy pasture.

After a few minutes, he heard the door behind him open and close, and the scrape of a boot on marble.

"You should not have come," Mariz said. "Showing such courtesy to the *senhora* may seem prudent, but in fact it diminishes her trust in me. Each time we speak in confidence, my relationship with her and the others suffers. I have told you this before, and yet—"

"My ghost says that the last spell came from me."

He faced Mariz, who gazed back at him, blinking in the brilliant daylight.

"I wasn't able to attempt a *revela potestatem* spell—there were too many people around me. And even if I had, I think we both know that it would have shown nothing at all. But as soon as the spell was cast, my spectral guide appeared, as he did the night Gordon beat Pryor."

Mariz started to argue, but Ethan cut him off with a raised hand.

"That is what happened, Mariz. You saw him; we both did. At the time, we couldn't know for certain, but after all that's happened since, I'm convinced it was my ghost who appeared in Pryor's room. Last night, when I asked him where the conjuring had come from, he pointed at me. I hadn't cut myself; none of my mullein was missing. But somehow, I cast the spell."

"What did it do, this conjuring you cast without knowing?"

"It started a row between a group of British soldiers and some of the young men who attended Christopher Seider's funeral. As it happens, I felt a spell that day, too. I was on Middle Street when Richardson shot the lad, and a short while before he pulled the trigger, someone cast a spell."

" 'Someone cast,' " Mariz repeated. "So this conjuring did not come from you."

"My guide didn't know where it came from. I believe that whoever is doing this is getting stronger and with each day is better able to use me as a conduit for his power."

"Was anyone hurt last night?"

Ethan shook his head. "No. But a second spell—one that also came from me—made one of the soldiers attack a friend of mine. I had to resort to a sleep spell to keep him from killing the man." He closed his eyes for a few seconds and took a long, steadying breath, trying to quell the panic rising in his chest. This was how he had felt throughout that week during the summer, as Ramsey unleashed horrors upon the city. He opened his eyes and asked Mariz, "Have you ever heard of a conjurer casting in this way?"

"I have not."

Ethan had expected as much.

"I believe I know what you are thinking, Kaille, for I am thinking it as well: you believe that Ramsey has returned and is responsible for these spells."

"The thought has crossed my mind."

"You should have told the *senhora*. She would have been more willing to let us speak."

"I was afraid she would immediately start hunting for him."

"Would that not be of help to you?"

"If Sephira and Ramsey go to war, innocent people will die. I won't shy away from a fight; if Ramsey is back, I'll kill him. He's left me no choice. But I would rather not endanger half of Boston if I can help it."

"He may not leave you much choice in that regard either."

Mariz was right.

The door opened and Nap joined them on the portico. "Sephira wants you inside, Mariz." He looked Ethan's way, but went back into the house without another word.

"I'm sorry if I've made your relationship with Sephira more difficult," Ethan said, once Nap had closed the door again.

The conjurer shrugged. "I understand now why you came. It could not be helped."

Ethan descended the steps to the cobblestone path.

"I sensed a finding spell this morning," Mariz called to him, making him stop. "Was that yours?"

"Aye. I should have known that Ramsey couldn't be located so easily, but I tried it anyway. I've also searched the waterfront for his ship, and found nothing. I did find another conjurer in the city, someone I don't know."

"Perhaps we are wrong, then, about Ramsey. Perhaps it is this other conjurer."

Ethan shrugged. "Maybe. I've wondered in recent days whether I'm so afraid of Ramsey's return that I'm incapable of rational thought."

"Where Ramsey is concerned," Mariz said, "fear *is* rational thought. You should be careful; turn your back on no one."

This much, at least, Ethan had figured out for himself. He raised a hand in farewell and walked away.

than's conversation with Janna went much as had his exchange with Mariz. She had never heard of one conjurer using another in the way this speller seemed to be using Ethan, which was a striking admission coming from her: Janna knew more about spellmaking than any conjurer he'd met. But though perplexed by what he told her about the spells, she remained unconvinced that Ramsey was behind the attacks.

"You're thinking' too much like a thieftaker an' not enough like a crazy man," she told him.

"That might be the nicest thing you've ever said to me."

She scowled. "You understand what I'm saying. Ramsey wants you dead, and he's not one for bein' subtle."

"What if this is all he can manage now, Janna? What if he was so badly hurt in the fire last summer that he's not strong enough for a battle? Maybe subtlety is all he has left."

She pondered this for some time before conceding that he might be right. Ethan would have preferred that she try harder to convince him he was wrong.

After leaving the Fat Spider, Ethan made his way back past the South End through Cornhill. He had planned to return to the Dowsing Rod, but as he drew nearer to Murray's Barracks, an idea came to him. He had gone to the Green Dragon to see if a conjurer in the Sons of Liberty could have been casting these mysterious spells. But there were others in Boston who might have something to gain from more violent confrontations between patriots and Tories. And his finding spell had revealed a conjurer in the center of the city, perhaps near the barracks.

Slipping off of Treamount Street before he reached the corner of Queen, Ethan made sure he could not be seen. Rather than risk calling attention to himself by removing his greatcoat, he bit down on the inside of his cheek and whispered, *"Velamentum ex cruore evocatum."* Concealment, conjured from blood.

The spell pulsed, and Reg watched as the conjuring settled over him.

"There may be conjurers where I'm going," Ethan said. "I don't want them to see you. *Dimitto te."* I release you.

The only thing Reg seemed to like less than being summoned was being dismissed. He glowered at Ethan as he faded from view. But Ethan had more pressing matters with which to concern himself. Walking through the city under a concealment spell was difficult under the best of circumstances, as he had to take care that he made no noise with his footsteps. But with fresh snow on the ground, his task became that much more complicated. He needed to place his feet only in spots where the snow had already been packed down by others.

He walked slowly, taking great care with each step. He passed groups of soldiers, watching them for any sign that they sensed his presence, but every man he saw ignored him. Reaching the entrance to the barracks, which was an old sugar warehouse owned by James Murray and James Smith, he waited as several men emerged from the building onto the street before easing inside.

Ethan wasn't sure what he had expected of the barracks, but upon entering he was shocked by the squalor of the soldiers' quarters. The air stank of sweat and urine and stale food. Though the warehouse was spacious, cots were crowded into it, leaving little room for walking; the men enjoyed no privacy. It was no wonder the occupying army had seen so many desertions over the past year and a half, or that such a large number of soldiers had resorted to thieving.

Still, the soldiers Ethan saw in the barracks, who had gathered in large and small clusters throughout the large space, seemed content to gamble at cards and laugh at one another's jokes. A few men in one corner of the room groused about "the damn'd dogs" they had encountered in the streets, and the "whores and mongrels" who served them in the various publick houses they frequented.

Ethan didn't remain with this group long enough to learn if they counted Kannice among them. Several times he heard men speak of using their muskets the next time they were accosted by gangs of toughs, but he thought this more bluster than anything else. Most of the men who said these things were young and appeared to be showing off for their older comrades.

He did not sense any conjurers among the regulars lounging in the barracks, but a skilled speller might have avoided detection. To be certain, he decided to try a spell. He moved to a spot near the center of the room, so that he could see most every man in the warehouse, and quietly removed three leaves of mullein from the pouch in his pocket.

Tegimen ex verbasco evocatum, he said in his mind. Warding, conjured from mullein.

He didn't anticipate that he would need the warding to protect himself, but a speller did not waste conjurings. Still, the warding was far less important than the act of conjuring itself.

Most of the men showed no sign of feeling the spell. But one soldier, a young, lanky man reclining on a cot near the southern end of the room, tensed and sat up.

"Abi!" Ethan whispered to Reg, who had appeared like spell-summoned fire next to him. Go away!

This command pulsed as had the first spell.

The young soldier was on his feet now, staring in Ethan's direction.

Cursing his recklessness, but glad to have the warding in place, Ethan backed toward the doorway, placing his feet with great care. When at last he reached the door he retreated into the street. Other soldiers milled about outside, but he avoided them and moved away from the barracks with as much speed and as little noise as he could manage. Still, he didn't go so far that he couldn't get a good look at the soldier should he appear at the barracks entrance. After a few seconds, the young soldier did just that, peering out into the street.

"Who's there?" the man asked in a low voice, the words tinged with a Scottish burr.

Ethan eased closer.

"Wha's the matter there, Morrison?" asked one of the men standing nearby.

"It's nothing. I thought I heard somethin'."

"Hearin' things now, are ye?"

"Aye," he said. Still he surveyed Brattle Street. It might have been Ethan's imagination, but he thought that the man's gaze lingered on him briefly. He didn't so much as draw breath.

"I'm gonna step outside for a bit," the man called to someone in the barracks.

He started in Ethan's direction, removing a knife from his belt as he walked. Ethan took a few more steps back, trying to match his footfalls with those of the soldier.

A chaise rattled past. Using the sound to mask his steps, Ethan hurried on to Queen Street.

He hadn't gotten far, however, when a spell growled in the ground. He knew it at once for a finding spell and spat a curse, turning the heads of some men nearby.

The spell rushed toward him, slipping over the street like an advancing tide over a sandy shore. It caught up with him in mere seconds, seeming to tug at his legs as might a retreating wave.

The young soldier had followed him as far as the corner of Brattle Street, shadowed by a pale form. It appeared to be the ghost of a man, also dressed in soldier's garb. With the sun shining down on the snow, Ethan could barely make out the figure much less determine its exact color, but it looked to be a pale blue. After a moment, the ghost lifted a shimmering arm and pointed directly at him.

Ethan knew that with his concealment spell still in place, the soldier couldn't see him. Nevertheless, he felt exposed, vulnerable. He turned and ran, knowing that he risked giving himself away. At the first corner, he turned southward away from the Dowser and kept running, his bad leg aching.

When he came to School Street, he turned again, this time toward the waterfront. He passed King's Chapel, where his friend Trevor Pell served as a minister, and entered the narrower lanes of the Cornhill section of the city. He had followed a roundabout path, but he didn't want the soldier following him either to the Dowser, or to his room over Henry's cooperage, where he was headed now. He needed to remove his concealment conjuring, but he feared casting the spell too close to the barracks, since the pulse of his own conjuring would be as effective as a finding spell in telling the soldier where he was. The farther Ethan was from the man when he cast, the more difficult it would be for the soldier to determine his location.

As Ethan passed Henry's shop on his way around the building to the stairway in back that led to his room, Shelly lifted her head and thumped her tail on the snow-covered lane. Dogs, Ethan had noticed in the past, could see through concealment conjurings; he had no idea why.

He climbed the stairs carefully, trying to make not a sound, and to keep his balance on the treacherous ice that covered the old wooden treads. Once he was safely in his room, with the door locked, he pulled off his greatcoat, cut his arm, and said, *"Fini velamentum ex cruore evocatum."* End concealment, conjured from blood.

Reg materialized directly in front of him, frowning the way Ethan's mother used to when disappointed in his casting.

"I know," Ethan said. "I'm a fool."

Reg nodded.

"But now I know that there's at least one conjurer among the ranks of the Twenty-ninth Regiment. And he didn't like that I was there. Perhaps he has more in mind than just keeping the peace."

Reg offered no response.

But Ethan remembered the soldier's finding spell. As reluctant as he was to conjure too much and draw the man to Henry's shop, Ethan knew that he had to attempt one more spell.

He cut himself again, dabbed at the welling blood, and marked his own forehead and face as he had done to Ebenezer Richardson several nights before.

"Revela omnias magias ex cruore evocatas," he said. Reveal all magicks, conjured from blood.

The rumble of the spell seemed to emanate from the foundation of the building. Ethan's face felt cool where the blood evaporated. And when he looked down at his legs, where the soldier's finding spell had touched him, he saw that at last one of his *revela* spells had worked.

On the street, in the sunlight, the soldier's spectral guide had looked as pale as ice. In the murky light of Ethan's room, however, his power was a far deeper shade of blue.

Reg pointed a ghostly finger at the glow on Ethan's legs and raised his gaze to Ethan's.

"You recognize that color, don't you?"

Yes.

Ethan had hoped for this. Reg's eyes wouldn't have been fooled by the daylight as his were. He would have seen the soldier's ghost in its true form.

"Did you see it on Middle Street? Was this the color of the ghost you saw the day Chris Seider was shot?"

The ghost nodded.

A part of Ethan wished that he had confronted the soldier— Morrison, another man had called him—rather than running from him, though he knew how dangerous that could have been.

"Did he cast the spell that made Richardson fire? Or the spells that sparked the confrontation during Chris Seider's funeral? Or even the one used against Gordon?"

Reg didn't answer right off. Eventually he shrugged, an apology etched in his ancient features.

"I understand; it's all right."

Considering his own question Ethan wasn't sure he believed that Morrison could have cast them. Those other spells left no residue, and at least two of them had been made to seem like they came from Ethan. The rich color of Morrison's magick indicated that he had some skill as a conjurer, but he had done nothing today to indicate he possessed enough power to have cast those other spells.

Which begged a different question: If Morrison's ghost was on Middle Street when Richardson fired into the crowd, did that mean he was working with someone else, who had cast those other spells? Was it possible that he was an associate of Nate Ramsey or even Jonathan Grant, the conjurer Ethan met at the Green Dragon? And had the soldier been on the street the previous night, when Ethan put himself between the regulars and the young men? He didn't remember seeing Morrison there, but he had been occupied with other matters.

Morrison might not have done anything to convince Ethan that he had power enough to cast these spells. But wasn't it more likely that he was responsible for the spells cast in recent days, than that Nate Ramsey had returned to Boston unnoticed?

With all of this to ponder, he left his room and again walked the length of Boston's waterfront, from Gibbon's Shipyard to Hudson's Point. As before, he did not find the *Muirenn* among the vessels in and around Boston's wharves. When he had finished, cold and exhausted, his bad leg screaming, he went to the Dowsing Rod, giving the barracks on Hillier's Street a wide berth as he left the North End.

He arrived at the tavern before most of Kannice's regular patrons, and took a seat in the farthest corner of the great room. Kelf placed before him an ale and a bowl of fish chowder. Ethan was ravenous, and was soon working on seconds of each. But as he ate, he brooded on how little he had learned this day.

Relieved as he was that he hadn't found Ramsey's ship, he wasn't entirely certain what he ought to do next. Chances were that Morrison wouldn't be leaving Boston any time soon. He was stuck here with his regiment, and unless he deserted, which didn't seem likely if he was plotting to sow conflict with these spells, Ethan would know where to find him. But while Ethan wanted desperately to question the soldier, he didn't think it wise to do so quite yet. Nor did he expect that a request made of Morrison's commanders for more information about the soldier would yield any results. The one person who might be able to learn something of Morrison was the sheriff, but as weary as he was, Ethan could not face a conversation with Greenleaf this night. With some reluctance, he vowed silently that he would seek out the sheriff come the morning.

The evening passed without incident. Diver and Deborah came in and sat with Ethan for a short while, but they seemed to be in the midst of a spat, and neither of them said much. Ethan was relieved when, earlier than usual, they left the tavern. He retired early as well, and did not hear Kannice when she joined him in her bed.

By the time Ethan awoke the following morning, she was already gone from the room; he could hear her moving around downstairs. He dressed and joined her there.

Seeing him, she came out from behind the bar and kissed him. "Good morning."

"I'm sorry I didn't hear you come in last night."

"It's all right," she said. "You slept; I'm glad." She glanced at his greatcoat, which he had carried down with him. "Where are you off to now, without any breakfast?"

He smiled. "I need to speak with the sheriff. And after that I'll probably search the waterfront again."

Concern furrowed her brow. "You're going to make yourself sick, walking so much in this cold. And if Ramsey is here, and has been since you felt that first spell, don't you think that you would have found his ship already?"

"I think that I'll find his ship when he's ready for me to find it, and I don't know when that's going to be."

If anything this made her look more worried. "Will you be back later?"

"Aye, I promise."

He left the tavern and walked once again to West Street and the stately home of Stephen Greenleaf. The sheriff was emerging from the house as Ethan arrived. Seeing him, Greenleaf scowled.

"What are you doing here?"

"I need information about a man, a soldier with the Twenty-ninth."

"And what in God's name made you think that I would be willing to help you? In case you hadn't noticed, Kaille, I work for the Crown, just as this soldier does. I'm not going to tell you—"

"He's a speller."

Greenleaf blew out a long breath, vapor billowing in the chill morning air. "And how would you know that?"

"His family name is Morrison. I don't know his given name. He speaks with a burr, so I assume he's a Scotsman. And I have cause to believe that he was on Middle Street when Christopher Seider was shot."

"Why do you need me? Why can't you find out whatever it is you want to know?"

"I'd need to speak with a commander in the army, and I don't think there are many British captains who would wish to share with a thief-taker information about the men under their command. But it may be that the sheriff of Suffolk County can get answers to questions I cannot."

Greenleaf made a small, impatient gesture, but he didn't argue. Instead, he said, "You didn't answer me, Kaille."

"I'd have thought you were used to that by now."

"What makes you think this man is a witch?"

"The devil came to my room last night and told me he was."

"I see. So, you're asking a boon of me, for the second time in less than a week, and once again you refuse to tell me what I wish to know. Why should I help you?"

"Because, Sheriff, I'm trying to help you do your job, and you're trying to have me hanged as a witch. I'm not sure the two are comparable."

"You're trying to help me do my job?" Greenleaf laughed. "It seems to me you're trying to make me do yours."

"That's not—This man, Morrison, he might well be responsible not only for the Seider boy's death but for a confrontation that nearly led to a second murder the night of the lad's funeral. And he might be—" He broke off, uncertain of how much he ought to tell the good sheriff.

"He might be what?"

Ethan shook his head. "He's a dangerous man, Sheriff. I'm sure of it."

"He might be what?" Greenleaf demanded again, enunciating each word.

Ethan didn't answer and after several moments, the sheriff turned and started away down West Street. "Good day, Kaille."

"He might be working with Nate Ramsey."

Greenleaf halted and whirled on his heel. "What did you say?"

"You heard me."

The sheriff glanced up and down the lane before walking back to where Ethan stood. "I heard you speak of a ghost," he said, his voice low. "Ramsey's dead. You've said you don't believe he is, but I've seen no proof otherwise and it's been months."

"He's not dead. And I believe he's back in Boston, though as of yet I have no evidence to prove it."

"Of course you don't. It's rather convenient for you, being able to sling Ramsey's name around when you want to alarm me, or get me to do your bidding, or divert my attention from other things."

"What other things?" Ethan asked, his voice rising.

"I don't know. That's for you to tell me. We can start with this Morrison fellow: What makes you think he's a conjurer and why didn't you mention before that you saw him on Middle Street?"

"I heard from someone else that he was on Middle Street. I didn't see him myself." *My spectral guide saw his spectral guide.* The mere thought of saying this nearly made Ethan laugh aloud. "As for Morrison's conjuring abilities," he said, pressing on, "he . . . he did things that raised my suspicions."

"What things?"

Ethan threw his arms wide. "What does it matter?"

"I thought as much," the sheriff said with a smirk. "You ask for my aid, but you're so concerned with keeping your neck out of a noose that you won't tell me what I want to know." He narrowed his eyes. "I don't think there was any conjurer on Middle Street but you. I don't think there was any conjurer at that damned funeral but you. I'd wager every coin in my pocket against every one in yours that you were responsible for those spells."

Ethan wanted to gainsay the man, but Greenleaf's guess had struck too close to the truth for comfort.

"I don't know what you're playing at," Greenleaf said, leaning closer to him. "But I won't be your dupe, and I won't waste my days chasing after witches and wraiths. If you truly believe that Ramsey's back you shouldn't be here, troubling me. You should be scouring the city."

Ethan glowered at him and then began to limp away. "Very well, Sheriff," he said over his shoulder. "I'll get the information some other way. Good day." He walked back to the street, but halted there and faced Greenleaf again. "And just so you know, I have been scouring the city. I've walked the length of the waterfront. All of it. Twice."

"And what have you found?"

"Nothing. I've seen no sign of the *Muirenn* or Ramsey."

"And yet you remain convinced that Ramsey is nearby."

"Aye," Ethan said. "Not because I wish to distract or alarm you, but because I'm determined that he will not catch us unawares again."

He strode away, and when Greenleaf called his name, he was tempted to ignore him. But at last he turned and saw that the sheriff had reached the street, and was walking after him.

Greenleaf stopped a few yards short of where Ethan stood, thin-lipped, his eyes pale in the bright morning light.

"Morrison, you say?"

"Aye. With the Twenty-ninth. I wouldn't be surprised to learn that he had recently been a seaman, perhaps on a merchant vessel." Many conjurers found employment with merchant captains, who were less squeamish than others about magick and more inclined to see the value of having a speller with them on the open seas.

"I'll find out what I can." Greenleaf stalked off without waiting for Ethan's reply.

Ethan watched him go, and then trod through the snow and ice to the waterfront. Kannice was right, he knew: Ramsey was not so careless as to let himself be found before he was ready for a confrontation. But Ethan couldn't bring himself to give up looking for him. He stood at the base of Fort Hill, near the South Battery, and he stared out over the icy surface of the harbor squinting against the sun and examining each ship he could see. None was a pink.

He thought about walking back to Gibbon's Shipyard, to begin his now-familiar route along the city shore, but his legs had grown leaden, and already the cold of the harbor breeze was carving through his coat. Instead, he made his way to Long Wharf and ventured out onto the pier as far as Minot's "T," from whence he could survey the harbor without walking such a great distance.

The dock was less crowded than it would have been had the waters around the wharf not been frozen solid, but still it bustled with sailors walking to and from their ice-locked ships and laborers carrying goods from warehouses to the city. Most of the men ignored Ethan, although a few eyed him, wariness in their stances and miens. Ethan soon realized that he could see little more from the wharf than he could from the streets that ran along the waterfront. After lingering on the pier for a few minutes, shivering within his coat, he made up his mind to return to the Dowsing Rod for the breakfast Kannice had wanted him to eat when first he woke.

But as he followed the "T" back to the main branch of the wharf, a spell rumbled in the wood beneath his feet. He knew without looking that Reg had appeared at his shoulder, diaphanous in the sunlight; he didn't spare the ghost so much as a glance. He started to scan the water again for Ramsey's ship, but stopped himself. Instead he looked back toward the street for some sign of Morrison or his blue spectral guide. He saw neither.

Someone near him shouted a warning. Ethan spun. Two laborers circled each other, fists raised, as others gathered around them. One of the men, the larger of the two, threw a wild punch; the other ducked under it and dug his fist into the first man's gut. This laborer doubled over but then charged his foe. They grappled for several seconds, each trying to get the advantage. After a minute or two of this, they fell to the ground, still grabbing at one another, flailing with their fists.

The men around them cheered; Ethan thought he heard several of them wagering on the outcome. Not wishing to see either man hurt because of a spell that had somehow drawn upon his conjuring power, he waded into the growing cluster of men, pushed his way past those closest to the fight, and tried to pull the men apart.

Several of the spectators voiced their displeasure, but two sailors joined Ethan in trying to separate the laborers.

The larger man bled from his nose and a cut on his lip. The other had a scrape on his forehead, but appeared to have gotten the better of their exchange.

"That's enough!" Ethan said, looking at each man in turn.

The smaller man held up his hands. "It wasn't me that started it."

Ethan looked at the larger man, who struggled to free himself from the grasp of the two sailors and renew his assault. His eyes had a glazed look; Ethan recalled Gordon's appearing much the same way that night in Will Pryor's room.

"Get away from here," Ethan said to the smaller laborer.

"I work here, an' like I told you, it was him that took the first swing at me. Tell him to go."

Ethan couldn't very well explain to him that the other man was under the influence of a conjuring. "I know it's not your fault—"

A cry of pain and shouted warnings stopped him.

Ethan pivoted again. The big laborer had thrown off both of the sailors. One of them was on his knees, bleeding from a gash on his arm, the other lay still, a bloody wound over his heart.

The laborer swung at Ethan, silver flashing in his hand. A knife. Ethan barely managed to throw himself backward and to the ground. The big man advanced on him, his fight with the other laborer now forgotten.

"*Discuti ex cruore evocatum,*" Ethan said, not caring who heard him. Shatter, conjured from blood.

The spell pulsed and the blade in the man's hand fractured with a sound like the ringing of coins. A murmur swept through the crowd around them. The laborer, though, did not seem to notice that his weapon was broken.

Ethan clambered to his feet and, as the man reached him, raised his fists.

The laborer tried again to hit him, but Ethan dodged the blow and struck one of his own, catching the laborer flush on the jaw. The man staggered.

Ethan bit down on the inside of his cheek and silently cast a sleep spell. *Dormite ex cruore evocatum.*

The laborer swayed and finally collapsed.

The men around them watched him fall, but then turned their gazes to Ethan. Silent, fearful, hostile; they eyed him the way they might one of the natives who had fought alongside the French during the Seven Years' War.

"What did you do to him?" one of them asked.

"I hit him," Ethan said. "You saw me do it."

"You didn' hit him that hard. An' we saw what you did to his knife, too."

"I did nothing to his knife."

Ethan pushed past the men to the two sailors. The one with the cut on his arm knelt beside his friend, who had not moved.

Ethan had used the prone man's blood for the shatter spell, but more had stained his shirt, and blood still seeped from the wound. His breathing was shallow, and his skin had a sickly gray hue.

"He's dyin'," his friend said. He looked up, meeting Ethan's gaze. He was younger than Ethan had thought; both of them were. "Can't you help him?"

Ethan shook his head. "I'm not—"

"I don't care if you're a witch. I've sailed with your kind, and I will again. But I know you can help him."

"It might be too late."

"Try. Please."

There was enough blood on this man's arm and the other man's chest for a healing spell, but the rest of the men were watching, listening.

Ethan decided that he didn't care, at least not enough to allow the man to die.

He placed his hand over the wound, and whispered, "*Remedium ex cruore evocatum.*" Healing, conjured from blood.

Healing spells were different from other conjurings. They didn't pulse so much as they echoed, like a distant pealing bell. He sensed the power flowing through his hand into the sailor's chest. He knew that beneath his palm and the man's coat and shirt, the skin was closing, knitting itself back together. He was but dimly aware of the men around him, but he guessed that they were watching. He knew that any one of them could well tell the sheriff what Ethan had done this day. Before nightfall, Greenleaf might finally have the evidence he needed to to send Ethan to the gallows.

"So be it," Ethan muttered, his eyes closed, his hand still trembling with the might of his conjuring. He didn't yet know how to stop this conjurer, whoever he was, from drawing upon his power to hurt others. But at least he could fight back in this way.

After some time, Ethan pulled his hand away from the sailor's chest. Leaning forward, he opened the slit in the man's clothes to examine the wound. There was a livid scar there, but the skin was closed, the bleeding had stopped.

"Will he live?" the sailor asked.

"I don't know." Ethan was too weary to stand. He remained on his knees, his head bowed.

"What's all this?"

He knew that voice too well. Greenleaf had come even sooner than he expected.

The sheriff shouldered his way through the crowd, only stopping when he stood directly over Ethan.

"Kaille. I should have known that I'd find you at the middle of it." He looked around at the other faces. "Well, what happened here?"

For several seconds no one spoke. Then one of the onlookers pointed at the sleeping laborer and said, "That cove started it." He pointed at the smaller laborer. "He started fighting with this one here. Then that one—the one you talked to—he stepped in and put this fellow down with one punch."

"Kaille did that?" the sheriff said, his tone as doubtful as such a claim deserved. "And what about these two? Who cut you?" he asked the kneeling sailor.

"That same cove."

"What happened to your friend?"

The sailor glanced at Ethan and then at his wounded companion, whose shirt no longer had any blood on it.

"That man hit him," Ethan said before the sailor could answer. He stood and pointed at the laborer. "It was quite a blow. This man hasn't moved since."

"Is he dead?"

"I don't think so."

"What is this all about, Kaille? Does it have anything to do with . . ." He looked at the others, appearing unsure of himself. "With those other incidents we've discussed?"

"Aye, it might. I can't yet be certain."

"Of course you can't. But you're at the center of it again, aren't you? Or did Ramsey do this, too?" Greenleaf surveyed the wharf one last time, regarding the other men and Ethan with suspicion and disgust in equal measure. "You should get that one to a surgeon," he said, waving a hand vaguely at the wounded sailor. "And the rest of you should get back to your jobs." He leveled a finger at Ethan. "That includes you."

Greenleaf turned smartly and left them. Ethan watched him go, feeling like he had cheated at cards and gotten away with it.

"The sheriff is right," he said to the sailor with the gash on his arm. "Take your friend to a surgeon. I've done what I can for him, but he lost a lot of blood."

"I will. Thank you."

"I believe I should be thanking you." He encompassed the others in his glance. "All of you."

"I don't usually hold with your kind," said one man in the crowd. "But if you can save that lad's life . . . well, your devilry can't be all bad."

Ethan wasn't sure what to say. He nodded to the man.

"I wish I could do what you did to that cove's knife," another man said. "You'd be handy to have around in a fight."

"My thanks, sir. I'm grateful to you for not telling the sheriff what you saw."

"You won't find a snitch on this wharf," the first man said, his tone hardening. "Nor on any other. You work the waterfront, you keep your mouth shut." He grinned. "Besides, there aren't too many down here who care for Greenleaf, that is unless you count the customs boys."

Others laughed at this, including Ethan.

"I should be going," he said. "Again, thank you."

"What's your name?" the man asked before Ethan could walk away.

After what they had done for him, he couldn't very well refuse to answer. "Ethan Kaille."

"O' course," one of the older men said. "From the *Ruby Blade*."

"That's right."

"You're a thieftaker, aren't you?"

"I am." He hesitated, wondering if he was about to give offense. "I know that none of you here would inform on someone, but I have to ask: Do you know a captain named Nate Ramsey?"

"I knew his father," the older man said. "Haven't see the son since summer."

No one else said a word.

"Very well. Good day."

Ethan returned to King Street and threaded his way through the South End lanes toward the Dowsing Rod. Uncle Reg walked beside him, his glow deepening in the shadows of the narrow streets.

"The spell that started the fight—it came from me, didn't it? Like the spells I felt the night of the funeral?"

Reg nodded.

"I didn't cast it." But Ethan knew his denial rang hollow. Whatever his intention, his power had sparked violence. Again.

Chapter
TWELVE

Once back in the Dowser, Ethan found that he was reluctant to leave the tavern again. He hated admitting to himself that he was afraid, but he could not deny that he feared setting off more conflicts. At least in the tavern, sitting by himself at the rear of the great room, he did not risk encounters with armed soldiers or excitable mobs.

As with everything else he had experienced during the course of the past week, his apprehension turned his thoughts to Nate Ramsey. The captain knew him too well; he understood that Ethan would choose to hide himself rather than put others at risk. Which meant that Ethan was doing exactly what Ramsey wanted him to do.

If Ramsey was behind these conjurings.

Damn him! Ethan thought. Self-doubt, confusion, fear—these were the captain's favored currencies. Ethan might not have proof of the man's return to Boston, but if Ramsey was not responsible for the malign spells cast in recent days, he didn't want to meet the conjurer who was. Knowing for certain that there were two men who could bedevil him so was almost more than Ethan thought he could bear.

Night fell, the Dowser filled up once more. Kannice had left Ethan to his thoughts throughout the afternoon, but now she approached his table with uncharacteristic diffidence.

"Are you feeling all right?" she asked.

"Aye. I'm fine."

She frowned at that. "You're not fine," she said, sounding more like herself. "You've been sitting here for hours. Not that I mind, but I expected you to be down at the waterfront, or asking questions of Janna, or risking a beating by going to see Sephira Pryce and her conjurer."

"Well, I would. But the food and ale here are too good. I can't bring myself to leave."

"Ethan," she said, growling his name, an eyebrow cocked.

"Sit," he said, indicating the chair opposite his own.

Her expression didn't change, but she lowered herself into the chair.

"I was at the waterfront," he said, dropping his voice. "While I was there I felt a spell, and it caused another fight. A man nearly died, and I had to conjure to protect myself. At least two dozen men saw me do it."

"The first spell—your ghost says it came from you?"

"Aye. So I'm here because I fear that if I'm out on the street, I'll do more harm than good. Probably I should go back to my room on Cooper's Alley. That would be safest."

She took his hand. "No, you should stay here."

"Eventually, I'll have to brave the world again. I'm not going to find the conjurer who's responsible for these spells by sitting at this table, gorging myself on your fine chowders and the Kent pale."

Their smiles were fleeting.

"But for now," Ethan went on, "I don't know what to do or where to go."

"I understand. You know that you're welcome here as long as you wish to stay. But . . ." She broke off, seeming to wince at what she intended to say.

"It's all right, Kannice. Go on."

"Don't be angry with me for suggesting this, but maybe you should leave Boston. Ramsey, or whoever this is, can't hurt you if you're not here, and he can't use you to hurt others."

"He can hurt you. He can hurt Janna and Mariz, Diver and Henry. And someone has to defeat him. Janna and Mariz can't do it without me, and I wouldn't want them to try."

"I'm sure that's true, but if you're just hiding from him . . ."

"I don't intend to hide forever. I'm going to find him, but right now

I don't even know where to look. Still, perhaps I should leave, because in the meantime, I'm not making any money."

"You know you don't need money to stay here."

"I do know it. Thank you. But I don't feel right taking your food and ale. And I'll owe rent to Henry before long."

Kannice stood. "I'll leave you. But know this: I was concerned for you; nothing more. You can stay here as long as you wish. I like having you here."

They both smiled.

She started to walk away, but then stopped and faced him again. "I haven't brought this up in some time, because I know that you don't want to discuss it. But if you lived here, and worked here, even some of the time, you wouldn't need to pay for food, and you wouldn't owe any rent to Henry."

It was a conversation they'd had many times before, though perhaps never under such dire circumstances.

"I'll consider it," he said.

Her smile returned. "You're humoring me again."

"Perhaps a little."

"Fine. Do you want another ale?"

He peered into his tankard, which was nigh to empty. "Please."

"I'll send Kelf over."

"Thank you. I'll be here, trying not to start any fights."

She laughed, but Ethan could see that as she turned away her brow was creased once more.

He didn't leave the Dowser for much of the following day, which was the first of March. He could have searched the waterfront again, and several times he reached for his greatcoat, intending to do precisely that. But he had little confidence that he would find the *Muirenn*, and he remained convinced that the risks of venturing into the city streets were too great to justify leaving the tavern.

Late in the day, however, a soldier arrived at the Dowser bearing a message. Ethan assumed that it was from the lieutenant governor, expressing his impatience for tidings about the Seider shooting. But instead the missive came from Geoffrey Brower, the husband of Ethan's sister, Bett. Brower, who worked as a customs official, offered little information in his note, but requested that Ethan come as soon as possible to the Royal Customs House on King Street.

Curious as to what Geoffrey could want of him, and glad to have some reason other than dark conjurings to venture out into the lanes, Ethan grabbed his greatcoat and strode toward the door, indicating to the soldier that he should lead the way.

"Who was it from?" Kannice asked him from behind the bar.

"My sister's husband."

"What does he want?"

"He didn't say. I'll be back."

Ethan and the regular stepped out into the cold, and followed Sudbury Street down to Queen. After being cooped up in the tavern for so long, Ethan was glad to be outside. The streets remained icy, and a cold wind off the harbor whistled through alleys and past shops. The sky was clear but had begun to darken, and the sun, low in the west, cast elongated shadows across the city.

As they passed Brattle Street and a cluster of soldiers, Ethan tensed, expecting at any moment to feel a spell. But no pulse of power came, and soon they were beyond the men.

Upon reaching the Customs House, a nondescript brick building to the east of the Town House, the soldier accompanied Ethan inside.

"Ah, here he is now." Geoffrey Brower stood near an oaken desk at the back of the room onto which the door opened. He was tall and thin, with a steep forehead and hook nose that gave him an aspect of superciliousness that matched perfectly his personality. He wore a ditto suit of forest green, and a plaited, powdered wig.

A second man stood with him. He was several inches shorter than Geoffrey and narrow-shouldered, with a straight nose, dark eyes, and a grave expression. He, too, wore a silk suit and powdered wig. Ethan knew without asking who this was, and he regretted having left the Dowser.

"Ethan Kaille," Geoffrey said, crossing the room on long strides, "I would like you to meet Mister Charles Paxton, of the Customs Board."

Paxton offered a thin smile, but made no effort to approach Ethan or proffer a hand in greeting.

"It is my pleasure, sir," Ethan said. "Geoffrey it's . . . it's good to see you again."

"And you, Ethan. Mister Paxton has recently suffered a most grievous loss, and I have been telling him that you are one of Boston's most skilled thieftakers."

Of course. Paxton was infamous throughout all of Massachusetts as one of only two Boston-born commissioners on the Royal Customs Board. Boston's Whigs considered him as much a villain as they did Francis Bernard, the former governor, and Andrew Oliver, Boston's first Stamp Tax collector. Not surprisingly, therefore, he was a hero to the city's Tories. More to the point, though, as a customs commissioner, he was also in a position to advance dear Geoffrey's career. This was the only reason Brower would ever have admitted knowing Ethan, much less being related to him, albeit by marriage.

Ethan was tempted to leave without hearing another word. But as he had mentioned to Kannice the night before, he needed work. Paxton was a man of means; Ethan intended to charge the commissioner accordingly for his services.

"I'm sorry to hear of your loss, sir," he said. "What can you tell me about the stolen items?"

"Most of what was taken belongs to my wife. A pearl necklace, a brooch set with sapphires and diamonds, and a few baubles. There was also a pocket watch that once belonged to my father. It's gold, but its value is more sentimental than pecuniary." He cleared his throat. "To be honest, Mister Kaille, I had planned to speak of this matter with Sephira Pryce. I have nothing against you personally, but she enjoys a sterling reputation. I've agreed to speak with you first as a courtesy to Mister Brower."

"Of course, sir, I understand. When were these items taken?"

"Only yesterday." He paused, as if casting about for something else to say. "Geoffrey tells me that you solved the Berson murder a few years ago?"

"That's right."

"Ethan also found those responsible for the deaths aboard the *Graystone*," Geoffrey added, sounding too eager.

"Yes, I had heard that. I take it you have had other successful inquiries aside from these."

"I have, sir," Ethan said. "But I've no interest in cataloging them for you."

"Ethan!"

"Be quiet, Geoffrey." Facing Paxton once more, Ethan said, "I have been a successful thieftaker in this city for the better part of ten years. I'm skilled at my trade, I'm honest, and I'm discreet. If you prefer Sephira Pryce, I understand. I'll say nothing against her, though I will tell you that I'm sure either of us can recover the items you've lost. Hire me. Don't hire me. The choice is yours."

Paxton stared openmouthed; one might have thought Ethan had struck his face with a glove. Ethan was certain that the man would tell him to leave. For his part, Geoffrey appeared apoplectic. To Ethan's great surprise, however—and no doubt Geoffrey's as well—the commissioner began to laugh.

"Well played, Mister Kaille. Well played. Very well, what do you charge for your services?"

For any other man, Ethan would have done the work for five pounds total. But not Paxton.

"Seven pounds, sir. Two and ten now, and four and ten when I recover what you've lost."

Paxton's smile lingered, but the look in his eyes grew flinty. "You don't lack for confidence, do you? Seven pounds is a good deal of money."

"Sephira Pryce will demand more."

"I've no doubt."

He produced a purse from his pocket, opened it, and counted out two pounds and ten shillings. He handed the coins to Ethan and slipped the purse back into his coat. Ethan pocketed the money.

"What now?" Paxton asked. "I've been fortunate; this is the first time I've had to hire a man of your profession. How does this work?"

"I take it these items were stolen from your home."

"That's right."

"Do you have any idea who might have done this?"

"None. The rear door was broken, my wife's personal effects were strewn about her dressing chamber and treated most barbarously. Whoever did this might well have been part of the rabble seen so often abroad in our city's streets. I put nothing past them."

"In that case, sir, I would suggest that I meet you at your home first thing tomorrow morning. I'll want to see the damage done to your home, as well as those jewels belonging to your wife that were not stolen. At the risk of inconveniencing you, I'll also need a written description of each stolen item."

"Of course."

"You see, Mister Paxton?" Geoffrey said. "Ethan is quite thorough. I think you'll be very pleased with his work."

Paxton barely glanced his way. Ethan had the sense that Brower was doing little to ingratiate himself with the commissioner.

"I'll look for you tomorrow morning, Mister Kaille."

"Yes, sir. Until then."

As Ethan turned to leave, a third man entered the main chamber from a small office at the rear of the building. He and the man recognized each other at the same time. Jonathan Grant, the patriot conjurer from the Green Dragon, froze at the sight of Ethan, his mouth agape, his eyes open so wide they made his expression comical.

"Ah, yes," Geoffrey said. "Mister Grant, this is Ethan Kaille. Ethan, this is Mister Grant, one of our clerks."

His tone was so dismissive, Ethan was surprised Grant didn't round on him in indignation. But Grant did not seem able to tear his gaze from Ethan. There was panic in his youthful face, and an entreaty as well.

Ethan proffered a hand to the man. "Mister Grant, it's a pleasure to make your acquaintance."

"A-and yours," the clerk managed, gripping Ethan's hand for an instant.

"Grant, have you found those manifests yet?" Paxton asked.

"Most of them, sir."

"Well, find the rest. Mister Kaille, I will look forward to our conversation in the morn. For now I have matters that demand my attention."

"Yes, of course, sir. Until the morrow. Good night, Geoffrey." He nodded once to Grant and left the Customs House, glad to be away.

The sky overhead had darkened to indigo, and a few stars had emerged, gleaming like gems in the velvet. The moon, a pale sickle, hung low in the west above a fiery horizon. Despite the cold, it was as lovely a night as Boston had seen in some weeks.

This might have had something to do with the coins that jangled in Ethan's pocket as he returned to the Dowsing Rod. Kannice would not be pleased with him. Nor would Diver. Mere days before he had stopped working for Theophilus Lillie, they would say, and now he was taking money from Paxton, who was even worse.

Ethan wouldn't go so far as to say that he didn't care—Kannice's opinion meant a great deal to him. But he also couldn't deny that he was happy to be employed again, no matter who was paying him.

Still, he was not looking forward to telling her why Geoffrey had summoned him.

Diver and Deborah were already at the Dowser when Ethan arrived. He had little choice but to take his ale back to their table. Kannice joined him there as he was still greeting his friends.

"What was that all about?" she asked, a towel draped over her shoulder, strands of auburn hair hanging across her brow.

"The message from Geoffrey, you mean?" Ethan asked, taking his seat.

Her periwinkle eyes narrowed and in that split second it came to him again just how well she knew him. "Of course that's what I mean. What did he want?"

"He found work for me, and I'm happy to have it."

"And who is it you'll be working for this time?" Diver asked, sounding every bit as suspicious as Kannice.

Ethan took a breath, bracing himself for their response. "Charles Paxton."

"Paxton!" Diver repeated. "You might as well be working for King George himself!"

Ethan lifted his tankard and took a sip. "Given what the king might pay, I could do worse." He glanced at Deborah, who appeared to be suppressing a grin.

"What are you doing for him?" Kannice asked. Ethan could tell that she was trying to conceal her outrage, and he appreciated the effort.

"I'm not protecting him, if that's what you're asking. His home was robbed, and he hired me to retrieve what was taken." He eyed Diver. "Surely we can agree that any man who's had his property pinched deserves to get back what's his, regardless of his political beliefs."

"I'm not so sure, where Paxton's concerned," Diver said. "Really, Ethan. It sometimes seems you go out of your way to work for the most despicable men in Boston."

"Not out of my way, no. But when they're offering coin, I don't avoid them either. You'll be happy to hear, though, that I asked for more than my usual fee."

This brought a smile to Diver's face. "And he agreed?"

"Aye. I'm making about as much as Sephira Pryce would."

"And why not?" Kannice said. "You're worth more."

"Does that mean I'm forgiven?"

"It might." A coy grin curved her lips. "We might need to discuss the matter further later this evening."

Ethan held her gaze before asking of Diver, "And you?"

The younger man shrugged. "A cove's got to work, doesn't he?"

It was a better ending to the discussion than he had expected, and, later, a nicer conclusion to his evening than he had anticipated.

Charles Paxton lived on Hutchinson Street perhaps one hundred yards south of Milk Street. His was the only residence on the east side of the lane, and an impressive home it was: a three-story brick structure with colonnades flanking the front entrance. It stood directly across the lane from the rope yard of John Gray and but a short distance from Green's Barracks, which housed those men of the Twenty-ninth Regiment for whom there was no space at Murray's Barracks. Indeed, Ethan had forgotten how close to the quarters Paxton lived.

The rope yard, one of several in this part of the city, was a grand enterprise that included a large warehouse, several other buildings including the Gray residence, and an open expanse that ran almost all the way from Cow Lane north to Milk Street.

Ethan arrived at the Paxton estate as the clocks on the nearby meeting houses struck eight bells. Journeymen and apprentices were arriving at the rope yards. Not far off, groups of soldiers congregated in the street, bundled in their red coats, their gazes following the workers.

Ethan felt uneasy as he waited for an answer to his knock on Paxton's door. The sooner he was inside the house and away from the regulars and workers, the better for all concerned.

He didn't have to wait long. The door opened and Paxton himself greeted Ethan.

"You're prompt, Mister Kaille. That bodes well for our association."

"Yes, sir."

Paxton asked him into the house and escorted him first to the rear of the house, where stood the broken door and doorjamb. Ethan knelt to examine the damage more closely, but from a mere glance he could see what had happened.

"The thief used his foot to break in the door," he said, still scrutinizing the shattered wood. "He would have kicked it here . . ." He pointed. "Beside the door handle. I take it the theft occurred during the day, while you were at the Customs House, and your wife was abroad in the city. I would imagine that your servants were gone as well, shopping for groceries, perhaps."

When Paxton said nothing, Ethan craned his neck to peer up at him.

"Very well done, Mister Kaille. That is precisely what happened."

"Yes, sir. No thief would have entered in this way when the house was occupied. It would have made a good deal of noise. I would guess as well that whoever did this had been watching your home for some time, educating himself as to your behavior and that of your wife, as well as those others who live with you." He stood.

"That doesn't surprise me," Paxton said. "You would have seen the sort of men who frequent the rope yard across the street from us. No doubt it was one of them."

"Or one of the soldiers billeted up the street."

He could see that Paxton wanted to argue the point; they both knew that he couldn't. Since the beginning of the occupation, soldiers had been responsible for many thefts throughout the city. They were paid poorly, were too often idle, and had little regard for the city's inhabitants.

"I suppose that's possible as well," Paxton said.

"Did you prepare a list of the stolen items?"

"Yes, of course. Wait here."

Paxton left through a doorway that led onto a narrow corridor. Ethan glanced at the door again, but really there was little more he could glean from it. Already he knew where this inquiry would take him. Before he was through, he would need to speak with Paxton's servants and pay a visit to Green's Barracks.

Paxton soon returned, clutching a piece of parchment. On it were listed nine items, including the necklace, brooch, and watch the commissioner had mentioned the night before. In addition, Mrs. Paxton had lost several gold rings, a pair of bracelets, and an ivory-handled hairbrush.

"Thank you, sir. This will be most helpful. I believe you said last night that these items were taken from your wife's dressing room?"

"That's right. Except for the watch, which was taken from my bedroom. I would allow you to see both, but there would be little use in it. We wasted no time cleaning up the mess left by this brute. There is nothing for you to see upstairs, and I don't wish to disturb my wife. As you might expect, she has been thoroughly unnerved by this ordeal. I would prefer that we not include her in any of our conversations, lest we upset her more."

"I understand," Ethan said. "Tell me though, is there anything unusual about the plan of this house?"

"What do you mean?"

"There's no delicate way for me to put this, sir. What I mean to ask it this: Would a stranger to your home have an easy time navigating its many rooms, or would he need some prior knowledge in order to find the things he stole?"

Paxton frowned. "I don't think I like your implication, Mister Kaille."

"No, sir, I didn't expect you would. I wish to speak with your servants, if I may. Particularly any young women who might work for you, and might have drawn the interest of one of General Gage's soldiers."

Paxton sighed. "That would be Louisa," he said. "I'm afraid she's not here at this time. Her parents live in the country and she left yesterday to spend the evening with them; her father, it seems, is elderly and infirm. She will return later today. You can speak with her tomorrow morning, if that suits you."

"That would be fine, sir."

"What will you do now?"

Ethan had no chance to answer, for at that moment a conjuring shook the floors and walls of the mansion. He knew it instantly for a finding spell, and he had no doubt that it had been cast to locate him. It rushed toward the house, putting him in mind of an advancing tide, as had Morrison's spell two days before. It reached him in mere seconds, and was followed immediately by another spell.

This time, as the house rumbled with conjuring power, Uncle Reg appeared between Ethan and Paxton, who was, of course, oblivious.

"Mister Kaille, I asked you a question."

"Yes, sir," Ethan said, desperate to leave at once and learn what this newest spell had wrought. "I plan to visit a tavern that is frequented by men who traffic in pilfered goods."

"You know of such a place?" Paxton asked, sounding indignant. "You should inform the sheriff at once."

"I would, sir," Ethan said, "but doing so would be a waste of time. Sheriff Greenleaf is well aware of its existence. If you can show me to the door?"

The customs man scowled. "Yes, all right."

Paxton led him back through to the front of the house, moving far too slowly for Ethan's purposes. It was all Ethan could do not to scream at the man to walk faster.

"I'll return tomorrow, sir," Ethan said as they reached the door. "Thank you for your time."

"Wait a minute, Mister Kaille. Do you mean to tell me that visiting this publick house is all you plan to do?"

"No, sir. I plan as well to speak with your servant, and to see if I can find any soldiers or journeymen working at the rope yard who might have lavished their attentions on her. But I intend to start at the tavern, because if I don't, and your property shows up there and is sold, you'll never see any of it again."

"Yes, but—"

"Mister Paxton, I have been a thieftaker for many years now. I wouldn't visit the Customs House and tell you how to do your job. Please don't presume to tell me how to conduct my inquiry."

Paxton's face shaded to crimson, but he essayed a thin smile. "Yes, very well. Good day, Mister Kaille."

"Good day, sir."

Ethan donned his hat and hurried back out to the street, but by the time he was close enough to the rope yard to see what was happening, events had already begun to turn ugly.

A soldier stood near the first of the ropewalks, trading insults with a journeyman as other workers looked on, laughing at each of the journeyman's barbs. Ethan could not hear all that was said, but he saw that the soldier's hands were clenched in fists, and that his face was bright red. Even as he shouted something back at the workers and took a step toward them, another man, using a nearby building to remain hidden, snuck up behind the regular and knocked his legs out from under him.

The soldier fell hard on his back, drawing uproarious laughter from the other men. Their mirth, however, was short-lived. A cutlass had slipped from within the soldier's coat when he went down. The man who had upended him grabbed the weapon and held it up for his fellow workers to see.

"Looks like I've got a prize," he said.

The soldier got to his feet, moving stiffly. He glowered at the men, but there were five of them, and he was alone and now unarmed. With a last dark look at the workers, he retreated toward the barracks.

After what he had seen at the Richardson house days before, Ethan knew better than to think that this was the end of the confrontation. He was not at all surprised when he felt another conjuring.

"Did that come from me?" he asked Uncle Reg.

The ghost nodded.

Ethan pursued the soldier, hoping that he might be able to dissuade the man from trying to avenge himself on the workers. But as he drew near, the soldier turned and pointed a trembling finger at him.

"You stay away from me!"

Ethan held up hid hands. "I'm not one of them, and I'm not trying to harm you."

"It's not me who'll come to harm! I'll have my sword back, and I'll have satisfaction! You'll see!"

"No good can come of this," Ethan said.

But the soldier dismissed him with a wave of his hand and ran on to the barracks.

Ethan stared after him, and then turned back toward Paxton's mansion and the journeymen. The laborers had returned to their work, though as Ethan reached them, they were still laughing and talking about how foolish the regular had looked as he fell.

"End this now," Ethan called to the men. "Return his cutlass and have nothing more to do with them."

The man who had taken the soldier's sword regarded Ethan with scorn, as Ethan had known he would. Why would these men want to end the conflict when they had gotten the better of its first skirmish? Another of the men called to his companions and pointed in the direction of the barracks. The other men gazed that way and fell silent.

Ethan didn't have to look to know what they saw, but still he turned. The soldier was striding down the center of the street, leading nine uniformed men, all of them carrying clubs.

The workers took shelter in the rope yard warehouse. Upon reaching the entrance to Gray's enterprise, the soldiers followed them inside.

"Damn!" Ethan started toward the building, then stopped himself, unsure of how to proceed. "What should I do?" he asked Reg.

The ghost lifted an arm and pointed northward, away from the warehouse.

"I should go to the barracks?"

Reg shook his head and pointed a second time, more emphatically.

"You're saying I should leave."

Reg nodded.

"But I'm responsible. The spells that started this came from me."

Again the ghost nodded, lifting his arm once more.

"You think they'll continue to fight until I'm gone."

The ghost offered no reply. He simply stared at Ethan, waiting.

Ethan knew that Reg was probably right, although he knew as well that there were spells he could use to keep the men from killing one another. The question was, how many times could he cast a sleep spell or some other sort of protective conjuring in front of others before someone decided to have him hanged for a witch? He had been lucky two days before on Long Wharf, and before that on the night of Chris Seider's funeral. He couldn't expect to be so fortunate forever.

He heard shouts coming from within the warehouse, and he watched as several more journeymen entered the building, all of them carrying woldring sticks, which they used to wind rope, but which would serve as cudgels as well. He had not felt another spell for several minutes, but apparently one wasn't needed; like a fire burning bright, this fight needed no more kindling.

ith one last glance at the warehouse, Ethan left Hutchinson Street, choosing to circle the base of Fort Hill rather than risk passing too close to Green's Barracks. He scanned the harbor and wharves as he walked, but his search for Nate Ramsey's ship proved as fruitless this morning as it had every time before.

Willing to try anything to keep the unseen conjurer from using him in this way, Ethan stopped on a stretch of empty road between the South Battery and Milk Street and pulled his pouch of mullein from the pocket of his coat.

"*Tegimen ex verbasco evocatum*," he said. Warding, conjured from mullein. The spell hummed in the street, a declaration to his enemy.

Ethan didn't know if the spell would work as he intended, but he had to make the attempt. If he could protect himself and those around him, he would have a better chance of finding whoever it was who had been casting these spells.

Shielded by his conjuring, Ethan continued on to the North End and what might have been the most disreputable tavern in all of Boston. The Crow's Nest sat at the southern extreme of Paddy's Alley, near the waterfront. Where Kannice did all she could to keep the Dowsing Rod free of fights, whoring, and other questionable behavior, the Crow's Nest seemed to exist for those things. It was run-down and filthy. The ale served there was swill; Ethan had never dared taste the food. He

wasn't entirely sure that the place served any. But for those who traf-
ficked in stolen goods—and thus, for thieftakers attempting to recover
those items—the Nest might well have been the most important establishment in the city.

In the ten years since Ethan's return to Boston from the plantation
in the Caribbean where he labored as a prisoner, the Crow's Nest had
seen a succession of ill-starred proprietors. Some had died; others had
been transported to the Caribbean for crimes they might or might not
have committed. The current owner, Joseph Duncan, was a slight, excitable Scotsman who had barely survived a bout with small pox back
in 1764. His face was pitted and scarred from the distemper.

When Ethan entered the tavern, Dunc was standing at the bar,
reading a newspaper, and, as always, puffing on a tobacco pipe and sending clouds of sweet smoke into the rafters.

Seeing Ethan, he turned his back on the door and raised the paper
so that it hid his face.

Ethan took off his hat and his gloves and stepped to the bar,
planting himself beside the man. He slid a half shilling onto the worn
wood.

"An ale," he said to the barkeep.

The man dropped the coin into the till and filled a tankard.

Ethan had no intention of drinking the stuff—it looked and tasted
enough like horse piss to make Ethan suspicious of its origins. But he
also wasn't going to pay Duncan for the information he sought, so he
thought that buying an ale was the least he could do.

Picking up the tankard, he turned and leaned back against the bar,
surveying the tavern. The men who sat at tables in pairs and groups of
three and four appeared perfectly at home amid the squalor of the Nest,
which told Ethan everything he needed to know about them.

Dunc still had not acknowledged him, though the amount of smoke
billowing from his pipe seemed to have increased.

"You can't ignore me forever, Dunc."

"Who says I can't?" he answered from behind the paper.

"*Imago ex cervisia evocata,*" Ethan said, his voice low. Illusion, conjured from ale.

The pulse of this spell was weaker than most of the others Ethan cast because it was an elemental spell. But it did what he had hoped it would: Illusory flames erupted from the pages of the *Gazette*.

Dunc jumped, dropped the paper to the floor, and stamped on it.

Ethan whispered. *"Fini imaginem ex cervisia evocatam."* Again, power pulsed, and the illusion vanished.

The other men in the tavern stared at Dunc the way they would at a lunatic.

"You're a bit skittish, aren't you?" Ethan said, grinning.

Dunc pulled the pipe from between his yellow teeth. "That wasn't funny, Kaille."

"I'd have to disagree."

Dunc put the pipe back in his mouth with a click of teeth on clay. "What do you want, anyway?"

Ethan raised an eyebrow. "You have to ask?"

"I'm not helping you find anything. You come in here every time you have a new job, and you seem to think it's up to me to find what you were hired to retrieve. Well, I'm through with that." Dunc gave a nasty smile. "Go talk to Pryce. Maybe she'll help you."

"You're right, Dunc."

"Well, you can think whatever you want, but—" He blinked. "What?"

"I said you're right. I shouldn't be asking you to do my work for me. So instead, allow me to help you out."

He pulled Paxton's list of pilfered goods from his pocket and unfolded it. All the while, Dunc watched him the way a fox would a hound.

"What's that?"

"The list of items I'm looking for."

"I just told you—"

Ethan held a finger inches in front of the Scot's nose, stopping him. "I heard you, Dunc. These things were stolen from the home of Charles Paxton."

"You're working for Paxton?" He grinned. "Things that bad then?"

"If any of these items come through the Nest, and word of it gets back to the customs boys, they'll shut you down. Even Greenleaf won't be able to talk them out of it."

Dunc's smile faded slowly. "Aye, you're probably right." He took the list from Ethan and perused it.

"Have you seen any of it?" Ethan asked.

"Not yet. When was it pinched?"

"I don't think it's been more than two days."

Dunc handed him back the parchment. "Have you any idea who cracked the house?"

"I have no proof, but forced to guess, I'd say it was one of the regulars billeted over at Green's Barracks."

"Well, I'm not going out of my way to tell you when these things show up here, but I'll make it clear to my fences that they're not to buy any of Paxton's stuff in my place."

"That's all I ask. My thanks, Dunc." He raised the tankard to his lips but thought better of taking a sip. He set it on the bar. "You really should serve better ale."

"I've told you before, coves don't come here for the drink."

"No, I don't imagine they do."

Dunc frowned. "Get out."

Ethan pulled on his gloves and picked up his hat off the bar.

As he did, a spell trembled in the walls of the tavern. He looked sharply at Reg, who gave a single nod.

But nothing happened. None of the men in the tavern started arguing or fighting. None of them so much as glanced Ethan's way. His warding had held. Or so he thought.

An instant later, a second spell shook the building, as puissant and clear as the pealing of a church bell. This time, Ethan felt the conjuring within his chest, as if the person who cast it had reached between his ribs and taken hold of his heart.

"Kaille? Are you all right?" Dunc asked, genuine concern on his narrow face.

"I don't know."

Chair legs scraped on the tavern's wooden floor. Two men who had been sitting at the nearest of the tables were now standing, glaring at Ethan. Seeming to respond to some silent command, both men drew their blades as one and started toward the bar.

Dunc backed away from them. "What the devil are you two doing?"

Ethan slid his knife from its sheath.

"Kaille?"

"Stay back, Dunc."

The men said not a word. Ethan didn't think that they even shared a look. But they separated, one stepping to Ethan's left, the other to his right. Both were tall, powerfully built. He had no doubt that they were skilled fighters.

Ethan still wore his greatcoat; he didn't think he could take it off before they attacked, and he wasn't sure he could fight them while wearing it. But he managed to pull off his left glove and cut the skin on the back of his hand.

"*Discuti ambo ex cruore evocatum.*" Shatter, both of them, conjured from blood.

Both men's blades broke, shards of metal falling to the floor with a sound like the tinkling of breaking icicles.

"Lord save us," Dunc whispered. Ethan kept his eyes on the men, who continued to stalk him. One of them lunged for him, moving faster than Ethan would have thought he could. He jumped back, acting on instinct. And a powerful forearm clamped down on his neck.

He struggled to get away, but the second man held him fast.

The first man reared back and hit him in the jaw, his fist like a brick. Ethan's vision swam; he tasted blood.

"*Discuti ex cruore evocatum,*" he said, using another shatter spell.

This time he heard bone break and a grunt of pain from the man behind him. The man's grip on his throat slackened. Ethan threw an elbow into his gut, drawing another grunt.

He grabbed the man's broken arm and twisted out of his grasp. The man howled.

His friend swung at Ethan a second time, but Ethan ducked out of the way and took a step back, and then another. The man matched him step for step.

Fortunately for Ethan, the brute was as clumsy as he was large. He threw another punch. Ethan ducked again and the man's fist whistled harmlessly over his head, leaving him off balance. Ethan planted his good leg and spun, using his bad leg as a club. His kick caught the brute in the kidney. The man collapsed to one knee. Ethan locked his hands together and hit him with every ounce of his strength, knocking him backward so that he sprawled unconscious on the floor, a trickle of blood flowing from his nose.

By this time, the other man was on his feet again. He held his broken arm cradled to his chest, but still he seemed determined to renew his assault on Ethan. He tried to hit Ethan with his good hand, but missed. Ethan threw a punch of his own, staggering the man. A second blow put him on the floor.

"Bloody hell!" Dunc said, staring at the men. "Do you know these two?"

Ethan was breathing hard, and his hands ached from the punches he had thrown. "I've never seen them before."

"Then why did they go for you that way?" Dunc's expression darkened. "And what was that you did to their knives?"

"I don't know the answer to the first question," Ethan said, flexing his right hand, "and you know perfectly well the answer to the second." He picked up his hat and set it on his head, eager to leave the Crow's Nest before another spell sent the rest of its patrons after him. "Remember what I told you about Paxton's property."

"Aye, I will."

"See you later, Dunc."

The Scotsman still stared at the two men. But as Ethan reached the door he said, "Hey, Kaille. Watch yourself."

"Aye," Ethan said. "I'm trying."

Once on the street again, Ethan cast a dark look at Reg and started back toward Mill Creek and the South End. He knew it wasn't the ghost's fault that his warding had failed, but he felt betrayed by his conjuring power, and Reg was the embodiment of that power.

"It seems a simple warding isn't enough," he said, walking with his hands buried in his pockets. "But I don't know what else to try."

Usually when confronted with his own ignorance about magicking, Ethan went to the Fat Spider to ask questions of Janna. But at the moment he didn't feel safe going anywhere: not to Janna's tavern or Kannice's. He even feared returning to his room on Cooper's Alley. What if Henry was hurt as a result of one of these spells?

He knew, though, that he couldn't remain in the streets; this was the most dangerous place, not only for him, but for any innocents who happened to cross his path. After some deliberation, he decided that his room was his safest refuge. He followed a serpentine path into the heart of the South End, taking the least crowded streets he could find, and adjusting his route whenever he encountered a crowd.

Any doubts he had harbored as to the identity of the conjurer who was harrying him had vanished with that last spell. Who else but Nate Ramsey was wicked enough to use conjurings in this way, and also strong enough to overcome Ethan's warding with such ease? But this certainty came as little consolation. How could he fight the man when he didn't even know where to find him?

He climbed the stairway to his room, locked and warded the door, and lit a fire in his stove to keep warm. Pulling out some of the herbs he carried, he then healed his bruised jaw. And as he did all of this, he cursed his inability to do more. Ramsey, he had little doubt, was laughing at him, mocking his ignorance and impotence, reveling in the success he had enjoyed thus far in this, their latest battle. Ethan realized as well that in the Crow's Nest he had made himself an unwitting ally in Ramsey's scheme. He had thought himself so clever using an illusion spell to scare Duncan. Instead, what he had done was tell Ramsey exactly where he was. He would need to be more careful in the future.

But of course Ramsey would want that as well. Slowly, one step at a time, Ramsey was weakening him, taking away every advantage Ethan might usually have enjoyed. Ethan had allies here in Boston, and so Ramsey sought to separate him from those on whom he relied. He was afraid now to set foot in the Dowser, or any other tavern, lest he cause another fray. Ethan and Ramsey were equals when it came to conjuring, but now Ethan was reluctant to conjure, lest he reveal his location to the captain.

Yet, even knowing this, Ethan was helpless to do anything about it. At least until he found Ramsey.

Though loath to go anywhere near Gray's Rope Works and Green's Barracks again, Ethan still had a job to complete, and he had promised

Paxton that he would return the following morning so that he might question the commissioner's servant.

He followed the same route to the Paxton estate that he had used when he left the previous day, thus keeping his distance from the barracks. But he couldn't avoid the ropewalks; all he could do was approach the mansion as quickly as his leg and the ice-covered lane would allow and get off the street.

Once more, Ethan's knock was answered by Paxton himself.

"Ah, Mister Kaille." He waved Ethan inside and closed the door. "I had feared that perhaps yesterday's events might keep you away."

Ethan felt the blood drain from his face. "What do you mean?"

"Simply that I watched from the window as the rabble at Gray's establishment assaulted that unfortunate soldier. And I saw as well that you attempted to intervene before leaving." He shook his head. "It was a bad business. Before all was said and done, some forty soldiers and nearly as many journeymen fought in the yard and in the street. Several men were wounded, and it would have been worse if not for old John Hill, who lives nearby. He somehow managed to keep those ruffians from doing worse to the uniformed men."

"Yes, sir," Ethan said. He was relieved to hear that the fighting hadn't resulted in any deaths, and also that Paxton had no inkling of his role in the incident.

Paxton led Ethan into a sitting room off the front foyer. "If you'll wait here, I'll fetch Louisa."

"Of course, sir. Thank you."

Paxton bustled away, only to return moments later leading a young woman in a plain blue dress. She had raven black hair, large blue eyes, and a pale oval face that might have been pretty had she not appeared so frightened.

"Louisa, this is Mister Kaille," Paxton said. "He's a thieftaker. I've engaged him to find the jewels that were taken from Missus Paxton's dressing room. I expect you to answer his questions truthfully. Do you understand me?"

The girl's head jerked up and down. Paxton was doing nothing to put her at ease.

"Good morning, Louisa," Ethan said, trying to keep his tone

gentle. "I won't take much of your time. I have some questions about people you might have seen near the Paxtons' home. All right?"

She nodded again.

"Have you any friends among the workers at Gray's Rope Works or the soldiers billeted up the street?"

Her gaze met his for the span of a heartbeat before darting away again; she began to wring her hands.

"Please answer him, Louisa."

"There's a . . . a s-soldier. But he's very nice, and I'm sure he's not . . . Well, I don't think he would take anything from my mistress."

"What's his name?" Ethan asked.

"James," she said. "James Fleming. He's just a private now, but he wants to be an officer. That's what he told me."

"Has he asked you questions about the house?"

"No," she said without hesitation. "Well—" She broke off and chewed her lip. "He wanted to know where my room was."

"Why did he want to know that?" Paxton asked, his brows knitting.

A faint smile lit her face and a bit of color warmed her cheeks. "It was rather sweet, really. He said that he wanted to know where to look at night when I was asleep and he was on patrol."

"Was that all he asked? Where your room was located?"

"Now that I think of it, I suppose he asked other questions as well." Ethan and the commissioner shared a look.

"What sort of questions?" Ethan asked.

"I didn't think anything of it." She turned to Paxton. "I swear to you, sir, I thought he was . . . he was only talking to me, because . . . because maybe he thought I was pretty. He'd prattle on about his fellow soldiers and the things he saw in Halifax before coming to Boston." A tear slipped down her cheek. "I've never been anywhere, so I had no stories to tell him. So I thought his questions were intended to let me talk, so that it wouldn't be him talking all the time."

"What sort of questions, Louisa?"

She faced Ethan again, her tears flowing freely now. "He asked about . . . about the rooms. Whose they were and where. I've never been in any house as grand as this one, and so I told him a lot. I suppose I wanted him to be impressed."

"Were there others?" Paxton asked, his voice flat. Ethan wondered if Louisa would still be employed here come nightfall. "Maybe one of the men from the rope yard?"

"No, sir," she said, shaking her head so forcefully that tears flew from her cheeks.

Clearly she thought that she was reassuring her master. Ethan thought it more likely that her response only deepened Paxton's anger. The commissioner would not want blame to fall on a British soldier.

"Is there anything else, Mister Kaille?" Paxton asked, sounding impatient for their interview to end.

The thrum of a conjuring kept Ethan from answering. It was a powerful spell, and it seemed to come from beneath Ethan's feet. Reg emerged from the shadows beside him, glowing with the color of dried blood. Ethan wondered if the soldiers and journeymen would be fighting again when he left the mansion.

Paxton leaned forward, peering into Ethan's face. "I said, is there anything else."

Ethan shook himself. "Aye. Yes, sir." To the young woman he said, "Can you describe James for me?"

She offered a watery smile. "He's about your height," she said, regarding Ethan with a critical eye. "He has red hair and brown eyes, and freckles across here." She ran a finger over the bridge of her nose. "And he also has a red birthmark here." She pointed to her temple.

"Thank you, Louisa. That's very helpful."

She looked at Paxton.

"You may go," he said, his tone and expression severe.

She curtsied and left them, dabbing at her tears with the cuffs of her sleeves.

"Foolish girl," Paxton said, when she was gone.

"She didn't know she was doing wrong."

"You needn't defend her, Mister Kaille. She can keep her job."

"Yes, sir."

"I suppose then that you'll go and speak with this man."

Ethan hesitated. He didn't like the idea of entering the barracks while he had so little control over his conjuring power. He liked even less the notion of neglecting his job because he was afraid.

"Well?"

"Yes, sir," Ethan said. "I intend to speak with Private Fleming as soon as possible."

"Good."

Ethan reached for his coat and hat. "I should be on my way, then."

"I should think," Paxton said. But he didn't lead Ethan back to the front entrance. "Did you learn anything yesterday? As I recall, you were going to visit some disreputable tavern."

"Yes, sir. I was there. The proprietor has not yet seen any of your lost items."

"So he says. Do you trust this man?"

"As much as I do anyone who associates with thieves."

"That's hardly reassuring, Mister Kaille."

"It's been but a few days since the theft. And if Louisa's friend was responsible, he won't have had much time to sell what he stole. If forced to guess, I would say that your watch and your wife's jewels remain hidden away in Green's Barracks even as we speak."

"I'll take your word for it, as I profess to have no knowledge of such things."

The commissioner led Ethan back to the foyer, but as he reached for the door handle, they both heard raised voices from out on the street.

"You shouldn't go out there yet," Paxton said.

They walked back into an adjacent room, the windows of which looked out upon the rope yard.

Three soldiers and an equal number of journeymen faced each other at the entrance to Gray's establishment. Once more, the regulars were armed with clubs, while the rope workers held woldring sticks. One of the journeymen said something, eliciting laughter from his companions. The soldiers leaped at them, and in seconds they were brawling in earnest.

"Damn!" Ethan strode back to the foyer.

"Mister Kaille, what are you doing?"

"I have to stop them."

"You can't! Don't be a fool! You'll get yourself killed."

Another spell shook the mansion, to be followed almost at once by a third. Ethan pulled the door open and stepped outside. Paxton eyed him from the window, limiting what he could do to put an end to the fighting.

After a brief, desperate deliberation, he concluded that he had but one choice. He bit down on the inside of his cheek and said to himself, *Dormite omnes ex cruore evocatum.* Sleep, all of them, conjured from blood.

He felt this conjuring as he had the others, but nothing happened. The men continued to fight. Had Ramsey once again found a way to keep him from casting spells, as he had months before? Every other spell Ethan had cast recently worked as he intended. Perhaps one of the conjurings he felt had been a warding intended to guard the journey-men and soldiers from his sleep spell. He had used such conjurings to great effect in recent days. Ramsey would have noticed.

He had no more time to ponder the matter. Bystanders had gathered to watch the confrontation, and now another journeyman emerged from the rope yard warehouse carrying two clubs. One he kept for himself, and the other he gave to one of the onlookers. Together, the two of them joined the other journeymen, turning the fight to their advantage. Outnumbered now, the soldiers tried to flee, but the workers would not let them go. One of the regulars took a blow to the head and collapsed in a heap. His assailant continued to beat him.

"No!" Ethan shouted. He bit down on his cheek again and cast the first spell that came to mind.

A wall of flame burst from the ground. The soldiers and workers fell back, breaking off their combat to stare wide-eyed at the flames.

Ethan allowed them to die away as he ran across the street, and helped the other two soldiers lift their injured comrade and retreat toward the barracks.

None of them said a word as they hurried away from the rope yard. The journeymen followed them down the street, but they didn't appear to be pursuing them in earnest. Rather, they shouted taunts for the entertainment of those who had gathered to watch the fight.

"Bastards," muttered one of the soldiers, a red-haired man who spoke with a thick burr. He was breathless; dark bloodstains mingled with the bright red of his uniform.

"What was that fire I saw?" the other man asked. "For just a second, I thought it was lightning."

His friend glanced at the sky, which was a clear, cold blue. "It wasn't lightnin'." He looked Ethan's way. "We're grateful to you, but we can carry him from here."

Ethan let go of the wounded man. The soldiers carried him on.

"There's a soldier I need to talk to," Ethan said, walking after them. "A Private Fleming from the Twenty-ninth."

"Jimmy?" the red-haired man asked.

"Aye. Do you know him well?"

"Well enough. What business have you got with him?"

"Nothing that he'd want me discussing with anyone else. Even a friend."

The soldier regarded him sourly. "Most times I'd tell you to go to hell. But you helped us back there, and that's worth somethin'. You can follow us."

"My thanks."

They soon came to the barracks, and the men carried their wounded friend inside. Ethan walked in after them, wary now, fearful of another spell. The accommodations here were more cramped than those at Murray's warehouse. There was no huge central room, but rather a series of somewhat smaller ones. Still the stink and noise of so many men reminded him much of the other barracks. They passed two rooms filled with cots, and as they neared a third doorway, the red-haired soldier looked back at Ethan and then nodded toward the door. "He should be in there."

"Thank you," Ethan said.

He paused on the threshold of this third room and scanned it for a soldier who matched the description Louisa had given him.

He spotted the young man in the far corner of the room, playing cards with several other men. His hair was fiery orange, and a wine-colored birthmark covered much of his right temple and cheek.

Already Ethan had the sense that this was a bad idea. He would have been better off waiting outside the barracks. Fleming had to leave the building eventually in order to patrol. But that meant remaining in the vicinity of Green's Barracks and the rope yard for hours. He might even have to come back a second day and a third before he managed to speak with the man. He wasn't sure he could risk spending that much time in the area. How many more fights might he cause? How many more men would be wounded?

He entered the room and made his way back to where Fleming reclined on one of the cots. Ethan had almost reached him when another spell growled like distant thunder. He faltered in midstride. None of the soldiers seemed to have sensed the conjuring—there were no spellers here. But they had noticed him, and silence had enveloped the room.

"Who are you?" asked one of the men playing cards with Jimmy Fleming.

Chapter

FOURTEEN

The soldiers regarded him the way a pack of street curs might an unfamiliar dog. Trapped under their hard glares, Ethan wasn't sure whether to proceed and interview Fleming as he had planned, or offer some excuse and hope that he could escape the barracks without getting himself killed. He expected that one of the soldiers who had led him here would mention him to Fleming, perhaps simply to ask what Ethan had wanted. If Fleming was in fact the thief who had cracked Charles Paxton's house, that might be enough to make him desert and flee the city. Or at the very least try to sell the goods he had stolen. Ethan's inquiry might well end in failure because of what he did in the next few seconds. And that was possibly the best outcome for which he could hope.

"I was hoping to have a word with Private Fleming," Ethan said, flashing a smile that was as bright and disarming as he could manage under the circumstances. This would be, he decided, like trying to take honey from a bees' nest. The warding he cast in the Crow's Nest was still protecting him. This new spell had done nothing to rile the men. If Ethan could avoid provoking them, he might escape without a fight.

"Not until you answer my question," said the man who had spoken. "Who are you?"

"My name is Ethan. I'm the brother of a girl he's been spending time with."

Most of the men turned to look at Jimmy. Only Louisa's beau continued to gape at Ethan.

"She doesn't have a brother," he said.

Ethan raised an eyebrow but said nothing.

"What have you been at, Jimmy?" asked another of the men. The others smirked; a few of them laughed.

"Is Jimmy in some sort of trouble?" the first soldier asked of Ethan.

"Not really," Ethan said, keeping his tone light. "She could do a lot worse than finding a soldier. But my Da wanted me to check on whoever it was she's spending her time with."

"She said your Da knew all about me!" Jimmy's gaze flicked from one of his comrades to the next. "I swear she did!"

"And so he does," Ethan said, his heart pounding. "But only from her. Can a father be blamed for wanting his son to take care of his little girl? Surely the rest of you lads understand. Perhaps some of you have sisters of your own."

Jimmy narrowed his eyes. "You look a little old to be her brother."

"More often than not I feel a little old, as well."

"Talk to him, Jimmy," said the first man. "There's no harm in talkin', is there?"

Fleming's mouth twisted. "Fine. Outside."

"Of course." To the others, Ethan added, "Thank you, gentlemen."

He left the room without bothering to see if Fleming had followed him. As he limped toward the door he felt yet another conjuring, but still he walked, half expecting to feel a bayonet pierce the flesh between his shoulder blades.

Only when he reached the street did he glance back. And so he was ill prepared when Fleming threw the punch; he had no time to ward himself or even raise an arm to block the blow. Jimmy's fist caught him on the side of the face, just below his cheekbone. Ethan staggered, tasting blood, but he didn't go down. One blow from a pup like Jimmy Fleming was nothing compared with the beatings he had taken from Sephira's men.

Jimmy tried to hit him again. Ethan jerked his head back out of the way and then struck a blow of his own, hitting the soldier below his eye. Fleming shook off the clout and came at him again. Still bleeding, Ethan didn't need to cut himself.

"*Pugnus ex cruore evocatus,*" he whispered. Fist, conjured from blood.

This conjured punch did what Ethan's fist could not: Jimmy fell to the ground, dazed though still conscious.

Ethan pulled the mullein from his coat pocket and pulled out three leaves, which he held in the curl of his fingers so that Fleming couldn't see them.

"*Quies ex verbasco evocata.*" Calm, conjured from mullein.

It was not a spell he had attempted before, though he had once seen his mother use it on a frenzied dog near their home in Bristol back in England. He didn't know if it would work against the conjuring that had made Jimmy attack in the first place, but he didn't wish to hurt the lad if he didn't have to. With the hum of the spell still shaking the cobbles beneath them, Jimmy blinked once and looked up at him.

"I hit you," the soldier said.

"Aye. I hit you back. Do you remember why you hit me?"

The lad sat up. "I don't . . . I was angry. I'm not even sure why. But I was as angry with you as I've ever been with anyone." He stared hard at Ethan. "What did you do?"

"Nothing that I can think of. Do you remember anything else?"

"No. I . . . I felt that I had to hit you. I *knew* it."

"You're not the first who's felt that way." Ethan smiled, then winced. The pup might not have been as strong as Afton or Gordon, but his blow would leave a bruise if Ethan didn't heal it.

"What's all this about your sister?" Jimmy asked, sounding groggy. "That's what we were talkin' about, right? Before I mean." He waved a hand absently at the door to the barracks. "Back in there."

"Aye. It wasn't really about my sister, but rather about you pinching jewels from the Paxton house."

Jimmy's eyes went wide. He tried to get to his feet, but Ethan placed a hand firmly on his shoulder, keeping him where he was.

"You lied to me," Fleming said. "She's not your sister, is she?"

"No. I'm a thieftaker. I was hired by Mister Paxton to recover the items you stole. But I thought you'd prefer that I not mention your thieving in front of the other soldiers."

"I didn't steal anythin'!"

Any doubt Ethan harbored as to the man's guilt vanished upon hearing this. Jimmy was a terrible liar. He didn't argue or challenge the soldier's denial, but instead continued to watch him and wait.

It didn't take long for Fleming to sag and drop his gaze. He glanced back into the barracks again, but he no longer appeared likely to bolt. "Did Louisa tell you?" he asked.

"Did she know you had done it?"

Jimmy's smirk was bitter. "She's better at this than I am. Of course she knew."

Ethan rubbed a hand across his brow. "She gave me your name, but she never let on that you were a thief, or that she had any part in what you'd done. At first she protested your innocence, but after some time she did say that you had asked her about the location of different rooms in the mansion."

A high, gasping laugh escaped the soldier. "I asked?" He shook his head. "I never asked her anything. She told me again and again, like a teacher giving a bloody lesson. I couldn't get her to stop talkin' about it until I could recite it all back to her. 'The mistress's dressing room is on the south side of the house, past the master's bedroom.' That sort of thing."

"Where are the jewels now, Jimmy? Do you have them in the barracks?"

Jimmy frowned. "Course not. That would be the worst place to keep them. Someone would find them in no time. One cove is always pinchin' somethin' from another."

"Then where did you hide them?"

Fleming's smile was as thin as a blade. "I didn't. Louisa did. That was her idea, too. I break in, steal the jewels, and give them back to her for safekeepin'. She said the Paxtons would never think to look in her room. And by the time they did, she'd have taken them elsewhere."

"Do you have any idea where?"

Jimmy gave a rueful shake of his head. "She didn' tell me, and I didn' think to ask. I trusted her; didn' see any reason not to."

"Could they still be in the——?"

Ethan felt himself go white. He knew exactly where Louisa had taken the jewels.

Her parents live in the country, Paxton had said. *She left yesterday to spend the evening with them; her father, it seems, is elderly and infirm.*

Her father was probably as spry as a colt. She had gone to her parents' home to hide the stolen jewels.

"Where do her parents live, Jimmy?"

"How should I know? You're the one who claimed to be her brother."

Ethan offered no response.

"They're in the country somewhere. She might have told me once, but I don't remember. None of the towns outside of Boston mean anythin' to me; their names all run together in my head. I think she said somethin' about the Middle Road to Dedham, but that's all I know."

Ethan knew that he would have to speak again with the girl, which meant another visit to Paxtons' house. But already there were journeymen standing on the street in front of the rope yard, across the lane from the Paxton house. They were staring toward Ethan and Jimmy. And every one of them held a cudgel. Moreover, Paxton was probably at the Customs House by now, and he had made it clear he did not want Ethan visiting his home when he wasn't present.

"You should get back in the barracks."

Fleming climbed to his feet, and following the direction of Ethan's gaze with his pale eyes, pulled himself up to his full height.

"I can get the others," he said.

Ethan put a hand on his chest, stopping him from going inside. "No. Go back to where I found you, and play cards. The last thing we need is another fight."

"They're the ones who have been causin' trouble."

Ethan wasn't about to get in an argument over which group had been more to blame for the brawling he had witnessed in the last two days, especially since he knew that he himself bore as much responsibility as anyone.

"Just go back to your friends."

"What's goin' to happen to me?" Jimmy asked. "Are you plannin' to bring the sheriff back here?"

"Mister Paxton hired me to recover the goods you stole. You haven't got them right now, at least that's what you tell me . . ."

"It's the truth!"

"I believe you," Ethan said. And he did. Everything Fleming had told him, aside from his initial denial, had the ring of truth to it. "I have an interest in finding what was stolen. When I do that, I get paid. I can turn you over to Sheriff Greenleaf—and I will if it turns out that you've been lying to me. But there's no profit in that. The profit lies in finding those jewels. Do you understand what I'm telling you?"

"Aye," Jimmy said, sounding wary.

Ethan looked up the road again. At least a half dozen journeymen were walking toward them. "Good. Now get inside."

Fleming nodded and stepped back into the barracks. Ethan cast one last glance up the road and hurried back toward his room in the South End. He hadn't gone far, though, when he changed his mind and headed instead to Boston's Neck and Janna Windcatcher's tavern. He didn't wish to put Janna and her establishment at risk, but he had no idea how to combat the conjurings that followed him around the city, and if anyone could help him find a way to defend himself, it was Janna.

The closer Ethan drew to the Fat Spider, the more difficult it became to walk on the icy road. This far out toward the town gate, Orange Street saw relatively little traffic, especially with fewer merchants coming into the city from outlying towns. By the time Ethan reached the tavern, his bad leg ached, and despite the cold he was sweating within his greatcoat.

He pulled the door open and entered, but then halted inside the door so that his eyes might adjust to the dim light of the tavern. Before he could see well enough to spot Janna, he heard her speak his name, drawing it out like an imprecation.

Ethan could barely make out the details in the great room. A fire burned in the hearth, and about a third of the tables in the tavern appeared to be occupied. Janna stood near the bar, a cloth in one hand, her other fist set against her hip.

"Well, come on," she said. "You'll want an ale an' a bowl of stew, an' the answers to a whole lot o' questions. Isn' that right?"

"It is."

He crossed to the bar, pulling off his greatcoat as he did. Janna disappeared into the kitchen only to return again a few seconds later bearing a steaming bowl of stew. It smelled of cinnamon and pepper and made his mouth water. Only now did he remember that he had eaten nothing all day.

He made quick work of that first serving and asked Janna for a second rather sheepishly. She retreated to the kitchen to refill the bowl.

"Where you been now that you're so hungry?" she asked after placing it in front of him again. "Ain't your woman feedin' you?"

"I stayed away from her tavern last night," Ethan said, keeping his voice low. "To be honest, I was afraid to come here."

"Why?"

"Do you remember what we talked about the last time I came?"

"Those spells you was feelin', the ones that made other people act crazy."

"That's right."

"I've been feelin' a lot of conjurin's the past few days. I assumed they were yours."

"Some of them have been, but not all. Not nearly."

"That conjurer still messin' with you?"

"Everywhere I go. Have people here been talking about the brawl at Gray's Rope Works?"

"The one yesterday?"

"Aye. There was another one today. I have a new client who lives across the street from the ropewalks. Those spells caused the brawls. Several days ago, I was almost stabbed by a laborer on Long Wharf, and yesterday two men attacked me in the Crow's Nest."

"And it was spells that did it each time?"

"Aye."

"So you came to ask me questions."

Ethan ducked his head. "I'm sorry, Janna. I'll pay for the food and ale, of course. And I can pay you as well for whatever you can—"

She laid a slender hand on his arm and shook her head.

"Not for this. You're in trouble."

"Thank you."

"You already tried to see the spell color, right?"

"Yes, several times. But whoever is doing this has hidden it well. Yesterday, I warded myself, and that seemed to work for a while. But then the conjurer cast a different spell, or a stronger one, and overcame my warding."

She raised her eyebrows. "Your wardin'?"

Janna straightened and indicated with a small, sharp gesture that he should follow her back into the kitchen. He walked around the bar and joined her in the small space. It was warmer here, and the aroma of her stew was far stronger.

Janna sat on a low stool near the cooking fire while Ethan perched on an old wine barrel.

"Now, what's this about a wardin'? Wardin' yourself from what?"

"From the conjurings," Ethan said. "I came to ask if you know of any way to keep another conjurer from using your power against your will?"

"So, are you tellin' me that these spells are comin' from you?"

"Aye. Every time one is cast, my ghost appears."

"But you're not castin' them?"

"Of course not."

She exhaled through her teeth, the breath coming out as a low hiss. "Damn, Kaille. That's not good at all."

"Has anything similar ever been done to you?"

"No," she said. "I've heard other folks tell of it, but I ain't never even known anyone who had it done to them. You say your wardin' worked for a while?"

"It worked once," Ethan said, his gut knotting. "Whoever is casting these spells tried something different and ripped through my warding like it was parchment."

Janna pursed her lips, her dark eyes trained on the fire. "Maybe the last time we talked I was too quick to say it's not Ramsey."

Rather than frightening him more, this admission on Janna's part came as some small relief. At least he wasn't the only person to sense the captain's scheming in these conjurings.

"He can find me anywhere—at least that's how it feels. I think he might have other conjurers working for him."

"That sounds like Ramsey."

"He has me hiding in my room, Janna. I'm afraid to go anywhere lest I start another brawl or get someone else killed."

"You didn' get anyone killed!" she said, her tone fierce. "And you didn' start any brawls either. That's Ramsey's doin'. Or whoever is castin' these spells. It ain't your fault, and thinkin' it is, well that's what Ramsey wants."

Ethan knew she was right. "How do these spells work?" he asked. "How can he have access to my power without my knowing it?"

"Usually, for magicking like this, he would need to have somethin' of yours. Best is somethin' from you—a lock of hair, a bit of your blood. Failin' that, he might have a piece of clothin' or somethin' that belonged to you. Anythin' that he can use to connect to you and your conjurin' power. After that, it's a matter of knowin' the right words, that's all."

"I was unconscious on his ship last summer—I don't know for how long. But he could have taken anything from me."

"Sounds like he did."

"Can I stop him?"

"I would have told you to ward yourself. If that ain't strong enough . . ." She shrugged. "There's other kinds of wardin' spells. You might wanna try some of them."

"I don't know them."

"Well, it's time you started learnin' more advanced spells. You can guard yourself from all sorts of magick. Like I say, it's just knowin' the words."

Ethan nodded, although he had no idea where to start looking for new spells to cast.

Janna leaned forward and patted his knee. "It's all right, Kaille. I've got some books you can borrow. You might find somethin' in them."

"Thank you, Janna."

"What bothers me is not knowin' for sure if it's Ramsey." She shook her head. "I never learned to hide my power that way—don't suppose I ever needed to. But you're sure that you're doin' your reveal spells right?"

"Aye, that spell I know. There was no residue on Richardson after he shot the boy or on Sephira's man after he beat that lad who had robbed Josiah Wells."

Janna winced, shaking her head once more and clicking her tongue. "Of course there wasn't. He's castin' these spells on you. That's where the color should be. On you."

"No," Ethan said. "I cast a *revela* spell on myself as well, after another conjurer used a finding spell against me. It revealed the residue from his spell, but nothing else. Believe me, Janna. If Ramsey's power had left a mark on me, I'd have noticed it. I know that color as well as I know my own."

"Let me try."

"But if my spell—"

"Be quiet and cut yourself," Janna said.

Ethan drew his knife, his pulse pounding, his stomach tight. He dragged the blade over his forearm, and as blood flowed from the wound, he dipped his finger in it and drew a line across his brow and down the bridge of his nose, over his chin, to his breastbone.

"*Revela omnias magias ex cruore evocatas,*" Janna said. Reveal all magicks, conjured from blood.

Her spell sang in the wood walls and the stone hearth, and her ghost, a glowing blue image of an old African woman, appeared beside her. A wash of cool air swept over Ethan's face as the blood vanished, and Janna took a quick, sharp breath.

He didn't want to look down, but what choice did he have?

His first reaction was one of revulsion—he imagined that this must have been how a smallpox victim felt upon noticing the first pustules of the distemper on his chest.

He was covered in the glow of another man's power. It shone from his chest, his gut, his limbs. Judging from the way Janna gaped at him, he assumed that it was all over his face.

The glow was unmistakable: a deep aqua, the color of the ocean on a clear, sunlit morn. Once, this had been among his favorite hues, a reminder of the years he had spent at sea, before the *Ruby Blade* mutiny and his conviction. Now it was the color of apprehension and uncertainty, of torment and pain. It was the color of Nate Ramsey's conjuring power. And it covered him like disease.

He slashed his knife across his forearm, drawing fresh blood. "Cast the counterspell, Janna. I don't want to see this."

She nodded, swallowed. "*Vela omnias magias,*" she said, her voice low. "*Ex cruore evocatas.*" Conceal all magicks, conjured from blood.

The glow of Ramsey's power began to fade, dying away slowly as Ethan watched. He wanted to shout at the magick, to make it vanish that very moment, but the spell Janna had cast didn't work that way. And truth be told, it mattered not. Now that he knew it was there, he could almost feel the captain's conjurings on him. His skin crawled with them.

When at last the glow of the spells had disappeared, Janna raised her gaze to his. She opened her mouth to speak, but stopped herself with a small shake of her head. At last she stood and smoothed her dress with the palm of her hand.

"I'll find you those books," she said, and left him.

Chapter
FIFTEEN

*J*anna returned several minutes later bearing three small volumes, all of them leather-bound and worn.

Ethan hadn't moved. Janna eyed him for several seconds before placing the books on the barrel beside him.

"Why would your spell work that way when mine didn't?" Ethan asked her, his voice taut.

"I don't know. But if he's found a way to use your power the way he would his own, hiding those conjurin's from you would be easy. Know what I mean?"

Ethan was far beyond his depth; his knowledge of spellmaking had not prepared him for anything like this. But he sensed that she was right, that if Ramsey could turn his magick against him in this way, concealing the residue of his spells would be a small matter. He picked up the books and examined their spines.

"I don't know what you'll find in those," she said. "But they're the best I've got. If you can't find it in one of them . . . Well, I think you probably can."

"My thanks, Janna." He stood, his legs feeling leaden. "I should go before he casts again and starts a fight in your tavern."

"You have mullein?" she asked.

"Aye. A pouch full of it."

"That's good. Ain't nothin' better for protection spells. You should have some betony and horehound, too. Spells in those books might call for them."

"All right. I'll have a pouch of each. How much will that cost?"

"A few shillin's is all." She was staring at the fire again; Ethan sensed that she was afraid to look him in the eye. "Maybe you should leave Boston. Just until you figure out how to beat him."

"Kannice said much the same thing."

"She's a smart woman."

"I have a job here. I need to finish it." As soon as he spoke the words, though, it occurred to Ethan that his job could well take him out of the city to the home of Louisa's parents. He balked at the very idea of it. Not because he couldn't leave Boston, but because he didn't want to. Or rather, because he refused to be driven from the city.

"For all I know, he wants me to leave," Ethan said, his words filling a growing silence. "Perhaps that's been his goal all along."

"His goal is to see you dead, and to take as many other people with you as he can. Clearly he's alive, but I'd wager every coin in my till that there's nothin' left of him but skin and bones and hate. And magick. I understand you not wantin' to leave. Your woman's here. Your friends are here. But don't tell me you're stayin' for a job. You're stayin' because you wanna fight him, and you don't wanna run."

"Aye," Ethan said. "That's it precisely. I don't want to run. I refuse."

Janna studied him, her expression as hard as obsidian. "All right then. When it comes time to fight him again, you know where to find me."

Ethan had to smile. "I do. And I'm grateful to you, Janna."

She waved away his gratitude as if it were a fly. "Let me get them herbs for you."

Janna left the the kitchen once more. Ethan picked up the books and followed her. His pulse had slowed, and an odd calm had settled over him like a cloak. The surety that Ramsey was in fact alive and back in Boston, the weight of Janna's books in his hand, his resolve not to leave the city until he had found and defeated Ramsey: All of these served to quiet his mind. He remained afraid of the harm Ramsey might do with one of his spells, and he still felt as though he were corrupted and diseased by the man's spells. But he would not surrender to Ramsey or to his conjurings, and he clung to that determination to fight the way he would a spar of wood in a storm-roiled sea.

"Here you go," Janna said, presenting him with a pair of fragrant pouches. "That's betony on the left and horehound on the right. If you forget which one is which, remember that betony is sweeter, horehound more bitter."

"Thank you, Janna. How much do I owe you?"

"Four shillin's."

Ethan pulled five shillings from his pocket and handed the coins to her. "That's for my supper and ale as well."

Janna glanced at them and slipped them into the folds of her dress. "I meant what I said. When it comes time to fight, you find me. Understand?"

"I will."

He reached for his tankard, which still sat on the bar next to his half-empty bowl of stew, and drained what was left of his ale. He picked up his hat, pulled on his greatcoat, and left the Spider for the cold.

Ethan knew that Kannice would be concerned about him, wondering where he was, but he returned to his room on Cooper's Alley, and after restarting the fire in his stove, he sat on his bed and began to thumb through the first of Janna's books.

He searched for any mention of a spell that enabled a conjurer to use the power of another, regardless of whether the second speller gave his consent for such a conjuring. Finding nothing in the first book, he tossed it aside and picked up the second, a volume titled *Spells and Incantations of the Necromancers*, which had been published in London in 1632. Ethan leafed through this book, once again finding nothing that could help him. He was about to give up on this one and look at the third book when he came upon a page describing "The borrowed incantation."

He sat up and lit a candle. And then he read.

It was not exactly what Ethan was looking for, but one line in the book's description of the spell caught his eye. "The borrowed incantation enables one witch to use the power of another to accomplish what he might not on his own."

There was no mention of the "borrowed incantation" in the remaining pages of the book, nor did he find mention of it when he again scanned the first book.

But the third volume, *A Collection of Spells and Conjurings*, devoted pages to it. According to the author, a man named Thaddeus Beralt, conjurers might borrow spells from allies or steal them from foes. He seemed to assume that this "borrowing" would always take place in the context of conjuring battles and would require that one conjurer be in close proximity to another. But in every other way, what he described resembled what Ramsey had been doing with Ethan's power.

"A determined necromancer might pilfer magick from another with ease provided that the second witch is unaware of what the first intends, and has taken no precautions against such violation."

Ethan frowned at this and searched adjacent pages for other references to the precautions a conjurer might take. He found none.

Returning to the beginning of the volume, he scanned each yellowed, brittle page with more care. Outside, the sky darkened; eventually Ethan had to light additional candles. He found several references to warding spells, as well as to herbs that might be used to enhance a "witch's" protection. To Janna's credit, mullein, betony, and horehound were mentioned more often than any other herbs.

But Ethan reached the end of the book without finding anything more about conjurings intended specifically to prevent the borrowing or theft of magick by another speller.

"*Veni ad me.*" Come to me.

An instant later, Reg stood over him, gleaming balefully in the small room. Ethan opened the second book to the page on which borrowed spells were mentioned and held it up for the ghost to see.

"Have you heard of these conjurings?" he asked.

Reg scanned the page, his bushy eyebrows bunched. Looking at Ethan again, he nodded.

"This is what Ramsey is doing to me, isn't it?"

The ghost hesitated, and when at last he nodded it was with some reluctance.

"Something similar, perhaps?"

Yes.

"Do you know how I can stop him from casting these spells? Is there a way to deny him use of my power?"

He knew from Reg's forlorn expression that the ghost would shake his head.

"But this book—" He picked up the third text and riffled the pages until he found the correct one. "It mentions 'precautions against such violation.' That must mean that there are wardings I can put in place, spells I can cast to keep him from using me in this way."

Reg opened his hands. *I don't know.*

"Very well," Ethan said. "*Dimitto te.*" I release you.

Once Reg was gone, he reached for the first book once more and began to read the volume more closely from the first page.

He stayed awake for much of the night and read through all three of Janna's books. Though he found a few more pages on which borrowed spells were mentioned, most of these were passing references. He read nothing that told him how to protect himself from Ramsey. When at last he lay down to sleep, he was as frustrated as he had been before studying the texts, and only slightly more knowledgeable.

His sleep was fitful and he roused himself with first light so that once more he could pay a visit to the Paxton mansion. He followed the same circuitous route to the commissioner's estate, but while he avoided the barracks this way, he did nothing to fool Ramsey. Even as he approached Paxton's door, a spell growled in the earth beneath him. He knocked on the door, gazing back at the rope yard and then down the street toward Green's Barracks as he did. But he saw neither soldiers nor journeymen. It almost seemed that the captain was toying with him, casting the spells for the sheer purpose of scaring Ethan. Reg had appeared beside him, but he spared Ethan not a glance. He, too, was watching for soldiers.

To Ethan's relief, Paxton answered his knock before Ramsey could cast a second spell.

"Mister Kaille," the commissioner said, clearly surprised to see Ethan on his doorstep once more. "I didn't expect you today."

The commissioner was dressed in a black silk coat and breeches.

Belatedly Ethan realized that it was Sunday morning and that Paxton and his wife would be on their way to church before long.

"No, sir. Please forgive the intrusion."

"Do you have news for me?"

"I believe I do. I was hoping I might come in and speak once more with your servant."

Paxton's expression darkened. "If you mean Louisa, I'm afraid that's impossible. She's gone."

A wave of nausea crashed over Ethan. "Gone where?" he asked, though of course he knew what Paxton would say.

"I've no earthly idea. She stole away sometime during the night. When my wife and I awoke this morning, she had already gone and had taken all of her things. Her room is completely empty."

"This is my fault," Ethan said, removing his hat and raking clawed fingers through his hair.

"Your fault? What do you mean?"

He donned his hat once more and looked Paxton in the eye. "Louisa and Private Fleming were working together. Her tears yesterday were a ruse, as was her visit with her infirm parents. I believe she has the stolen items hidden in their home."

"I'm deeply sorry to hear that," Paxton said. "But in what way is this your fault."

"I spoke to Fleming yesterday and wrung the truth from him. I should have called the sheriff straightaway, but I didn't think that Fleming would desert, nor did I believe that Louisa would run off. I assumed that I would have this chance to confront her."

Paxton's frown had deepened. "I must tell you that I'm disappointed, Mister Kaille. Geoffrey Brower led me to believe that you were a skilled thieftaker. I expected better from you."

"And you shall have it, sir. You have my word."

"What will you do?"

"What is Louisa's family name?"

"Allen. At least this is what she told me."

"And where is her parents' home?"

"She said it was in Medfield, but you have proved her false, Mister Kaille. Shouldn't we assume that everything she told me was a lie?"

"Not necessarily, sir. Sometimes a succession of small truths can conceal a larger falsehood. And Fleming mentioned to me that her parents' home was along the Middle Road."

"I have little personal experience with such things and so have no choice but to place my trust in you again. But I do so reluctantly."

"I understand, sir," Ethan said, starting away from the door. "But I swear to you that your property will be found."

Ethan didn't wait for a reply, nor did he tarry by the rope yard, though he could see that once more Ramsey's spell had drawn soldiers and journeymen into the ice-covered lane.

He left Hutchinson's Street at its south end, and followed Cow Lane down to Summer Street. Soon, he stood again before the entrance to Sephira Pryce's mansion. Afton opened the door this time, and glowered down at him.

"What do you want now?"

"I need to speak with Sephira."

The brute set his jaw and Ethan thought he would refuse and send him away. But then he said, "Right then, wait here," drawling the words. Though he closed the door, Ethan could hear him lumber through the house.

He pulled the door open again moments later and held out his hand. Ethan handed over his knife and his pouches of herbs. Sephira's man eyed these dubiously, but gestured for Ethan to enter. After shutting the door once more, he led Ethan into the common room, where Sephira stood before a blazing fire. She wore a dress of dark blue satin, rather than her usual breeches and waistcoat. He had to admit that she looked even more beautiful than usual. But while her garb was different, the amused, somewhat mocking expression on her face was all too familiar. Nap, Gordon, and Mariz stood nearby, looking far more grim than she.

"Ethan. What a surprise. You're starting to make a habit of this. Does your little friend with the tavern know how much time we've been spending together?"

"Good day, Sephira."

"Have you come to speak with me, or with Mariz?"

"With you," Ethan said. "I have a business proposition for you."

She considered him briefly, then gestured toward the chair next to hers. Ethan removed his greatcoat and sat.

"A business proposition," she repeated. "Explain yourself, and do it quickly, please; I was about to make my way to the meeting house."

Of course; that would explain the dress. Ethan could hardly imagine Sephira attending church. He considered saying as much, but thought better of it.

"I was hired by Charles Paxton to retrieve some jewels that were pinched from his home."

"Yes, I'd heard," she said. "I hadn't yet decided whether or not to let you keep that job. Paxton isn't as wealthy as Josiah Wells, but he is a man of some means. I would have preferred that he come to me."

Ethan smiled. "Well, then this should be rather simple. You can have the job. I'll even tell you where to find the jewels, so that you can collect the balance of what he owes me."

"Why would you do this?"

"Because I have more important matters to which to attend. I can't take the time to retrieve Paxton's property."

Sephira bristled. "And so you thought to give me your castoffs? Of all the impudent . . . I should have Nap and Gordon here beat you bloody."

"Forgive me, Sephira. I phrased that poorly. Under most circumstances, I would gladly get the jewels myself, but I can't now. It's not that I have a better job; it's that my life is in danger, and I can't afford to leave Boston right now."

This seemed to do little to mollify her. "We would have to leave Boston?"

"Aye. Paxton was robbed by a soldier named Jimmy Fleming, a private with the Twenty-ninth. But he was working with one of Paxton's servants. Her name is Louisa Allen. According to Fleming, she has the jewels hidden at her parents' home in Medfield. Louisa left the Paxton home last night—I assume that Jimmy is with her, though I could be mistaken. In any case, we haven't much time. She must know that Jimmy told me where she took the jewels; she won't remain there for long."

"How much is Paxton paying you?"

"He gave me two pounds ten when I began my inquiry. Upon returning the jewels to him, he'll pay another four and ten."

"Seven pounds," Sephira said, raising an eyebrow. "You're learning, Ethan." She picked up a goblet from a small table beside her chair and sipped her wine. "Still, I'm not sure it would be worth our time to travel all the way out to Medfield for a mere four and ten."

"You want me to give you more?"

"I want you to *tell* me more," she said, still holding the wineglass.

"I've told you everything that—"

"Not about Paxton and his servant. I want to know what or who has you so fearful that you would offer me coin we both know you need."

He remained wary of telling her that Ramsey was back in Boston— she hated the man too much. He didn't trust her not to get herself killed, and Ethan and others along with her. He didn't know, however, that he could convince her to help him without telling her.

"It's a private matter, Sephira."

She shook her head. "It ceased to be private the moment you walked into my home."

"Isn't it enough to say that—"

"I want the truth—all of it. And you're going to tell me, because you need my help even more than you need that four pounds ten. We both know that you wouldn't come to me unless you had a good deal at stake." She regarded him through narrowed eyes. "I would surmise that you learned the truth of what had happened but didn't act soon enough. Thus, you let this soldier and his girl escape Boston, and then you had to admit as much to Paxton. Which means that your reputation as a thieftaker is at risk." She sipped her wine again. "Do I have it right so far?"

"Don't you always?"

Her smile was radiant. "Yes, I do. Now, tell me what this about."

Ethan kept silent as he considered his options. The truth was, he had precious few.

Apparently, Sephira misinterpreted his silence. "Very well. Retrieve the jewels on your own. Nap, Gordon, I believe it's time for Ethan to leave."

The two men took a step toward him.

"Ramsey is back."

Sephira raised a hand, and her toughs froze where they were, her single gesture as powerful in this house as a spell. "Nate Ramsey?" she asked, ice in her voice.

"Aye."

"You are certain of this?" Mariz asked. "You have suspected—"

"I'm certain. He's been using me to cast spells, including the one that made Gordon attack Will Pryor."

"You knew about this?" Sephira demanded of Mariz.

"He knew nothing," Ethan said, drawing her gaze. "When last Mariz and I spoke, I mentioned that the spells being used against me were the sort that Ramsey might try. But it was conjecture; that's all. Only yesterday did I determine that he is in fact alive and in Boston once more."

Again, Sephira appeared dissatisfied with his assurances. And no doubt this exchange was further eroding her trust in Mariz.

"What is it he wants?" Sephira asked.

"He wants to hurt me; his ultimate goal, no doubt, is to see me dead. But he's in no rush to kill me. Right now he is using my power to cast spells that make others behave violently. I've been the cause of brawls between soldiers and workers, I've been attacked, I might well bear some responsibility for the death of Christopher Seider.

"He wants to make me an exile in my own city; he wants me to doubt my every action, and he wants me fearful not only for my own life but for those of the people I love. Once he's accomplished all of that, he'll come to finish me."

"Do you know where he is?" Mariz asked.

"No. I've searched the waterfront for his ship, and several days ago I tried a finding spell. But until Ramsey wants to be found, his location will remain a secret."

"I'll help you kill him," Sephira said.

"Before this is over, I'll be grateful for your help. For right now, though, I would ask that you retrieve Paxton's jewels."

She made an impatient gesture, nearly spilling her wine. "We'll see to that today. What shall I do with the soldier and the girl?"

Ethan hadn't even considered this. "To be honest, Sephira, I don't care."

"Well, now I know that Ramsey has you scared."

"Aye," Ethan said.

"I assume you'll wish to consult with Mariz. Until Ramsey is dead you have my leave to do so whenever necessary."

It was Ethan's turn to cock an eyebrow. "I guess you're scared of him as well."

"I fear no man. But I do want the bloody bastard dead."

"That's a common sentiment where Ramsey is concerned. Thank you, Sephira." To Afton he said, "I'll need my blade and my herbs."

Afton held them up, but Mariz took them from him, and turning to Ethan said, "I will see you out."

With one last nod to Sephira, Ethan picked up his hat and coat and walked back to the foyer. Mariz followed.

"What are these spells Ramsey is using against you?" the conjurer asked, handing Ethan his knife and the leather pouches.

"Have you ever heard of borrowed spells?"

"Borrowed?"

"The translation to Portuguese might not be exact. In essence, Ramsey has found a way to use my power to cast spells, regardless of distance or simple wardings. The residue of his conjurings is all over me, and so far I've not been able to do a damned thing to stop him."

"So he is using conjurings to make you cast spells for him—spells you do not wish to cast. Is that right?"

"Aye, that's close enough."

Mariz removed his spectacles and rubbed the lenses with a handkerchief. "Last time we spoke, I might have been too quick to say that I had never heard of such things. Your phrase—'borrowed spells'—has stirred a memory. There is a kind of conjuring, one that I heard mentioned back in my country, long ago. We call them stolen spells, but I believe they involve the same magick."

"Stolen spells sounds more apt. Do you know how to prevent them? Is there a warding that you can teach me?"

"I am not certain. There may be something. I have a teacher, a man back in Lisbon who taught me much about casting. I can ask him."

"Not by letter, Mariz. I haven't time."

"I understand. I will find out what I can."

"My thanks."

Ethan pulled open the door and stepped out onto the portico.

"Kaille, have you considered——?"

"Leaving Boston?"

Mariz nodded. "I see that you have. But you have decided to stay."

"What would you do? Would you allow yourself to be hounded from your home?"

The conjurer gave a small shake of his head, his spectacles catching the glare from outside. "You and the *senhora* are much alike in many ways."

"Thank you, Mariz," he said, his tone dry. "That's what I wanted to hear."

Mariz grinned before pushing the door shut.

Chapter
SIXTEEN

*I*t being Sunday morning, the streets were relatively empty. Ethan took advantage of the circumstance by following Summer Street to the edge of the Common and then walking up Common Street to Treamount and finally on to Sudbury and the Dowsing Rod.

As he neared the tavern, he saw Kannice emerge from within, a red woolen cape draped over shoulders, her auburn hair shining in the morning sun. She locked the door and turned to make her way toward the West Meeting House. Noticing him, she halted.

They stood thus for what seemed an age. Kannice's expression remained grave.

"You're alive," she said, breaking the hard silence.

"Aye."

"I would have liked to know that. I would have liked to know something."

"I didn't . . ." He shook his head, unsure of exactly what he had intended to say.

"You didn't what? Didn't stop to think that perhaps I'd be concerned? Didn't take the time to send a note or get word to someone?"

She walked to where he stood, eyeing him critically, her gaze lingering on the spot where Fleming had hit him: a bruise he had forgotten to heal.

"You don't look so bad," she said at last. "Have you been hurt? In gaol? Held captive by Sephira Pryce?"

"None of those, no."

"Then what's happened to you, Ethan? Where have you been for the past two nights?"

"Cooper's Alley, alone in my room."

"Why?"

"Because I'm afraid of what might happen if I'm in your tavern with a crowd of men. Because I don't trust my conjuring power anymore. Because Nate Ramsey is alive and back in Boston, and everywhere I go he's using me—my power—to wreak havoc."

She canted her head to the side, her brow creasing. "I'm sorry. That's . . . You're sure it's Ramsey?"

"Aye, beyond doubt."

A church bell began to toll to the north and west. Kannice looked over her shoulder and then faced Ethan again, an apology in her blue eyes.

"I have to go."

"I know. I'm sorry, Kannice. You're right. I should have . . . I should have gotten word to you somehow, even if just to say that I was all right and that I was missing you."

"It doesn't sound like you're all right. Why did you come here?"

"I thought it would be safe, at least for a while. And I wanted to see you."

She smiled at that. Glancing once more toward the church, she pulled out her key and handed it to him. "Go inside. Wait for me. I'll be back in an hour or so."

He took the key from her; he wanted to kiss her, but he sensed that she didn't want him to, which was something new and entirely unwelcome in their relationship. "All right," he said. "Thank you."

Her gaze lingered on his for a second longer. Then she turned and hurried away.

Ethan let himself into the tavern. A fire burned low in the hearth, and the great room smelled faintly of chowder and fresh bread. He removed his gloves and coat, put another log on the fire, and pulled a chair up in front of the hearth.

She had every right to be angry with him; he knew this. There was no shortage of ways he might have let her know that he was safe—he could even have sent an illusion spell to her. She deserved such consideration given all that she did for him, and all that she had endured in their years together.

He sensed, though, that she wanted more from him, or else nothing at all. She had made no secret of her wishes: She wanted him to give up thieftaking and his room over Henry's shop, to live with her here at the Dowser and help her run the tavern. She had never said that she wished to marry, at least not in so many words. But that might have been because he had made clear to her years ago that he never had any intention of marrying.

Once more he thought of the night more than a week before when he had seen her at the bar, laughing with a stranger. He didn't doubt the love they shared, nor did he think that she would ever cuckold him. But perhaps she had started to imagine for herself a different life, one in which the absence of her man from her bed didn't make her worry that he had been killed in the streets of Boston. She was as beautiful now as the day he met her, and still young enough to bear children. He didn't know if she wanted that; he had never thought to ask, and she knew him too well to bring it up.

He was still sitting and staring at the flames, ruminating on all of this, when Kannice returned from church. He stood as she came inside. She faltered at the sight of him, but then she walked behind the bar, hung her cape on a hook, and tied her hair back.

"Have you eaten anything?" she asked.

"No."

"What can I fix for you? I'm going to have some eggs and ham."

"I'm not really hungry."

"You're saying that to save me work. It's no trouble." Her smile was too bright, too brittle.

"I thought you'd want to talk," Ethan said.

"That's all right. I'm sorry for the way I spoke to you earlier. I shouldn't have said those things." She pointed toward the kitchen. "I'm going to have some breakfast. You should have something."

"You were right to say what you did. And I want to talk to you about it."

Her smile faded. Ethan pulled another chair from a nearby table and set it next to his own before the hearth.

"Come sit with me."

Kannice's cheeks had gone pale. She joined him by the fire and sat, her hands folded in her lap, her gaze fixed on the flames. They said nothing for several minutes; Ethan thought that he ought to start the conversation, but he wasn't sure how to begin.

"Some nights back," he began, "when I was still working for Lillie, I was here, sitting with Diver and Deborah, and I saw you speaking with another man."

She looked at him. "I speak with lots of men."

"I know that. This one was young and handsome; he made you laugh. And—"

"Do you think I'm interested in another man, and that's why I said those things to you?"

He shook his head. "No. But it made me think that you could do better than to spend your time with me."

She started to object, but he raised a finger to his lips.

"Do you want children, Kannice?"

Her eyes went wide. "Children? Dear Lord, Ethan, what were you thinking about while I was gone?"

His cheeks warmed. "You. The two of us. Do you want children?"

She gazed at him for some time before heaving a sigh and turning back to the fire. "There was a time when I did. Rafe and I spoke of having children. We were very young and newly married, and having children was what a young, newly married girl was supposed to do."

"And now?"

"And now I'm thirty-two and a widow and I own a tavern, and I don't know how I would fit children into my life." She reached over and took his hand. "But, Ethan, I wasn't angry with you this morning because I want children, any more than I was angry with you because I want another man in my life. I have the man I want."

"But . . . ?"

She took a breath. "But I want a different life with him than the one we have now. And I'm not sure he wants the same thing."

"You want me to give up thieftaking."

He thought she would demur, but her gaze remained steady as she said, "Yes."

Ethan looked away. "It's been hard recently, I know."

"It's always hard. If it's not Sephira Pryce trying to kill you, it's Ramsey, or Simon Gant, or Caleb Osborne, or half a dozen others I can think of off the top of my head. When I heard nothing from you two nights ago, I was worried. When you didn't show up last night, I thought . . . I thought you might be dead." Tears glistened in her eyes. "I'm not sure how much longer I can live with that kind of fear."

"I'm good at what I do. I've been thieftaking for ten years now, and I haven't been killed even once."

A choked laugh escaped her, but then she sobered once more. "You can't stay young forever."

"I'm not sure I'm young now."

She smiled, offering no reply, her silence a pointed acquiescence.

Ethan laughed. "You could argue a little."

"Why bother when you're making my argument for me?"

Ethan lifted Kannice's hand to his lips. "You know that even if I decide to go into the tavern business, I can't simply stop thieftaking right now. Ramsey is out there, and he won't forgo his vengeance because I happen to change professions."

"I understand."

"And if I start living here, working here, spending every minute with you, you might find that you don't care for me as much as you thought."

"I've considered the possibility," Kannice said, eyes dancing.

"And . . . ?"

"I'm willing to take my chances."

He nodded, looked at the fire.

"Are you truly considering this?" she asked.

"Aye. If the alternative is losing you, then I'll give up thieftaking."

She stared at him, as if seeing him for the first time.

"You're surprised."

"Very," she said. "I didn't think . . ." She shook her head. "It doesn't matter. I'm grateful to you."

"Didn't think what?"

She dropped his hand and stood. "How about that breakfast?"

Ethan caught hold of her again. "You didn't think what, Kannice?"

"I wasn't . . ." Tears welled in her eyes again. "I didn't think you loved me that much," she whispered.

Ethan felt his heart constrict. He stood and took her in his arms. Her sobs shook them both.

"I love you more than I can say," he said, breathing the words into her scented hair. "And the fact that you doubted it . . . I'm sorry; it's my fault."

He held her for what seemed a long time. Her sobs subsided slowly, and at last she pulled away and brushed a strand of hair from her face. Her eyes were red-rimmed and puffy.

"I'm sorry," she said.

"You needn't apologize."

Before they could say more, the tavern door opened and Kelf walked in. Seeing them, he halted, his face turning even redder than the cold had made it.

"G'morning, Kannice. Ethan, it's good to see that you're . . . alive."

"Good day, Kelf," Ethan said.

Kannice grinned. "I think it's time I made breakfast." She gave Ethan a quick kiss and hurried back to the kitchen.

Ethan remained by the fire, watching as Kelf took off his coat and stepped behind the bar. "I suppose I owe you an apology, too."

Kelf shrugged. "It might be helpful if you told her when you plan on stayin' away and when you plan on bein' here. There's only so many ways for a fella to say, 'No, I don't think he's dead,' before it starts to sound insincere."

Ethan chuckled. "Fair enough."

He joined Kannice in the kitchen. She had eggs frying in a pan along with several slabs of bacon.

"I should go," he said.

"Why?" she asked, with equal measures of surprise and disappointment.

"Because the more people who come to the Dowser, the more dangerous it is for me to be here." He glanced toward the great room to make certain that that barkeep wasn't close enough to hear. When he went on, it was in a softer voice. "If Ramsey were to cast another of his spells right now, and Kelf were to attack me, I'd have no choice but to use conjurings against him. I don't want to risk hurting him or you."

"I don't understand this, Ethan. What is it Ramsey is doing? And how are you so sure it's him?"

"I've seen the residue of his conjurings—his color. It's all over me. He's found some way to turn my spellmaking to his purposes, and he's making people attack each other, and attack me. You've heard of the fights over at Gray's Rope Works?"

"Aye. A soldier had his skull fractured there yesterday."

"Damn," Ethan said. "I saw it happen. I made it happen, or rather Ramsey did using my power."

"But that's only one—"

"I was the cause of a brawl on Long Wharf, two men attacked me in the Crow's Nest, and I'm more convinced than ever that I'm to blame for the death of Christopher Seider."

"Even if this is true, Ramsey's to blame, not you."

Janna had told him the same thing. "You're right. But still, staying here is too great a risk."

"When was the last time you ate?" she asked, in a tone he knew all too well.

"Fine. I'll leave after I eat."

He and Kannice ate at the bar as Kelf worked. Kannice offered to feed the barkeep as well, but he assured her that he had eaten. He seemed intent on giving the two of them as much privacy as possible.

Once Ethan had finished eating and had helped Kannice clean up, he put on his coat and gloves, and retrieved his hat.

"You'll be in your room?" Kannice asked.

"Aye."

"And then what?"

"I don't know. I have to find a way to protect myself so that I can search for Ramsey without being the cause of another brawl." *Or another death.*

Her brow had furrowed again. Ethan thought he knew why.

"I can't leave Boston forever," he said. "And when I return, he'll still be here, waiting for me. I have to end it; best I do it now."

"I'm sure you're right," she said, sounding anything but sure.

He put his arms around her and kissed her forehead, hoping to smooth away the creases.

"I don't know when I'll be back, but I'll try to get word to you when I can."

"Yes, all right."

They kissed, and he left. Out on the street again, he thrust his hands in his pockets, lowered his head, and walked as swiftly as his bad leg would allow. He hurried past clusters of soldiers and wended his way through crowds of workers, dreading the touch of a spell or the appearance of Uncle Reg. But he made it back to his room above Henry's shop without incident.

After rekindling his fire, he reached for Janna's books once more and began to read all that he could about warding spells. He soon discovered that the wardings listed in Janna's books were far more sophisticated than the basic warding spell on which he usually relied. According to these texts, there were countless variations of wardings, each of which worked best against certain kinds of spells. If a speller knew that a specific conjuring would be used against him, he could ward himself against that spell. Most of the time, Ethan had no idea what spell his latest foe would use against him, but in this case, with Ramsey back and using borrowed conjurings against him, he knew exactly what he wanted to guard against.

Unfortunately, none of the wardings listed in the books were specific to this sort of conjuring. Eventually, however, as night fell, he began to recognize patterns in the spells these books described, and he wondered if he might create his own warding. The herbs Janna had recommended to him were mentioned again and again in the volumes, convincing Ethan that whatever warding he created should use all three of them.

Holding three leaves of each herb in the palm of his hand, Ethan said, *"Protege meam magiam contra violationem, ex verbasco et marrubio et betonica evocatum."* Protect my magick from violation, conjured from mullein, horehound, and betony.

The spell rang like the harp of God in his walls and floor. Reg stood in front of Ethan, staring avidly at the books and pouches of leaves.

"That was powerful," Ethan said to him. "Don't you agree?"

The ghost nodded.

He pulled out three more leaves from each pouch and held them the same way. "*Protege meam magiam contra violationem, ex his herbis evocatum.*" Protect my magick from violation, conjured from these herbs.

This second conjuring was easier and quicker to say, but when it hummed in the wood around him, it felt far less puissant than had the first version he tried.

"What do you think?" Ethan asked the ghost.

Reg held up one finger. *The first.*

"Aye. That's what I think."

"Teaching yourself wardings. Such diligence."

Ethan jumped up and grabbed for his knife, knocking Janna's books and at least one of the pouches to the floor. He didn't care.

Nate Ramsey stood in his room, arms crossed, a smug smile on his face.

"Easy, Ethan," he said. "If it was really me, you'd be dead already."

Ethan didn't answer, nor did he relax his grip on his blade. But he eyed the figure before him more closely.

It was, he realized, an illusion, created with a conjuring. Ramsey looked just as he had the first time Ethan met him—tall, lean, with a long face and a dark, unruly beard. His eyes were palest blue, and his teeth, bared in a feral grin, were yellow and crooked. He wore a silk shirt, tan breeches, and a bloodred coat.

Ethan knew that this couldn't be what Ramsey looked like now, for he was unmarked, unscarred. And that was impossible. Ramsey was a powerful conjurer—perhaps the most powerful Ethan had encountered in all his years—but during their final battle the previous summer, he had been trapped in a deadly fire, buried beneath flaming rubble. Such an inferno would have killed most men, and there had been times in the intervening months when Ethan had thought—hoped—that the captain must be dead. Even the most skilled conjurer would emerge from such an ordeal with some scars.

"How do I look?" Ramsey's illusion asked, in a voice that was thinner than Ethan remembered, but only a little.

"I was thinking that you look well."

"I did that for your benefit. Thanks to you I'm actually not as handsome as I used to be."

"You started the fire, Ramsey, not I."

The figure shook its head. "Arguing with me already. And here I came to see you and to offer you a gift."

"What gift could you offer to me?"

"The lives of people you love, of course. Think, Kaille. This is going to be a terribly boring conversation if you can't follow along."

"Where are you, Ramsey? This isn't like you—cowering somewhere in hiding, attacking me from afar. Tell me where I can find you and I'll come now. We can settle this today, without anyone else getting hurt."

"I don't think so. I've had a long time to think about our next encounter. I have it all planned. Letting you find me too soon would ruin everything." The figure looked down at the books and the herbs. "I am impressed, though. You must be learning quite a lot."

"Then at least you can tell me where you learned to do borrowed spells?"

A smile split the illusion's face. "I was most proud when I mastered those conjurings. I'd been hearing about them since I was a child, but never knew how they worked until now. Imagine how differently our past battles might have gone had I known then how to cast them."

Ethan suppressed a shudder. "Where, Ramsey?"

The illusion's expression turned stony. "I'm not going to tell you that. Don't mistake me for a fool."

"Thanks to you, a boy is dead. He was all of eleven years old, and in your desperate attempt to avenge yourself on me, you killed him. You might not have pulled the trigger, but his blood is on your hands."

"Let's talk about my gifts for you," the illusion said, as if it hadn't heard.

"Because you don't wish to speak of Christopher Seider?"

"Because I choose what we will discuss!" Ramsey's voice echoed in the small room. "Because if I wanted to I could kill them all, and there would be nothing you could do to stop me! Because I'm giving you . . ." The figure faltered, and when next it spoke, it was in a calmer, softer tone. "A gift."

"Fine, Ramsey. What 'gift' are you offering?"

The smile returned. "A hint, so that you can be prepared when the time comes."

"Prepared for what?"

"Your choice."

"What?"

Ramsey's image merely grinned at him, his pale eyes wide, like those of a child desperate to share a secret.

"You're mad," Ethan said.

"You know better. You understand how dangerous it would be to dismiss me as nothing more than a lunatic."

Ethan had no desire to engage in this pointless battle of words, but he hoped that if he kept Ramsey talking long enough the captain might reveal something of his whereabouts or his intentions.

"Have you used a concealment spell on your ship? Is that why I can't find it?"

"You can't find it—can't find me—because I am not yet ready to be found. You don't seem to understand, Ethan: I control everything. I control you, your magic, your friends. Think of what I've accomplished thus far. You're afraid to go to that tavern your woman owns. You're afraid to walk through the city. You're afraid to do the job you were hired to do. You think I'm mad, and yet here you sit, alone in this small, shabby room, reading books and trying to teach yourself wardings that are destined to fail." The illusion leaned forward. "You can call me mad," it said in a confidential tone, "but I'm winning. Again."

"Perhaps it's time I summoned the spirit of your father, as I did the last time we confronted each other in this room. It angered you then. How would you feel about it now?"

"By all means, make the attempt. Do you honestly believe I failed to anticipate the threat?"

Ethan tried to conceal his disappointment, but knew that he hadn't succeeded. The illusion laughed.

"Was that the only weapon you had? I thought it might be."

The image of Ramsey looked gleeful. If Ethan could have killed him in that moment, he would have done so gladly.

"I think I'll be leaving now. I have much to do and I'm afraid you need to spend a good deal more time with those books of yours. So far, they don't seem to be doing you much good. Remember. Make your choice."

Ethan had no chance to answer. A conjuring rumbled in the wood and a sudden wind whipped through his room, rattling the door and the shutters on his window, and extinguishing the candles, so that an instant later, when the image of Ramsey vanished, the room was plunged into darkness.

The only light came from Uncle Reg, who glowed like a low-hanging moon, the dismay on his face a mirror for Ethan's emotions.

"That spell came from me, didn't it?" Ethan said.

To which the ghost could do naught but nod. Ethan's wardings had failed once more.

Chapter
SEVENTEEN

*H*e had cast not one warding but two, using the herbs from Janna and the wording he had worked out from reading through her books. And still Ramsey had mastered his power as easily as if it were his own.

Ethan lit the candles again and picked up the books off his floor, but though he opened one, he didn't bother to read. He had no idea what to look for in its pages. Muttering a curse, he tossed it aside.

He removed several leaves of mullein from a pouch and, on the off chance that Ramsey had lied to him, tried to summon the spirit of Ramsey's father, Nathaniel Ramsey, whom Nate had tried to bring back from the dead during the summer. The spell thrummed, but the ghost did not answer the summons. Ramsey had told him the truth.

He reached for *A Collection of Spells and Conjurings* and read once more all the pages that mentioned borrowed spells, thinking—hoping—that perhaps he had missed some vital clue that would tell him how Ramsey was using his power. But he learned no more this time than he had all the others. At last, frustrated and weary, he blew out the candles and climbed into bed.

While it took him little time to fall asleep, he awoke at every creak of the building, every whistle of cold wind outside his room. When morning came, he felt no more rested than he had when he went to bed. He sensed that time was running short. Ramsey would not have come to him, even as an illusion, unless he was sure that he could prevail in a battle, and unless he was prepared for their final confrontation.

And yet Ethan had no idea what he ought to do. He hated the thought of "cowering in hiding," as he had so brashly accused Ramsey of doing. But neither did it make sense for him to leave the safety of his room merely for the sake of doing something.

Eventually, hunger drove him out-of-doors. He went to the nearest grocer and bought a small round of cheese and some bread. While he was there, he also took a copy of the week's *Boston Gazette*, which bore this day's date, 5 March 1770. He had thought he might learn more of what had happened to the soldiers and journeymen who fought at Gray's Rope Works. But the newspaper offered no details on the confrontations, except to say, "The particulars of several encounters between the inhabitants and the soldiery the week past we are oblig'd to omit for want of room."

Much of the paper was taken up with descriptions of Christopher Seider's funeral, and further denunciations of Ebenezer Richardson and George Wilmot. Apparently discussions of one tragedy caused by Ramsey and by Ethan's power had taken up so much room that the paper could say nothing more about the other victims of the captain's scheme. Ramsey would have though it an amusing paradox.

Ethan returned to his room, ate his meal, and scoured his mind for answers. None came to him.

But late in the day, as the sky darkened and another clear winter's night settled over the city, Nate Ramsey used a second illusion spell to appear in Ethan's room.

"Still here, eh?" the figure asked. "Still playing with your books and your leaves."

"What do you want, Ramsey?"

"It's time for you to choose."

"I still don't understand what you're talking about."

"That's because you spend too much time alone. I worry about you, Ethan. You need to get out and mingle with the people of Boston."

"Aye, you'd enjoy that wouldn't you?"

"My enjoyment is irrelevant. But perhaps you've met a friend of mine, a soldier." The illusion watched him, avid, expectant.

"What are you playing at?"

"I'm not playing. I'm only pointing out that I don't need for you to be in the streets to do what I have to."

"Morrison," Ethan said in a breathless whisper.

"His name is Daniel. He's a fine lad and a decent conjurer. Not that he'll have to do a thing. I can use his power—I can use anyone's really— the same way I've been using yours. I won't even have to worry about those irksome wardings you've been casting."

"Then do it," Ethan said. "Why should this bother me? As long as you're not using my power again, I don't care."

Ramsey's illusion flashed a delighted smile. "But you do! That's what makes you such a wonderful adversary, Kaille. You do care. You care that innocent people might be killed. You care that one conflict might lead to bloodier ones. But mostly you care about your friends, including that young man who has cast his lot with Samuel Adams and the Sons of Liberty."

Diver. Somehow Ethan was on his feet, a rigid finger leveled at the figure like the barrel of a musket. "If you do anything to hurt him, I swear to God, I'll spend my last breath hunting you down."

"It seems Adams and his rabble have something planned for this evening. I assume that your friend will be there. I know that I'll have friends there." Ramsey's image began to fade. "Time to choose, Kaille."

He still didn't know what Ramsey meant by that last, unless he referred to the choice between remaining in his room while Diver was in peril and putting others at risk by venturing out into the streets to find his friend and protect him. But the captain had made that choice for him. If Morrison would be in the streets, thus allowing Ramsey to cast his spells, then it didn't matter if Ethan was there, too. And he couldn't allow Diver to be hurt or killed.

Ethan decided to go first to the Dowsing Rod. Perhaps he could find Diver before his friend ventured into the lanes to attend whatever assembly Adams had planned for this night.

He paused long enough to cast another warding, this time using more of the herbs than he had the previous night. He held out little hope that the spell could stop Ramsey, but it was worth the attempt.

Then he rushed out into the night, throwing on his greatcoat as he dashed down the wooden stairway and into the street.

Ethan didn't bother with side streets and byways on this night. Ramsey had plans for him and Ethan could do nothing to distract or dissuade him from whatever that larger purpose might be. He walked through crowds and past clusters of soldiers, and for the first night in more than a week, he did not fear the touch of a spell.

Nor did he hesitate to enter the Dowsing Rod when he reached Sudbury Street. The tavern was crowded with Kannice's usual patrons and some whom Ethan did not recognize, but he made his way through the great room without faltering, stepping first to the bar.

"I didn't expect to see you here tonight," Kannice said, favoring him with a brilliant smile.

"I know. But an old friend paid me a visit today."

She heard the catch in his voice, and her smile slipped.

"I use the word 'friend' loosely."

"He came to your room?" she asked in a whisper.

"He used an illusion spell to speak with me. But there's no doubt as to who it was."

"And so it's safe for you again?"

"Not really. He told me that Diver's life is in danger. I'm not sure what twisted game he's playing now, but I need to find Diver and warn him. Is he here?"

"I don't know," she said. "We've been so busy. I'm sorry."

"It's all right. If he's here, I'll find him."

She nodded, fear in her eyes. Ethan gave her hand a quick squeeze, and waded into the crowd, away from the bar.

He searched for Diver at the rear tables, and when he didn't find his friend there, searched the rest of the tavern. But Diver was nowhere to be seen, and neither was Deborah.

Convinced that Diver must be abroad in the city somewhere with the rest of Samuel Adams's followers, Ethan started back toward the tavern door. Kannice had emerged from the kitchen with Kelf, a large tureen of chowder held between them. Ethan caught her eye again and gave a small shake of his head. She frowned, but was then distracted by one of her patrons. She responded with a forced smile before looking at Ethan again. He raised a hand in farewell, and she did the same. Her brow creased once more, and Ethan sensed that she wanted to ask him something, perhaps whether he would be back later in the evening.

She never got the chance.

A powerful conjuring vibrated in the floor of the tavern. Abruptly, Reg was next to him, his eyes as bright as the flames in the tavern's hearth. But Ethan barely noticed the ghost.

Ahead of him, two men started to grapple with each other, one of them shouting curses, the other saying nothing. This second man threw off the first, but then advanced on him again. Another patron shouted a warning. Ethan tried to get to the men before they could hurt anyone. But by now, of course, others in the tavern were crowding around them, eager to get a clear view of the fight.

Another conjuring rumbled and the shouts from in front of him grew more strident, more urgent.

Ethan pushed at the throng, desperate to see what was happening.

Kannice yelled for the men to stop their brawling. Ethan swayed, his heart seeming to stop.

"No!" he shouted. "Kannice get away from them!"

But he had little hope that she could make out his warning above the din.

More shouts echoed in the great room: Kannice's voice once more, and then Kelf's thundering baritone. Ethan clawed through the crowd, pulling men out of his way, pushing between others, ignoring their protests and threats.

At last he could glimpse the combatants ahead of him, though there still were men blocking his way. The silent man remained at the center of it all, and though his first foe was nowhere to be seen, others had stepped in to take his place. Kannice still ordered the men to stop, but to no avail. And she was far too close to the fight for Ethan's comfort.

"Kannice, get away from them!" he called to her again.

She heard him this time. Her gaze flew to his, and her eyes widened. At last it seemed to dawn on her that this was more than a simple tavern brawl.

But even as she tried to edge away toward the kitchen, silver flashed in the candlelight. A knife in the hand of the silent man—the man who had been touched by Ramsey's spell. And Ethan's power.

With one final herculean effort, Ethan pushed past the last of the patrons in his way. And as he did, the silent man plunged his blade into the chest of one of the men he had been fighting. This man dropped to the floor, blood gushing from the wound and spreading like flame over his shirt.

A second man already lay on the floor, unconscious, his face bruised and bloodied. But the knife-wielding stranger wasn't done. Faster than Ethan would have thought possible, he spun away from the man he had stabbed and lunged, leading with an upward stroke of his blade.

Not at Ethan. Not even at Kelf, who had planted himself in front of the man, his huge hands fisted.

But rather at Kannice, who remained barely within his reach.

"*Discuti ex cruore—*"

Before Ethan could finish speaking the shatter spell, Kannice screamed. Kelf hammered a fist into the silent man's temple, knocking him to the floor. But the man's blade remained, jutting downward from below Kannice's breastbone, a crimson stain blossoming around it, darkening her dress.

"Ethan?" she said, half question, half plea, her voice weak.

Ethan caught her as she started to fall. Her eyelids fluttered.

"Ethan," she said again, breathing his name.

"I'm right here. I've got you. Someone call for a surgeon!" he shouted.

The commotion continued; Ethan was vaguely aware of men subduing the stranger while others crowded around the man he had stabbed. But he cared only about Kannice. He carried her back into the kitchen, dropped to his knees, and laid her down on the floor.

"Ethan!" Kelf loomed in the doorway. Kelf, who didn't know that Ethan was a conjurer. "I've sent someone for a doctor. How is she?"

"Get out, Kelf."

"What?"

"Get out. Shut the door."

"Ethan, I'm—"

"*Get out!*" Ethan bellowed, tears hot on his cheeks.

Kelf glared at him, and Ethan was sure he would refuse. But his gaze dropped to Kannice, and the anger drained from his face. He stepped back from the doorway and closed the door.

Ethan looked down at her again. Her trembling pale hands had wandered to the hilt of the knife protruding from her chest. He could see that she was trying to pull it free.

"No," he said, covering her hands with his. "You have to leave it in. Or else you'll bleed—" The words "to death" stuck in his throat. "You'll bleed all over your dress."

"It hurts," she said, tears seeping from the corners of her eyes.

The stain over her heart continued to spread—more slowly than it would have had one of them removed the blade, but inexorably. Her hands had gone cold, and her face was shading toward gray. He had no doubt that the wound would prove fatal if he didn't use a conjuring to save her. Or at least make the attempt. He had never healed a wound as deep and dangerous as this on his own, not even the other day on Long Wharf. He didn't know if he could.

"I know it hurts," he said. He leaned over and touched his lips to her brow. Her skin felt clammy, despite the warmth of the cooking fire beside them. "I'm going to heal you."

"Can you?" she said, the words like the whisper of wind over grass.

"I—I'm sure I can."

"All right."

But he had to remove the knife first. If the spell didn't work fast enough, she would bleed out and die. And Ramsey had access to his power. Could the captain keep him from conjuring? Would he wait until the knife was out, and then keep Ethan from casting his spell?

"I have to pull out the knife to heal you."

"But you said—"

"I know. I'll heal you before . . . It'll be all right. But it's going to hurt when I remove the blade. I need you to be strong, all right?"

He took her hand and squeezed it as he had moments before in the great room. She tried to return the gesture, but the pressure was barely perceptible.

"Are you ready?" he asked.

She mouthed, "Yes."

Ethan closed his eyes and whispered a prayer, something he hadn't done in years. Grasping the hilt of the knife, he pulled it from her chest.

Kannice let out a soft, anguished cry, her back arching. Then she sagged to the floor again. Blood pulsed from the wound, soaking her dress.

He placed his hands over the wound and said, "*Remedium ex cruore evocatum.*" Healing, conjured from blood.

The spell vibrated in the floor and in the stone of the kitchen hearth, and his hand tingled with the power of his conjuring. He glanced at Reg, who knelt beside him, concern etched in his glowing features.

"The spell is working," Ethan said. "I can feel it."

Reg nodded. Kannice murmured something that Ethan couldn't make out. He remained as he was for several minutes, the spell flowing through his hands into her chest, his eyes never straying from her face. But though he could feel the conjuring, he saw no improvement in her color, no strengthening of her breath.

He wore his greatcoat still, and did not dare stop to remove it. So, leaving one hand in place over her heart, he drew his knife, flipped it so that the blade landed in his palm, and wrapped his fingers around the honed edge. Then he tightened his grip on it until he felt the blade bite through his skin. Blood ran through his fingers. He dropped the knife and, placing his bloodied hand over the wound once more, spoke the healing spell a second time.

While this second conjuring still hummed in the tavern floor, the door opened again.

"How is—"

Ethan looked up. Kelf stared at him, openmouthed, murder in his eyes.

"What in the hell are you doin' to her?"

Ethan had hoped to avoid this, but he met the man's gaze steadily, never for an instant allowing his conjuring to slacken. "Close the door."

"Not until you—"

"Close the door, Kelf."

The barman kicked the door so that it shut with a loud bang. Ethan glanced at Kannice, but she did not stir.

"Now tell me what you're doin'."

"I'm saving her life."

"And how in God's name are you doin' that?"

Ethan turned his gaze back to Kannice. "I think you know."

"Never mind what I know an' don't, I want to hear it from you. How are you savin' her?"

"It's called a healing spell. The Latin is *remedium*." He wasn't sure why he said it—Kelf wouldn't care. Perhaps he thought that if he could explain what he did, the barkeep might accept it and put away his fear and his anger. He should have known better.

"Witchery." Kelf said the word as if it were a curse.

Ethan shook his head. "Conjuring."

Kelf didn't answer right away. For some time he merely stood there, looming over Ethan and Kannice. Ethan feared that he might lash out with a fist, or yank him away from Kannice. But whatever his feelings about magick, he loved Kannice nearly as much as Ethan did, and he seemed to sense that to stop Ethan would be to harm her.

"This is why you told me to leave."

"Aye," Ethan muttered.

"Look at me, Kaille!"

Ethan flinched. Never before had Kelf called him anything but Ethan. But he forced himself to look the barman in the eye; Kelf deserved that much. "Aye! This is why I sent you away. Because I was afraid you might try to stop me, and she was dying!"

"Does she know?"

"Aye. She has for many years. Almost since the day we met." He hoped that this would mean something to Kelf, that it would allow the barman to move beyond his own fear and disapproval.

"How do I know you're not makin' matters worse?"

"I love her, Kelf. You've seen that I love her; that's how you know."

"And how do I—?" Kelf straightened. "Where's all the blood? There was blood all over her, and now it's gone."

"Aye. That's how I cast the healing spell. I need the blood to make the conjuring work."

Kelf regarded him the way he might a leper. "Stay away from me," he said, shaking a meaty finger at Ethan. "She might choose to have you around, but I want nothin' more to do with you."

"I'm keeping her alive, Kelf!"

"Even so."

He turned on his heel and yanked the door open once more.

"Kelf, wait."

The barman halted but didn't face him.

"Say nothing to anyone else. Please. For Kannice's sake if not for mine."

Kelf said nothing, made no gesture. He simply left the kitchen.

Alone once more, Ethan retrieved his knife with one hand and cut himself again. For a third time, he cast the healing spell, allowing the power to flow into Kannice's body. There did not seem to be any more blood flowing from the wound, and she breathed still, though her breaths were shallow. He wasn't yet ready to look at the wound; he didn't know if a third conjuring would do her any good, but he feared what he would find when at last he pulled his hands away to see what Ramsey's spells had wrought.

Ramsey's spells.

He had come here looking for Diver, and instead he had come within a blade's breadth of getting Kannice killed.

Time to choose, Kaille.

He heard the captain's warning once more, understanding at long last. This was what he had meant. Time to choose between the people who mattered to him most, between his love and his oldest, dearest friend.

He had to save Kannice's life. There had been no choice in that at all. But what was happening to Diver? What peril faced him? Ethan had not noticed any other spells in these last harrowing moments, but being so intent on Kannice, he wasn't sure that he would have.

When at last his third healing spell had run its course, Ethan removed his hands and looked through the slice in her bodice to see the skin beneath. The scar below her sternum was livid still, but the skin had closed. He laid his head on her breast and heard her heart beating, slow but strong. Her chest rose and fell with her breathing. She might well have been sleeping, save for the pallor of her cheeks.

"Thank God," he whispered, fresh tears on his face.

He stood, his knees protesting as he straightened his legs. He took a pair of towels from beside the stove, folded them, and slipped them under Kannice's head. They were a poor substitute for a pillow, but he didn't wish to move her. And, he had to admit, he didn't want others out in the tavern to see her and wonder, as Kelf had, why the blood on her dress had vanished. But if she was to remain here for now, she would need a blanket.

Ethan stepped to the door and opened it, only to find Kelf in the act of reaching for the door handle. He held a blanket in his arms.

Face-to-face with Ethan, he scowled.

"I was coming to get a blanket," Ethan said.

"Well, here, take this one." The barkeep thrust the blanket into Ethan's hands and walked away.

He watched Kelf move to the far end of the bar before returning to Kannice's side and laying the blanket over her. Bending closer to her, he touched her cheek with the back of his hand. It might have been his imagination, or his desperate wish to see some improvement in her condition before he left the tavern, but he thought that her skin might have felt a bit warmer.

He kissed her forehead. "I have to go," he whispered. "I'll be back as soon as I can, and in the meanwhile, Kelf will take care of you. I love you."

Ethan stood once more, walked out of the kitchen, and approached the barman. Kelf stiffened as Ethan approached, and would not look at him.

"What happened to the other man who was stabbed?"

"He's upstairs with a surgeon. But he lost a lot of blood."

"And the man who stabbed him and Kannice?"

Kelf shrugged, his eyes still trained on the bar. "I took him outside, hopin' to find a man of the watch. But I couldn't—seems there's some business goin' on in the streets tonight. I even heard some lads yellin' 'fire.' I didn't want to waste much time on him. So, in the end I left him lyin' in the street. And good riddance to him. I hope he freezes."

Ethan would have liked to explain that it wasn't the man's fault, that he had been controlled by a spell. But he knew that Kelf wouldn't want to hear any of it, and their friendship already lay in tatters.

Moreover, it sounded as though he needed to see to the other half of the "choice" Ramsey had given him.

"Where were they yelling 'fire'?" he asked.

"I don't know. Does it matter?"

"I have to go."

Kelf did look at him then, though only for an instant.

"Diver's in trouble, and I have to find him. Kannice should be all right now, but I don't know how long it will be before she wakes. You'll have to watch her."

"I plan to."

Ethan hesitated. "Kelf—"

"Diver needs your help. Go find him."

He nodded and left.

Chapter

EIGHTEEN

The wind had died away, leaving the night cold but pleasant. A quarter moon shone in a clear sky, its glow reflected off the snow to light the streets and buildings of the city. Ethan smelled no smoke in the air, but he did hear raised voices coming from several directions, and for a moment, standing outside the Dowsing Rod on Sudbury Street, he wasn't certain where he should begin his search for Diver.

It occurred to him then that Ramsey, intentionally or not, had given him a hint. If he could locate the conjurer Morrison, he might find Diver as well.

He slipped his hand into his pocket and pulled out three leaves of mullein.

"*Locus magi ex verbasco evocatus.*" Location of conjurer, conjured from mullein.

Reg, who had stayed with him as he healed Kannice, watched, appearing eager. The spell rumbled in the icy street and spread outward. Before long, Ethan felt it pool around a conjurer near Murray's Barracks only a short distance away. Ethan took a step in that direction, only to halt as his conjuring found a second speller, this one nearer the Town House.

"There are two," he said to the ghost.

Reg nodded.

"Grant and Morrison?"

The ghost gazed back at him, offering no response.

Ethan started toward the barracks, and the nearer of the two conjurers. The closer he drew to Brattle Street, the more people he heard shouting and calling to one another. Gangs of young men rushed through the streets, most of them carrying sticks and clubs. Groups of soldiers marched in the lanes as well, their muskets fixed with bayonets. Whatever the patriots had in mind for this night, General Gage's men were taking it seriously.

Reaching the corner of Brattle Street and Hillier's Lane, Ethan saw that a large crowd had gathered in front of the barracks, pressing into the street. The bells of the Brattle Street Church began to peal. Young men taunted the soldiers and pelted them with snowballs and ice, as had the pups Ethan had seen several nights earlier. Others yelled "Fire!" and "Town-born, turn out!"

Both cries were intended to bring more men and boys out-of-doors: very useful when there was, in fact, a fire burning in the city, but folly on a night such as this, when calling more people into the street increased the danger to all.

He didn't see Morrison outside the barracks, nor did he spot Diver among the men converging on the soldiers' quarters. His trepidation mounting, Ethan turned away from the barracks and strode eastward, toward King Street and the Town House.

Before he reached the building, with its great clock tower, the bell of the Old Brick Church, on Church Square near King Street, began to toll as well, which promised to summon still more people to the gathering. He had yet to feel another conjuring, and he could see no evidence that Samuel Adams or others among the leaders of the Sons of Liberty were directing events. Rather, it seemed that circumstances themselves were conspiring to make matters ever worse.

King Street teemed with men of all ages—an even greater mob than that which had gathered at the barracks. Ethan thought that more were streaming onto the lane from Dock Square to the north. Repeated cries of "Fire!" went up all around him, and the bells at the churches continued to ring. The mob was already perilously large, and it was growing rapidly.

Ethan could barely see for all the people around him. The memory of fighting through the patrons of the Dowsing Rod to reach Kannice made his heart pound. This felt too familiar. He still did not see Diver anywhere, nor did he see Morrison. Indeed, it seemed that only one soldier stood near the Customs House—a young man who appeared terrified, and justifiably so.

Still more people joined the throng on King Street, some of them carrying buckets and other items intended to help the victims of what they truly believed to be a fire. They seemed bemused by what they saw in the lane. Several men pulled a pair of fire engines onto the street and set them in front of the Town House.

Others, however, clearly had known that this was no fire. They arrived on the street carrying weapons—mostly cudgels, although a few bore cutlasses and even broadswords. Ethan heard glass shatter, and straining to see over the heads of those around him, realized that some of the men were attacking the Brazen Head tavern, which belonged to William Jackson, a well-known violator of the nonimportation agreements.

Some in the throng shouted at the lone soldier, daring him to use his weapon.

"Fire!" several called. "Damn you, fire!"

They pelted him, and swarmed near him, only to retreat again as the man jabbed his bayonet at them. Other spectators pleaded with the man to hold his fire, and with the boys who were molesting him to leave off and let the man be.

A disturbance to the west, back toward Murray's Barracks, attracted Ethan's notice.

Shouts of "Make way! Make way" echoed off shop fronts and homes, and several more soldiers, grenadiers, judging by the high, bear-fur hats that they wore, hurried past him, no doubt intent on giving aid to their solitary comrade. They pushed through the onlookers, making no effort to be gentle about it. A few slashed with their bayonets at those they passed, drawing cries of pain and outrage, and more than a bit of blood.

They joined the young man in front of the Customs House, and leveled their weapons. With them was an officer Ethan remembered from eighteen months before, when he was hired by the Customs Board to learn what had befallen the sailors and soldiers aboard

HMS *Graystone*, a sloop that had sailed into Boston Harbor as part of the occupying fleet.

He remembered the army captain's name as Preston—Thomas Preston. He was tall, gaunt, with a rough, sallow face and a manner to match. But he acted with practiced efficiency, barking orders to the men so that they positioned themselves in a tight arc at the mouth of the narrow lane between the Customs House and the Royal Exchange tavern. Once they were set to his satisfaction, he paced in front of his men, eyeing the mob with manifest uneasiness. They were still only ten or so, including the captain, against a mob many times larger.

The boys and men gathered around the Customs House gave no indication that the appearance of more armed men had done anything to cool their appetite for confrontation. If anything, the arrival of the men, and the manner in which they had forced themselves through the crowd, had further inflamed the passions of those surrounding them.

Ethan wanted to be away and quickly. But he had yet to find Diver, and he feared leaving his friend to whatever plans Ramsey had for him. His fears only increased when he recognized several of the men standing with Preston from the brawl at Gray's Rope Works a few days before.

He sensed that Preston wished to lead the men away, back toward Murray's Barracks. But the crowd, which had advanced and retreated like the tide, pressed forward again, blocking their way.

"Damn you, you sons of bitches, fire!" a voice rang out. "You can't kill us all!"

"Fire and be damned!" called another.

Preston raised his hands and spoke to the young men closest to the soldiers, his voice raised.

"Go home now, lads!" he said. "Lest there be murder done!"

His words were met with jeers and more taunts. Snowballs and ice rained down on the captain and his men. Some in the crowd were close enough to Preston and his men to strike the barrels of the soldiers' muskets with their sticks. Ethan heard the ring of wood on steel.

From the near side of King Street, closer to the Town House, came more voices, some shouting that a magistrate had come to disperse the mob. And Ethan did see one skulking figure who dodged salvos of ice chunks and ran away down Pudding Lane.

Turning back toward the Customs House, Ethan caught sight of a familiar face: youthful, framed by dark curls. He stood a good deal closer to the soldiers than did Ethan, in the middle of King Street, a few yards behind a tall mulatto man.

"Diver!" Ethan called.

His friend showed no sign that he had heard.

But someone did, and it seemed that this was what Ramsey and whoever was working with him had been awaiting.

The spell that roared in the stone and ice beneath his feet dwarfed even the most powerful of the conjurings Ethan had sensed in recent days. He glanced to his right for confirmation of what he already knew. The conjuring had come from him. Reg stood beside him.

"Diver!" Ethan shouted again, panicked now.

Diver turned, searching for the person who had called to him.

Ethan called his name a third time and waved his hand over his head.

Diver's face brightened. Ethan was sure his friend thought he had come for the assembly rather than for anything having to do with him. He didn't care.

He started to wend his way through the crowd, even as Diver took a step toward him. As he walked, using the herbs in his pocket, Ethan cast a calming spell like the one he had used on Jimmy Fleming a couple of days before. He might as well have thrown handfuls of sand at an advancing tide. His spell hummed in the street, but it was nothing compared to the conjuring he had felt moments ago. It had no discernible effect on the mob or the soldiers.

Another object flew from the crowd toward the soldiers, spinning end over end, arcing high over the street, white, shining with moonlight. At first Ethan thought it a large piece of ice; a second later he realized it was a short, thick cudgel.

It seemed to descend slowly, guided by some unseen hand. Ethan watched it tumble toward the ground and then hit the musket of the soldier standing at the far left of the formation Preston had arranged.

The soldier staggered and fell, but immediately scrambled to his feet.

"Damn you, fire!" he shouted at his comrades.

And aiming his weapon he did just that.

The report sounded flat, muffled. Had Ethan not seen flame leap from the muzzle of his weapon, he would have doubted what he heard and questioned the source of the cloud of gray smoke that hung around the grenadier, a pale halo.

Everyone on the street froze, most seeming as incredulous as Ethan. A soldier had fired into the crowd. Ethan saw no sign that anyone had been hit, and after that initial silence, men and boys hurled more taunts at the men and again urged them to fire. A few lunged at the soldiers, and a scuffle broke out between Preston and a man Ethan didn't know. Others swung their sticks at the soldiers, baiting them once more. More people called on the men to fire.

Perhaps it was the spell Ramsey had cast using Ethan's power. Perhaps it was the mere fact that one of their own had already fired a shot. But this time the soldiers under Preston's command took up the challenges flung at them by the mob.

Musket fire crackled like a raging blaze. Flames belched from the barrels of the weapons and more smoke rose into the night air.

The mob erupted with cries and shouts—not taunts this time, but terror and pain.

Ethan looked for Diver once more, but could hardly see for the tumult that surrounded him. The crowd, which only moments before had pressed in on the soldiers in front of the Customs House, now dispersed, running in every direction. A few fearless souls continued to harass the soldiers, pressing toward them again, even as the men reloaded their weapons and raised them once more.

Dodging those who fled, Ethan pushed toward the middle of the frozen street. He had only taken a few steps, though, when he slowed and then halted again, his head spinning. A man—actually he looked to be little more than a boy—lay near the edge of the street, a torrent of blood from his chest darkening the ice. Ethan started toward this figure, but then spotted another nearby. This second man bled profusely from wounds to his hip and side.

Men had gathered next to both of the wounded, but they did not appear to know what to do for them. Several of those running from the scene were shouting for surgeons, so perhaps help would arrive soon. In the meantime, however, Ethan noticed more people moving past with bloody wounds. One man had been shot in the arm. He trudged alone past where Ethan stood, clutching his injury, blood running through his fingers. Another man was supported by two friends, having been struck in the thigh.

Ethan forced himself into motion. He had to find Diver. He had taken only a few steps when he halted again, the blood draining from his cheeks. A short distance from the man bleeding from his hip and thigh lay a third man, facedown.

"No," Ethan said, the word coming out as might a grunt after a blow to the gut. This man was long of limb with dark, unruly hair.

Ethan ran toward him, his feet slipping on the ice so that he sprawled to the ground beside the figure. He faltered for an instant, then lifted the man to examine his face.

His relief was tempered by his horror. It was not Diver. This lad was several years younger than Ethan's friend. He, too, had been struck in the chest as well as in the shoulder. In the pale moonlight, the snow and ice beneath him appeared black and slick with his blood.

Ethan laid him down again and stood, scanning the street for Diver, and eyeing the soldiers as well. He was far closer to them now, and directly in their line of sight. They had their muskets held ready, and Ethan knew that if they fired again, he would be fortunate to survive.

"Diver!" he called.

"Ethan."

The reply came from ahead of him and slightly to his right. His friend's voice sounded weak, strained. Ethan's heart began to labor. *Not Diver, too.*

"Where are you?"

A prone figure stirred, raised a hand before letting it drop again. Ethan ran to him.

Diver lay on his side, breathing heavily, his eyes squeezed shut. Blood pooled in the crusted snow beneath him.

"Diver . . ."

"It hurts, Ethan. It hurts more than anything."

The wound was on his arm. Seeing this, Ethan let out a breath he hadn't known he was holding. His relief was short-lived, however. Diver was bleeding profusely; his teeth chattered and his entire body seemed to be quaking.

Ethan helped him lie down on his back. Diver gritted his teeth and let out a low, quavering moan.

For the second time in less than an hour, Ethan laid his hands on someone he loved and whispered a healing spell. *"Remedium ex cruore evocatum."*

He kept his hands over the wound for several seconds, but nothing seemed to happen. Blood continued to pulse from the ravaged arm at an alarming rate, running over his fingers and soaking his breeches.

"Damn," he said through clenched teeth.

"What?" Diver asked.

Ethan didn't answer. Pulling his hands away, he bent to inspect Diver's injury more closely, and nearly vomited in response to what he saw. The arm was a mess. The musket ball appeared to have splintered the bone, so that shards of it were embedded in the surrounding muscle. And he could tell as well that the ball had severed the artery. That was why it bled so.

"Ethan?"

The wound was beyond his talents as a healer, and his friend was bleeding out before his eyes. Ethan could let him die, or he could do the one thing he knew would save Diver's life, though at a potential cost that sent a shudder through his body.

He hesitated for all of two seconds.

He didn't know any better way to do what he had in mind, and so he cast a fire spell, aiming it at the artery and sourcing it in Diver's blood. His conjuring pounded in the lane, and he smelled flesh burn as his spell cauterized the wound.

Diver screamed. When he could speak again, he said, "What . . . what did you do?"

"I've stopped the bleeding," Ethan said, the words scraped from his throat. "But we need to get you to a surgeon."

He pulled off his scarf and, as gently as he could, made a sling of it, to keep the arm immobile. As he did, he took a moment to survey the scene before him, and to try to get his bearings.

The tall mulatto man he had spotted ahead of Diver before the shooting began lay near the soldiers, unmoving, the blood on his chest shining in the moonlight. A second man, no more than two or three feet away from the first, had been struck in the head. Ethan thought he must have died before he hit the ground. Long had he expected that the occupation of his city would lead to bloodshed and even death, but never had he imagined a scene like this.

Tearing his gaze away from the dead men, he looked to the south, considering what options he had. Dr. Church's house was too far from here. He wasn't sure he could carry Diver such a distance, and he didn't know how long his cauterization would hold. But there was another doctor to whom he could take his friend.

"Am I dying?" Diver asked, his voice faint.

"Not tonight, you're not," Ethan said. "You'll be back in the Dowser sipping ales with me before you know it."

A grimace flitted across the young man's face and was gone; Ethan thought he was trying to smile.

"I'm cold, Ethan. I can't feel my hands."

"Which is why I need to get you to a surgeon, straight away."

"All right."

"I have to lift you, and it's going to hurt."

Diver gave a slight nod.

Ethan slipped his arms under his friend's back and legs and lifted him into his arms.

Diver gasped. "Oh, God! Oh, God, Ethan, that hurts!"

"I know," Ethan said, rasping the words as he struggled to his feet. He nearly fell, but righted himself and staggered toward the Town House. He glanced at the clock tower; it was a few minutes before ten o'clock. He wondered whether Kannice had awakened yet.

Once past the Town House, Ethan followed Queen Street to Brattle. For once, he cared not a whit about walking past Murray's Barracks. Let one of the soldiers accost him. Let Morrison show his face. Ethan would incinerate with a thought anyone who troubled him this night.

Reaching Hanover Street, his bad leg aching, his breath coming now in great gasps, he walked past several doors until he reached a modest home on the left. Even as he approached the front door, however, he heard quick footsteps behind him. He spun, the words of a shatter spell on his lips.

But the man striding in his direction was none other than the one he had sought in coming here.

"Doctor Warren!"

The doctor hardly spared Ethan a glance, so intent was he on Diver.

"He was on King Street?" the doctor asked.

"Aye, and was struck in the arm."

The doctor regarded him. "I was on my way to retrieve my bag. Others require my services as well. But you're here and I'll not turn you away. Follow me." He pushed open his door and entered the house, gesturing sharply for Ethan to follow.

It was warm within, the air carrying the familiar bitter scent of spermaceti candles. Warren lit several with a taper, and at the same time pointed at a sofa in the middle of the sitting room.

"Put him there."

"But the blood . . ."

"Aye, the blood. Elizabeth will have my head, but there's naught to be done."

"I've stopped much of the bleeding," Ethan said, lowering Diver onto the sofa as gently as he could. "I was afraid he might bleed out. But the ball remains in him and—"

"Wait," Warren said. "You stopped the bleeding?" He stared at Ethan, recognition flashing in his eyes at last. "Mister Kaille!"

"Aye, sir."

"Forgive me. I didn't . . ." He shook his head. "Elizabeth accuses me of being lost to the rest of the world when absorbed in my work. Perhaps she's right. This man is a friend of yours?"

"Aye."

"Then, let us see to his recovery, shall we?"

"Thank you, sir."

Together they stripped off Diver's coat, waistcoat, and shirt. Warren bent over him and probed the wound with practiced fingers. Diver, who had passed out somewhere between King Street and Warren's house, stirred but did not wake.

"When you said it was an arm injury, I didn't think much of it," the doctor murmured after some time. "But this . . . The ball is in there still, right next to the brachial artery, which has been severed." He looked at Ethan. "There must have been a great deal of blood."

"Aye, there was. I thought . . . I cauterized the artery, thinking it was the only way to stop the bleeding."

"It was. You saved his life."

Ethan heard a catch in the man's voice.

"Can what I did be repaired?"

Warren continued to examine the wound, wincing at what he saw, or perhaps at Ethan's question. "I fear not. The damage to the artery is . . ." He shook his head. "I don't believe it can be mended; it never could be. And . . . and as a consequence of what you did, the lower part of his arm has been denied blood for a long time."

Ethan closed his eyes.

"But hear me," Warren went on. "The ball has shattered the humerus—the arm bone—beyond repair, or at least beyond my capacity as a surgeon. He was doomed to lose this arm as soon as the ball struck him."

"But surely a physician of your skill—"

"I can't work miracles, Mister Kaille. I'm afraid that's your bailiwick, not mine. Did you try to mend the bone?"

Ethan shook his head, feeling ill. "I was afraid even to make the attempt, lest I make matters worse. This healing lies beyond my talents as well. My one goal was to stop the bleeding."

Warren assayed a smile, but failed. "As it should have been. You did the right thing, Mister Kaille. I offer this as both a surgeon and a friend." He briefly rested a hand on Ethan's shoulder. Then he left the room. Ethan turned back to his friend.

"This is the second time I've gotten you shot," he whispered, smoothing Diver's hair off his brow. "And I may have cost you . . ." He couldn't bring himself to speak the words, even with Diver unconscious. "Forgive me."

Sooner even than Ethan had expected, Warren returned, carrying a black leather case, several cloths, and some white material that Ethan guessed was for a bandage. He carried as well an amputation saw, with a curved iron frame and a serrated blade that made Ethan's stomach heave. The doctor placed these items on a table beside the sofa and removed from the case a small pair of forceps and two small blades.

"We'll deal with the ball first," Warren said. "Do you have much experience with surgeries?"

"Very little, and none that was good."

"Well, do the best you can. I can't handle all of this on my own."

Ethan nodded. And for the next several minutes he watched as the doctor went about his work with grim efficiency. When Warren asked for his blades or the forceps, Ethan handed them to him, but he held his tongue, and knew a moment of profound relief when at last Warren extracted the bullet, held it up for Ethan to see, and then set it on a small cloth.

"That was the easy part," he said. He peered down at Diver's arm once more, his mouth set in a thin hard line, his brow furrowed. "I'm afraid there's nothing for it, Mister Kaille. I can't repair the bone or the artery, and therefore it's too dangerous for him to keep the arm. I'm sorry."

"Let me try again."

Warren raised his gaze. "With witchery, you mean?"

"With a conjuring, yes."

"Are you sure that's wise? If the bleeding starts again—"

"I won't let that happen. Please."

"Very well."

Ethan had been standing by the sofa, but now he knelt beside Diver. Blood still seeped from his friend's injury, which meant that he would not have to cut himself. Casting a quick, self-conscious look at Warren, Ethan placed his hands over the wound and whispered the words of the healing conjuring. The spell groaned and Reg appeared beside the sofa, but Warren gave no sign of noticing either.

The power of the spell tingled in the palm of Ethan's hand, as if he were holding a dozen buzzing bees. He closed his eyes for several seconds, delving into the wound with his magick, trying to sense what effect his conjuring was having on the shattered bone and the burned end of the artery. But he wasn't trained as a healer; he didn't have as much experience with such spells as he should have. When he opened his eyes again, he found Warren watching him, avid, his eyes wide and shining with candlelight.

"Is this all there is to it?" the doctor asked, his voice loud after the long silence.

Ethan nodded. He had cast a good deal this night, and under heart-rending circumstances. He was weary. Warren fell silent and said nothing more. When the spell had spent itself, leaving Diver's wound bloodless but still livid, his flesh ravaged, Ethan pulled out his knife and cut himself, drawing a sharp breath from the doctor. Ethan ignored him. He muttered the spell again, and held his hands over the wound for several minutes more, until finally, this second conjuring spent as well, he pulled his hands away and rocked back on his heels.

Warren edged closer and bent low to scrutinize the injury. After a second's hesitation, he probed the wound with practiced fingers. At first he wore a look of wonder, but as his examination went on, his mien turned grim once more.

"What you've done to the bone is remarkable," he said, after some time. "More than I could ever have hoped to do. But still, there is too much damage, and the artery remains as it was."

Ethan raised his blade to his forearm. "I can cast again."

"Is there any reason to believe that your efforts would be more effective this time?"

He had no answer.

"We need to remove the arm now; the longer the delay, the greater the danger to your friend."

Still Ethan kept the blade poised over his forearm, his gaze fixed on Diver, his vision blurred with tears.

"The hardest part of my profession is knowing when to give up, when to admit that the wound or disease has won. You can't help him anymore. And there are others in Boston tonight who require my care. You saved your friend's life, and that is no small thing. But there's nothing more we can do to save his arm."

Every breath Ethan took seemed to come at great cost, and his hands had begun to shake.

"Help me move him. We should do this on the table in my dining room." The doctor spoke in even tones. Not light, by any means. But steady, reassuring, purposeful.

Ethan sheathed his blade. Together they carried Diver to the dining room and positioned him on the table. Warren returned to the common room to retrieve his tools and supplies, leaving Ethan alone with his friend. He could think of nothing to say, and before long Warren was beside him again, arraying his tools on the table.

"I need you to hold him," the doctor said, his voice gentle. "He's unconscious, which is a blessing—for him and for us—but nevertheless, you must keep him still. Do you understand?"

Ethan nodded, the motion jerky.

"Look away. Don't watch any of it. It won't take long, and aside from keeping him still, I can do everything else myself." He pointed to two spots on Diver's lower arm. "Grip him here and here."

He nodded again, bile rising in his throat. He took hold of Diver's arm where Warren had indicated and stared at the wall opposite where he stood. A portrait hung there: a young woman, pretty, dressed in a blue satin gown. Ethan wondered if this was Warren's wife. Whoever she was, he refused to tear his gaze from her.

Still, keeping his eyes averted helped only so much. He could hear it all. The quiet ring of metal tools, the soft shudder of a blade carving through muscle and skin, and worst of all, the horrific rattle of that sawblade on bone. Tears slid down his cheeks and his pulse pounded in his ears. The procedure seemed to take forever, and yet it ended abruptly, sooner than Ethan expected.

"Don't look yet," Warren said, though out of the corner of his eye Ethan saw him take up the bandages. "But you can release the arm."

Doing so felt like the most evil of betrayals.

Forgive me, Diver.

And then another thought: *Ramsey, you will pay for this in blood and torment.*

"Why don't you step outside, Mister Kaille. I'll join you there shortly."

Without speaking a word, Ethan left the house. The cold air was a mercy, and he took a long, unsteady breath. Church bells continued to peal, echoing up and down the deserted lane. Ethan listened for musket fire, but heard none. He glanced up at the sky, bright with stars and moonlight, and tried to summon a prayer for Diver and for Kannice, tried to feel the Lord's presence, just as he had when he was a boy in Bristol, standing with his parents and sisters in the cathedral there. But he felt naught but anguish and fury and heartache.

He stood thus for a long time, until at last the door opened behind him and Warren joined him on the ice-covered walk that led from the house.

"He's resting. I don't imagine he'll wake for some time. My wife and children won't be home this evening. Samuel feared violence this night, and suggested that our families lodge elsewhere. So, he can remain here, but if he does wake, he'll probably be alone. I'd like to move him, but I dare not so soon after the surgery."

"I understand. He lives near here, on Pudding Lane. Perhaps tomorrow we can see him back to his room." *If I survive the night.*

"That would be fine. I'll check in on him when I can." The doctor hesitated. "What you did in there—earlier, I mean . . . I know that we didn't save his arm, but your powers are most remarkable. I heard you say something as you . . . as you conjured."

"It was Latin," Ethan said, weary beyond measure. "Roughly translated, it means 'healing conjured from blood.'"

"I have others to whom to attend this evening. I could use your help."

Ethan took another long breath. "Diver is a friend, Doctor Warren. He's known me for many years. He trusts me, and the power I wield. And you're a learned man who is more accepting of . . . phenomena with which you are unfamiliar than most would be. There are some who would rather die or lose a loved one than be healed by what they consider witchery."

"I doubt that."

"I assure you it's true. I know as well that there are many who would see me hanged before they allowed me to cast a healing spell."

Warren grimaced. "That I believe."

"Will you also believe that I have other matters to which to attend this night that are every bit as important as healing the wounded? I seek to prevent more deaths and injuries."

"Very well, Mister Kaille," the doctor said, but he sounded disappointed.

"You have my deepest thanks for all that you did for him." Ethan dug into his pocket. "I have a pound or two—"

"No," Warren said, his tone brooking no argument. "Not for this wound, not on this night. There will be a price to pay in blood and death before all is said and done. But I'll not make coin from it."

"Again, my thanks."

"We should move him back to the sofa. He'll be more comfortable there."

Ethan followed the doctor back into the house, his legs leaden. Reaching the dining room, he faltered in midstep, his gaze falling to the bandage that covered what was left of Diver's arm. It was stark white, save for a small circle of crimson staining the center, like a target.

"He's better off now than he was when you brought him here," Warren said. "Please believe that."

Ethan didn't answer. They moved Diver to the sofa, and Warren laid a blanket over him. Ethan didn't want to leave, but he knew as well that there was nothing more he could do. And what he had done had been woefully inadequate.

You saved his life. Kannice's voice.

I cost him his arm.

He thanked the good doctor one last time and let himself out of the house.

Glancing once more at the night sky, Ethan headed back toward the Dowsing Rod to see how Kannice fared. He knew that he couldn't remain there long, but he had to see her. And after that, he had other places to go.

This deadly night was far from over.

Chapter
NINETEEN

hurch bells pealed all across the town—not only at the Brattle Street and Old Brick churches, but, it seemed, from every sanctuary in Boston. Ethan saw others hurrying through the city streets, their heads lowered, their expressions uneasy, their gazes darting furtively. But no one spoke a word, not of vengeance or resistance or even mourning. Aside from the tolling of bells, a strained silence had settled over the lanes and shops and houses. Grief and rage, apprehension and anticipation—the emotions of thousands seemed to hang like a low storm cloud in the chill air.

As Ethan trudged along the icy street from Warren's house back toward the Dowsing Rod, he began to tremble, his mind reeling, his chest tight.

For the second time in as many weeks, people had died in the streets of his city. *Diver has lost his arm.*

And once again the spell that caused all of this had been sourced in his power. Never mind that Ramsey was responsible; the captain was wielding him as if he were nothing more than a weapon, insensate, without will of his own. He was too weak, too ignorant of the conjuring Ramsey was using. Due to his failure people had died, just as had Christopher Seider on Middle Street.

Ethan halted in the center of Queen Street, swaying, his hands covering his face. A sob escaped him, but no tears fell from his eyes. He took several quick, deep breaths, trying to compose himself, knowing that he could not afford to give in to his frustration and sense of help-lessness.

Because not only had he allowed Ramsey to use him to kill, he had also allowed the captain to strike at Kannice, and at Diver. And, he knew, Ramsey would make the attempt again. He would see to it that everyone Ethan loved died, and then he would kill Ethan as well. The man was mad, cruel, brilliant, and bent on revenge.

"*Where are you, Ramsey?*" Ethan bellowed at the sky.

Others on the street halted and gaped at him. Ethan didn't care.

"Show yourself, you son of a bitch! Come out in the open where I can see your face before I kill you!"

The echo of his words died away, leaving only the murmur of low-ered voices and the muffled beat of footsteps. Ethan glanced around. Those who still watched him averted their eyes at the touch of his gaze.

He started walking again, his hands shaking, his heart beating like a war drum. But with each step he took, his pulse slowed, and his hands stilled. There would be time later to mourn and reflect on all that Ramsey had done with his power. For now, he needed to see that Kan-nice was all right. After that, he would resume his hunt for the cap-tain.

When he reached the Dowsing Rod, he found that the door was locked. He pounded on the wood with a gloved fist and waited.

He heard heavy footsteps and the click of the lock. The door swung open, revealing Kelf, implacable and huge, his cleaver in hand. The bar-keep glared at him and didn't move.

"Are you going to let me in?" Ethan asked. "Or am I going to have to fight my way past you?"

"Do you think you could?"

Ethan looked him directly in the eye. "I know it."

Kelf considered him, and for the first time in the many years of their friendship, there was a hint of fear in his gaze. He took a step back out of Ethan's way.

"Where is she?" Ethan asked, as he swept past the man.

"Where you left her. I've been sittin' with her."

"Has she awakened?"

"No. But there's some color in her cheeks."

Ethan made his way into the kitchen and knelt beside Kannice. Kelf was right: there was a blush to her cheeks that hadn't been there when he left. Her breathing was steady and stronger.

His eyes stung.

He kissed her lightly on her brow, which felt warm again. "Kannice? Can you hear me?"

Her head moved slightly, and her eyelids twitched but then were still again.

"Kannice?"

She mouthed his name.

"Aye, it's me."

Kelf came to the doorway. "Did she say somethin'?"

"My name; nothing more." Ethan smoothed her blanket and kissed her again, but she had fallen into a deep slumber and said no more. Ethan stood. "I can't stay." He kept his eyes on Kannice, but he said it to Kelf.

The barkeep seemed to understand. "I'm not goin' anywhere. Not tonight at least."

"Thank you, Kelf."

"I'm not doin' it for you."

Ethan met his gaze. "Thank you just the same." He stepped past him into the great room, and crossed back to the door.

"Did you find Diver?" Kelf called.

"Aye. He was shot."

"Shot?" Kelf said, his voice sharp. "Is he all right?"

"He'll live." The words almost caught in his throat. He couldn't bring himself to say more.

"Shot by who?"

"Have you heard yet what happened on King Street?"

"No."

"You will," Ethan said, and left.

He started back toward the Town House, walking at a swift pace, his hands in his pockets. Despite what Ramsey's illusion had said to him, Ethan had not seen Morrison on King Street or in front of the barracks. And when Ramsey cast his spell, he used Ethan's power rather than someone else's. This was significant in some way; Ethan was sure of it. But he didn't yet know why.

Following Queen Street eastward, Ethan was forced to stop well before he reached the Town House. A great many soldiers, likely every man billeted at Murray's Barracks, had gathered at the near end of King Street, with the Town House at their backs, and had taken up firing positions. The men in the front row were on one knee, their weapons raised. Behind them, soldiers stood in rows ready to take their places after the men in front fired. Preston stood at the end of the front row, his cutlass in hand, and he eyed yet another mob that had formed before him.

With the church bells ringing, and word of the shootings on King Street spreading through the town, more and more people crowded the street. Boston was moments away from more killings.

More to the point, Morrison stood with his fellow soldiers, in the second or third row behind the kneeling men. He scanned the angry faces arrayed before him, as did his comrades. But Ethan sensed a purpose to Morrison's search; the man was looking for him.

Ethan edged away from the mob, taking care not to draw attention to himself. When he could no longer see the soldiers, or be seen by them, he hurried on to Dock Square. Here, too, an angry crowd of men had gathered and were shouting insults at a pair of retreating figures, who made their way west and south, back the way Ethan had come.

"Damn you, Hutchinson!" cried one man bearing a cudgel. "Stand like a man!"

Others around him laughed. Ethan wondered if one of the figures in retreat was truly the lieutenant governor.

Once again, though, he was surrounded by men, many of them bearing weapons of one sort or another. He continued past and through Dock Square, before heading south on Merchant's Row. He intended to follow it past King Street, thinking that surely it would not be safe to return to that bloodied lane.

But as he crossed the street and gazed westward, back toward the Town House, he saw that the area in front of the Customs House was now largely deserted. Unsure of why he did so, Ethan turned and walked back to the scene of the shootings.

Aside from a few stragglers who wandered the street, their eyes drawn to the bloodstains on the ice and snow, most of the mob had moved on, as had the uniformed men. The rest of the wounded, he hoped, were being attended to; the dead had been removed. Only the blood in the street told of the recent tragedy.

"Is that you, Kaille?"

Ethan spun, reaching for his knife, but the man approaching raised his hands in a placating gesture.

"It's all right," Sheriff Greenleaf said. "It's just me."

Ethan exhaled, vapor billowing in the night air, and let his blade hand drop.

"Who did you think I was?"

"Nate Ramsey, or someone working with him."

Greenleaf nodded, but said nothing. His gaze wandered the street. It was a measure of how calamitous this night had been that Ethan's mention of Ramsey drew so little response from the man.

"Were you here when it happened?" the sheriff asked.

"Aye."

"You seem to have come through unscathed." There was no goad in the words; it was merely an observation.

"I was fortunate," Ethan said. "A friend of mine was shot: Diver Jervis."

Greenleaf looked at him. "Dead?"

Ethan shook his head. "I suppose he was fortunate, too. How many died?"

"Three so far. But some who were hit won't last the night."

"There's another mob on the far side of the Town House. And Preston has his soldiers lined up to fire. This isn't over."

"Aye," the sheriff said. "The lieutenant governor was on his way, but another mob chased him off. I'm not sure where he is now. We know how bad this night has been; we're trying to keep it from getting worse."

Ethan said nothing. The pealing of bells echoed through the street, but thus far he had heard no more musket fire.

"What did you see?"

"I'm sorry?" Ethan said.

"You were here; you saw it happen. And I'm asking what exactly you saw."

"I hardly know where to begin. The soldiers were besieged—outnumbered, surrounded by a mob that was shouting insults and pelting them with snow and ice. One soldier was hit by an object thrown at him; it appeared to be a stick. He fell, got back up, and fired. Before those in the street could flee, the rest of the soldiers—perhaps eight in all—opened fire as well."

"Did they fire more than once?"

"Not that I saw," Ethan said. "But after the initial volley, I took Diver away to a surgeon. Why?"

"The soldiers claim they only fired the one volley. But we know of three dead, and many others wounded. More, frankly, than can be accounted for given the number of regulars present."

"Perhaps they double-loaded their weapons," Ethan said. "I've heard of soldiers doing that."

"As have I. You may be right. Did Preston give the order to fire? I've spoken to a number of witnesses who say he did."

Ethan hesitated. "As you may recall, I have no love for Thomas Preston." Captain Preston, along with the sheriff himself, had arrested Ethan during the *Graystone* affair. Ethan passed a miserable night in the town gaol, the memory of which still gave him nightmares. "But I heard no order. There were people in the mob yelling for the soldiers to fire; it would have been easy for someone to mistake these taunts for an order."

"My thanks, Kaille. That will be helpful to us."

"You should know something else, Sheriff. Before the first man pulled the trigger, before he was struck by that thrown club, I felt a conjuring." He didn't mention that the power for the spell had been his. Greenleaf's understanding of conjurings was rudimentary at best, and despite the civility of this conversation, he still would have been glad for an excuse to put Ethan back in prison.

"Was it like the one you felt the day the Seider boy was shot?"

"Aye. And I know now beyond any doubt that Ramsey is back in Boston. What happened tonight may have been as much his doing as it was Preston's or anyone else's."

"I want him caught, Kaille. I want him dead."

"No more than I do."

He thought Greenleaf might argue, but the sheriff merely nodded again, his gaze straying once more toward the Town House.

"I need to be on my way," Greenleaf said. "I have men to question tonight, and already there's talk of a town meeting tomorrow at Faneuil Hall. We could see more blood before this is over. But, still, I want to know when you find Ramsey."

"You will."

Greenleaf tipped his hat and strode off toward the western end of King Street.

Ethan watched him go, wondering how he might win access to Murray's Barracks once more. He wanted to speak with the soldier Morrison. If he was going to find Ramsey, he would need information from the man helping the captain.

Even as he thought this, however, another man he recognized meandered by. This young gentleman, wearing a woolen cape and carrying a brass-tipped walking cane, halted a few paces from where Ethan stood to stare down at a large, red stain in the snow.

"Mister Grant?" Ethan said.

The young conjurer Ethan had met in the Green Dragon tavern started at the sound of his name, and took a step back. He gawked at Ethan for a few seconds, recognition dawning in his expression.

"Mister Kaille?" he said, sounding unsure of himself.

"Aye." Ethan walked over to the man and proffered a gloved hand, which Grant gripped briefly.

"Terrible business," the clerk said, looking down at the blood again. "I was here when it happened."

"I was as well," Ethan said.

"Then you know. I feared this day would come. I suppose we all did when the occupation began."

The realization came to Ethan as an epiphany. "Wait! If you were here, then you must have felt the conjuring as well. Seconds before the first soldier fired his weapon."

Grant's eyes widened. "Yes, I did! I thought at the time that I had imagined it."

"Would that you had," Ethan said. "It was a powerful spell; I don't see how you could have confused it for anything but what it was."

Under the light of the quarter moon, Ethan saw the man's cheeks color. "I'm not as skilled in matters of spellmaking as I should be," he said. "But . . . but you say it was real?"

"Aye."

Before Ethan could say more, shouts went up from beyond the Town House. He froze, listening again for the report of muskets. But he heard naught but voices. He wondered if the mob had seen Hutchinson or the sheriff. Neither would be well received on this night.

"What do you suppose is happening there?" Grant asked. "Shall we go and see?"

"I think I would be better off remaining here."

"Yes, you're probably right. There's no sense tempting fate a second time."

Ethan regarded the man through narrowed eyes. "Why were you abroad tonight, Mister Grant? I can't imagine you would have chanced being part of Mister Adams's assembly."

"No, of course not. But I was on my way back to the Customs House to see to some ledgers Mister Paxton wanted. When I arrived, the mob had already started to congregate."

It made sense. And yet something in the man's manner gave Ethan pause.

"And you, Mister Kaille? What brought you here? From what I understand, you've shown little interest in casting your lot with the patriot cause."

"That's true. I was drawn here by something else. I can't say what."

"Can't or won't?"

Ethan offered a thin smile. "Won't."

"I see."

Another memory stirred in Ethan's mind, one that should have come to him sooner.

"Did you feel my finding spell earlier this evening?" he asked.

"Naturally."

"And you knew it was mine?"

Grant faltered, then forced a smile. "Not until this moment, no."

"You're lying. You knew I had cast it, and so knew that I could place you here. Perhaps more to the point, you might have guessed that I was on my way to King Street. And you would have had time to communicate that information to someone else."

"To whom would I communicate it?" Grant's laughter was brittle. "You think quite highly of yourself, Mister Kaille, to assume that your comings and goings are the stuff of my conversations."

"How long have you been working for him?"

"For whom?"

"Nate Ramsey."

Grant's mouth twitched.

"He chose poorly in you," Ethan said. "You don't lie well, and your face gives you away."

"He chose well enough. *Dormite ex—*"

Before he could finish the sleep spell, Ethan lashed out with his good leg to kick the man in the stomach.

Grant grunted a curse and collapsed to one knee. But moving faster than Ethan had expected, he swung his cane, hitting Ethan solidly in the side of his bad leg. Ethan fell.

Grant got to his feet and fled, moving awkwardly, one hand gripping his gut where Ethan's foot had connected.

Ethan forced himself up and hobbled after the man, who led him off King Street onto Leverett's Lane. As he ran, he bit down on the inside of his cheek.

"*Pugnus ex cruore evocatus,*" he said. Fist, conjured from blood. The conjuring pulsed and abruptly Reg was running alongside him.

He aimed the blow at Grant's back. As he had hoped, the spell was enough to knock the clerk off balance. He sprawled onto the ice, his cane clattering out of reach.

Ethan heard him mutter something and had time to think that it must be a spell. He felt it hum, saw Grant's ghost, the finely dressed woman with the pale orange glow, appear on the narrow lane.

An instant later, a ball of fire crashed into Ethan's chest, pounding him to the frozen ground and setting his greatcoat ablaze.

Ethan rolled right and left until the flames were extinguished. By then, though, Grant was on his feet once more, and but a few strides from the corner of Water Street.

Sitting up, Ethan grabbed his knife and cut the back of his hand. *"Discuti ex cruore evocatum!"* Shatter, conjured from blood.

Grant cried out, crumpled in a heap, and grabbed at his broken leg.

Ethan got to his feet and advanced on the man. As he did, he pulled leaves from his pouch of mullein. *"Tegimen ex verbasco evocatum."* Warding, conjured from mullein.

His spell pulsed, and was followed only an instant later by a second conjuring. This one struck Ethan as a blow, knocking him back on his heels, but doing no more damage. His warding had held against whatever spell Grant had attempted.

The clerk made a sound like a trapped animal. Ethan saw that he had a knife in hand. Before Grant could cut himself to conjure again Ethan covered the remaining distance between them and kicked the blade out of the man's hand. It hit the wall of the nearest building and vanished in a small pile of loose snow.

Grant bit down, probably on his tongue or cheek, as Ethan himself had done while pursuing the man. A spell rang in the street, and once more Ethan was hammered by the power of Grant's conjuring. But as before, the spell had no other effect on him.

He kicked the clerk in the side, making him retch.

"I'm warded," Ethan said. "And you're not conjurer enough to overcome my spell. Now you're going to answer some questions for me, and then I'll decide whether to give you to the sheriff or kill you myself."

"Save your breath," Grant said, panting the words. "I'll tell you nothing."

"I want an answer to my question: How long have you been working for Nate Ramsey?"

He saw the man's mouth move and knew that he was trying to conjure again. Ethan dug the toe of his boot into the leg he had shattered with his conjuring. Grant howled.

"How long?"

When Grant didn't answer, Ethan kicked him a second time.

While the clerk sobbed in pain, Ethan retrieved the man's knife from the snowbank. Returning to Grant's side, he squatted beside him, grabbed his collar with one hand, and with the other set the point of the blade at the corner of the clerk's eye.

Grant stiffened.

"Answer me, or I swear I'll take out your eye."

Tears coursed from the clerk's eyes, and snot ran from his nose, so that he resembled an overgrown boy who had taken a beating. But his expression could have flayed the skin from Ethan's bones.

"I know of no one named Ramsey," he said.

Ethan increased the pressure of the blade against the man's skin, though he took care not to draw blood.

"It's the truth. But I . . . I was hired by someone. I don't know who it was."

"How long ago?"

"Not long. Perhaps a fortnight."

"This person came to you?"

Grant pressed his lips together.

Ethan tapped the point of the knife against his face. "Did he come to you?"

"I was approached by a man claiming to be the agent of another. He gave no names—not his own, nor that of his employer."

"He offered you money."

"That's right."

"How much?"

The clerk's mouth twisted. "Five pounds. And I've been promised five more."

It was a sizable amount, but not necessarily beyond Ramsey's means.

"And he told you to seek me out?" Ethan asked.

Grant laughed, though with little mirth. "You do have a mighty high opinion of yourself, don't you? Of course he didn't. Nor did I do any such thing. If you remember, you found me in the Green Dragon."

"But you were there for him."

"I was there as a supporter of the Sons of Liberty. His instructions were to watch for conjurers—any conjurers. I didn't have to change my daily routine. Indeed, the man with whom I spoke made it clear to me that I was not to do so."

Ethan shook his head. None of this was as he had expected. "He merely told you to search for other conjurers?"

"Not even to search for them. To keep watch, to tell him of any spells I felt or spectral guides I happened to see."

"Did he tell you why?"

"No. But I believed—" He clamped his mouth shut, his gaze sliding away.

"You believed what, Grant?" When the clerk didn't respond, Ethan tightened his hold on the man's cape and shook him. "What did you believe?"

"It might have been foolish of me, but I believed I had been hired by a friend of the patriot cause, someone who suspected that . . . that loyalists were using spellers to spy on Adams and the others. I suppose that sounds ridiculous."

Ethan had battled such a conjurer several years before. He shook his head. "Not so ridiculous, no." He adjusted his grip on the man. "What were you to do if you found anyone? What did you do after our encounter at the Green Dragon?"

"I was to write a missive describing who and what I had seen, and deliver it to a predetermined location."

At last. Ethan's pulse quickened. "Where? Where did you take those missives?"

"That's quite enough, I think."

Ethan sprang to his feet and spun, gripping his knife. At first he saw no one. But then Ramsey—or rather the faintly glowing, conjured illusion of him—appeared from the darkness, like a ship emerging from mist.

The figure did not spare Ethan a look, but stared straight at the clerk. It wore Ramsey's familiar sardonic smile, but its eyes gleamed as would embers in a hearth.

"I'm disappointed in you, Grant."

Grant appeared more perplexed than frightened. "Who are you?"

"The man who gave you those five pounds you've been telling Kaille about. I would have thought that much money bought not only your cooperation, but also a modicum of discretion."

With Ramsey's illusion still watching the clerk, Ethan slowly moved his blade hand toward the other. If he could draw blood and cast a finding spell while Ramsey was conjuring, he might locate the captain in spite of whatever precautions he might have—

"Don't do it, Kaille. Whatever spell you're trying to cast will only make matters worse."

"Worse for whom? For you, Ramsey? Do you think I care?"

"You've outlived your usefulness," the figure said, addressing Grant again. "Not that you were terribly useful to begin with. But nevertheless . . ." He smiled again.

A conjuring surged through the ground beneath Ethan's feet. He couldn't keep himself from glancing at Reg. The ghost was already watching him.

Grant let out a strangled cry and clawed at his chest. His mouth was agape, but he did not seem to be able to draw breath.

Ethan knelt next to him. "Grant?" He glared up at Ramsey's illusion. "What are you doing to him?"

"Nothing at all. You're doing it."

"Grant!" Ethan said again.

The clerk's eyes had gone wide. His hands still clutched his heart. He fell over onto his side, his unbroken leg kicking spasmodically.

Ethan fumbled in his coat pocket for the three pouches of herbs. Removing several leaves from each—he didn't bother to count them—he said, "*Tegimen nobis ambobus ex verbasco et marrubio et betonica evocatum.*" Warding, both of us, conjured from mullein, horehound, and betony.

The conjuring rumbled, an answer to Ramsey's spell. But Grant continued to flail silently.

"No," said Ramsey's illusion. "I'm afraid that didn't work."

"Damn you, Ramsey!"

"Damn me?" the illusion said. "Damn me? Thus far, I've done you a favor Kaille. You ought to be thanking me!" He pointed at the clerk. "I can kill him in as many ways as you can conjure. I can slice open his throat or shatter his neck, or do any number of things that will make it seem that he has been killed on this deserted lane by a more powerful man, a man seen with him on King Street only moments before. Or I can let him die as he's dying now, in a manner that will draw little notice. Earlier it was your choice that mattered; now it's mine. Depending upon what I do in the next few moments, you could be gaoled tonight and hanged tomorrow. You shouldn't be damning me; you should be begging."

Ethan stared back at him, shaking with rage, at Ramsey and at his own impotence.

The illusion cocked its glowing head to the side as if considering options. "What to do. On the one hand, I'm not done with you yet. And when you die, it will be by my hand, not Greenleaf's. Then again, I would so enjoy seeing the great Ethan Kaille brought low."

Grant's movements were growing feeble.

Ethan pulled more leaves from the pouches.

"Save your herbs, and your breath. He'll be dead in another minute, and one way or another it will have been your power that killed him."

Ethan held the herbs in his open palm, but he could think of no conjuring that would work against Ramsey's conjuring.

"Time to choose," the illusion whispered.

And even as the glowing figure spoke the words, another spell rumbled in the lane. Ethan didn't have to ask Reg to know that it was his own power he felt. Blood spurted from a sudden gash on Grant's neck and sprayed in a broad, dark fan across the ice.

Ethan was still on his knees, the leaves in his hand, and he fell back, scrabbling away from the man and his blood. "God have mercy!"

"I think he won't," Ramsey said.

Ethan stared at the clerk, watching in horror as he gave one last weak kick and moved no more. He felt nauseated and utterly disgusted with himself. Mostly, though, he detested Ramsey as he had no man ever before.

"What do you want of me?" Ethan asked, the words scraped from his throat.

"I want revenge. I want you to suffer and then to die. Haven't I been clear?"

"I mean," Ethan said, looking up at him, "what do you want to make this stop? You say you want to kill me. Fine. Tell me where to go, and I'll go there. We can fight to the death. And if you prevail, so be it."

"No, Kaille. No. This is better by far than killing you could ever be. You're weak, desperate, filled with guilt and self-loathing for all that your power has wrought. These past few days have brought me more pleasure than I imagined they would. And I am in no hurry for them to end." He glanced once more at Grant's body before facing Ethan once more and smiling. But he didn't vanish. Not yet. Instead he turned, facing back toward King Street. "Murder!" he cried. "Murder most foul!"

Ethan saw figures gathering at the mouth of the lane, pointing in his direction.

"Until next we meet," Ramsey said.

The illusion faded much as it had appeared, withdrawing into the inky darkness, and leaving Ethan alone with the corpse of Jonathan Grant.

Chapter
TWENTY

He remained on his knees for a moment after the conjured figure disappeared. Ramsey was exactly right. He was desperate and filled with self-loathing. In their previous encounter, Ramsey had used spells to burn him, to break his bones, to keep him from drawing breath. Indeed, the spell he had used to choke Grant might well have been one that he used to torture Ethan the previous summer. Yet nothing Ramsey did to him then hurt half as much as what he had made Ethan endure this night. So great was Ethan's anguish that as he watched the clerk die, he had been ready to give up his life to make it end.

But he would not die by the hangman's noose.

The crowd at the end of the lane was growing, and a few intrepid souls were edging toward him, perhaps trying to catch a glimpse of his face and to make sense of the scene before them.

Ethan lurched to his feet, driven by cold and fear and the knowledge that he hadn't the power to undo his own failure, which had cost Grant his life. He dashed out of the lane and across Water Street, keeping his head lowered, hoping that no one abroad at this hour would recognize him by his limp or his clothes or his features.

He needed help, and the last time he had spoken to Sephira Pryce, she had made an uncharacteristically generous offer.

Running as fast as his bad leg would allow, he continued southward until he reached the New South Meeting House, with its soaring spire, which gleamed white in the glow of the moon. The bells in the church still pealed along with those of the city's other sanctuaries, but here at the southern end of Boston, the tolling drifted across pasture-land and fields, incongruously peaceful on such a bloody night.

Ethan turned up Summer Street and soon stood once again at Sephira's door, breathing hard, his eyes streaming with the cold.

Despite the late hour, Sephira's windows were alight with candle flame. He knocked, and could not have been more surprised when Sephira herself opened the door.

"Mariz has been expecting you," she said without preamble, and walked away from the door. Ethan entered the house, closed the door, and followed her into the sitting room.

Sephira had already taken a seat by the hearth. Mariz and her other toughs were arrayed around the room.

"You knew I'd come?" Ethan said to the conjurer.

"Yes. I sensed many spells, and I feared for you. They came from the center of the city, but I could not locate them precisely enough to find you. I thought that, if you survived, you might come here."

Ethan didn't know what to say. Here was more kindness than he had thought to find.

"What's happened, Ethan?" Sephira asked, her tone as gentle as he had ever heard it, at least when directed at him.

He gave a high, choked laugh, and at the same time blinked away fresh tears. "Ramsey is using me . . . The shootings tonight on King Street—you've heard about them?"

She nodded.

"I was there. The spells that caused them to fire . . ." He broke off. He knew he wasn't making sense, but he was torn between his need and his fear of confessing too much to this woman who had tormented him so over the years. "A friend of mine was shot. He also used me to start a brawl in a tavern, and the woman I love was stabbed."

"Is she—?"

"I healed her in time."

"And your friend?"

"He'll live as well. But . . ." Even now, he couldn't bring himself to say out loud that Diver had lost his arm. "But just now," he went on, "as I was about to learn something of value from another conjurer, Ramsey appeared as an illusion. This other conjurer is dead. People saw me looming over him. They think I did it."

"I don't understand," Sephira said. "You say he used you. Used you how?"

Ethan looked to Mariz.

"He is casting spells using Kaille's power," Mariz said, watching Ethan even as he spoke to Sephira. "I do not know the magick, but it means that Ramsey does not have to be present to cast; wherever Kaille is, Ramsey can conjure."

"Including here?"

Ethan felt himself go pale. "Aye. I'm sorry, Sephira. I wasn't thinking. I'll leave right away." He headed back to her door.

"Ethan, come back here." She sounded more annoyed than frightened, like a parent summoning a wayward child.

"It's not safe for you," he said, remaining by the door.

"I would think that would make you all the more willing to come closer."

He had to grin. But he didn't move.

Seconds later, Sephira joined him in the foyer. "I told you the other day, I'm not afraid of Ramsey."

"You should be. I'm terrified of him."

"I'm sorry about your woman. I'm glad she's all right."

"Thank you."

"Come back inside."

"I came to speak with Mariz. He and I can go outside and talk there. That would be the more prudent thing to do."

"I find prudence boring. Didn't you know?"

He smiled again.

"Let me see if I understand," she said. "Ramsey is using you to hurt others, including the people who mean the most to you. Am I to infer that it was your witchery, wielded by Ramsey, that caused tonight's shootings?"

"Aye."

"And now he's managed to make it seem that you're a murderer."

"That's right."

"Impressive."

Ethan looked to the side, his mouth twitching.

"Relax, Ethan. I have no intention of helping Ramsey or of taking advantage of what he's done to you." She grinned. "At least not right now."

"Why not?" he asked, facing her.

"Because he killed Nigel. And because someday I'm going to ruin you myself, and I certainly don't need his help."

Ethan couldn't help but laugh, though his chest ached.

"Mariz," she called.

The conjurer joined them.

"Ethan wants a word with you. I think he'd be happier discussing these matters outside."

"Of course, *Senhora*." Mariz retreated into another room, only to emerge again, shrugging on a coat.

"You and I will speak again soon," Sephira said.

"Did you go to Medfield?" Ethan asked.

"Nap and Gordon did. They found the girl and the jewels. The soldier is gone, I think. But you have my thanks." She flashed a dazzling smile. "It was the easiest four and ten I've earned in some time."

"My pleasure."

He and Mariz stepped outside onto the portico. Ethan gazed northward toward the lights of Cornhill. Mariz pulled the door shut.

"I have communicated with my mentor as I told you I would," the conjurer said, coming forward to stand beside Ethan. "He has heard of borrowed spells and even knew of a conjurer who used them against another man. But he could tell me nothing about how to guard one's power from the use of another. The magicking, he said, was beyond any he had learned."

Ethan's disappointment was mild; he had not expected anything more. "Thank you for trying. I've never sent an illusion so far to speak with someone. Was it difficult?"

Mariz shrugged. "He is in the city of my youth. I know the place well, which made it easier. But it is Ramsey's illusion of which I wish to speak. You have spoken to him?"

"Aye. But I'm not sure there's much to be gained in talking about it. He can do what he wants with my power, at a time and place of his choosing."

"And you can do nothing to stop him?"

"Wardings don't work, even sophisticated ones. And I can't hurt an illusion. I believe there may be another man working with him—a soldier with the Twenty-ninth Regiment who's billeted at Murray's Barracks. But on this, of all nights, I won't be able to get near him. The last I saw of him, he was guarding the Town House with his comrades."

"We can use a concealment spell. Perhaps we can get close enough to speak with him when he is no longer on duty."

In spite of everything, Ethan smiled at his use of the word "we."

"Thank you, Mariz."

"Tell me about these wardings you have tried."

Ethan described for him the spell he had taught himself using the herbs he purchased at the Fat Spider.

"I have never cast such a warding myself, but I know that in Portugal, there are no herbs more valued for protection spells than the three Miss Windcatcher sold you."

"Right," Ethan said. "The spell should work, but for some reason it doesn't."

"Then let us find the soldier; perhaps he can explain this."

"All right."

Mariz slipped back inside to tell Sephira that they would be leaving for a time. He returned moments later.

Ethan raised his blade to the back of his hand, intending to cast the concealment spell. Mariz, though, put out a hand to stop him.

"I will cast it," he said. "Ramsey knows your conjurings. He may feel when you cast, and even recognize the spell. He is not as familiar with me and my power."

It was a fair point. "Very well."

Sephira's man cut himself and spoke the concealment spell for both of them. The conjuring trembled in the ground, and then settled over Ethan, like a cool mist on this frigid night. Concealed as they were by the same spell, Ethan and Mariz could see each other. They would be invisible to others, however, including any conjurers they encountered. They dismissed their spectral guides—Reg scowled when Ethan muttered, *"Dimitto te"*—and set out toward Cornhill and the western end of King Street.

So late at night, and at this end of the city, away from the mob that no doubt still crowded the lanes around the Town House, the streets were empty. Ethan and Mariz placed their feet with some care to avoid making too much noise as they walked, but for now they were in little danger of being heard. And for the time being, Ethan didn't have to worry about being identified as Grant's murderer.

"This soldier we seek—"

"His family name is Morrison."

"What else do you know about him?"

"I know he's a conjurer, and that his spectral guide was on Middle Street the day Christopher Seider was shot. Beyond that I don't know anything for certain. But I believe Ramsey hired Grant—the man he killed tonight—because he had ties to the Sons of Liberty. And I think he wanted to have a soldier working for him as well. What better way to sow as much conflict as possible in a garrisoned city?"

"But to what end, Kaille? I did not think that Ramsey cared about politics. He hates you, and has been driven by that hatred all along. Why bother with all of this?"

"I don't know. He may believe that I care even if he doesn't. And no doubt he remembers that Sephira worked for importation violators last summer; he hates her as well, and may wish to pit us against each other."

Mariz did not appear convinced. Ethan wasn't sure that he believed all of this either. But as they neared the corner of Cornhill and King streets, another thought came to him, one that he had first voiced to Janna.

"The illusion Ramsey used looked just like him." There were more people on the streets here, and Ethan said this in a whisper. "Or rather exactly as I remember him from last summer."

Sephira's man frowned at him and shrugged. "If you were to cast such a spell, would you not have it appear as you do?"

"Of course I would. But think, Mariz. He was trapped in that burning warehouse. He should have been scarred; as skilled as he is with conjurings, he couldn't have escaped completely unscathed."

"He is prideful. Perhaps he would not want you to see his scars."

"I'm sure he wouldn't," Ethan said. "But what if there is more at work here than mere pride? What if he's not merely scarred, but truly maimed? What if he's using these spells against me because he can't strike at me more directly? What if I can't find his ship because he is no longer capable of captaining a vessel?"

"It is possible. I had not considered this, but yes, it makes sense. This would make him easier to defeat, would it not?"

"It probably would. But it will also make him more desperate, more extravagant in what he's willing to do."

They passed the Old Brick Church. Its bell still tolled, testimony to how far Ramsey might go in his quest for revenge. The church stood only a few paces from the Town House and the western end of King Street. Remarkably, the crowd had dispersed, or perhaps had moved elsewhere. The soldiers were no longer guarding the building.

"They must be back at the barracks," Ethan said.

"Then this will be easier."

According to the clock on the Town House, it was past two o'clock in the morning. Still, Ethan and Mariz continued on to Murray's Barracks, stopping outside the entrance. The door was shut, and they couldn't open it without giving themselves away. They heard enough voices from within, though, to know that the soldiers were not yet abed.

"What now?" Mariz asked, his voice low.

"Now we convince him to join us outside. *Veni ad me*," Ethan said. Come to me.

Reg winked into view, bright russet in the gloom. He still appeared to be annoyed at having been dismissed as they made their way to the barracks.

"I didn't want someone spotting us too soon," Ethan said. "But now I need you to draw the soldier-conjurer outside. Do you know which man I mean?"

The ghost grinned and nodded.

"Good. Then go."

Reg glided to the doorway and passed through the wood and into the warehouse.

"This way," Ethan said.

He led Mariz farther up Brattle Street, past Hillier's Street, to Wings Lane, which was deserted. They waited at that corner, watching the barracks entrance, both of them with their blades drawn. After a few moments, Reg emerged onto the street once more and turned unerringly in their direction. Halfway up Brattle Street, the ghost halted and peered back over his glowing shoulder.

A few seconds later, the door to the sugar warehouse opened and out stepped a lanky uniformed soldier, his musket in hand. He glanced up and down the street. Spotting Reg, he strode after him.

Reg glided toward Ethan and Mariz, turning the corner at Wings Lane and then passing them, so that Morrison could not see him anymore.

The soldier quickened his pace.

Ethan and Mariz retreated a short distance onto the lane. As they did, Mariz looked at Ethan and mimicked holding a musket. Then he shook his head.

Ethan understood: This confrontation promised to be far more dangerous if Morrison was armed. Before he could respond, however, Morrison reached the corner. Reg had stopped a few strides beyond Ethan and Mariz, and now stood in the middle of the lane.

Seeing him there, Morrison slowed, his weapon held at waist level, the bayonet glinting with moonlight.

Ethan was close enough to see by the moonlight that his eyes were dark, and his chin bore a white scar. The soldier crept in his direction, his gaze sweeping the narrow street.

"Who are ya?" the soldier said. "Show yourself."

Mariz stood several feet from Ethan and Morrison had inadvertently positioned himself between them. Ethan caught Mariz's eye and pointed at him. Sephira's man appeared confused, but Ethan knew that he would catch on soon enough.

"Put down your weapon," Ethan said.

Morrison whirled toward him and raised his weapon as if to fire. Mariz stepped behind the man, and kicked his legs out from under him. The soldier fell to the ice, the musket slipping from his grip. Ethan covered the distance between himself and the soldier in a single stride and kicked the weapon beyond Morrison's reach.

Still on the ground, though now sitting, Morrison grabbed for his blade. For a half second, Ethan considered casting another shatter spell. But he didn't wish to draw Ramsey's attention if he could help it. Instead, as Morrison pulled his knife free of the sheath on his belt, Ethan kicked him in the side. The weapon flew from the soldier's hand, its blade clattering on the street with the ring of steel on ice.

Gasping, the soldier nevertheless tried to get up. Ethan planted his foot on the man's chest and shoved him down. The man grabbed Ethan's leg with both hands.

"Don't try it," Ethan said, putting more weight on Morrison so that the lad struggled to draw breath. "There are two of us, conjurers both. Even if you were to throw me off, you'd die before you could get away or cast the simplest of spells."

Morrison glowered. "Who are ya?" he said again, wheezing the words. "You came to the barracks before. Days ago. Isn't that right?"

"Let go of my leg."

The soldier remained still, except for his eyes, which darted from side to side, perhaps seeking some clue as to where Mariz stood.

Sephira's man squatted beside him, grabbed a handful of Morrison's hair, and laid the edge of his knife along the side of the soldier's throat.

Morrison dropped his hands to his side.

"Show yourselves then," he said, his voice still strained. "I'll not treat with men I can't look in the eye."

Ethan and Mariz shared a glance. Sephira's man appeared doubtful, and gave a small shake of his head. But Ethan wanted to see if Morrison recognized him. He nodded.

Mariz frowned, but then acquiesced with a shrug. He cut himself and said, *"Fini velamentum ex cruore evocatum."* End concealment, conjured from blood. With the pulse of the conjuring, and the appearance of Mariz's spectral guide, Morrison grew watchful and wary. Concealment spells did not wear off instantly, and so the soldier peered in turns at Ethan and Mariz, squinting, trying to see them more clearly.

When at last he was able to make out Ethan's features, he could not conceal the flash of recognition in his eyes.

"Aye," Ethan said. "You know me, don't you? Ramsey has seen to that."

"I don't know what you're talkin' about."

He was a better liar than Grant, but not by much. Ethan removed his foot from Morrison's chest and motioned for Mariz to release him.

"Stand up," he said.

Morrison eyed them both, but then climbed to his feet. He was several inches taller than both of them. Ethan could see that he was already thinking of possible routes to safety.

"You've been working for someone," Ethan said. "A conjurer. You were given five pounds initially and promised more. The person who paid you said to watch for conjurers here in town, and to leave a missive somewhere when you found one."

"I told you, I—"

Ethan stopped him with a raised hand. "Don't lie to me, lad. I've no time for games, and even less patience. You weren't the only one he hired, and I've already learned a good deal."

Morrison glanced at Mariz again. Sephira's man held his knife over his arm; it might as well have been a pistol, full-cocked and aimed at his heart.

Morrison huffed a sigh. "What is it you want to know?" he said.

"Let's start with where you're supposed to deliver your missives."

"The burying ground on the Common. The old one with the granary."

The Granary Burying Ground. It was almost funny. The last time Ethan and Ramsey fought, it was over the souls of the newly dead. They had faced each other in that cemetery. Had Ramsey found one more way to mock him?

"Where exactly?" Ethan asked.

"Just by the gate."

"Are you to meet someone, or leave the messages and go?"

"I'm just to leave them."

"Did you meet someone when you were first paid?"

"Aye. But he was no conjurer, at least not that I could tell. I think he was a sailor."

Maybe Ramsey still had his ship after all, and so still commanded a loyal crew.

"Is there a signal of some sort, a way to let this person know that you've left word?"

"Aye. I'm to place the message at the base of a tombstone, one near the entrance, and then I'm to cast a spell: a simple wardin'. I was told that my spells would be recognized and that someone would come an' retrieve the message."

"And how were you to be paid the balance of what you're owed?"

Morrison shrugged. "They haven't said yet. But they were good for the first five pounds; I expect they'll pay me the rest."

"What if they don't?" Ethan shook his head, forestalling an answer. "Allow me: You believe that though they haven't said as much, the people you're working for are loyalists who seek to weaken the patriot cause. You were happy to be paid, but you would do this work for nothing if it meant helping to defeat Samuel Adams and his rabble. Isn't that right?"

The way the soldier gawked at him one might have thought he had sprouted wings and flown in circles over the city. "How did you know that?"

"You're not the only conjurer Ramsey hired."

"You mentioned that name before. Ramsey. Who is he?"

"He's no loyalist; I can tell you that much. He's a merchant captain, a conjurer, and a madman. None of what you've been asked to do will help your fellow soldiers or hurt Samuel Adams and his allies. Ramsey wants vengeance. That's all he cares about."

"Vengeance on who?" Morrison asked.

"On me."

"I don't believe you," Morrison said, narrowing his eyes.

"I don't care. You're going to help us find him."

The soldier's expression hardened. "And what if I don't?"

"Then every man in your regiment will learn that you're a witch."

"I could do the same to you. To both of you," he added with a quick look at Mariz.

"You could, but it wouldn't prevent your court-martial, would it? You don't have to do anything you wouldn't otherwise," Ethan said.

"You'll come with us to the burying ground, cast your spell, and be on your way. We won't trouble you again, and you'll have done nothing to violate the terms of your agreement with Ramsey."

"What about a message? I'm supposed to leave one for him."

"And so you will. We're to be your message."

Ethan could see that the soldier didn't like this idea at all. He was eyeing the two of them again; Ethan thought he might be trying to determine if he could fight them off long enough to retrieve his musket.

"I've had a long night, Morrison," Ethan said. "I was on King Street when your friends opened fire. And that was far from the worst part of my evening. If you so much as glance in the direction of your weapon, my friend and I will shatter every bone in your body, heal them all, and then break them again, one by one. Through no fault of your own, you've been drawn into a blood feud. Ramsey wants me dead, and I'm determined to kill him if I have to. Please don't make me hurt you, too."

The soldier hesitated but then nodded.

"Shall we make our way to the burying ground?" Ethan asked.

"I suppose."

"Come along then." Ethan turned to Mariz. "Walk behind us. If he takes a step in the wrong direction, snap his neck."

Mariz turned to Morrison and smiled. "With pleasure."

"What about my knife and musket?"

"It's half past two in the morning. Leave them there; they'll be waiting for you when we're done at the burying ground."

The soldier didn't seem satisfied with this response either, but he fell in beside Ethan and they began the short walk from Wings Lane to the burying ground.

"Why does this man Ramsey hate you so much?" Morrison asked after some time.

"That's a long tale," Ethan said, unable to keep the weariness from his voice. "Long ago we found ourselves at odds, and we never managed to make peace."

This left Morrison looking more confounded than satisfied, but he said nothing more until they reached the burying ground gate.

Once inside the grounds, the soldier led Ethan to one of the grave markers near the entrance.

"This is it," he said. "This is where I'm to leave the missives."

"All right then," Ethan said. "Cast your spell. Carefully, Morrison. There's still two of us and only one of you."

The man reached for his knife, but of course it was no longer on his belt. Ethan drew his own and handed it to the man hilt first. Morrison took it, clearly surprised by the trust Ethan had shown him. He cut himself and muttered his warding spell. When the thrum of the conjuring had died away, he returned Ethan's knife.

"What now?"

"Go back to your regiment, lad. You'll have no more trouble from me." Ethan proffered a hand, which the man gripped after a moment's hesitation.

The soldier cast one last look at Mariz, before trudging through the snow back to the street.

"I am not sure it was wise to let him go," Mariz said, watching the soldier.

"Perhaps not. But I've seen too many men die tonight. I'm not willing to watch Ramsey kill him, too."

Mariz didn't argue. "So now we wait for another man to come."

"Aye," Ethan said. "We won't be so gentle with this next one."

hey left the burying ground and found a vantage point near the corner of School Street from which they could see the cemetery gate. Lifting his collar against a light, cold wind off the harbor, Ethan leaned against the side of a building and closed his eyes. He longed for sleep.

"Are you certain that Ramsey will send someone tonight?" Mariz asked. "It is very late."

Ethan didn't bother opening his eyes. "He'll send someone. He killed Grant tonight because he's afraid I'm getting too close to finding him. He'll want to know what Morrison has learned."

"And when he figures out that Morrison has deceived him, what will he do? Did you really spare Morrison, or have you sent him to his death?"

At that, Ethan opened his eyes. "I can't control Ramsey. All I can do is find him and kill him before he does more harm."

"You were reluctant to kill him the last time we fought him."

"Not anymore," Ethan said.

Mariz nodded his approval.

Sooner even than Ethan had expected, he heard the sound of footsteps, boots crunching the frozen snow. He spotted the sailor, who was coming not from the South End waterfront, as Ethan had expected, but from the north. He might have come from the North End, or perhaps even from New Boston, as the West End was also known. The man followed what in the summer months was barely more than a dirt path from Beacon Street around the back of the burying ground to the gate Ethan and Mariz had been watching. He carried a torch and, after entering the cemetery, walked directly to the tomb Morrison had indicated.

Ethan and Mariz made their way back to the cemetery gate as well, making as little noise as possible.

The sailor had stopped at the gravesite and appeared to be searching the ground. Seeing nothing, he lowered his torch so that it would cast more light on the grave marker.

"Have you lost something?" Ethan asked.

The man spun, nearly dropping his torch. "No, I—" He fell silent, his eyes going wide as he recognized Ethan and Mariz. This was one of the crewmen Ramsey had with him the previous summer, when he desecrated graves in all three of Boston's oldest burying grounds, including this one.

He drew his knife and lowered himself into a crouch, the blade in one hand, the torch in the other. Mariz had his knife at his arm, ready to cut himself for a conjuring. Ethan held his blade ready as well, but he didn't wish to conjure. Doing so would only draw Ramsey's attention.

"Those won't do you much good against two conjurers."

"I'll take my chances," the man said.

Ethan had to admire his courage, though he knew it would do the sailor no good. A dark and eerie calm had settled over him. Never before had he done what he contemplated now. But never before had he been so desperate.

"It needn't come to a fight. I want to see your captain; that's all. I know he's been eager to see me as well. Tell me where he is and you're free to go."

"I ain' tellin' you nothin'."

"Do you carry a pistol, Mariz?" Ethan asked quietly.

The conjurer glanced his way. "Yes, I do."

Ethan held out his hand. "Give it to me."

The sailor had started to back away. Ethan feared that he would flee.

"Now!" he said, his voice carrying across the burying ground.

Mariz reached into his coat pocket, removed the flintlock, and handed it to Ethan.

Ethan wasted no time. He raised the weapon, took careful aim, and fired. The report of the pistol was deafening and seemed to echo in every corner of the city. The soldier collapsed, wailing, clutching his bloodied thigh. He had dropped his knife and torch—the latter sputtered and went out when it hit the snow.

Ethan walked to where the man lay and pocketed the dropped blade.

"Now," he said, kneeling next to the man. "Let's begin with something easy, shall we? What's your name?"

"Go to hell," the sailor said through clenched teeth.

"You're unarmed, you're hurt, you're cold and tired. I can heal you. I'd be glad to. Or I can kill you, very, very slowly."

"Kaille—"

"Quiet, Mariz." To the sailor he said again, "Tell me your name."

"Go ahead and kill me."

"You believe that I won't. Perhaps Ramsey has convinced you that I'm weak, that even when circumstance calls for ruthlessness, I'm incapable of it. Not long ago, there might have been some truth to that. But after what your captain has done to me these past few days, I assure you, I am willing to do whatever I have to find him." He flipped Mariz's pistol in the air and caught it by the barrel. And still holding the sailor's gaze, he pounded the butt of the flintlock on the bullet wound in the sailor's leg.

The man roared his pain, tears springing from his eyes.

"This is going to get much, much worse if you don't start answering my questions."

When the sailor merely glared back at him, Ethan said, "You don't wish to tell me your name. That's fine. Tell me where Ramsey is."

Silence.

He hammered at the wound a second time, drawing a howl from the sailor.

"Ramsey has been using my power to cast spells. Did you know that? Because of him, I bear some blame for the death of a young boy." He hit the man again. "For the fracturing of a soldier's skull." He struck another blow. "For a tavern brawl that almost killed the woman I love." Another blow. "And for tonight's shooting, which killed at least three men and cost my dearest friend his arm." He hit the soldier four more times.

By now the soldier was writhing in agony, and whimpering like a beaten cur. Tiny spots of blood dotted the snow near his leg, and the butt of Mariz's pistol was sticky and red.

"What would you propose I do?" Ethan asked Ramsey's man, his voice sounding disturbingly calm to his own ears. When the sailor didn't answer, he said, "I'm at a loss as well. I can't allow this to go on. And with you here, I have the opportunity to ascertain where Ramsey can be found. So you see, I have no choice in the matter. I bear you no malice, but I also have no particular reason to spare you. Ramsey hasn't cared who he hurts or kills in seeking to avenge himself on me. Why should I be any different?"

A voice in his head—Kannice's—answered his own question: *Because you are.* But he ignored this, his eyes fixed on the sailor.

He held out the pistol for Mariz; the conjurer took it from him. Ethan held up his blade for the sailor to see.

The man looked away, fresh tears on his face, his breathing ragged.

"Surely you understand by now how desperate I am. How much are you willing to endure for the sake of Ramsey's blind vengeance?"

"He's my captain," the man said. He shook his head. "You wouldn't understand."

"I would, actually. I was once a seaman, as you are."

The sailor sneered. "You were a mutineer. A traitor. I'm nothin' like you."

Ethan shrugged, and in one swift, brutally quick motion he stabbed down with his blade, burying it in the man's leg an inch below the bullet wound.

The sailor screamed. Mariz let out a sharp hiss and grabbed Ethan's shoulder.

Ethan shrugged him off before pulling the blade free.

"Where is Ramsey?" he asked.

The sailor had fallen back onto the ice. He sobbed softly, his eyes squeezed shut, bloody fingers gripping his mutilated leg.

"He is not going to tell you," Mariz said, his voice low but hard.

"Not yet. I don't wish to alert Ramsey to our presence here, but you may have to conjure after all."

"I won't."

Ethan looked up at him. "You know what Ramsey has done. And you know as well that if Sephira were here, she would be doing exactly as I am."

"Yes, Kaille, she would! Does that not tell you how wrong this is? You are not like her. That is one of the reasons I have been pleased to call you my friend." He gestured at the sailor. "But this . . . This is precisely what she would do."

Ethan turned back to Ramsey's man, who still lay on his back, his chest rising and falling. Ethan's hands had started shaking again. His hatred for Ramsey churned in his gut like bile. But Mariz was right. This man lying before him had done nothing to him. "What am I supposed to do?" he whispered, his throat tight.

"I do not know," Mariz said. "Not this, though. Surely not this."

Ethan exhaled through his teeth, his shoulders slumping. He reached for the sailor's hands, but the man flinched and tried to crawl away.

"It's all right," Ethan said. "I'm going to heal you."

Still the man resisted; why wouldn't he?

"Mariz."

The other conjurer knelt beside him and removed the sailor's hands from his leg. Ethan placed his hand over the two wounds and whispered, *"Remedium ex cruore evocatum."*

At the first touch of the healing spell, the sailor tensed and inhaled sharply through his teeth. But after a few seconds his fists unclenched and his breathing eased a little.

When the wounds had healed over enough to stop bleeding, Ethan sat back on his heels. The sailor was watching him.

"You'll need to have a surgeon work on that leg," Ethan said.

The man spoke not a word.

But a voice from behind them said, "What's the matter with his leg?"

Ethan had expected this. He stood and faced the illusion Ramsey had conjured. "I shot him. Stabbed him, too. Even now, you inspire great loyalty in the men of your crew. He told me nothing."

"You tortured him?" the figure asked.

"Aye."

"And then you healed him."

"I suppose that makes me weak."

"It doesn't make you weak, but it is symptomatic of your weakness."

"If you care to tell me where you are, I'll bring him to you. Perhaps you have a surgeon among your crew who can tend to his wound."

"My thanks, but I'll send men for him. You'd best not be there when they arrive. There will be many of them, and they'll all be armed."

"I'm going to find you eventually, Ramsey."

"Perhaps. You might die first." The figure grinned.

Ethan turned and walked away. Mariz followed.

"Harm one of my men again, and those you love will suffer even more."

"Do not answer him," Mariz said, whispering the words. "Keep walking."

"Kaille!"

Ethan heeded Mariz's advice.

"Damn you, Kaille!"

A spell rang in the icy ground. Reg appeared beside him, a warning in his brilliant eyes. Ethan had little time to wonder what spell Ramsey had cast now using his power.

Pain exploded on the side of his head, behind his ear.

Ethan stumbled and fell to his hands and knees. Mariz kicked him in the gut, flipping Ethan on to his back.

Ramsey's illusion laughed.

Mariz cut the back of his hand.

"*Tegimen ex verbasco evocatum!*" Ethan said, blurting the words, and using the mullein he carried to protect himself. He didn't know if he was still warded, and with Mariz being spell-crazed he wasn't taking any chances.

Mariz's conjuring hit him an instant later, pounding his body like a mighty wave, but doing no further damage. Ethan didn't know what spell Sephira's man had cast; he knew only that his warding had held.

He kicked out, his boot catching Mariz just below the knee. The man lurched back a step but then righted himself.

Ethan tried to get to his feet, but Mariz directed a second conjuring at him, and he was thrown to the ground once more. His warding protected him from the effects of the spell, but as long as Mariz continued to hammer at him with conjurings Ethan would be unable to get away from the cemetery before Ramsey's men arrived.

Unwilling to give the man the chance to conjure again, he sliced the skin on his hand and spoke a sleep spell. The conjuring pulsed, and Mariz reeled, as if kicked by a mule. But the spell did not put him to sleep.

"You'll have to do better than that, Kaille. A sleep spell won't defeat his wardings. You're going to have to kill him, too."

With his next conjuring, Mariz did not attack directly. Rather, he made the torch Ramsey's man had been carrying fly at Ethan's head. Dark as it was, Ethan didn't realize what he had done until it was too late; he only saw the torch at the last moment. It hit his forehead as hard as it would have had the man swung it like a club. Once more Ethan was knocked to the ground. Addled, dizzy, he lay still for several seconds, trying to clear his vision.

He had no chance to get back up. Mariz loomed over him, the torch in hand. He aimed a blow at Ethan's face, but Ethan managed to roll out of the way before the torch hit him. As it was, he heard it whistle past and slam into the ground. Shards of ice hit his head and neck.

Mariz struck at him again, hitting his side. Ethan let out a grunt; he thought he felt ribs crack.

He bit down on the inside of his cheek, tasting blood. He whispered a shatter spell. The wood splintered, slivers of the torch rained down on him. Before Mariz could kick him again, or worse, he rolled away and clambered to his feet.

Sephira's man was stalking him now, knife held ready, his eyes blank, passionless.

"Mariz," he said. "It's me. Look me in the eye."

Mariz leaped at him, leading with his blade. It was a clumsy assault: too rushed, too reckless. Clearly Sephira had hired the man for his conjuring ability, not his skill as a fighter. Ethan dodged the attack, and struck a blow of his own to the side of Mariz's head. Mariz reeled. Ethan dove at the man, pressing his advantage even as he sucked his breath at the pain in his side. Grabbing Mariz around the midsection, Ethan drove him to the ground. He punched him once, and a second time. The knife slipped from Mariz's fingers. Ethan grabbed it and shoved it into his pocket.

He started to his feet, only to feel the pulse of another conjuring. It struck him squarely in the chest, lifting him off of his feet and slamming him down. He thought it might have been a blade spell, one that would have sliced him in half but for his warding. He realized, though, that the type of conjuring was of little importance. Ramsey wanted to keep them fighting; nothing else mattered.

"Mariz! Look at me!"

Sephira's man was standing once more, searching for his blade or for the torch. Seeing neither, he took a step in Ethan's direction.

"He won't listen to you, Kaille," said Ramsey's illusion. "And he won't stop unless I tell him to." The figure grinned. "And I won't."

Ethan didn't wish to hurt his friend, but it seemed he had no other choice. He cut himself and cast a fire spell, knowing that the conjuring would slow Mariz down without penetrating his wardings. Or assuming as much. As his conjuring drummed in the earth, a second spell made the ground tremble as well. And when the fire spell hit Sephira's man it not only knocked him over, it also engulfed his coat in flames. Ramsey had used Ethan's power to remove Mariz's warding.

Ethan swore and ran to his friend, pulling off his own coat so that he might smother the blaze. Mariz flailed at him with his fists and feet, more intent on fighting Ethan than on saving his own life. But Ethan used his coat to subdue the man and extinguish the fire. And then he hit Mariz again and again until the conjurer lost consciousness.

He heard a sharp sound and looking up realized that Ramsey's illusion was applauding, that same mocking grin on the lean face.

"Well done, Kaille. I had hoped you would have to do more damage, but it was entertaining nevertheless. And next time I'll turn a more worthy opponent against you." He looked back northward. Following the line of the figure's gaze, Ethan saw in the distance many men approaching, several of them carrying torches. "My crew," Ramsey said, facing Ethan once more. "You might want to be on your way."

Breathing hard, the burns on his hands throbbing, Ethan swung his coat back on, though it was still smoking. He lifted Mariz, grunting with the effort, his battered ribs aching, and slung the man over his shoulder.

"I can make you kill him right now," Ramsey said. "You know that, don't you?"

"Aye, I know it. What do you expect me to do, Ramsey? Surrender?"

"No, Kaille! I know you won't. That is what makes this so delicious. You won't surrender. I can count on that. But I think killing him sounds like a fine idea. You don't really want to carry him anyway, do you?" Ramsey's image laughed.

"Kaille!"

They both turned at the sound of the voice. Stephen Greenleaf stood a short distance off, a flintlock pistol in his hand. But that hand had dropped to his side and his eyes were fixed on the glowing figure, his mouth hanging open.

Ethan saw the sheriff's lips move and knew that he said the captain's name. But he heard nothing.

Ramsey's illusion laughed again and glanced Ethan's way. "I suppose your friend has just been given a reprieve. I assure you, it's only temporary."

An instant later he winked out of sight.

Ethan exhaled. Ramsey's men were approaching and he didn't wish to be here when they arrived. But with the sheriff now hurrying toward him, he couldn't flee. Not yet.

"That was Ramsey!" Greenleaf said. "Or at least a ghost of him."

"Aye," Ethan said, shifting his grip on Mariz. "It was a vision Ramsey conjured to speak with me."

"So, he's alive!"

"I told you as much earlier this evening."

"I remember. I didn't believe you."

"Of course not."

The sheriff looked down at Ramsey's man, who still lay in the snow, the blood on his leg appearing black in the moonlight. "Who's this?"

"One of Ramsey's crew."

"What happened to him?"

"I tortured him." Greenleaf's gaze snapped to Ethan's face, but Ethan didn't pause. "In an attempt to learn where Ramsey is hiding."

"You shot him."

"Aye."

"That's what drew me here. I heard the gunshot." He lifted his chin toward Mariz, who was still slung over Ethan's shoulder. "And who's that?"

"Sephira's man. Mariz. I beat him senseless after Ramsey used a spell to make him attack me."

The sheriff blinked. "Busy night."

"You could say that."

"Did you also murder a man on Leveret's Lane?"

"Jonathan Grant," Ethan said. "I was there when he died, but it was Ramsey who committed the murder, again with a spell." He glanced once more toward the approaching men. They were close now. He could hear their voices so clearly they could have been speaking to him.

"It didn't look like a spell," Greenleaf said. "It looked like someone slashed his throat. You carry a knife, don't you, Kaille?"

"It was a spell, Sheriff. Ramsey's spell."

"Damn you witches! I don't care what you call it: conjuring, witchery, black magick. It's the devil's work. I should hang the lot of you." He narrowed his eyes. "How do I know you're not lying to me? How do I know you didn't conjure that image of Ramsey to fool me?"

"You don't. Can we be moving, Sheriff? Those are Ramsey's men, and they're not going to be happy with me after what I've done to their friend."

Without waiting for an answer, Ethan started away. His back and shoulders already ached, and he had a long walk ahead of him.

"Tell me about Grant," Greenleaf said, falling in step beside him.

Ethan explained to the sheriff what he could, taking great pains to avoid saying anything that Greenleaf could point to as evidence of his conjuring abilities. The resulting narrative served only to deepen the sheriff's frustration.

"I understand little of this," he said, "and I believe even less. I should throw you in the gaol and hang you come the morn."

Ethan was too weary to argue. "Perhaps you should. And then you can fight Ramsey on your own."

"I'm not sure Ramsey—"

Ethan halted, swaying under Mariz's weight. "Ramsey is here, in Boston. He is responsible for murders and bloodshed. You can believe that or not, but it's the truth. I intend to kill him when I find him, and then you'll know that I wasn't lying to you. But for now either help me carry this man the rest of the way to Summer Street, or leave me in peace."

Greenleaf regarded him for several seconds, his lips pressed in a flat line. "Kill him then. I want to see the body. If you can do that, I'll not trouble you about Grant. But if you can't, you'll swing for his murder. I guarantee it." He started to say more, but then seemed to think better of it. In the end, he merely turned and stalked back toward the center of the city.

Ethan watched him go, adjusted his hold on Mariz, and marshaled his strength for what remained of his walk to Summer Street.

The first faint glow of dawn had touched the eastern sky over the harbor when Ethan again rapped on Sephira's door. He had longer to wait this time, and when the door opened Ethan found himself face-to-face with an African servant he had never before seen. The man was as tall and brawny as Afton and Gordon, but he wore a suit rather than the clothes of a street tough.

"I have Mariz," he said, barely getting the words out. He was breathless. His legs shook with the effort of remaining upright. "My name is Kaille."

The man bent low to peer up at Mariz's face. He seemed to recognize him, because he motioned Ethan into the house and shut the door.

"I'll wake Miss Pryce," the man said. He pointed toward the sitting room. "You may set him on the daybed."

Ethan carried Mariz to the sitting room, lowered him onto the daybed, and collapsed to the floor. There he sat, with his back cushioned against the sofa as he tried to catch his breath. When he could muster the strength, he pulled off his coat, slipped his knife from his belt, and cut himself. With his first spell, he lit several candles in the room. When he could see well enough, he cut himself a second time, dabbed some blood on the burns that covered Mariz's neck and jaw, and cast a healing spell.

He still held his hands over the burns when Sephira entered the room, her eyes bleary with sleep, her hair in tangles. It was, he realized, the first time he had seen her look anything less than perfect. And still she was lovely.

"What happened to him?" she asked, her voice more of a rasp than its usual purr.

"A fire spell," Ethan said. "He has burns on his neck and face."

"From Ramsey?"

Ethan answered with a small shrug. "In a way. Ramsey used a spell to turn Mariz against me, the same way he made Gordon attack Will Pryor. Mariz and I battled with spells, and since Mariz had warded himself, my spells didn't do much more than knock him back a step or two. But as I cast a fire spell, Ramsey removed Mariz's warding."

"So you did this to him."

Ethan met her gaze. "Aye. It wasn't my intention, but I did it."

"And the bruises on his face?"

"Those I did intend. I didn't want to use conjurings to subdue him, so I beat him."

She nodded. "You don't appear to be hurt; are your spells that much stronger than Mariz's?"

"Not at all. Ramsey didn't remove my warding; that's the only reason my spell worked when Mariz's didn't. And as for not being hurt,

I'm reasonably certain that your friend here broke one or two of my ribs."

Sephira smirked. "Remind me to increase his pay."

Ethan's laugh quickly turned to a wince.

"You haven't healed yourself?"

He shook his head. "Mariz's injuries are worse than mine. And I'm responsible for them."

"I don't pretend to know much about your witchery, Ethan, but from all that I gather, you're not responsible. Mariz attacked you. Isn't that right?"

"Well, yes."

"And you thought that he was protected when you cast your spell, didn't you?"

"Aye, I was sure of it."

"Ramsey is terribly clever," she said. "And as much as I hate him, that's a difficult admission for me." She ran a hand through her knotted curls. "Your greatest weakness has always been that you're too kind, too sentimental."

"Aye, you've told me as much."

"And Ramsey is using that weakness to his advantage. You're not responsible for the things he does, even if he uses your magicking to do them. But you're so racked with guilt, you can't see that."

"Are you trying to help me, Sephira?"

She scowled. "It's the hour. If the sun was fully up, I'd be more than glad to see you suffer."

Ethan smiled. He removed his hands from Mariz's burns and leaned closer to see how they had healed.

"He should be all right," Ethan said.

"The burns on his coat are blackening my daybed."

"Aye. You can take it out of his increased wage." He cut himself a third time, and lifting his shirt, rubbed some blood on the skin over his sore ribs. He could feel the broken bone—a clean break. He'd been more fortunate than Diver.

"*Remedium ex cruore evocatum.*" Healing, conjured from blood.

Sephira watched him, her eyes luminous in the candlelight.

"So what do you suggest?" Ethan asked, avoiding her gaze, feeling oddly uncomfortable with her eyes upon him.

"I don't know," she said. "I don't suffer from this particular malady—guilt and kindness don't come naturally to me—and so I have little experience with banishing them from my thoughts. But that, it seems to me, is what you need to do. These are Ramsey's crimes, not yours."

Ethan felt the bone knitting beneath his hands. After a few moments more, he was able to move and draw a deep breath without too much pain. He pulled down his shirt and stood.

"We need to wake him."

A frown furrowed Sephira's brow. "The night Gordon beat that boy, you were afraid to wake him lest he renew his assault."

"I remember. But if I'm to defeat Ramsey, I'll need Mariz's help, and I can't afford to wait another day. We'll wake him, and if I have to, I'll use a spell to put him to sleep. Ramsey removed his warding; I don't think he put it back in place."

Sephira did not look happy. "I don't want a conjuring war in my sitting room."

"Neither do I."

He pushed up his sleeve and cut his forearm, allowing the blood to well from the wound. "Wake him," he said.

Sephira eyed his knife and bloody arm the way she might a pistol in the hands of a rival. But she knelt beside the daybed and gave Mariz a gentle shake.

"Mariz, wake up. I need to speak with you." He didn't stir, and she glanced up at Ethan again.

"Try again," Ethan said. "Use my name."

Her frown deepened. "Mariz, Kaille is here. He wants a word with you. Wake up now. You need to speak with him."

Mariz gave a low moan, his eyelids twitching but not opening.

"Mariz—"

"Yes, *Senhora*," he said, sounding groggy. "I hear you. You say that Kaille is here?"

Sephira looked at Ethan again. "That's right."

Ethan tightened his gripped on his blade.

"That is good," Mariz said. He opened his eyes, squeezed them shut, but only for a second. His eyes found Sephira first, then shifted to Ethan. He sat up and touched the burns on his face.

"Ramsey set me against you," he said.

Ethan nodded and allowed himself to relax. "Aye, he did."

"He should not have. I know where he is."

Chapter TWENTY-TWO

Ethan hardly dared hope that he had heard the man correctly. "How is that possible?"

"I sensed his conjuring, as I would if he had cast the spell on his own rather than through you. I do not know why I was able to— perhaps because to control me in that way he had to use both his power and yours. But I believe I can lead you to him."

"Where?" Ethan asked. "Where is he?"

"In New Boston, near the spur of land that juts into the Charles River."

"Barton's Point?" Sephira asked.

"Yes, near there."

"There are shipyards there," Sephira said to Ethan. "Warehouses. There's also a rope yard along Wiltshire."

"Aye. He and his crew could be in any one of those."

She stood. "Nap, Gordon, and the others will be here before long. We'll go with you."

"No," Ethan said. "I can't risk taking anyone with me. Ramsey will use my power to control you, and we'll wind up fighting each other instead of him."

"We've fought each other before," Sephira said. "We're rather good at it."

"I'm serious, Sephira."

"So am I. Do you honestly believe that you can defeat him on your own? Despite all evidence to the contrary?"

"I don't know. But I'm certain that if I have you with me, or Mariz, or Janna, or anyone else, it will be more difficult to fight him rather than less."

"There must be some way for you to ward yourself against him," Mariz said. "All spells can be defeated; our task is to determine how."

"I've tried different wardings, and to no avail. He knows my conjurings too well."

Mariz stared back at him, his eyes widening a bit.

"He knows *my* conjurings too well," Ethan said again, excitement seeping into his voice. "But not yours. What if you were to put a warding on me using the herbs I bought from Janna. The spell would be every bit as strong, but because it wasn't mine, Ramsey might not find a way past it."

"This could work," Mariz said. "Although, I was warded tonight as well, and he mastered me using your power."

"I had forgotten that." With the memory, came a dampening of Ethan's initial enthusiasm.

"Still, Kaille, it might slow him, even if only for a moment. Perhaps that will be enough."

It wasn't much; it was hardly anything. But it was all they had, and Mariz was right. If they could confound Ramsey, even for the briefest instant, it might give them the advantage they needed to destroy him. He pulled the pouches of herbs from his coat pockets, removed three leaves from each, and handed the leaves to Mariz.

The conjurer placed the leaves in his palm and opened his mouth. But then he closed it again. "I am not sure of the wording," he said after a few seconds.

"Your warding on me," Ethan said. "Sourced in the herbs. That would be simplest. And use my name. The more specific the spell, the more powerful it seems to be."

"Yes, all right." Mariz held out his hand again, the leaves piled in his palm. "*Meum tegimen pro Kaille, ex verbasco et marrubio et betonica evocatum.*" My warding over Kaille, conjured from mullein, horehound, and betony.

The spell growled like some beast from hell, seeming to shake the mansion to its foundations. Mariz's spectral guide, the young man in Renaissance garb, appeared beside him and eyed Ethan with interest.

"The leaves are gone," Sephira said in a hushed voice.

"Aye," Ethan said. "Let's hope that means it worked."

"Now you'll take us with you?" she asked.

He hesitated, but not for long. He would need her help getting past Ramsey's crew, just as he would need Mariz's help to overcome the captain's conjurings. "I'd be grateful," he said.

Sephira nodded. "Good. I'm going to dress. When was the last time you ate?"

Ethan allowed himself a breathless laugh. "I couldn't tell you."

"I assumed as much. I'll have breakfast prepared. We'll eat, and then we'll hunt."

⁓≈⁓

By the time the sun was up and shining through Sephira's windows, Nap, Gordon, and Afton had arrived at the mansion. So, too, had several of Sephira's other toughs, men with whom Ethan had but limited contact. Sephira had returned to the dining room, dressed as usual in black breeches, a white silk shirt, and a waistcoat that fit her with unnerving snugness.

Nap and the two brutes Ethan knew so well could not mask their surprise at finding him already in the house, supping with Sephira at a table laden with breads, cheeses, eggs, and sweet pastries. Nap and Gordon exchanged a quick look; Nap even raised an eyebrow. Ethan suppressed a grin. Let the men believe what they would. For this day, at least, he and Sephira were allies, as they had been when last Ramsey cast his spells in Boston.

"We need to locate Ramsey and his men more precisely," Sephira said, sipping coffee and watching as Ethan filled his plate yet again. "You can find him with your witchery, can't you?"

"I can," Ethan said, "but I won't."

"Why on earth not?"

Ethan shifted his gaze to Mariz. While Sephira would be more than willing to help Ethan kill Ramsey, she would be less eager to follow Ethan into the coming battle. She trusted in her own leadership, and no one else's, and Ethan assumed that this was merely the first in what would be a series of questions regarding his decisions. This day would be easier if Mariz would explain at least some of the choices Ethan made.

Sephira's man appeared to understand.

"The conjuring of which you speak, *Senhora*, is a finding spell. It will allow us to locate Ramsey, but it will also alert Ramsey to the fact that we are coming. He will feel the conjuring and thus prepare himself for our arrival."

"He doesn't think we have any idea of where he is," Ethan said. "For the first time since all this began, we have an advantage, however small it might be. I won't squander it for convenience."

Sephira didn't mask her displeasure at having her suggestion dismissed, but she acquiesced with a curt nod.

Ethan ate what remained of his breakfast, and pushed back from her table, feeling considerably better for having eaten a decent meal. He could have done with a few hours' slumber, but he didn't dare delay their confrontation with Ramsey any longer.

Sephira stood as well. "Have my carriage brought around to the front of the house," she said to Afton.

The big man lumbered toward the back entrance.

"The two of you will ride with me," she said to Ethan and Mariz. "The others will follow us."

"Aye, all right. But heed me, Sephira. Ramsey's men are not the enemy. Mariz and I will try first to put them to sleep. Failing that, you and your men will have no choice but to fight them. If some try to escape, let them go. If you can overcome them with blades and fists, do so. Only resort to pistols if nothing else works."

"Are you truly trying to instruct me in the art of fighting?" she asked, her voice cold, the look in her eyes as hard as sapphires.

"I'm telling you not to kill them unless they leave you no other choice."

"Do you expect Ramsey's men to be so gentle? Will he instruct them to spare our lives? Or will he direct them to do murder, and will he do a bit of killing himself, as he did when Nigel died?"

It was the first time either of them had spoken to the other of Nigel Billings, the man in her employ whom Ramsey had killed with a spell, since the yellow-haired man's funeral the previous summer. Ethan had no answer for her righteous rage.

"We go to fight," she said. "If I tell my men to hold back, I put their lives at risk. Even you should understand that."

"We're better than he is, Sephira. We should fight that way."

She shook her head. "I'm not."

"Yes, you are," he said, surprising himself and her. "You're better than Ramsey. He doesn't scruple to kill, even if his victims have done nothing wrong other than get in his way. You're . . . different . . ."

Her smile was thin, and yet somehow genuine. "Saying it doesn't make it so. I'm more like Ramsey than either you or I would care to admit. I'm helping you today because I've sworn to avenge Nigel's death. And you're allowing me to come with you because you need me, and you need Mariz. But let's not lie to each other. I've killed for no more reason than you assigned to Ramsey's crimes. And I will again. You of all people know this. Tomorrow, when Ramsey is dead, and you and I are no longer allies, you'll hate me once more, as you did before you knew that Ramsey was back in Boston."

"And you'll hate me."

Her smile this time was reflexive and cruel. "No, I won't, Ethan. You're not important enough to me to inspire such passion one way or another."

Ethan laughed, but his mirth was short-lived; he and Sephira were left eyeing one another.

"You can try your sleep spell," she said. "And my men will use pistols as a last resort. But we fight as we always fight, and woe to Ramsey's men if they dare stand against us."

It was more than Ethan had expected from her, and as much as he could reasonably ask. She was right: If her men fought timidly, afraid to strike a killing blow, they would imperil their own lives.

"Fair enough."

They left the mansion a few minutes later, Sephira wearing an elegant black cape over her street clothes. She and Ethan sat in the carriage opposite Mariz and Nap, while Gordon perched on the box and took up the reins. Behind the carriage, Afton stood with ten more men, all of them armed with blades. Ethan had no doubt that they all carried flintlocks as well, but for now they kept them concealed.

The day had dawned clear and cold, though not as biting as recent mornings had been. The sun on Sephira's snow-covered gardens was almost blinding, and a flock of jays, their plumage a match for the cloudless sky, scolded from a bare birch tree at the front of the house. It was too fine a morning for what they were about to do.

They followed Summer Street to Winter, and Winter to the edge of the Common. Here, they turned and skirted the open land, rolling by the Granary Burying Ground and past King's Chapel onto Treamount Street and then Sudbury, so that they passed in front of Kannice's tavern. Sephira watched Ethan as they went by the Dowser, curiosity in her cold eyes. Ethan gazed back at her, impassive. But he did wonder what Kannice would have thought had she seen him in such company.

A short distance beyond the tavern door, they turned onto Hillier's Lane and then Green Lane, which took them through the heart of New Boston. The men walking behind the carriage had been speaking in low voices, but they fell silent now. Ethan felt his apprehension rising and saw that Sephira's expression had turned grim. She stared out the carriage window, the muscles in her jaw bunched.

"Near here, Mariz?" Ethan asked.

"Farther, I think. Closer to the point."

They reached the corner of Leveret's Street and turned due north. Ethan pushed open the carriage door and hopped out onto the lane. He slipped on the ice but righted himself without falling. Mariz joined him, and then Sephira and Nap.

"I take it we're walking now," Sephira said, her voice dry.

"I'm not sure what we're looking for," Ethan said, shielding his eyes against the glare with an open hand, and scanning the road. "But I assume that wherever Ramsey is hiding will be guarded by at least one man."

The northern end of New Boston sloped gently to the water's edge, affording them a view of the streets and buildings to the north. Near Barton's Point and Berry's Shipyard sat several rope yards and their warehouses. Ethan paused and pointed, looking at Mariz.

"There?" Ethan asked.

"I am not certain. Perhaps."

They walked on, trailed by the carriage, now empty, and Sephira's gang of toughs.

"He may not have men guarding whatever building he is in," Mariz said. "It is possible he believes detection spells are more reliable."

It was a fair point. Detection spells were conjurings that worked much as did a spider's web: They only took effect when someone or something came in contact with a primary spell. Once disturbed, this first conjuring tripped a second. Ramsey had used them against Ethan and his allies during their last encounter.

Sephira regarded them, fists on her hips. "So, it's possible that we could be attacked by witchery at any moment, without warning. Is that right?"

"Aye," Ethan said.

"Whatever your faults, Ethan, outings with you are never dull."

They walked on past Lee's Shipyard. No one spoke, but the turning of carriage wheels and the footsteps of more than a dozen on ice-crusted snow were loud enough to alert all to their approach. Ethan felt exposed on the open road; it was only a matter of time before Ramsey's men spotted them.

Ethan kept his eyes trained on the rope yard warehouses. He saw nothing there that made him believe one of them held Ramsey and his crew, but still his gaze was drawn to the buildings. When they reached the lane, Ethan turned westward.

"Why are you turning here?" Mariz asked.

"I don't know. I sense that Ramsey is in one of those warehouses. If you think he's elsewhere, say so. Otherwise I'm going this way."

Mariz shared a glance with Sephira and shrugged. They followed him.

The street ended at Wiltshire; Ethan turned to the north once more. And as the others joined him on the broader lane, he caught a glimpse at last of what he had been searching for. The door to one of the warehouses swung open and then closed again with a sharp crack that reached his ears a second later.

"Did you see that?" Ethan asked, pointing again.

"I heard something," Mariz said. "That is all."

"Someone entered that warehouse."

Sephira gave a doubtful look. "And you think it was Ramsey?"

"I don't know. Whoever it was couldn't be seen. I believe he was under a concealment spell."

"So, Ramsey knows now that we are coming." Mariz removed his spectacles and wiped the lenses with a kerchief. "Perhaps it is time to use a spell."

"What sort?" Ethan asked.

"I would like to know if he has cast detection spells. During our previous encounter, he nearly killed us all with them."

"You know such a spell?" Sephira asked.

"We do now," Ethan answered. "Each of us made a point of learning it after our last battle." To Mariz he said, "As you say, they know we're here; there's no longer any reason not to cast it."

Sephira's man shrugged off his coat and pushed up his sleeve. Ethan did the same.

"I can cast the spell, Kaille."

"We'll cast together," Ethan said. "As we did the last time we fought him. Our spells will be stronger."

Mariz nodded.

"Ensnarements of magick," Ethan said. "That would be the wording, I think."

"Yes, that is how I learned it as well."

Taking care to match their movements, they cut their forearms and then said together, *"Pateant omnes insidiae magicae, ex cruore evocatum."* Let all ensnarements of magick be unveiled, conjured from blood.

The spell roared in the street, spreading from where they stood as would a finding spell used to locate a conjurer.

An instant later, Sephira let out a small gasp.

Mere feet in front of them, a thin wall of aqua power shimmered faintly in the bright daylight. Several yards past this barrier stood another. A third wavered in the sun closer to the warehouse, and still another awaited them just before the warehouse door. As the spell he and Mariz had cast continued to wash over New Boston, other walls appeared blocking other routes to the warehouse. There were even barriers shimmering over the water. He could see no way to approach the building without setting off at least three conjurings.

"There must be a dozen of them," Sephira said. "How can that be? These streets aren't as crowded as those in other parts of Boston, but they're not deserted, either."

"I would imagine," Ethan said, "that they only work if a conjurer disturbs the primary spell. If Mariz touches that barrier, or if I do, the second spell will be made active. But you and your men can walk through them at will. Ramsey doesn't fear you."

"He should."

Ethan didn't answer, and Sephira, despite her brave words, gave no indication that she intended to go on without him.

"We should ward them," Ethan said, after considering the detection spells for some time.

Sephira shook her head. Ethan knew that she disliked relying on "witchery" for anything, much less the safety of herself and her men. "I thought your wardings didn't work against Ramsey's spells," she said.

"My wardings can stop spells such as these. But they haven't worked against whatever conjuring he is using to gain access to my power. It was for those spells that Mariz cast the warding in your home."

"Fine," she said, sounding impatient. "Get on with it."

Together, Ethan and Mariz placed a warding spell on their entire company—themselves, as well as Sephira and her other men. Ethan hoped that it would hold against the detection spells Ramsey had cast.

Uncle Reg had appeared beside Mariz's spectral guide and was regarding Sephira with unconcealed hostility. Even if Ethan was willing to trust her for this day, his ghost remained wary.

I want you to stay with me. He didn't speak the words aloud, but Reg perceived them anyway. The ghost's gaze found his and he nodded his assent.

"You and your men should wait here," Ethan said to Sephira. "Mariz and I will go ahead. When we've dealt with all the spells, you can join us."

"That's not what we agreed to back at my home."

"I didn't know then how many detection spells Ramsey would cast. Let me do this, Sephira. You can't help us with these spells, but you can be killed by them."

She glowered, tight-lipped, her eyes shockingly blue in the bright glare of the sun and snow. "Fine."

Ethan and Mariz edged closer to the first shimmering barrier. If the detection spells Ramsey had used last summer were any indication, this first spell would simply alert Ramsey to their approach—it would be the second, third, and fourth that were intended to kill. Then again, Ramsey could hardly be called predictable.

They halted inches from the spell and exchanged looks. Ethan raised his hand to the level of his chest.

"Are you ready?" he asked.

Mariz planted his feet and dipped his chin once.

Ethan extended his hand to the glowing wall of magick.

As soon as he grazed the barrier with his palm, the ground shook with the power of Ramsey's conjuring. A ball of fire flew from the wall, striking Ethan in the chest and lifting him off the lane.

He landed on his back almost at Sephira's feet, dazed, his back and chest aching. Flames burned on his waistcoat and licked at his face and neck and chest. Heat, pain; for a panicked instant, he thought that his warding had failed and that he was on fire. He began to roll back and forth, only to realize that the flames were neither spreading nor going out. Indeed, though he could feel the heat of them, they weren't actually burning his clothing or his flesh. He stopped trying to put out the fire and climbed to his feet, feeling like he had been run over by Sephira's carriage.

"So much for the spells only warning him of our approach," Ethan said under his breath.

Sephira watched him, seeming unsure of whether to be alarmed or amused. "What?"

"It doesn't matter," Ethan said. The flames still clung to his chest, the heat rising to his face. Even knowing that it wasn't doing any damage, he found the sensation disconcerting to say the least.

He cut his arm. *"Exstingue ignem,"* he said. *"Ex cruore evocatum."* Extinguish flames, conjured from blood.

The fire vanished with a small pop, like the crackle of dried wood in a hearth.

Ethan walked back to where Mariz stood.

"You are all right?" the conjurer asked.

"Aye."

The first barrier had vanished with the fire spell. The second one still glimmered in the sun a few paces farther down the street.

"Shall we?" Ethan said.

They walked on until they reached the next shimmering wall. Sephira and her men advanced as well, though they stopped well short of the detection spell.

Once more Ethan reached out toward the conjuring. He didn't relish the idea of being assaulted again, but he knew that he would face far worse from Ramsey before the day was out. He couldn't allow himself to be cowed by one detection spell.

As soon as his hand touched this second spell, a ring of flame burst from the ice, encircling him and Mariz. Immediately, the ring began to contract, closing on them like a fiery noose.

Mariz already had blood on his arm. Ethan cut himself as well.

"Extinguish flames," he said. "Quickly!"

"Exstingue ignem," they said as one. *"Ex cruore evocatum!"*

Their spell pulsed; the blaze wavered as from a gust of wind. But this time nothing else happened. The heat of the fire was growing more intense, melting the ice and snow on the road and still pressing in on them. He sensed that these flames, unlike the first that had struck him, would burn them despite their wardings.

"Perhaps we can escape them without conjuring," Mariz said.

Ethan nodded. Shielding their faces with their arms, they ran toward the edge of the flames, only to find that the ring of fire moved with them, even as it continued to tighten. Ethan could almost hear Ramsey chuckling.

"Opposite directions," Ethan said.

He ran one way and Mariz the other, but the ring elongated and narrowed to match their movements. There would be no escaping the flames in this manner.

"I would entertain any ideas you might have," Ethan said, his voice tight as he and Mariz walked toward each other once more.

"I was about to say the same."

Ethan judged that they had but one option left. "I used this when I was trapped in the warehouse at Drake's Wharf. It saved my life and kept me from burning, but I could still feel the heat."

"What is the wording?"

"Protection from fire," Ethan said. The flames were almost upon them.

"All right. Let us try."

They cut themselves and said together, "*Tegimen contra ignem ex cruore evocatum.*" Protection from fire, conjured from blood.

The spell pulsed and the blood vanished from their arms. Ethan looked at Reg to see if the ghost thought the spell had worked, but already the spectral guide was standing in the fire. Ethan could see nothing of him save his glowing eyes.

A moment later the flames reached them. Ethan couldn't keep from screaming at the pain. Mariz roared in agony as well. For several terrifying seconds, which might as well have been an eternity of torment, they were in the flames, surrounded by them. Ethan thought his skin must be peeling away; with every breath he felt like he was inhaling molten steel.

And then the ring was small enough that they could stagger out of it on the far side. Ethan collapsed and was vaguely aware that Mariz had, too. But when he looked at his hands and his clothes he saw that, as in the burning warehouse at the wharf, he had come through this ordeal unscathed. The ring of flame had become a narrow cylinder, and as he watched, it closed on itself and vanished in a puff of pale gray smoke.

"It's fire," Ethan said, his voice sounding thin. "All of these detection spells will be fire conjurings of one kind or another." He looked at Mariz. "It's his revenge for what happened at Drake's Wharf."

"Does that mean you know how to stop them?" Sephira asked, walking to where he still lay.

"No," Ethan said. "We know what to expect, but that's all."

"What does it matter if you can't prevent it?"

Ethan forced himself to his feet. "I suppose it doesn't."

He helped Mariz up, and they continued toward the end of the lane and the next detection spell, which still glowed with Ramsey's aqua power. Sephira and her men followed more closely than Ethan would have liked. But he had warned her once, and he didn't wish to argue with her again.

"I should thank you for that last spell," Mariz said as they walked. "I believe I would have died had I been alone."

"You're welcome. But thinking about it, I'm not entirely convinced that we would have died, even without the protection spell. I don't believe he wishes to kill us with these conjurings. He wants to defeat me in combat. The spells are intended to make us suffer, and to demonstrate his cleverness and his power."

"That bodes ill for this next spell."

Ethan couldn't argue. They stopped before this glowing barrier as they had before the first two. Taking a long breath, Ethan touched it, wincing in anticipation of pain at the hum of power.

For the span of a heartbeat, nothing happened. One of Sephira's men shouted a warning. Ethan spun, but was pushed to the side before he could see what had prompted the cry. He fell. And an instant later, a ball of flame crashed into the ground, hitting the spot where he had been standing.

He hadn't time to thank Mariz for saving him. In the next moment, blazing spheres the size of snowballs were pelting down on all of them. He smelled burning hair and clothing, heard screams of pain. And he could do nothing more than cover his head and neck. Fiery missiles scorched his arms and legs, his back and head. Their warding offered no protection; there seemed to be no escape.

Ethan knew that his waistcoat had caught fire, but he didn't dare roll to put out the blaze, lest another ball of flame strike his face or chest. He cowered and endured the assault, which seemed interminable.

And then it was over. As suddenly as the salvo began, it ended. Ethan managed to smother the flames burning on his back, though he could feel that his waistcoat was mostly gone. His flesh was tender, probably blistered.

Most of the others were in a similar state. Sephira's cape was charred in several places, and some of her hair had burned. Ethan wasn't sure he had ever seen her look more angry. Several of her toughs bore ugly burns on their arms and faces. One man lay on the ground, most of his clothing and hair burned away, his body livid, his skin melted in places.

"I swear I'm going to kill him," Sephira said, staring down at her wounded man. "And I'll enjoy doing it."

Mariz's injuries were similar to Ethan's. This time it was he who helped Ethan to his feet.

"One more," he said.

Grim, and every bit as angry as Sephira, Ethan trudged on to the warehouse and the final barrier, Mariz beside him.

Ethan and the others halted just outside the rope yard warehouse. He had yet to see any of Ramsey's crew; he assumed that the sailors awaited them inside. Sephira, he noticed, had her flintlock in hand, as did several of her men. He eyed the weapon before raising his gaze to hers. She stared back at him, eyes blazing, daring him to tell her that she should put the pistol away.

He said nothing, but turned back to the last of Ramsey's conjured barriers.

A simple fire spell, a ring of flame, fireballs raining down upon them. What had Ramsey saved for this final spell?

"The ground," he whispered. Then louder, so that Mariz and Sephira would hear, he said again, "The ground. It's going to melt or turn to flame, or something of the sort. That's what this last conjuring will do."

"How do you know?" Sephira asked.

"I'm guessing. But I trust my instincts in this."

"So what should we do?"

"I'm less certain about that." He raised his hand and held it a hairsbreadth from the barrier. "Be prepared to run."

He pressed his palm into the shimmering wall and felt the familiar release of power.

The ground beneath him started to give way.

Behind him, several men cried out. Rather than retreating toward them, Ethan leaped forward and crashed into the warehouse door. His teeth rattled with the impact and pain blossomed in his shoulder. But the doorjamb gave way with a rending of wood. He toppled into the building, sprawling onto the dirt floor, which was as solid as the ground outside had been before Ramsey's last detection spell.

"At last," came a rasping, uneven voice from the far side of the warehouse. "Now our battle can commence in earnest."

CHAPTER
TWENTY-THREE

*E*than jumped up, expecting to be beset by spells and armed sailors. But no attack came, and he was left to stare across the great room, his mouth agape as he struggled to comprehend the scene before him.

Earlier this very day—before sunrise, although it seemed as though weeks had passed—Ethan remarked to Mariz on the appearance of Ramsey's illusion, and the possibility that, because of the fire at Drake's Wharf, the captain had made the figure look as he once had, rather than as he did now. But never had he thought to see Ramsey in such a state.

He sat propped up by pillows in a large bed, blankets covering him to above his waist. Even from this end of the warehouse, Ethan could see that his unruly dark hair and unkempt beard were gone. The lone window in the building had been covered, and the only light came from a few candles that had been set on barrels and crates, and from a vast shining aqua dome of power—faint, transparent, but, Ethan was sure, as impermeable as steel—that surrounded the bed and its occupant. Still, Ethan could see that his skin was waxen and pale.

Ten sailors stood around the bed, some armed with knives and lengths of rope, others with pistols. They watched Ethan, like wolves guarding their pack leader.

"Come closer, Kaille," Ramsey said, his voice barely discernible above the shouts from outside of Sephira and the others. "Come see what you've done to me."

Ethan glanced back at the door, which stood ajar, pieces of the splintered jamb on the floor. He hadn't noticed before, but Uncle Reg still stood with him, his bright eyes fixed on that aqua shield.

"They can't help you. I'm not entirely sure that they can help themselves."

Ethan started toward the bed with deliberate steps, his gaze sweeping over Ramsey's men. Reg followed him. Ethan held his knife ready, though he had little doubt that the captain had warded the sailors.

"You needn't fear them. They have strict orders not to touch you. They are here to guard against interference from others. I've made it clear to them that you are mine."

The closer Ethan drew to the bed, the more horrified he grew at what he could see of the man lying in it. Ramsey, who once had been as dashing and vital as he was mad, now was disfigured almost beyond recognition. The flesh on his face and head appeared to have melted like ice in the spring and then solidified again, misshapen and hideous. His lips had been burned away, so that his mouth was a slanting gash across his face. His nose was little more than a flap of skin. He had no eyebrows or eyelashes, and the skin around one of his eyes drooped, so that it was barely open.

It was as if a careless child had begun to mold a face from clay, only to tire of his art and leave the visage unfinished.

The only aspect of the captain's face that struck him as at all familiar were the eyes themselves. Pale, almost ghostly, they were intelligent and hard and they peered out from the ravaged mien with such hatred Ethan had to resist the urge to flinch away.

"I'm glad you're here, Kaille. I feared that you might allow some other conjurer to fight this battle for you. I thought you'd bring Miss Windcatcher with you, or Pryce's pet conjurer. It came as some relief to see you fly through that door."

Ethan couldn't bring himself to speak. He stared at the man; the face, the emaciated form, the thin, bony hands, which were as scarred and grotesque as his mien.

Ramsey's mouth quirked in what might have been intended as a grin. "Hideous, aren't I? You did this to me."

"No," Ethan said, finding his voice. "You started the fire. You started the war. You did this to yourself. I'm no more responsible for your burns than I am for the deaths of Christopher Seider and the men who were shot last night."

"You left me to burn!" Ramsey said, his voice rising to a rough screech. "You were content to let me die! But I saved myself, and I healed the burns."

Ethan winced.

"Aye, that's right! I healed myself. As terrible as this face might seem now, it is better by far than it was in the days and weeks after we sailed from Boston."

Ethan tore his gaze from Ramsey and considered the shield of power that covered the bed. It was the same hue as the detection spells, and it glimmered similarly, its lustrous surface reflecting the candlelight as might a glass bowl.

"You can't defeat it," Ramsey said. "Not without killing me. And yet, you cannot kill me without defeating it. A conundrum, wouldn't you say?"

"I thought you wanted to fight me, Ramsey. And instead you hide in this conjured cocoon. That hardly seems fair."

"Fair?" the captain said. "*Fair?* I can't walk, Kaille. I can't hold a weapon. I have nothing left but magicking. And you dare speak to me of fairness?"

"Ethan!" Sephira's voice.

He looked back toward the door once more.

"They cannot enter. The building is surrounded by flames and molten stone, as from the great volcanoes of the Mediterranean. Have you seen them?" Ramsey asked, abruptly sounding wistful. "Etna, Vesuvius?"

Ethan shook his head.

"I have. My father took me once, and I have been back since. But no more. Never again shall I captain my vessel past Gibraltar or along the shores of Italy. The life I have known is lost to me, and so I seek to deprive you of your life, as small recompense."

"How have you used my power for your conjurings, Ramsey? What manner of spell allowed you to do that?"

The captain offered no answer save to lift the corners of his scarred mouth in a ghoulish smile.

"Come now," Ethan said. "One of us will be dead before this morning ends. Surely no harm can come of revealing your secret now."

"The harm comes from telling you nothing, from allowing you to die in ignorance, without the satisfaction of knowing how you have been bested again and again and again. How is your woman, by the way? Did that man in her tavern kill her, or did you rescue her in time?"

Ethan's arm was bleeding and the spell was on his lips before he knew what he had done. *"Discuti ex cruore evocatum!"* Shatter, conjured from blood!

Ethan's conjuring thrummed, and at the same time, the aqua dome shielding Ramsey seemed to shudder. He had time to realize his mistake, but could do nothing more before the spell rebounded and struck him. His warding held; the shatter spell did not break any of his bones. But once more he was knocked off his feet so that he landed hard on the dirt floor.

Ramsey's laugh was dry as brittle wood. But that was of little interest to Ethan, who had noticed something else. At the moment his conjuring touched the aqua shield, Ramsey's spectral guide appeared beside the captain's bed. The old, bent figure of a sea captain remained in view for but an instant before vanishing again. But that was enough to tell Ethan that the captain was using a different sort of power to maintain his domed warding. Reg appeared when Ethan cast his own wardings, but not each time another conjurer's assault tested his defenses.

Ramsey held no knife in his hands; Ethan wasn't sure he could. And yet he had no doubt that the captain expected this encounter to end with a battle of conjurings. What was Ramsey using as the source of his power? Were some members of his crew conjurers? Was he using them as he had used Ethan this past fortnight?

Ethan brushed himself off and got to his feet. Ramsey cackled.

"Did you believe a simple conjuring would defeat my warding? Or did my mention of your woman banish all reason from your mind? Perhaps she is dead then, and that particular barb found its mark."

Saying nothing, Ethan edged closer to the bed. Despite Ramsey's assurances, the sailors guarding him stepped forward, blocking his way.

"I thought we were to fight without interference, Ramsey," Ethan said.

"You're close enough, I believe. You could stand with your nose but an inch from my warding and it would do you no good."

"Then why not allow me to do that?"

He gave the captain no time to reply. Slashing at his arm again, he said, "*Falx ex cruore evocata.*" Blade, conjured from blood.

It was not a spell he would have used under ordinary circumstances. Blade spells were vicious conjurings that could literally carve a man's body in half. But he assumed that Ramsey's crew were warded, and would survive the assault. And few spells struck at their victims with such force, which was exactly what Ethan wanted.

The spell pulsed, and the men went down like ninepins. Ethan strode past them, cutting his arm again as he went, only to halt and sway at what he saw on the far side of Ramsey's bed.

A second spell pulsed—it might have been a blade spell as well. Ethan was tossed backward as if he were no more than a rag doll. He landed in a heap near where he had been standing before he advanced on the bed.

But now he knew.

"Damn you, Kaille!"

He had managed a glimpse, no more. But the image would not soon fade from his mind.

Beyond the large bed that held the captain, but still within the protection of the dome, stood a smaller, lower pallet. And on it lay a man—one of Ramsey's sailors perhaps, or more likely some hapless innocent brought here for the captain to use and discard.

This poor creature was naked to the waist, his body covered with bloodless gashes. He appeared to be unconscious; Ethan wondered if Ramsey had him under some sort of conjured thrall. And beside him, on a low stool, also hidden from view and also warded, sat another man—definitely a sailor—who held a knife over the one bloody wound on the torso of his victim. Ethan guessed that the sailor cut the man after each of Ramsey's conjurings, so that the captain would always have blood for his next spell. He wondered how many men Ramsey had bled to death since his arrival in Boston.

Most of Ramsey's men were back on their feet, tending to the few who had yet to recover from Ethan's spell. The captain, though, paid them no heed. He stared daggers at Ethan, his disfigured face twisted with rage.

"You're barbaric," Ethan said. "You know no shame."

"What choice do I have? I can't grip a blade or pluck leaves of mullein from a pouch as you are wont to do. I have only this."

"How many of them have you killed?"

"Fewer than you think," Ramsey said, in a tone he might have used to discuss the recent snowstorm. "There is a good deal of blood in the human form, and our spells require surprisingly little."

"And what of the unfortunate soul who must wield his blade on your behalf? What damage have you done to him?"

"Don't pretend to care about my men, Kaille. You fool no one. He understands my need, and he was one of several who offered themselves for this particular service."

Ethan wasn't sure if he was bothered more by what the captain's man had to do, or by the fact that he believed Ramsey when he said the sailor had volunteered for such gruesome duty. But he knew this to be Ramsey's greatest weakness, and he believed that if he could convince the sailor to stop cutting his victim, or if he could incapacitate the sailor even for a short while, he might break through the shield that guarded Ramsey.

Once more he thought of how Ramsey's spectral guide had appeared when his spell struck the aqua dome. Was it possible that Ramsey had to cast a spell—and thus needed fresh blood—each time the warding was tested?

He had no chance to satisfy his curiosity. Ramsey muttered something that might have been "Enough." A conjuring hummed in the floor and walls, and Ethan was struck once more by the force of a spell. It seemed to be directed at his bad leg, which was swept out from under him. He dropped to the ground. But if it was a shatter spell intended to break the bone, it failed.

From where he lay on the ground, with blood still on his arm from the last cut he had made, Ethan countered with a conjuring of his own.

"*Aperi hiatum ex cruore evocatum.*" Open chasm, conjured from blood.

He aimed the spell at the ground beneath the dome, hoping the opening would swallow the bed and Ramsey with it. But once more the dome shuddered and the spell turned back on Ethan. The floor opened, seemingly rent by giant unseen hands. The widening split raced toward him. Ethan rolled to the side, tottered on the edge of the crack, and with one last racking effort, threw himself onto solid ground.

Again, though, he had noticed that when his conjuring hit the shield, Ramsey's ghost appeared, albeit for the blink of an eye. He felt certain that in maintaining the protection of the dome, the captain had taken still more blood from the unconscious man beside him.

"Our wardings serve us well," Ramsey said, watching Ethan as he climbed to his feet yet again. "You escaped my fire spells out on the street. I might have been too gentle with them."

This time the pulse of power brought another ring of fire. Like the last, this one began to press in on Ethan, the heat of it making him shield his face with an upraised arm.

"The circle of fire created by the detection spell was meant to cause you pain," Ramsey said, pitching his voice so that Ethan could hear it above the roar of the blaze. "This one will only contract so far. How long can your endure such agony, Kaille? For how long will your warding against flames work?"

Too long, Ethan knew. His spell would protect him from the flames as long as he remained alive, and so if he could not escape this fiery ring, the agony would go on and on. He assumed that another extinguishing spell would not work, and he could not leap through the fire to safety. But what if he convinced Ramsey to extinguish the flames for him. Ethan ran toward Ramsey's bed, and as he expected, the circle of fire moved with him, as it had on the street. He veered off just as he reached the domed shield and pressed himself to the warehouse wall.

The flames licked at the wood and then caught. Ethan heard the crack and snap of burning lumber.

"No!" Ramsey said, barking the word. *"Exstingue ignem ex cruore evocatum."*

The fire sputtered and went out, leaving a small section of the wall charred and smoking.

"You fool!" Ramsey was trembling and breathing hard, a sheen of sweat on his face.

"Fool you say." Ethan wiped sweat from his own brow. "I thought it was rather clever of me. In fact . . . *Ignis ex cruore evocatus.*" Fire, conjured from blood.

Flame flew from his hand into the still smoldering wall. The building shook, and in seconds, the section of wall nearest to Ramsey's bed was engulfed.

Ramsey shouted another extinguishing spell, his voice spiraling upward in panic. As he put out that fire, Ethan used another spell to light a second blaze on the wall behind Ramsey's men.

The captain used a conjuring to douse these flames as well, but he was wide-eyed with terror now.

"Kill him!" the captain said. "I don't care how! But I want him dead!"

The men advanced on Ethan. A half dozen of them drew pistols and cocked the hammers. Ethan hacked at his arm and cast another blade spell, knocking them back, although not before one of men got off a shot. The ball whistled past Ethan's head, too close for comfort.

While the men were still sprawled on the floor, he cast again— *"Impedimentum ex verbasco et marrubio et betonica evocata"*—drawing upon the herbs he carried to conjure a barrier, a gleaming wall not unlike Ramsey's shield. This one glowed russet, the color of Uncle Reg, and it surrounded Ramsey's men, hemming them in against the wall.

Ethan didn't believe it would prove as effective as the captain's, but it didn't need to. None of the men were conjurers; he only wanted his barrier to hold them back and block the bullets from their flintlocks. As if responding to the thought, one of the men sat up, aimed his pistol at Ethan, and fired. The ball rebounded off the barrier and an instant later struck the wall behind the man. He ducked belatedly and gaped at his weapon, seeming to realize how close he had come to killing himself.

"It's just the two of us now, Ramsey," Ethan said, turning back to the captain. "Shall I light another fire?"

"I should have resorted to this already," Ramsey said, sounding as though he hadn't heard. "I've been wasting time."

This conjuring felt all too familiar. Ethan shuddered at the touch of it and looked to Reg, only to find that the ghost was watching him.

But nothing else happened.

"Impossible!" the captain said in a rasp. "Impossible!"

He glanced to his side, toward the man on the cot and the sailor who was cutting him. Another conjuring shook the warehouse, but again whatever Ramsey had intended did not result.

"I don't understand!"

Ethan could not quite believe that having Mariz ward him from the conjurings had worked so well, but he concealed his amazement as he said, "I found a way to stop you. You can't use my power anymore."

"But I can!"

A third spell rumbled and failed. Ramsey let out a skirling, inarticulate scream.

"What will you do now, Ramsey?"

"It doesn't matter," the captain said. He licked his lips and said again, "It doesn't matter at all."

Another conjuring slammed Ethan to the floor. He didn't know what kind of spell it was, and didn't have time to ponder the matter. A second spell hit him, and a third. Each failed to penetrate his warding, but each battered him with the force of an ocean breaker. A fourth made his vision blur, a fifth left him addled. And still the assault went on. He feared he might pass out, and that if he did, his conjured barrier would fail, allowing Ramsey's men to kill him.

Desperate, not knowing what else to do, he dragged his knife across his arm and cast another fire spell. He didn't aim it, but simply let it fly from his hand. He heard it hit wood, heard the crackle of spreading flames.

Ramsey broke off his attack to extinguish the fire. Ethan cast three more fire spells in quick succession, directing them at the ceiling, the wall near the captain's bed, and the wall nearest the door through which he had entered the warehouse.

The captain cast his spells as quickly, snuffing out the flames before they could spread. But this gave Ethan the respite he needed. He knew that he was forcing Ramsey's man to draw more and more blood from the unfortunate lying on the pallet, but he could think of no way to prevent this without surrendering to the captain.

This thought, however, gave him another idea. He wasn't certain that he could do what he had in mind; he didn't know how much conjuring power Ramsey's barrier could block. But if he succeeded, the tactic he was contemplating might allow him to defeat the man, finally and for all time. He threw another ball of fire at a wall, and as Ramsey put out the blaze, Ethan staggered to his feet and approached the bed.

And before Ramsey could aim a spell at him, he cast once more.

"Ignis ex cruore evocatus." Fire, conjured from blood.

This time, however, he did not bother to cut himself. Instead, he drew upon the blood he knew was already available on the man beside Ramsey's bed. The act of conjuring blood from a wound caused the wound to stop bleeding; this was why Ethan had to cut himself anew with each spell he cast. If he could take blood from the man Ramsey had been using in this manner, he would not only fuel his own conjuring, he might also deny blood to Ramsey until his sailor could cut the man again.

But could he reach the man's blood? The barrier Ramsey had created was meant to repel attacks, both conjured and physical. Ethan sought not to breach the warding for an assault; he simply wished to use for his spell a source that was located within the shield.

And Ramsey's warding could not prevent this.

Another flaming sphere flew from Ethan's hand, striking the ceiling directly above where Ramsey lay.

"Falx ex cruore evocata," Ethan said, once more drawing on the blood of Ramsey's hapless victim, this time for a blade spell.

The conjuring crashed against the barrier like a wave and spent itself, as Ethan knew it would. But the glowing wall rippled noticeably, and this time Ramsey's spectral guide did not appear when the shield was tested. Ethan could tell by the slight fading of its color and the dulling of its glimmer that the barrier was weakened by the impact of his spell. Something in Ramsey's conjuring, be it the sheer strength of the barrier or whatever spell the captain had used to create it, made it vulnerable to such attacks. It seemed it could hold against anything, but it needed to be renewed constantly. Therein lay its one flaw. And Ethan sought to make the most of it.

He cast again—another blade spell. He didn't expect that this one would reach the captain either. But as long as he kept conjuring and denying Ramsey access to the blood he so desperately needed, the shield would continue to grow dimmer and less powerful.

"Cut him faster!" Ramsey hissed the words, his widened eyes on the flames which still burned the ceiling above him.

"*Discuti ex cruore evocatum,*" Ethan said. Shatter, conjured from blood.

Enraged, unable to tear his gaze from the fire, unable even to form words, Ramsey screamed again and pounded his fists on the bed.

And still Ethan conjured. A fire spell. And rather than aim it at the walls or ceiling, he directed it at Ramsey, knowing once more that it wouldn't penetrate the shield, but knowing as well that it would terrify the man.

At the sight of the fireball, the captain raised an arm, and turned his head, flinching back against his pillows despite his warding.

The aqua barrier held against this spell, but it sagged under the force of the conjuring, like a ship's sail that suddenly catches a leeward wind. The spell even rebounded off the barrier with less force than had Ethan's earlier spell; it barely even staggered him.

"Cut yourselves!" Ramsey shouted to the men Ethan had trapped with his conjured wall. "All of you! I need blood!"

The captain's men were quick with their blades. Ethan managed to cast two more blade spells, each of which made Ramsey's conjured dome flicker and quake. He thought that a third spell might get through and strike at the captain, but he didn't get the chance to cast it. Before he could speak another spell, he felt a pulse in the warehouse floor and saw Ramsey's ghost flash into view.

The captain's conjuring fell upon Ethan, driving him to the ground and crushing the breath from his chest.

He didn't believe that his warding had failed; if it had, this spell would have killed him. But whatever conjuring Ramsey had aimed at him was more powerful by far than any other the captain had cast this day.

By the time Ethan could raise his head again, the flames above the bed had been extinguished and Ramsey's barrier had regained much of its hue and substance.

"That was well done, Kaille. I hadn't thought you could be so clever. But you won't catch me off my guard again. Indeed, you've reminded me that I have as much blood at my disposal as I could possibly want. Thank you for that."

A spell made the warehouse tremble and the weight crashed down on Ethan again, stealing his breath, making his heart labor. It was like having Afton and Gordon both stand on his chest. Even with his warding intact he feared that the sheer might of the conjuring would kill him.

"How long can you endure this, Ethan?" Ramsey asked, seeming to sense his desperation. "I have all day."

Chapter
TWENTY-FOUR

*E*than had little time left, and no idea how to regain the upper hand in his battle with Ramsey. He cut his arm, but rather than aim a conjuring at the captain or his men, Ethan cast an illusion spell, sending an image of himself out of the building and up the road to where Mariz stood with Sephira.

"I need help," Ethan made the figure say. "An attack, Mariz. Or a distraction. Anything. I don't know if the warehouse is warded; I expect it is. But if it's not, light it on fire. I'll get out somehow. If it is warded, then an illusion of some sort. Ramsey is terrified of fire. Try—"

Within the warehouse, another spell hit him, tearing a gasp from his beleaguered lungs. He opened his eyes to the dim light of the building and the glow of Ramsey's power.

"I felt that," the captain said. "An illusion spell. You were speaking with Sephira's conjurer, or perhaps Miss Windcatcher. They can't help you. Not from that distance."

The building shook. Ramsey glanced up at the ceiling and then laughed.

"A fire spell. You told them to burn us out. You're a desperate fool, Kaille. Of course I warded the building."

Ethan rolled off his back and pushed himself up to his hands and knees. Glancing at Ramsey's crew, who remained behind the wall he had conjured, he saw that all but one or two of them had blood on their arms.

And then, with a pounding of magick, the blood was gone. All of it. Ethan was mashed to the floor; it felt like the warehouse roof had fallen in on top of him. He could not keep his arm from being trapped beneath him. The bone snapped and he howled with pain.

So much blood. If Ethan could have drawn upon it he might have been able to defeat the captain's warding. But as it was . . .

He had been in such straits before. The memory of one such circumstance came to him now. He had cast the killing spell that took the life of a dog, Pitch, Shelly's mate. It had been an act of last resort, and to this day he had not forgiven himself. He had vowed that he would never cast such a spell again. And if his choice was between dying and taking the life of one of Ramsey's sailors, he would choose to die.

But there was someone else. The man lying on that low pallet beside Ramsey's bed was going to die. Ramsey would kill him with his spells; Ethan himself had robbed the man of blood. He doubted that the poor soul could survive much longer. Wouldn't it be a mercy if he could take the man's life with a single conjuring?

He started to recite the conjuring under his breath—another blade conjuring. Sourced in the life of another it might be strong enough to carve through Ramsey's warding and kill the captain. But after a few words, Ethan stopped himself. He had made this choice once, and had justified it to himself with the belief that he hadn't acted to save his own life, but rather to save the life of Holin, the son of Marielle Taylor, his former betrothed. If he cast such a spell now and managed to survive his battle with Ramsey, how would he excuse it this time?

Better to die than to live with the knowledge that he had traded his own life for that of an innocent.

But perhaps there was one other way.

Of course I warded the building, Ramsey had said. But both of them knew that he had only warded it against attacks from outside. Ethan had already proven that the walls within could be burned. Clearly the captain assumed that Ethan had tried to burn them in order to distract him from the maintenance of his shield and from his attacks. Perhaps Ethan had made the same assumption. Not anymore.

He cut himself. *"Ignis ex cruore evocatus."*

And before the flames he threw had reached the near wall, next to Ramsey, he cast a second spell.

"Tegimen et impedimentum ex verbasco et marrubio et betonica evocata." Warding and barrier, conjured from mullein, horehound, and betony.

The rumble of another spell followed on the heels of this one, but it had no effect. The blaze began to spread along the warehouse wall, and the shimmering russet shield Ethan had conjured over it rendered Ramsey's extinguishing spell impotent. He cast the spell again, using more of Janna's herbs. He would fortify the conjuring every time Ramsey attacked, so as to make certain that it held. He knew that his supply of leaves wouldn't last forever, but he thought that he could maintain the conjuring with blood if he had to. And he wasn't sure Ramsey could tolerate flames in such proximity for very long.

Ramsey tried to douse the fire again, and again he failed.

Ethan cast his spell once more.

"Enough of this, Kaille." The captain sounded panicked. "You won't kill yourself to kill me."

"Actually, I will."

Ramsey seemed to know better than to argue. "What about my men? You won't let them die. I'm sure of it."

"I can't say what I'll do. I haven't decided yet. But what about you, Ramsey? Would you let them die to save your own life? I believe you would. Your men have faith in you. They think that you'll protect them. Look at them now, and tell them that you would rather die than see them perish."

The captain looked to his men, wet his scarred lips. "I would," he said. "I would die for them."

"Discuti ex cruore evocatum," Ethan said. Shatter, conjured from blood.

The wall of the building just to the side of Ethan's barrier shattered like glass.

"Reloca impedimentum ex verbasco et marrubio et betonica evocatum."

Ethan's conjured shield shifted a few feet, enough to give the men access to the hole he had made in the warehouse wall.

"Tell them to leave. Without delay, Ramsey. The fire is spreading."

Ramsey stared up at the flames and tried to slide himself to the far side of his bed. He said nothing.

"I thought as much," Ethan said.

Smoke began to billow into the rafters of the building and the fire continued to grow, creeping along the wall toward Ramsey like a bright spider.

"Make it stop!" Ramsey said.

"No. If burning this building to the ground and dying by my own conjuring is the only way I can rid the world of you, then so be it."

Ethan cast his barrier spell again so that the warding widened to cover the spreading flames. But he also started to recite in silence a second spell, in anticipation of what he thought Ramsey would do next.

He knew the man well.

"Cut yourselves, damn it!" the captain called to his men.

The sailors had been eyeing the flames, but now they cut themselves once more, drawing more blood.

Prepared as he was, Ethan might still have failed to finish his conjuring before Ramsey cast whatever spell he had in mind. But at that moment, another spell whispered in the wood. It was weaker than those Ramsey and Ethan had cast over the past several minutes. But that hardly mattered.

It was an illusion spell: Bright yellow flames erupted from the floor in the middle of the warehouse, near to where Ethan stood. He was certain Ramsey knew that this fire wasn't real. But with flames burning so close to where he lay, and with his face and body covered with scars from the Drake's Wharf fire, the captain couldn't help but be distracted, albeit for only an instant.

That was enough. Ethan cut his arm and spoke the last words of his conjuring. Once more, he cast a blade spell, this time drawing not only upon his own blood, but also on that of Ramsey's crew. Eleven men in all.

The spell shook the warehouse to its foundations. And when Ethan's attack struck the aqua dome—the warding that had guarded Ramsey from so much—light flared, forcing him to shield his eyes. When he looked again, the dome was gone.

Ramsey cried out—fury, dismay, terror. Already Ramsey's men were hacking at their arms with their blades, ready to give more blood to save their captain.

Ethan didn't wait for them. He cut himself, and, hoping his aim was true, shouted one last time, *"Falx ex cruore evocata!"*

The blade spell thrummed. Ramsey had started to shout out a spell of his own, the Latin ringing high and clear. But his voice was cut off abruptly, the last sound from him sharp, choked.

And then his head rolled off his neck and blood fountained across his pillows and blankets.

Ethan could hardly believe what he had done. He stared at the body, at the head, at the torrent of crimson that stained the blankets and bedding. His hands shook, and he could hear that his breathing was uneven, ragged.

After some time he became aware of Ramsey's men, who made not a sound, but stared at the bed. Some wore expressions of shock, others revulsion. As he watched, they turned individually and in pairs to look at him.

"Go," he said, his mouth dry. "I've no quarrel with any of you. Stay far away, and you needn't fear me."

He didn't know if they would heed his words. He should have. These men, perhaps more than any others in Boston, understood the power a conjurer could wield. They dared not challenge him. Rather, they filed out of the warehouse through the jagged opening his shatter spell had created.

Ethan cast one spell to remove the warding he had placed before the warehouse wall, and a second to extinguish the flames.

Smoke continued to gather in the building. He knew he should leave, but he couldn't bring himself to do so. Not yet.

He stood, and walked toward the captain, his steps stiff. Only when he was within a few strides of the foot of the bed did he remember the last of Ramsey's men, the one who had been harvesting blood on the captain's behalf.

The man had been hiding, crouched on the far side of the bed. Now he lunged at Ethan, his blade held high. Ethan raised his uninjured arm to block the blow, felt a searing pain below his elbow. Ramsey's man pulled the blade from Ethan's arm and raised it to attack again.

"*Discuti ex cruore evocatum!*" Shatter, conjured from blood!

The blade broke, and the sailor's eyes widened. Ethan stepped and spun, kicking him in the side with his bad foot. The man let out a grunt, his body seeming to crumple. Before he could do more, Ethan kicked him again in the the side of the head.

"That was nicely done, Ethan! As I've said before, you should come and work for me."

Ethan turned. Sephira stood by the doorway, a pistol in her hand. She strode toward him, her boot heels scraping on the rough floor.

"Is that Ramsey?" she said, pointing at the blood-soaked form in the bed as she halted beside him.

"Aye."

Her gaze lingered on the corpse and her voice was more subdued as she said, "Once again, nicely done."

"There's another man lying beside the bed. Ramsey was harvesting blood from him for spells. He needs healing; I'll see to his wounds when I return. Otherwise he's not to be touched."

"And what about you? You look like you could use a bit of healing as well."

Ethan wanted to refuse. He didn't have time even for this. But one arm was bleeding and the other was broken. "I need to find the sheriff and bring him here."

"That arm looks broken."

He hesitated. "It is."

"Then don't be a fool. Let Mariz heal you and then you can find the sheriff."

She was right. They went outside, where Ethan was surprised to see that the sun still hung in the eastern sky. It was not yet midday, though his body felt as it might if he had battled Ramsey for hours upon hours.

Upon spotting Ethan and Sephira, Mariz strode toward them, concern on his face.

"He needs healing," Sephira said. "And he's in a bit of a hurry."

"Then I shall work quickly."

Mariz cast spells to heal both of Ethan's arms. The break was a clean one—Ethan thought of Diver, and his breath caught in his throat—and the knife wound, though deep, was straight and not overly long. Within a few minutes, much of the pain from both wounds had subsided. The arm that had been broken remained tender, but at least he could use it again.

"Thank you, Mariz."

"Of course. You have other wounds?"

"None that matter. It's time I went in search of Greenleaf." To Sephira he said, "I've let Ramsey's crew go. But they might return for their captain's body."

"Should we let them take it?"

Ethan considered this. "They can have the body, but the head remains here. I have to prove to the sheriff that Ramsey is dead."

To his surprise, Sephira blanched. "All right."

He started up the lane.

"I've never seen you this way before, Ethan. So . . . cold."

He faltered in midstride, but then walked on, saying nothing.

At the first corner he reached, he paused, unsure of where he ought to look for Greenleaf. It was a few seconds before he recalled their exchange on King Street during the night. There was to be a town meeting in Faneuil Hall. He hurried back toward Cornhill.

Had he not witnessed it himself, Ethan would never have believed that so many people would fit into Faneuil Hall for any reason, and certainly not for a town meeting. But the previous night's events had left the citizenry of Boston shaken and angry. Forced to guess, Ethan would have said that there were at least three thousand people in the building and the streets surrounding it. There were soldiers here as well, and tension hummed in the air like a conjuring.

It was no small feat for Ethan to gain entrance to the building, much less to thread his way through the throng to the front of the chamber, where Samuel Adams and others negotiated the wording of a formal message to the lieutenant governor, calling on him to have the British soldiers removed from the city.

Adams, Ethan could see, was in his element. The events of the night before had given him the upper hand in his ongoing battle with Hutchinson over the fate of Boston and, some would argue, all the American colonies. His demeanor remained appropriately somber— only the most partisan of observers could accuse him of gloating, or of taking pleasure in the tragedy that had befallen their city. But neither could they say that he had wilted in the face of a crisis. Ethan had missed much of the discussion, but he could see that Adams and his allies—including Otis, John Hancock, and a man Ethan heard others refer to as William Molineux, whom he recognized as the broad-shouldered gentleman who had kept Ebenezer Richardson from being hanged the day Chris Seider was shot—had convinced the mob to express their rage and grief through political petition rather than additional violence. He wondered if the result would have been different if Ramsey yet lived, and could cast more of his spells.

On the thought, he surveyed the throng and soon spotted Sheriff Stephen Greenleaf leaning against the wall at the far end of the great chamber, his eyes watchful, his expression characteristically grim.

Ethan made his way to the sheriff, who didn't notice him until Ethan was but a short distance from him.

"Kaille," he said. "I thought you didn't fancy yourself part of Adams's rabble."

A few men standing nearby stared daggers at them both.

"I came looking for you, Sheriff."

Greenleaf frowned and eyed Ethan's shirt, coat, and breaches, which looked a mess from all that Ethan had endured in the warehouse on Wiltshire Street. "More trouble with Ramsey, I take it."

"He's dead."

The sheriff's gaze sharpened. "I've heard that before."

"Not from me you haven't. You know that as well as I."

"Aye, I remember. You're sure he's dead."

"If you'll come with me, I'll show you the body."

Greenleaf, scanned the chamber and appeared to convince himself that he wouldn't be missed. "All right, then," he said. "Take me to him."

They left Faneuil Hall, strode past the barracks on Brattle Street, and crossed through New Boston. Greenleaf's strides were long and quick; Ethan struggled to keep pace. In no time, his bad leg had started to ache. But he was as eager to show the sheriff that Ramsey was dead as Greenleaf was to see the corpse for himself. The nearer they drew to the rope yard and its warehouse, the more uneasy Ethan grew. He knew what he had done and seen; he knew Ramsey was dead. But a part of him couldn't help but wonder if somehow the captain had managed to bring himself back, to use the awesome power he wielded to cheat death one last time.

When at last they reached the warehouse, however, they found Sephira and her men waiting outside, appearing bored and impatient.

"Good day, Miss Pryce," Greenleaf said, removing his tricorn.

"Sheriff."

"Why are you out here?" Ethan asked her.

Sephira regarded him as she might an insolent child. "Because I didn't wish to remain in there with that dead . . . thing."

"Have Ramsey's men come back?"

She shook her head. "Not yet. I'm not convinced they will."

Ethan entered the warehouse, Greenleaf behind him. Sephira, he noticed, followed them.

To Ethan's profound relief, the inside of the warehouse appeared exactly as it had before he left to find the sheriff. The body of Nate Ramsey still lay in the bed, half covered by his blood-soaked blanket and bed linens. The captain's head lay on the bed as well, a pool of blood beneath it.

"Damn," Greenleaf whispered. He stepped past Ethan, and approached the bed, moving with caution, perhaps fearing that at any moment the corpse might animate itself and attack. "He was bedridden?"

"Aye," Ethan said. "The burns from the Drake's Wharf fire left him incapacitated."

"And yet he could do his mischief."

"He remained a powerful conjurer until the very end."

The sheriff glanced back at him. "But not so powerful that you couldn't defeat him."

"I was fortunate."

"You call it fortune. I call it witchery."

Ethan was too weary to argue.

Greenleaf grinned and faced forward once more. He halted at the foot of the bed and bent low to examine the hairless, fire-ravaged head. He made no effort to touch it. "You're sure this was Ramsey? It looks nothing like him."

"I'm sure," Ethan said.

"I saw him last night and—"

"You saw an image Ramsey conjured for my benefit and that of anyone else who saw him. He might have been cruel and mad, but he was also proud. He wished to hide from all the world what he had become. But this is him. I swear it."

"It's true, Sheriff," Sephira said.

"But . . ." Greenleaf straightened and shook his head. "Very well. I've little choice but to believe you."

"I wanted him dead as much as you did. Probably more. I've no reason to lie to you."

"You have every reason! Jonathan Grant's murder remains unexplained, and your life hangs in the balance!"

"Ramsey killed him. I've told you that."

"I would have preferred to hear it from Ramsey."

Ethan threw his hands wide. "You wanted Ramsey dead! You can't tell me to kill him and then hear his confession. That is, unless you're a witch."

Greenleaf's face shaded to crimson. Sephira snorted.

"Fine," the sheriff said at last, the word clipped. "What of his crew?"

"I let them go," Ethan said. "Though there was one who I beat senseless." He looked at Sephira.

"He awoke while you were gone," she said. "I told him to leave."

"They're guilty of crimes as well," Greenleaf said. "They gave aid to Ramsey in all he did."

"Then I would suggest that you find them before they sail the *Muirenn* out of the harbor. But you'll have no help from me in that regard. I defeated Ramsey, as I told you I would. I'll not fight the crew for you as well."

He thought the sheriff would argue, but instead he said, "Very well,

Kaille. I assume that after today, I won't have to hear again of Nate Ramsey and his damned witchcraft."

"I assume so as well," Ethan said.

Greenleaf eyed the head and body again then turned and strode back toward the warehouse entrance. "I should return to Faneuil Hall. The lieutenant governor wants me to keep an eye on Adams and his friends."

"I'm sure he does."

The sheriff's expression soured. "You'd best watch yourself, Kaille. With Ramsey dead, you won't have anyone else to blame for the magicking that happens in this city. It'll be you and that African woman who thinks she's so smart. And eventually I'll find a way to slip a noose around both of your necks."

"You're welcome," Ethan said. "I was glad to help."

Greenleaf frowned. If anything, Sephira's laughter served only to deepen his consternation. He regarded them both and then stormed out of the building.

"He doesn't like you very much," she said, staring after the man.

"Neither do you, if I remember correctly."

Sephira smiled. "Not very much, no. But I do find it convenient to have you around, for the entertainment you provide, if nothing else."

Ethan grinned. "Thank you for all that you did today. And also for allowing Mariz to help me."

She waved away his gratitude, much as Janna often did. "Greenleaf has a point, you know. Ramsey was a common enemy. Now that he's dead, you and I have no one left to fight but each other."

"We've done that before."

"Yes, we have. And I look forward to our next encounter." She sauntered toward the door.

"Sephira."

She stopped, turned.

There was much Ethan wanted to say, but not to her, not yet. There were others to whom he would have to speak first.

She quirked an eyebrow. "You have something else to say to me?"

"No. Again, my thanks."

Sephira gave a small shrug and left him there in the warehouse. Ethan took one last look at the body of Nate Ramsey and then at the damage his own fire spells had done to the building. He walked around to the far side of the bed, where lay the unfortunate man from whom Ramsey had been taking blood for his spells, the man whose life he had considered using as the source for a spell of his own. Sitting on the floor beside the man, he cut his own arm, dabbed his blood over the worst of the man's many wounds, and whispered a healing spell.

While his spell was still humming in the floor and walls, he heard footsteps behind him. He looked to see who had come, fearing that Ramsey's men had returned. But it was Mariz.

"I sensed your conjuring. What are you doing?" He halted at the sight of the man. "*Ah, meu Deus!* What happened to him?"

"Ramsey was using his blood for spells. I couldn't bring myself to leave him here. So I'm healing him."

"I can help you, if you would like."

"I'd be grateful."

Mariz joined him beside the man, cut himself, and cast a healing spell. And for the next hour or more, Ethan and Mariz cast spell after spell, until the worst of the man's wounds had been mended. When they were done, Ethan took the bloodstained blanket off of the bed and draped it over the man.

"He'll wake eventually," Ethan said. "And hopefully he won't remember too much from this ordeal."

He covered Ramsey's body and head, so that they wouldn't be the first things the man saw upon opening his eyes.

He and Mariz walked outside into the brilliant sunlight; Ethan blinked against the glare and shaded his eyes.

"What will you do now?" Mariz asked.

"I need to speak with Samuel Adams, and also with Thomas Hutchinson."

Mariz's eyebrows went up. "These are important men. They will speak with you?"

"I hope so." Ethan proffered a hand, which the conjurer gripped.

"My thanks, Mariz. Without your help, and without your warding, I would never have survived my battle with Ramsey."

"I am glad to have helped you, Kaille. And though I know that you did not wish to kill Ramsey, I am pleased that he is dead."

"So am I," Ethan said. "More than I can say."

Chapter TWENTY-FIVE

s it turned out, Adams and Hutchinson were together by midafternoon. Those who first met at Faneuil
Hall had dispatched Adams, along with several other del-
egates, to the Old South Meeting House, where they presented to
Hutchinson their demand that General Gage's soldiers be removed
from the city and sent to Castle William, a fortified island in Boston
Harbor. The meeting had been intended for the Town House, but
the crowd that followed Adams, Hancock, and the others was so huge
that the discussion had to be moved to a building that could accom-
modate all who wished to attend.

This time, Ethan was not able to push his way through the mob,
and so had to be content with hearing of the encounter from others,
who, no doubt, had themselves heard of it from those fortunate enough
to be present.

It seemed that Adams had not been the only man to speak with
eloquence of the dangers of keeping the soldiers in the city. If the regulars did not leave, Royall Tyler was said to have warned, ten thousand
men from the countryside would descend upon the city and kill them
all, "should it be called rebellion—should it incur the loss of our char-
ter, or be the consequence what it would."

Unable to see either Adams or Hutchinson, Ethan waited in the
street for word of what was to be done with the billeted soldiers. When
word came that Hutchinson and Colonel Dalrymple, who was in com-

mand of the men in Boston, had capitulated and would be sending the soldiers out of the city, he surprised himself by shouting his approval with the others, and, like so many standing with him, wiping a tear from his eye.

As night fell and the air grew cold he retreated to the Dowsing Rod, where the celebration had been fully joined. As he entered, Tom Langer, one of Kannice's regulars, was standing on a table slurring a toast to Samuel Adams and the Sons of Liberty.

Kelf spotted Ethan and his expression darkened. Undaunted, Ethan stepped to the bar.

"How is Kannice?" he asked.

"She's restin'," the barman said, not meeting his gaze. "She was asking after you. But she doesn't need to be cookin' and servin' and she definitely doesn't need you . . . gettin' her all worked up, if you catch my meaning."

"I do," Ethan said. "She's in her room?"

Kelf scowled. "Aye."

"My thanks."

The barman turned away without a response.

Eventually, the two of them would have to find some way to repair their friendship, but for now Ethan was more concerned with seeing Kannice. He climbed the stairs and followed the corridor to her room. There he knocked on the door—he couldn't remember the last time he had done so.

"Come in," Kannice called. Her voice sounded strong. Once more, his eyes welled.

He pushed the door open and was greeted with a radiant smile.

"I was wondering when you'd come to see me."

He crossed to the bed, sat, and kissed her brow.

"I would have come sooner. I'm sorry. I've been . . ." He shook his head. "It's been a long day."

"Ramsey?"

"Ramsey's dead. I killed him."

"No doubt?"

He smiled. "No doubt."

She closed her eyes. "Thank God."

Ethan took her hand. "How are you feeling?"

"My chest is sore—it hurts if I take a deep breath. But other than that, I'm fine."

He nodded. "Good. Let me see the scar."

She pulled down the front of her nightgown, exposing the wound. It was an angry shade of red, but the skin around the wound did not appear to be swollen or fevered.

"You'll be fine in another day or two," he said. "As long as you rest."

"Aye," she said, her tone arch, "like you always do when you've been hurt."

He grinned and took her hand once more. She smiled as well, but not for long.

"What happened between you and Kelf?"

Ethan looked away. "Why? What did he tell you?"

"Nothing. Just that you had saved my life. But there was something in the way he spoke of it that made me wonder. And when I told him that I wanted to see you, that he should send you up here as soon as you reached the tavern, he grew sullen."

Ethan faced her again. "He knows I saved your life."

"Well, of course, but that's—" She stopped, her eyes going wide. "Oh, Ethan. I'm sorry. I should have understood."

He shook his head. "It's not your fault. It's not Kelf's either. But I don't know if he'll ever accept . . . what I am."

"He'll have to. He works here, and you're going to be coming around for a good while longer. At least I hope you are."

He raised her hand to his lips. "I am."

"Then, Kelf will have to get accustomed to it."

Ethan wasn't convinced that it would be quite that easy, but he kept his doubts to himself.

"Did you hear about what happened on King Street?"

He had to smile. Only someone who had been confined to her bed all day could even ask such a thing. "I was there. I saw it all, and felt the spell from Ramsey that made it happen."

"He did that, too?"

"Aye. Diver was shot."

She paled. "Is he all right?"

"I assume he's still alive. I haven't seen him today. But I kept him from bleeding to death, and then I carried him to the home of Doctor Warren. He . . . he lost an arm."

"Dear God. Ethan, I'm so sorry."

He nodded, unable to speak.

She scrutinized his face. "When was the last time you slept?"

A small laugh escaped him, sounding more like a sob. "It's been some time."

"You should lie down." She started to slide over and make room for him.

Ethan gave her hand a squeeze, stopping her. "I'll sleep, but in my room at Henry's. You need rest even more than I do."

"I'm not so sure."

"Well, I am. And I think that if I dare spend the night, even if just to sleep, Kelf will have my head."

She gave a small pout. "All right."

"Are you hungry?"

"Yes, I am."

"Then allow me to bring you some chowder and a bit of Madeira. I'll even sup with you."

Her face brightened. "I'd like that."

He left her and descended the stairs to the tavern. Kelf was being run ragged serving all the drinks and taking care of the food as well. And it seemed to Ethan that the barman took some satisfaction in making him wait. But eventually Ethan managed to buy two bowls of the fish chowder, a cup of Madeira, and a tankard of ale. It took him two trips to carry all of this to Kannice's room, but soon he was sitting with her once more. To his pleasure, Kannice made short work of her chowder, prompting Ethan to get her a second bowl.

When he returned, he again joined her on the bed, and for several moments he kept silent, searching for the best way to say what was on his mind.

"So, I have a question for you," he began at last.

"Hmm?" Kannice said, intent on the chowder.

"Are you still willing to have me as a partner here at the tavern?"

She nearly dropped her spoon, and she did manage to spill a good deal of stew onto her blanket, though she hardly noticed. "Are you serious?"

"Aye. This business with Ramsey . . . I've had enough. I'm too old to be making my living in the streets, risking my life day and night. And I would much rather pass my days with you than with Sheriff Greenleaf and Sephira Pryce and Thomas Hutchinson."

"We've been talking about this for a long time, Ethan, and all along you've resisted the idea. Even the other day when you said that you would consider it, you were soon gone again, back in the lanes looking for Ramsey. Thieftaking is in your blood, as running a tavern is in mine. Don't get me wrong: It's still what I want. But I think perhaps you're saying this because of what you've been through these past weeks, and because of what was done to me. I don't want you waking up in a month's time and realizing that you've made a terrible mistake."

"I woke up last night," he said. He took both of her hands in his. "I watched that man stab you in the heart, and I woke up. I'm not saying that it will be easy; I'm sure I'll miss it now and then. But I want this, and I'm ready to give up my room on Cooper's Alley, and live here with you. As . . . as husband and wife, if you'll have me."

She made a small sound—half laugh, half gasp. "You're full of surprises tonight, aren't you?"

"I should have asked long ago."

She shook her head, her eyes shining with tears. "No," she said. "You needed to come to it when you were ready."

"Does that mean you'll marry me?"

She grinned, eyes dancing. "Well, I'll have to think about it, won't I?"

"Of course," Ethan said. "I don't want you waking up in a month's time and realizing that you've made a terrible mistake."

Kannice threw her head back and laughed. Then winced and raised a hand to her chest.

Ethan leaned forward and kissed her; she returned the kiss hungrily.

"I should go," he whispered.

"Why?"

"Because we both need rest. And because you have a good deal to ponder."

"No, I don't! Ethan, I was—"

He touched a finger to her lips, silencing her. "Yes, you do. Think about it, Kannice. The Dowser is yours; yours and Rafe's. Before you accept me as a partner, and as a husband, you should think about whether you'll be happy working and living with me for the rest of your life."

"I will be," she said. "I've no doubt. But go, and we'll speak of it again tomorrow."

"Aye, we will."

He kissed her again, stood, and stepped to the door. There he paused, though, and looked back at her. "In all honesty, I'll be in the lanes again tomorrow morning. Ramsey may be dead, but there are still matters to which I must see. I thought you should know that."

"I assumed as much. It's all right, Ethan."

He nodded, and let himself out of the room. He left the Dowser and made his way to Pudding Lane. Despite the late hour, he wished to pay a visit to Diver so that he might see how his friend was faring. Upon reaching the small byway, he saw that a light still shone in his friend's room. He climbed the stairs and knocked.

Deborah answered, looking young and pale.

"Mister Kaille!"

"Ethan."

"Yes, of course," she said. "Ethan. Please come in."

He removed his hat and entered the room. It was warm within and the air smelled of spermaceti candles. Diver lay in bed, his shirt off, a fresh bandage on his shoulder, as bright as newly fallen snow. His face was ashen and gaunt, and at the sight of Ethan he averted his gaze.

"How are you feeling?" Ethan asked, approaching the bed.

His friend didn't answer.

"Diver, I was . . . I did everything I could."

"What happened?" Diver asked, still not looking his way, his voice flat.

"What do you remember?"

"I remember being on King Street when the soldiers started shooting, and I have a vague memory of being hit, of you being there and telling me that you had stopped the bleeding and were going to take me to a surgeon. But after that I don't recall a thing."

"I carried you to Warren's home. You passed out along the way. He removed the ball from your arm, and we both tried to heal the artery and the bone. We couldn't."

"So, you were there when he . . ."

"Aye."

"Doctor Warren said you saved his life."

Ethan glanced back at Deborah. "I kept him from bleeding out, but I . . . I couldn't do more. And before I saved him, I got him shot. Again."

At her questioning look, Ethan related to them both all that had happened with Ramsey over the past several days, concluding with their confrontation in the warehouse.

"It's not your fault he was shot," Deborah said when he finished. "You can't blame yourself for the spells this man Ramsey cast. I don't understand much about conjuring, but I do know that much."

Ethan nodded. He would have preferred to hear this from Diver, but his friend remained silent, still staring at the wall.

"My thanks." He traced a finger along the brim of his hat. "I should go. I didn't wish to intrude, but I did want to see how you were doing." He crossed back to the door, Deborah trailing behind him.

"I'm grateful to you, Mister Kaille. Derrey is, too. He just needs time."

Ethan found it hard to speak. He had come breathtakingly close to losing the two most important people in his life. And though he felt confident that Diver would live, he knew that this wound would be a long, long time in healing.

"How is Kannice?" Deborah asked.

He swallowed. "She's better. Thank you for asking."

"And he's really dead? Ramsey, I mean."

It seemed a common question where the captain was concerned.

"Aye. I killed him myself. You have my word."

The next morning, following the first decent night of sleep Ethan had enjoyed in more than a fortnight, he returned to the Green Dragon, and after some wrangling with several different men, managed to gain entrance to the small chamber off the rear of the great room. There he found Joseph Warren, Paul Revere, James Otis, and, most important, Samuel Adams.

Adams greeted him with more warmth than Ethan had expected, gripping Ethan's proffered hand and placing his other hand over it.

"Joseph told me that a friend of yours was wounded on King Street. I'm terribly sorry."

"Thank you, sir. He's recovering, and for that I'm deeply grateful."

"I'm glad to hear it. Would that others had been as fortunate."

"Yes, sir."

"What can I do for you, Mister Kaille?"

"I come bearing tidings, sir. When last we spoke, I told you that a conjurer had used a spell to cause the shooting of Christopher Seider. That conjurer is now dead."

Adams gazed toward the chamber's small window, his head shaking with his palsy. "I would never claim to take pleasure in any death, but I'm relieved to hear that this man can't trouble us further."

"Yes, sir. You should know, though, that he also played a role in the events of March the fifth. His spells might have influenced the behavior of the soldiers who fired and the men who provoked them."

"Provoked them?" Otis repeated, his voice sharp. He took a step in Ethan's direction. "You dare suggest that—"

"That's enough, James," Adams said, casting a quick look toward his friend. He shifted his gaze to Warren and nodded once.

The doctor approached Otis and spoke to him in a low voice. Ethan could not make out what was said, but after a moment the two men left the room.

"You do seem to have a knack for angering James," Adams said, staring after them.

"I assure you, sir, it's not my intention."

Adams faced him. "I believe you, Mister Kaille. James is not a well man." He took a breath. "The fact is, the soldiers *were* provoked. I don't condone their use of firearms—I want to be perfectly clear about that. Moreover, I do not believe that armed soldiers should have been in Boston at all. Ultimately responsibility for this . . . massacre rests with those who garrisoned those men here in the first place. What happened the other night was both tragic and utterly predictable. The soldiers were provoked, and they in turn provoked that mob. Their mere presence here is a provocation."

"I understand that they are to leave."

"Yes," Adams said. "I hesitate to claim that any good can come of such terrible events, but they'll be sent to Castle William, and that is a small blessing."

"Yes, sir. As to the conjurer, I feel that I must emphasize the importance of his role in what occurred. If those soldiers are to be charged with murder, as I hear some of them will, I must bring this information to the attention of the proper authorities."

"Of course you must, Mister Kaille. But you're speaking to the wrong man."

"Well, sir, I expect that you'll be advocating for their punishment."

"No, I won't. I intend to play no role in their trial. I'm well known as a champion of liberty. Any part I play in the legal proceedings will distract attention not only from the actions of the soldiers, but also from the ill-conceived policies that lay at the root of these events."

"I see," Ethan said. "Well, I had planned to speak with the lieutenant governor as well. Perhaps I should see him now."

Adams smiled. "When I said that you were speaking to the wrong man, I didn't mean Hutchinson. Perhaps I should have said that you're speaking to the wrong Adams."

Ethan frowned. "I don't understand."

"My cousin, John Adams, has consented to represent in court Captain Preston and the soldiers he commanded."

Ethan had no idea what to say.

"You're surprised."

"To say the least, sir. Do you approve?"

"My approval or disapproval is of little consequence, but yes, I do. John is a man of great integrity. The soldiers will get a fair hearing, and in so doing may convince those who doubt our motives and tactics that we believe in justice for all, foe and friend alike. My point, though, is that of all people, John most needs to know of this conjurer and his role in the shootings."

"I've never met Mister Adams."

"With that, I can help you." Adams stepped to a desk against the near wall of the small room. He found a piece of parchment, dipped a quill in a well of ink, and penned a short missive. He then folded the parchment and placed it in an envelope, which he sealed with wax. "Here you are, Mister Kaille. Present this to John when you see him. He will speak with you."

"Thank you, sir."

Ethan crossed to the door.

"Do I dare even ask if you're now ready to join us?" Adams asked before Ethan could let himself out of the room.

"I think I may be, sir."

Adams looked every bit as amazed as Kannice had the night before. "Because of what happened on King Street?" he asked.

Ethan shook his head. "Because of the woman I mentioned the last time we spoke."

Adams was still laughing when Ethan pulled the door shut.

The law office of John Adams stood on Queen Street, directly across from the gaol and the Court House, and adjacent to Murray's Barracks. Ethan had no desire to go anywhere near the soldiers' quarters, but he had little choice in the matter.

Upon entering the office, he was greeted by a young, well-dressed man who introduced himself as William Tudor. When Ethan requested a word with Mr. Adams, the young attorney demurred.

"I'm afraid you'll have to come back another time. Mister Adams is quite busy at the moment."

"I've no doubt that he is," Ethan said, pulling the envelope from the pocket of his greatcoat. "But I carry a letter of introduction from his cousin, Mister Samuel Adams. I believe Mister Adams will wish to speak with me."

He handed the missive to Tudor, who took it into a second chamber, off the main room. As Ethan expected, he soon returned.

"Mister Adams will see you, Mister Kaille."

Tudor held the door open as Ethan entered this smaller chamber, and then closed it, leaving Ethan alone with the gentleman standing at a polished wood desk.

John Adams bore little resemblance to his cousin. Where Samuel was handsome, even a bit dashing, John was odd in appearance. He was several inches shorter than Ethan and portly, with a weak chin and dark eyebrows over expressive hazel eyes. He wore a gray wig, and a black silk suit.

He greeted Ethan solemnly and indicated a pair of chairs beside the hearth.

They both sat.

Adams held up the message from his cousin. "Samuel informs me that you have information pertaining to the recent events on King Street." He spoke in a strong, rich baritone that belied his undistinguished appearance.

"Yes, sir."

"He also indicates that I am to accept as truth whatever you tell me, no matter how fanciful, even preposterous, it might sound."

Ethan smiled, silently thanking Samuel Adams for his foresight. "Aye, sir. What I have to say may well seem to stretch the bounds of credulity." Speaking slowly, his voice low, Ethan then explained all that had happened in the past fortnight, beginning with the shooting of Christopher Seider.

Long after Ethan had finished, Adams remained silent, his eyes fixed on the fire. When at last he stirred and regarded Ethan, it was with the same even expression he had maintained since Ethan's arrival.

"You tell a most remarkable tale, Mister Kaille."

"Yes, sir."

"Am I to assume then that you believe Captain Preston and the men under his command should be acquitted?"

"I'm neither a lawyer nor a judge, sir. And I have no idea if what I've related to you can even be spoken of in a court of law. But I thought that you should know."

"I'm grateful to you. It may be that I will need to call on you before the trial; perhaps even during it. But to be honest I have every confidence that these men will be acquitted, even if I never mention witchery and conjurings."

"You do?" Ethan said, unable to mask his surprise.

"That surprises you. I suppose that's to be expected. But already I have spoken with many who were there that night. These men were abused most foully. They were taunted and insulted, pelted with snowballs and rocks. A club was thrown at them. Many of those in the mob shouted for the men to fire. Most in Boston would like to see them convicted; I know this. And there can be no doubt that by their actions, they caused the deaths of four men. But facts are stubborn things, and the facts tell us that these men acted out of fear for their own safety. Who among us would have behaved differently?"

Ethan had heard men speak of the brilliance of John Adams, but until then he had not understood fully what they meant. An hour before, he would have wagered every pence he had that Preston and the others would be found guilty. No longer.

"I fear I've wasted your time, sir," he said, getting to his feet. "You require no aid from me."

For the first time since Ethan's arrival, Adams smiled. "You're kind, Mister Kaille. And I'm grateful to you for coming here. Many men, particularly those who keep company with my cousin, would have kept such information to themselves rather than give aid of any sort to these soldiers."

Ethan didn't bother to gainsay the man's assumption that he supported the Sons of Liberty. He allowed Adams to escort him to the building entrance and bid him farewell.

Adams's office was but a short distance from the Town House, and so Ethan next paid a visit to the chambers of Thomas Hutchinson. He had expected that he would have some difficulty convincing those who worked for the lieutenant governor to grant him admittance to the man's office. He was wrong.

Within moments of his arrival, he stood before Hutchinson. Recent events had left him looking even more weary than he had during their previous encounter. Ethan doubted that he had slept in the past two days.

"Sheriff Greenleaf tells me that the conjurer of whom we spoke—the one you thought responsible for the Seider boy's death—is dead," Hutchinson said. "Moreover, he tells me that you killed him."

"Yes, sir, that's right."

"The sheriff suggests that we owe you our gratitude."

This was the last thing Ethan had expected him to say. "Mister Greenleaf is too kind, sir."

Hutchinson gave a wry grin. "I think we both know better. I think as well that the province owes you five pounds. I assume that is why you came."

"I came to inform you that before he died, Ramsey cast spells that may well have caused the shootings on King Street."

Hutchinson's mouth fell open. "What?" he said, breathless.

"He used his conjurings against the mob and the soldiers, as he did the day of the shooting on Middle Street. I have just now informed John Adams of this, so that he might make use of the information in his defense of the men."

"Thank you, Mister Kaille. That was most fair-minded of you."

"You may find this hard to credit, sir, but the idea was not my own. It came from Samuel Adams."

Hutchinson pondered this, a faint smile on his lips. "Yes, I'm sure it did. Whatever else he might be, there can be no doubt that he's canny." The lieutenant governor stood unmoving for some time before returning to his desk and retrieving a purse that rang with coins. "Your five pounds," he said, untying the drawstrings and pouring out the contents of the purse. He counted out Ethan's payment and then glanced his way. "And what of our arrangement, Mister Kaille? Do I owe you an additional three pounds? Did Samuel Adams's motives prove to be as pure as you believed?"

"You know they didn't, sir. You owe me five pounds and nothing more. I spoke to Adams on your behalf and tried to dissuade him from organizing more assemblies like the one outside Ebenezer Richardson's house. I failed, as we both knew I would. But I did fulfill my part of our wager."

"Very well," said the lieutenant governor, holding out the coins to Ethan.

Ethan took his payment and pocketed it without bothering to count the coins.

"Thank you, sir. Good day."

"Thank you, Mister Kaille. As you well know, I have no love for your kind. Witchery is a scourge on this province and has been for more than a century. But the sheriff is right: You've done us a service, and I'm grateful to you."

Ethan could think of nothing to say. He nodded once to the man and left the chamber, grateful to be done with Hutchinson, at least for a while, and grateful as well for the coins jangling in his pocket. Upon reaching the street, he paused. He owed a visit to Janna; she would want to know that Ramsey was dead. But all he wished to do was sit with Kannice. He walked back to the Dowsing Rod, taking care to avoid the barracks of the Twenty-ninth Regiment.

Only when he entered the tavern, however, did he remember that he would have to face Kelf before he could see Kannice.

Kelf stood at the bar, polishing the wood with a cloth. A few patrons sat at tables eating oysters and drinking flips, but the tavern was mostly empty. When the barman spotted Ethan, he dropped his gaze and rubbed at the wood with enough force to strip it of its finish. Ethan approached the bar.

"We're going to have to talk eventually," he said.

"I thought I told you to keep away from me," Kelf said, running his words together in an angry jumble.

"Aye, you did. But that's not going to happen, and you know it. So we need to talk."

"I've nothin' to say to you."

"Why, Kelf? Because I saved her life?"

"Because you're a witch!"

The patrons looked their way. Ethan stared back at them, daring them to say something. Before long, they returned their attention to their flips.

"Keep your voice down," Ethan said, facing the barman once more.

Kelf muttered an apology.

"I'm a conjurer, not a witch, and I have been for as long as you've known me. In what way does this change me?"

"I don't know, but it does. It's . . . it's not natural."

Ethan chanced a smile. "Actually it is. I was born this way, as were my mother and both of my sisters."

Kelf did not respond.

"I'm going to marry her, Kelf. I'll be living here, helping the two of you run the Dowser. You and I have to be able to work together."

"Maybe she won't want to keep me. She doesn't need both of us."

"Of course I do."

Kelf looked past Ethan toward the stairs. Ethan turned. Kannice stood at the foot of the stairway, a shawl wrapped around her shoulders. She had more color today, though she still looked pale.

"You shouldn't be out of bed," Ethan said.

Kannice crossed to the bar, ignoring him for the moment. "The Dowsing Rod wouldn't be the same without you, Kelf, whether or not Ethan is here."

The barman wouldn't meet her gaze.

"But you have to accept that he's a speller," she went on, dropping her voice. "If you can't do that, we have a problem."

"It doesn't bother you?" Kelf asked. "Truly?"

"No, it doesn't. He's a good man, as you well know. And thanks to his conjuring, I'm alive."

"He used blood."

"Aye, I did," Ethan said. "I can also conjure with leaves, with fresh wood, with grass. For some simple spells I need no more than air or water. But to save Kannice's life I needed to cast a powerful spell, and blood works best."

"Have you ever spelled me?"

"No, I've never had cause. But if I needed to cast in order to save your life, I would." He grinned. "There was a time though, some years ago, when I used a spell on the door, and in the morning you couldn't get in."

"I remember that," Kelf said, a smile creeping over his features. "I almost broke down the door."

"Aye, but I removed the spell before you did."

Too soon, Kelf appeared to remember what it was they were discussing. His smile faded. He eyed Ethan and then Kannice, frowning once more. "Wait. Did you say that you're goin' to marry her?"

Ethan glanced her way. "I will if she'll have me."

Kannice took his hand. "Aye, we'll be married before long. And we want you there with us."

The barman ducked his head. "I'm happy for you both. But I need some time to get used to this—to get used to you, Ethan."

Kannice's expression hardened. "What time—?"

"That's fine, Kelf," Ethan said. "There's no hurry. I plan to be around here for a long while." He turned to Kannice, who still glared at Kelf. "You should be in bed."

"I'm done lying in bed," she said, in a tone he had learned long ago not to challenge. "I want a bite to eat, and then I want to work in my kitchen."

Ethan and Kelf shared a grin. "I'll fetch her some food," Kelf said. "And then I'll clear out of her way."

He lumbered into the kitchen.

"You were more understanding than I would have been," Kannice said, once she and Ethan were alone.

"He's trying," Ethan said. "I can't ask for more than that." He took her in his arms and kissed her. "I'm glad to see you up and about, even if you should be in bed."

A coy grin touched her lips. "The next time I'm in bed, I won't be alone."

"Well then, you should definitely be in bed."

"Later," she said, laughing as she pulled away from him. "Right now, I want to cook. It's been too long, and this place will be filling up soon enough."

Ethan said nothing, but gazed back at her, reliving for an instant the terror he'd known upon seeing her with a knife in her chest. How would he have gone on without her?

"Ethan? Are you all right?"

"I'm fine," he said. "More than fine. I'm glad you're well enough to be making chowder again; I've no doubt Tom Langer will be, too."

She smiled, though her brow remained creased.

"I love you," he said.

Her brow smoothed. "Good."

Late in the afternoon of the next day, March 8, nearly every shop in the city closed, church bells began to peal, and a crowd of mourners that most agreed numbered more than ten thousand converged on King Street to honor the memories of Crispus Attucks, James Caldwell, Samuel Gray, and Samuel Maverick, the four men who died as a result of the shootings there.

At least one of the other victims, a young Irish laborer named Patrick Carr, remained grievously wounded; few expected him to survive.

Men and women came to the city from Roxbury, Charlestown, and other nearby communities; the resulting procession dwarfed that which accompanied Christopher Seider to his final resting place. Walking six abreast through the city streets, the mourners bore the coffins from King Street to the Liberty Tree and finally to the Granary Burying Ground.

Though Ethan tried to remind himself that Ramsey's spells had caused these deaths, he could not help but feel that he, too, was responsible in some small way. Had he discovered sooner the secret to warding his power from the captain's influence, he might have saved these lives.

He was flanked on the icy lanes by Kannice and Diver, Kelf and Deborah. Kannice held fast to his hand. Deborah supported Diver, who had insisted upon taking part in the procession despite Ethan's and Deborah's misgivings.

It was as solemn and momentous an occasion as Ethan had ever witnessed. There were no incidents, no confrontations between mourners and soldiers. But it seemed to Ethan that he and the others participated not merely in a funeral, but in a demonstration of the growing might of Samuel Adams's movement for liberty. *The next time British soldiers take up arms against Boston's citizenry,* they seemed to say by their mere presence in the streets, *this is what they will face.*

The honored dead were interred in a single vault, beside the grave of Chris Seider. After, Ethan, Kannice, and the others returned to the Dowser and drank a solemn toast to the fallen men.

"I'd like to drink a toast to Mister Kaille as well," Deborah said, as they stood by the bar. "Were it not for him, Derrey would have been buried today, along with the rest."

Diver kept his eyes lowered, but nodded as she spoke. Kelf and Ethan shared a glance as the barman said, "Hear, hear," along with the others.

"Thank you, Deborah," Ethan said. "But I did it out of selfishness. Diver owes me for more ales than I can count, and I have every intention of collecting."

Most of them laughed—even Diver managed a faint smile—but once more Ethan's breath caught, this time at the thought of how close he had come to losing his dear friend.

He was not a religious man, nor a vindictive one. But at that moment he hoped with all his heart that Nate Ramsey was burning in the fires of hell.

TWENTY-SIX

Ethan left his room on Cooper's Alley a few days later, bidding a fond farewell to Henry, and promising to visit the cooper whenever he had the opportunity. On March 18, the day after Samuel Adams arranged another massive funeral, this one for Patrick Carr, Ethan and Kannice were married in a humble ceremony before a magistrate at the Town House. Diver and Deborah were there as witnesses, as were Kelf, Henry, and even Janna, who made a point of telling anyone who would listen that she could have seen them wed years earlier if only Ethan had paid her for one of her love spells.

In the days that followed, Ethan tried to make himself useful around the tavern. He certainly was not as fine a cook as Kannice, nor was he as strong as Kelf. But, it turned out, he had some skill with wood-work, and he soon took it upon himself to repair all the uneven tables and squeaky chairs in the great room, which was no small task.

While working on one such chair in the middle of a warm, sunny afternoon later in the month, he heard the tavern door open and close, and then the soft scrape of boot leather on the wooden floor.

"If I didn't see it with my own eyes, I wouldn't have believed it."

Ethan stood and turned. "Good day, Sephira."

She had come alone, or perhaps she remembered that Kannice had ordered her toughs from the Dowser the one other time she came to the tavern, and so left Nap, Mariz, Afton, and Gordon in the street.

She looked as lovely as always, her cheeks flushed, her dark curls shining.

"I heard a rumor that you've given up thieftaking. Is it true?"

"Aye," Ethan said. "I've given up my room on Cooper's Alley as well. I live here now. Kannice and I are married."

"Why, Ethan, how quaint." Her smile was overly sweet. "You've been domesticated."

"Is there something I can help you with? Or did you come here just to mock me?"

"The latter," she said, strolling around the great room, eyeing the bar, the tables and chairs, the hearth. "I'm not sure I see the appeal. I suppose it's a nice enough place; a bit on the shabby side, but charming nevertheless." She halted not far from where he stood. "But this is not the life for a man like you."

"I disagree." He said the words forcefully enough, but he found it difficult to meet her gaze.

"No, you don't. You know as well as I that you'll be bored before long. You'll miss the search for thieves, the fights in the lanes, the satisfaction of finishing a job." She stepped closer. "You might even miss me."

He laughed. "You think I'll miss being beaten to a bloody mess by your brutes? Having my life threatened time and again? Being hounded by Sheriff Greenleaf? You're mad."

"So you say now. But mark my word: You're not the type to be penned and saddled. You'll be chafing at the halter before long, looking for any excuse to be back in the streets."

"I don't think so," came a voice from behind them.

Sephira's gaze shifted, and a cruel smile curved her lips. Turning, Ethan saw that Kannice had emerged from the kitchen and now stood behind the bar.

"Congratulations, Missus Kaille," Sephira said. "Having not been invited to the wedding, I wanted to come by and wish you both great happiness."

"Is that what you were doing?" Kannice said. "That's not how it sounded."

Sephira's smile deepened. Facing Ethan again, she said, "Though

I'm loath to admit it, I know there may be times when I'm presented with jobs that lie beyond my . . . talents. On those occasions, I may seek you out."

"What about Mariz? You've been boasting for more than a year now that you can match me conjuring for conjuring. Why would you need me?"

"Come now. We both know that Mariz is no thieftaker. I find it convenient having access to magick, but I wouldn't trust him with an inquiry."

He knelt beside the chair he had been repairing. "I'm no longer a thieftaker. You'll have to find help somewhere else."

"No, you won't," Kannice said. "If he can help you he will. For half of whatever fee you're paid."

Sephira blinked, then laughed. "Oh, I like her, Ethan. I remember her as fiery, but who knew she could be so shrewd as well. She knows you better than you know yourself. Perhaps I was wrong before. She won't allow you to grow bored. She's too smart for that."

"Shouldn't you be crawling back under your rock?" Kannice asked.

Sephira stilled, putting Ethan in mind of a wolf. "Have a care, my dear. You may be clever, but no one speaks to me that way."

Ethan, who still carried his knife on his belt, drew it now and stood once more. "I think you should leave."

She smiled once more. "Very well. But I'm not through with you, and eventually I'll lure you back into the lanes. You'll see." She cast one last look at Kannice, and sauntered out of the tavern.

"You need to be more careful with her," Ethan said, watching the door, his blade still in hand.

"I can't help it; she brings out the worst in me."

"Oh, I understand. Believe me. But you must never forget how dangerous she is."

"I know." Kannice came out from behind the bar and joined Ethan where he stood. "Evil as she may be, she's right, you know: You are going to get bored."

"No, I won't."

She nodded. "Aye, you will. And that's all right. If a job comes your way, and you wish to take it, you should."

"I thought you didn't want me thieftaking anymore."

"I don't. But more than that, I don't want you to be unhappy, or to feel trapped. And if you say that you're never going to work in the lanes again, that's what will happen."

"So, I'm to be a tavernkeeper by day and a thieftaker by night?"

She put her arms around his neck and kissed him deeply. "You won't be thieftaking every night," she murmured. "I'll see to that. But perhaps now and then."

He glanced toward the door before kissing her again. "Now and then," he repeated, his breath stirring her hair. "I believe I can live with that."

Historical Note

With each of the Thieftaker books, I have looked for ways to blend my fictional elements—Ethan's life, his conjurings, his anachronistic profession, his loves and friends and rivals and enemies—with the historical details of 1760s and, now, 1770s Boston. Finding that balance between fact and fiction, and weaving the fantastic and historical together in a manner that leaves the boundary between the two all but invisible to my readers, has always been the greatest challenge of writing this series.

And in none of the books was this challenge more formidable than in *Dead Man's Reach*. The circumstances and progression of occurrences leading up to what has come to be known as the Boston Massacre were as complex as those surrounding any event in the pre-Revolutionary period. The seeds of this watershed tragedy were actually planted in 1768, when customs officials seized John Hancock's ship *Liberty*, prompting riots and, eventually, the occupation of Boston by British troops. These events were chronicled, loosely of course, in *Thieves' Quarry*. Over the following eighteen months, the presence of soldiers in the city fed a growing tension that often threatened to spill over into bloodshed.

In February 1770, the violence erupted at last. The shooting of young Christopher Seider by Ebenezer Richardson happened much as it is described in these pages, including the initial demonstrations in front of the shop of Theophilus Lillie. So did the grand funeral arranged by Samuel Adams and his fellow patriots, down to the complications created by the tremendous blizzard that struck New England just days before the demonstration.

In the days and weeks that followed, conflicts between soldiers and Boston's citizenry continued. The fights at Gray's Rope Works followed the progression described in this novel, as did the moment-by-moment escalation of emotion on the night of March 5, 1770, when soldiers opened fire on the mob that had gathered near the Customs House on King Street.

Therein lies the challenge I mentioned. Not only did I wish to blend my fictional narrative with historical events, but I also did my best to make my story follow the historical timeline as closely as possible. It wasn't always easy, but it was a great deal of fun.

Of course, Ethan's blood feud with Nate Ramsey played no role in these events, and we have no evidence that magick did anything to ratchet up the emotions of those who gathered in Boston's streets. But that is a discussion for another time and place.

In piecing together the sequence of historical occurrences, in particular those surrounding the Seider shooting, the fights at Gray's Rope Works, and the massacre itself, I relied on two books: Hiller B. Zobel's *The Boston Massacre* (W. W. Norton, 1970) and Richard Archer's *As If an Enemy's Country: The British Occupation of Boston and the Origins of Revolution* (Oxford University Press, 2010).

For more information on the scholarly and primary sources I have used for this and other Thieftaker books and stories—along with a good deal of other information—please visit my website: www.dbjackson -author.com.

Acknowledgments

As with the other Thieftaker novels, I owe a great debt to several people who have helped me get my facts (and fictions) straight. My thanks to Dr. John C. Willis, for his help with the history; Dr. Christopher M. McDonough, who translated more spells for me; Dr. Robert D. Hughes, who educated me on the arcana of Anglican Church matters; and Dr. Thomas Spacarelli, who translated a bit of Portuguese for me. Any mistakes that remain despite the best efforts of all these very smart people are entirely my own.

As always, I wish to thank the Norman B. Leventhal Map Center at the Boston Public Library, in particular Catherine T. Wood, the center's office manager, for allowing us to use the map of Boston that appears at the front of the book.

Lucienne Diver is a superb agent, a terrific critical reader, and a wonderful friend. I am grateful to her for all that she has done for my books and my career. My sincere thanks as well to Deirdre Knight, Jia Giles, and the great people at the Knight Agency.

I've been fortunate to work on this book with several fine editors at Tor Books, including Marco Palmieri, Stacy Hill, and Christopher Morgan. Their insights, patience, and wisdom added immeasurably to the finished product, and I am indebted to them all. I'm also deeply grateful to Tom Doherty, Irene Gallo and her staff, Cassie Ammerman, Leah Withers, Diana Pho, and all the terrific people at Tor, and also to Terry McGarry.

ACKNOWLEDGMENTS

Thank you as well to: Faith Hunter, Misty Massey, A. J. Hartley, John Hartness, James Tuck, Carrie Ryan, Mindy Klasky, Diana Pharaoh Francis, C. E. Murphy, Charles Coleman Finlay, Kat Richardson, Blake Charlton, Kate Elliott, Eric Flint, Mary Robinette Kowal, Alethea Kontis, Stephen Leigh, Lynn Flewelling, Joshua Palmatier, Stuart Jaffe, Edmund Schubert, Kalayna Price, Robert Sawyer, and Patricia Bray, all of whom have helped me with ideas or world-building, character or plotting, phrasing or research, not to mention promotion of the series.

At the end of the day, as at the beginning, my wife and daughters are the source of my greatest happiness and, on a day-to-day basis, the lion's share of my laughter. I couldn't do any of this without their love and support.

About the Author

D. B. JACKSON is the award-winning author of more than fifteen fantasy novels, many short stories, and the occasional media tie-in. His books have been translated into more than a dozen languages. He has a master's degree and Ph.D. in U.S. history, which have come in handy as he has written the Thieftaker novels and short stories. He and his family live in the mountains of Appalachia.

Visit him at www.dbjackson-author.com.